SECRETS AND WISHES

STONE CREEK BRIDES
BOOK TWO

KATHLEEN ROUSER

WILD HEARt
BOOKS

Unless otherwise indicated, all Scripture quotations are taken from the Holy Bible, Kings James Version.

Cover design by: Carpe Librum Book Design

ISBN: 978-1-942265-86-3

PRAISE FOR KATHLEEN ROUSER

"Take a leisurely, well-researched romp into the past with a strong and vibrant heroine and other endearing characters. Fans of Christian historical fiction will not be disappointed with this sweet romance!"

— LINORE ROSE BURKARD, AWARD-WINNING AUTHOR OF *THE HOUSE IN GROSVENOR SQUARE*

"Kathleen Rouser's *Secrets and Wishes* touches the hearts of readers who have ever had to start again after a devastating loss. Set in the backdrop of 1901 Michigan, the story brings to life the characters and their everyday lives so much so that I felt I was watching a movie rather than reading a book. A delightful story to lose yourself in."

— CINDY THOMSON, AUTHOR OF THE ELLIS ISLAND AND THE DAUGHTERS OF IRELAND SERIES

"Kathleen Rouser has once again written a superb, thought-provoking story which has a strong spiritual theme woven throughout. In *Secrets and Wishes*, she follows the developing romance of Maggie Galloway and Thomas Harper, an apothecary in 1901 Stone Creek, Michigan, while at the same time keeping you guessing as to the outcome. Historically accurate, the story carries the reader back to a time when the roles of the apothecary included stitching up wounds and handing out minor prescriptions without a doctor's signature. I found the herbs and remedies used at the turn of the nineteenth into the twentieth century intriguing."

— CATHERINE ULRICH BRAKEFIELD, AWARD-WINNING AUTHOR OF *WILTED DANDELIONS*

"*Secrets and Wishes* is a delightful follow-up to *Rumors and Promises*. It brings with it all the charm and imagery which made the first book so notable. Depicting loss and grief and showcasing the struggles of blending families makes this poignant story applicable to modern readers while also depicting historical Michigan at the turn of the twentieth century in amazing ways. Kathleen takes readers on an unforgettable journey of love discovered again and the joy of being set free from blame or guilt, all while effortlessly weaving in a gentle faith in God without being preachy. Highly recommend!"

— AMBER STOCKTON, CBA BESTSELLING AUTHOR OF *LIBERTY'S PROMISE* AND TWENTY-ONE OTHER FAITH-BASED NOVELS

For my children, Jesse, Leslie, and Matthew. I am thankful for the gift of each of you. For my daughter-in-law, Jessica. I am thankful for the gift that you are to Matthew and to our family. And for Pei-Lin, your faith has been an inspiration to me.

A merry heart doeth good like a medicine:
but a broken spirit drieth the bones.

— PROVERBS 17:22 (AUTHORIZED
KJV)

CHAPTER 1

*M*aggie Galloway hiked up the front hem of her skirt as she raced across the schoolyard when she first spied the commotion. She held tight to her hat with her free hand.

"Yeah, get him, Philip!" A tall boy from the group of children surrounding the scuffle thrust a fist into the air.

A girl gasped. "I'm telling Miss Oliver!" She marched toward the schoolhouse.

A full red head of hair bobbed in the center, a definite sign of trouble. *Her* Philip? *Unbelievable.* Maggie's heart thudded at the sight of her son. She dropped her hem, stopped to regain her breath as far as her corset allowed, and held a palm to her chest. "Boys." She paused to inhale again. "Stop this fighting right now!"

Naomi Oliver stomped out the door of the schoolhouse toward the little crowd. Some of the children made way for their teacher while the errant boys' fists flew toward each other,

1

only hitting their mark half the time. "What is the meaning of this?" She grabbed hold of Philip's collar.

The other students backed away and scattered. Everyone, that is, except Philip and his enemy. The other boy turned and ran.

"Zeke Harper, come back here!" Miss Oliver strode in Zeke's direction, pulling Philip along with her. The other boy slowed and looked over his shoulder.

Maggie waited, giving Naomi space to do her job. An older woman pushed past the teacher and grasped Zeke by the collar. "I will gladly take care of him."

"No, Mrs. Peaberry, I'll behave, I promise." Zeke's blond hair fell into his eyes, and he flailed his arms.

"Since when? You're coming with me. We're going to tell your father what you have been up to." The severe-looking woman shoved him away from the crowd and held onto his ear.

Who was this boy, called Zeke, who no doubt had provoked her son to fisticuffs? And the pinched-faced biddy leading him away?

Maggie turned back to Philip. A shock of his red hair stood like a coxcomb. His shirt—untucked, dirty, and missing a button—added to the disheveled look. He swiped a hand across his soiled face. Her little gentleman had been transformed into a ruffian! Perhaps she'd grown used to his usual exemplary behavior, though always thankful for it. After all, he was Reverend Ian McCormick's nephew.

Miss Oliver held his shoulders. A pouf of soft brown hair surrounded the young lady's face. She pressed her lips together while shaking her head.

"Mrs. Galloway, I'm so sorry you had to witness such a thing." The glance Miss Oliver slanted toward Philip contained a mixture of affection and disappointment.

"What is this all about?" Maggie wet her thumb with her tongue and wiped the streaks of blood and dirt from his cheek.

Philip frowned and pulled away. She didn't like the look of the cut to the side of his eye.

"It's not the first time it's happened here. I'm afraid they've been taunting one another all day. I should have seen it coming."

Maggie shook her head. "I will talk to him and make sure he's disciplined."

"Both young men will have chores to do—together." Miss Oliver smiled.

Anger flashed in Philip's eyes. "I hate Zeke Harper!"

"Philip. You mustn't say such things." Maggie took a clean white handkerchief from her reticule to wipe her son's face. He jerked his hand up to push hers away.

"Hold still for a minute." She grasped his chin.

"He said his dad was the best pharmacist in Michigan. I told him Pa...used to be..." Philip sniffled. "I told him Pa used to be the best in the world!"

"That's not a reason to hit him." She stopped dabbing her son's face.

"Yeah, but then he laughed and said it didn't count 'cause Pa's dead." Philip burst into tears. Maggie knelt in front of him, gathering him into her arms. He so much wanted to be a man but was still so very much a little boy.

"Young men sometimes do get overzealous in defending their fathers' honors." Miss Oliver gave Maggie a knowing look. Then she cleared her throat. "I'll leave you two for a few minutes. I'll be inside."

Maggie could only nod. In her own grief and the busyness, she hadn't realized how deeply her son's hurt still ran. She'd been preoccupied with keeping house for her brother when they had first moved to Stone Creek.

"I...miss...Pa," Philip managed to choke out between sobs. As much as it stabbed her heart to see the wound of grief opened afresh, relief filled her that he could finally admit to his loss. His Grandfather Galloway had entreated him to be the man of the house at Robert's funeral. He'd meant well, but it was a tall order for a little boy. Had Philip taken those words too seriously?

Maggie swallowed hard. "So do I, dearest. So do I." She let her son cry himself out.

Maggie blinked back her tears in silence and held her baby tight. She set her jaw at the thought of what the Harper boy said. How could some people's children be so inconsiderate?

"Is there something I can get for you?" Miss Oliver's soft touch on Maggie's shoulder gave comfort when she came back outside to check on them.

"Thank you, no." Maggie appreciated Naomi Oliver's thoughtfulness.

"The Harpers are new in town. Their father has his hands full. His wife passed on less than a year ago, leaving him alone to rear four children." Caution edged the teacher's voice.

"Of course." Maggie only knew that a family had moved in above the pharmacy and the sign now proclaimed it *Harper Apothecary*. What should she do next to remedy the situation?

"Philip." With gentleness, she took him by the shoulders and looked him in the eye. "Zeke is hurting too. He recently lost his mama. When we hurt, sometimes we say things we don't mean."

Philip nodded as he sniffled.

"It's all well and good that you defended your father's... memory." She swallowed against the narrowing of her throat. Would the painful grief never heal? "But what does Jesus ask us to do?"

He barely returned her gaze. "Turn the other cheek?"

"Well, it's a bit late for that now. Isn't it? But you can forgive Zeke and tell him you're sorry for your part in it."

"Aw, do I have to?"

"You most certainly do. We are going to march right over to

Mr. Harper's pharmacy. Mr. Starks was kind enough to bring me to town since he had errands to do for Mrs. Myles. We mustn't keep him waiting long, so get to it."

*T*homas Harper attempted to roll out the tension creeping into his shoulders. He stared up at the clock. Only a few more minutes of peaceful quiet before his children arrived home from school. He'd sent his most recent housekeeper, Mrs. Peaberry, to retrieve them, hoping to keep things calm between his three sons and his daughter.

He picked up a book left on the counter and sighed. *Treasure Island* by Robert Louis Stevenson. Thomas looked forward to the end of the day when the children would gather with him in the cozy sitting room and listen to him read aloud the pirate story before they climbed into bed. At least they would listen with rapt attention, and at peace, for that half hour before bedtime.

His three sons were as spirited as the pirates sometimes. The task of training them to become good men loomed before Thomas. He had a soft spot for his daughter, but he treasured each one of his children. He needed to find a better way to go about things since he became a widower.

The back door clattered open, and he placed the book back on the counter.

"Stop pulling my pigtails!" Abby Harper yelled from the hallway.

The mischievous chuckles of her younger brothers, Lyle and Josiah followed, along with scuffling sounds.

That would do wonders for business. If I had any customers to begin with. He stood in the midst of what was left of his unpacked crates. Organization had never been his strong suit.

He needed her now more than ever. He leaned against the

counter and closed his eyes. *Bess.* Somehow his lovely wife kept their spirited brood under control. Not only that, but she helped him with the books. Anything out of place in the store miraculously found a spot on the right shelf. She would have had the soda fountain up and running by now, making sure the store was already profitable.

Who was he kidding? It was likely his dependence on her which brought her to an end. Worn out, she'd succumbed to influenza. It should have been him instead. He hung his head. It had been his job to find the right medicine to give her. The pain of not seeing his wife's sweet smile again this side of eternity cut a deep gash in his heart.

"Papa, Lyle and Josiah are being horrid to me again." Abby stood before her father with hands fisted at her sides and her pigtails askew.

"And where is Mrs. Peaberry?" Thomas looked around the corner.

"Pa won't be mad at us once Zeke gets back." Josiah smirked and hiked his thumb back toward the door.

Lyle covered his mouth while he bumped into Josiah.

Thomas shook his head at all three. He placed a hand on his daughter's shoulder. "No need to tattle, little dove." He turned to the boys. "You can work at being better gentlemen."

He paused as Josiah's words settled on him. "Now what has Zeke gotten into?"

"They aren't far behind us. I'm sure of that." Josiah averted his gaze.

"Josiah, I asked you a question." The back door clattered open again.

"And furthermore, young man, I've never seen the likes of you or your brothers. There's no reason for this kind of behavior. School is for learning. Not fisticuffs." Bess's image dissolved as the high-pitched voice of Mrs. Peaberry scraped at his nerves. "And how do you expect me to get the grass stains out of your knickers? I've got more than enough to do already."

"Ow, Ow! Let me go, you old battle-ax." The back door pounded shut against the frame.

Mrs. Peaberry dragged Zeke down the hall with one hand grasping his collar and the other his ear.

"That is quite uncalled for, Zeke. Apologize to Mrs. Peaberry immediately." Thomas crossed his arms and did his best to convey his sternest glare.

"But she's hurting me."

"And as far as you're concerned..." Thomas faced the house-keeper. "Unhand my son's ear." He flitted his gaze toward the other children, who snickered. Perhaps he should be more careful about how he dealt with Mrs. Peaberry in front of them in the future.

"Well, I can't believe this." The housekeeper's grin turned to a grimace when she let go of Zeke and placed her hands on her hips.

A smug grin sprang up on Zeke's face, which wouldn't do at all.

"Excuse me. I brought up six well-behaved sons, and all of them have perfect hearing."

"I'm not implying you would try to hurt the boy, but please leave us, and I will try to remedy this situation." Why was he trying to deal with every problem instead of the other way around? He needed a woman who wouldn't only discipline the children but also had an ounce of compassion for them. Someone who would smooth the way between his offspring and himself. Someone like Bess.

"If you think an apology is all that's necessary, you're sorely mistaken. The child needs proper discipline. That's the problem here. Such disrespect is not to be tolerated. Now, if you'll excuse me, I'll get onto other chores." Mrs. Peaberry marched toward the stairway with head held high. The clomp of her boots on the stairway echoed in the little shop.

Tow-headed Zeke had hair so much like his mother's, but it was more tousled than usual. The rest of the boy's disheveled appearance included a bruise underneath his right eye. He'd been fighting. Again. "Son, I thought we were going to start over in Stone Creek. We agreed you weren't going to fight anymore."

"It's my first one, Pa, and I was defending your honor." Zeke had a point. He hadn't fought in over a month.

"I thought you didn't want people to think you're a bully."

The boy jutted out his chin. "Mrs. Peaberry's a bully."

"We're talking about you, young man, and that's not acceptable talk." Thomas cleared his throat and lowered his voice to a whisper. "Perhaps if you behaved better, so would she. Now, go get cleaned up. And I expect you to explain to me what happened at school, not to mention, have some kind words for Mrs. Peaberry when you've calmed down." Thomas placed his hand on his son's shoulder for a passing moment. He connected with the pain in Zeke's eyes. Thomas could never make up for the absence of a mother, nor for the void in his own life.

A scrape and a thud were followed by Mrs. Peaberry's ear-piercing scream. "I can't take any more of this. Get back here, you rapscallions!"

Josiah and Lyle fairly flew down the stairs, followed by Abby, her pigtails bouncing behind her.

"I didn't do anything." Abby's voice held a pleading tone. She frowned above her round, wire-rimmed glasses and hugged a book close.

The boys tried to contain their chuckles, but the laughter escaped in waves. When one calmed down, the other bent over again in a fit, barely able to catch a breath.

"What have you done now?" Thomas feared the worst of

the boys' shenanigans. Couldn't he have one day of peace in his home? His life? He passed a hand over his hair.

"I'll tell you what happened." Mrs. Peaberry appeared at the bottom of the stairs. The front brim of her dark gray hat curved downward, giving her a hawk-like appearance. "I found a snake in my drawer. A snake!"

Next, she held up a banana peel. "And they were all too happy, with their unsanitary practices, to leave this on the floor of my room. I turned and ran only to fall on my...on my...posterior." Her voice lowered as her face reddened.

Thomas put his hand out to receive the brown fruit skin, as empty and disheveled as he felt. "Children," he began in his most serious tone.

"Don't waste your breath, Mr. Harper. This brood of vipers is hopeless. I am leaving your employ this very minute."

"But..."

"Nothing would entice me to stay. *Nothing*. You can send my bags and the remainder of my wages to the Pink Hotel. That is where I will be staying tonight. Good day!"

Thomas stared after the ill-tempered woman as she walked out onto the boardwalk, slamming the door behind her, which resonated throughout the shop.

"Go do your homework." He couldn't even look into his children's eyes. Their footsteps retreated up the stairs. For one afternoon, anyway, Thomas was relieved at the lack of customers.

～

*W*istful thoughts of a chubby toddler tugged at Maggie's memories as Philip squared his shoulders and promised to follow close. He brushed away her offered hand. Without a father, Philip instinctively pushed himself to become the man of the house.

The new Harper Apothecary on Main Street, with freshly painted letters on its sign, showed Stone Creek's progress. Some townspeople were concerned its presence might cut into Dr. Moore's income, as he had been the only one to offer medicine thus far. However, others saw help for the aging doctor, someone to provide services when he was busy elsewhere. He couldn't ever take the doctor's place. The wise older man welcomed such growth in Stone Creek. Hopefully, it would prove to be the healthy alliance the dear physician expected.

Maggie stopped short to examine the show globe displayed in the picture window. The tall, rounded jar stood proudly in the center. An ornate stopper plugged the clear glass container filled with liquid bluer than any summer sky. "This reminds me so much of your father's show globe. Do you remember?" The liquid shimmering in the daylight had at one time attested to the apothecary's prowess, or as it had been further in the past, their skills at alchemy. Through the ages, the show globe had become symbolic, but still an artful representation for the profession. She recalled the day Robert had explained it all to her as though it was yesterday. Maggie sighed.

"Yes, but Pa's was prettier. It was green."

He set his freckled face in determination and, she feared, a bit of defiance. Still, she had to smile. *Loyal to the end, isn't he?* "You're right, but before you were born, he mixed it up blue for a while."

The door opened, a bell jingling in its wake. The older woman she'd seen earlier strode out of the shop as though escaping the plague. "Snakes." The woman shook her head ignoring Maggie as she pushed past them. "A...most ill-behaved brood...of...vipers."

Philip, wide-eyed, sidestepped the woman. "Mama, is that lady addle-pated?"

"Sh, that's not a polite thing to say. Now, let's stay on the task before us. Have you decided what you're going to say?"

"Yes, ma'am." Philip nodded, looking none too happy.

He held the door open for her, and Maggie waited after passing through so they could face his enemy together.

The medicinal odor, wrapped in a strange mixture of valerian and peppermint, forced her back in time. Maggie half expected to see Robert standing behind the counter, mortar and pestle in hand. Instead, a taller man emerged from the afternoon shadows. His sad hazel eyes emanated weariness. A curly wisp of sandy brown hair fell across his rather high forehead. Lines furrowed the brow of his handsome face, though he didn't look as though he was yet forty. "May I help you, ma'am?"

Maggie reached out her hand, wanting to keep things businesslike. "Mrs. Maggie Galloway."

His brows rose as though surprised at her confidence. He gave her a firm but polite shake. A gentleman. "Thomas Harper."

"I believe my son, Philip, had a scuffle with your son Zeke this afternoon?" She arched an eyebrow with the question.

"Ah, yes." Mr. Harper glanced toward the stairway before returning her gaze with an expression of sincere remorse. "I'm sorry he behaved in such a way. Zeke..." He paused. "Zeke has been a bit of a bully since he lost his mother. He wasn't always like this. He and I are working on correcting his bad habits."

Though Mr. Harper was immediately apologetic, tension hung between them.

"I brought Philip to make up with your son. I think they should work this out."

Mr. Harper smoothed his hair back, then wiped his hands together. He looked at the floor and then up at her, then down again. Did he expect the boy to rise up out of the floorboards? Maggie glanced toward the ticking clock. Mr. Starks would want to return to Apple Blossom House, the estate where she rented a cottage, soon.

"Would you mind calling your son, sir?"

As if he despaired of doing such a thing, Mr. Harper sighed. "If you insist."

Really. Who was in charge here? This man? Or his child?

He retreated toward the stairs to the left of her and tucked just into the hallway. "Zeke. Please come down here right now." He walked toward her again. "Is there anything I can help you with while we wait?" A strained smile revealed a dimple in the man's right cheek. Endearing.

Maggie surveyed the store. Jars of different sizes perched too near the edges of dusty shelves with empty gaps where there should be important remedies. "Hmm." She hadn't meant to say that aloud.

Mr. Harper's questioning look unnerved her. Maggie didn't want to criticize the man when he was new in town. She bit back her comments.

A boy not much bigger than Philip slid down the banister. His feet hit the floorboards with a thud.

"Hi, Philip!" he called out as though seeing a long-lost friend.

Philip raised his hand in a curt wave. Maggie placed a firm hand on his back, urging her son forward.

"Hi, Zeke. Sorry I punched you." Philip rubbed his neck.

"You're all right. I shouldn't have said what I did." The other boy shifted his weight to one leg. He possessed an attitude and stance beyond his years.

"Shouldn't you two shake hands on it?" Did she have to tell them how to do everything?

"What a good idea. Don't you think?"

Does Mr. Harper think he's taking charge now?

"You're all right too." Philip nodded and smiled, putting forth his right hand. The boys grasped hands and pumped them up and down as though they were operating the lever on a water pump.

Finally, the smile returned to her son's face. His grief was forgotten for the moment, and what a relief he'd made up with Zeke. Maggie glanced beyond the two children. Two more boys and an older girl peered over the railing of the stairs.

"You want to see my pet snake?" Zeke motioned Philip toward the stairway.

"Is it poisonous?" Maggie looked to Mr. Harper.

"No. Most assuredly, it's a harmless garter snake. I want you to take it back out to the garden now, Zeke."

"Aww, Pa." But he must have seen the pleading look in his father's eyes. In fact, the man seemed too tired to produce anger.

"Yes, Pa." Zeke turned to Philip. "Come on. You can help me bring down the box he's in."

"Really?" Philip followed at the other boy's heels. The rest of the Harper children greeted him with eagerness.

Maggie hadn't seen such enthusiasm in her son all day. "We have to leave as soon as you're done." She hated to keep them from mending their acquaintance. Surely, it would make things easier for the kind Miss Oliver as well if the children got along.

Tick. Tick. Tick. Silence ensued. Maggie turned to find Mr. Harper watching her as though sizing her up. For a moment, her gaze stuck on his. She was dangerously close to being drawn in by the sadness of those eyes.

Her glance swept around the shop in a desperate attempt to think of what she needed. "White willow extract." The words left her mouth, unbidden. "Do you have some?"

"Certainly, but have you tried aspirin?" He searched the shelves. "I've taken the powdered drug, all the way from Germany, and pressed it into tablets which are much easier to swallow." He held up the preparation.

"Mr. Harper, I prepare my own remedies with the best ingredients I find available." Maggie sniffed. "I'm not interested in newfangled products. If I wanted a form of some medicine man's chicanery, I could find it at Neuberger's Mercantile."

The pharmacist held the bottle closer to her. "I assure you, this is an exceptional product. The chemical base is the same, but more potent and exacting in each dose. The future of pharmacology, I'll warrant you."

"If my husband were still alive, I'm sure he would beg to differ." Maggie's voice rose. "He didn't rush into selling newfangled remedies like some snake oil salesman." She narrowed her eyes at Mr. Harper.

"I see. Then I take it you know so much because you had the same amount of training as your husband or I?" He drummed his fingers on the counter.

"Your point being?"

"I've heard your snickerdoodle cookies are legendary in this town, but I wouldn't pretend to know what spices to put in a cookie—"

"I'm sure you wouldn't." She sucked in her breath and stepped back from the counter. "I'm guessing I know a bit more about pharmacology than you do about baking."

For the first time, a sparkle of humor appeared in the man's eyes, a twitch of his lips. How dare he make fun of her? "I'll be taking my leave now." She glared at him before calling her son. "Philip!"

Mr. Harper snickered. "And not share your wealth of knowledge first?"

To Maggie's horror, all five children stood at the foot of the stairs staring at the two of them. How had she not heard them make their way back down the stairs? Zeke carried a box.

"If you'd like, I can still get some willow extract for you." The former worry returned to Mr. Harper's face.

"If you can find it in this mess you call an apothecary." Maggie shook her head and waved her hand about.

"No, Ranger!" Too late, Zeke Harper tried to push the

escaping reptile back into its box, but it flipped out of his grasp onto the floor.

Maggie screamed and grabbed Philip by the hand, doing a staccato dance around the slithering snake. She managed to pull her son out the door and down the street toward the Myleses' buggy.

"But I was having fun," Philip whined.

Maggie didn't slow down.

"You sure got mad at Mr. Harper. Don't you owe him an apology?"

The sincerity in her son's eyes melted her.

"I mean, doesn't Jesus want you to be sorry when you hurt someone?" Philip pressed her further.

Maggie opened her mouth, but what could she say? By her own words, she'd been condemned. Perhaps it wasn't only the snake she sought escape from, but also from a handsome widower who needed the balm of compassion. Well, that balm was going to have to come from someone else.

CHAPTER 2

$\mathcal{T}$homas barely noticed the commotion as the boys scrambled around him to retrieve their pet. He stared toward the door, where the auburn-haired spitfire had escaped. That woman had a lot of nerve telling him what he should or shouldn't be selling. Didn't she know he'd been properly educated for this profession? Who did she think she was, anyway?

Yet he couldn't forget her aqua eyes, almost as dark as the sapphire-blue dress she wore. They had bored into him in a most provocative way, as though she could read his mind and heart.

Women. The only one he had ever loved or thought worthy of his regard had been Bess. They'd been childhood sweethearts. He couldn't imagine being married to anyone else. They'd had enough love and happiness for a lifetime. He could only commit to spending the rest of his life single.

All three boys were down on their bellies, scooting after Ranger. Abby watched, silent. She shook her head. The snake disappeared through a hole in the floor. The boys all made a lunge, heads crashing together.

"Ow!" they cried, nearly in unison.

"Well, that's just fine. All Pa needs is a snake in the cellar." Abby took her position as the oldest, crossing her arms. "You better go find it."

"Yes, ma'am." Josiah, one year younger than Abby's thirteen, gave her a mock salute.

"Boys, see what you can do to recover the snake." Thomas raised his voice as his frustrations mounted. "I have quite enough to do." His sons looked askance at their usually calm, steady father. Well, he wasn't perfect, and he didn't possess the angelic joy their deceased mother had. "Get to it!"

The boys scurried off like frightened mice.

Abby curled an arm around her father's, laying her head against his shoulder. "Papa." She called him by his favorite name. "I could make us cheese sandwiches for supper if there's any bread left."

Thomas patted his daughter's shoulder. "I'm not hungry, but perhaps you should fix something for you and your brothers."

She nodded. "I miss Mama."

"So do I." They didn't often say the words to one another because the statement wouldn't bring Bess back. In fact, admitting this exposed the empty spot in their hearts and their lives all the more. But he knew if anyone felt the absence of her mother, it was Abby.

His daughter was a studious bookworm, a melancholy dreamer as he had been. He'd tried to avoid thrusting her into the role of mothering her feisty brothers, but Mrs. Peaberry had been his third housekeeper, and she'd lasted all of two weeks.

"We'll be all right." Thomas hugged her awkwardly. The child would soon become a young lady, and he wasn't sure what to do with her—except perhaps lock her away from every suitor until a knight in shining armor came along. How was he supposed to navigate this uncharted territory alone?

His children needed a mother—and he missed his wife.

~

"*J*hope I have not kept you waiting too long, Mr. Starks. We had a little problem at the school and some additional business to take care of. We certainly didn't mean to take so much of your time." The butler helped Maggie up into Gloria and Asa Myles's buggy.

"I am at your disposal, ma'am." Mr. Starks tipped his hat. "I was detained, as well, at the mercantile."

Philip scrambled into his seat. "Was Mr. Neuberger talking a lot again? Mama says it always takes longer when he gets chatty and nosey with the customers."

"Philip. What's gotten into you? You're absolutely incorrigible today." Maggie's voice rose higher than she would have liked.

The usually stoic Mr. Starks covered his mouth with one leather-gloved hand. His shoulders shook with humor. "No offense in the truth, ma'am. I think a bit of spring has gotten into the boy."

"Well, perhaps you can help me find some extra chores for him to work that bit of spring out."

Philip's impish grin turned into a pout. His shoulders slumped.

"There were a few pieces of mail for you at the post office. I took the liberty of procuring them since you were detained." Mr. Starks handed Maggie several envelopes.

"Why, thank you." Maggie's heart tripped a little. Riffling through the small bundle, Maggie found the envelope she'd anticipated from the Silver Leaf Flour Company and tore it open.

Dear Mrs. Galloway,

We are pleased to convey our most hearty congratulations on your securing second place in our Silver Leaf Don't Rest on Your Laurels Baking Contest. While Mrs. Edwina Beardsley will wear the first-place genuine Silver Leaf Laurel, you will be awarded the second-place Silver Leaf Laurel pin, which will be presented to you in person by none other than our own Midwest Regional Director, Mr. Giles Prescott of our Chicago, Illinois, office. Mr. Prescott will contact you directly to arrange a convenient time for your presentation. It is our sincerest wish you take the time to collect and invite your dearest friends and closest neighbors to include them in this august occasion. We are also honored to assure you that your original Pecan Snickerdoodle recipe will appear in our latest nationally distributed Silver Leaf Cookbook. Your continued patronage, high regard for, and recommendation of our finest Silver Leaf Flour products remains one of our most treasured assets.

Sincerely,

C. Horace Stockwell III, President

Silver Leaf Flour Mill, Minneapolis, Minnesota

"*W*ell, what do you know? I won't be going to Minneapolis to have the Silver Leaf Laurel placed upon my head, but second place isn't so bad." Maggie reread the letter which included a familiar name—Giles Prescott. Could this executive possibly be the Giles she once knew?

"Is the prize for your new cookies, Mama?" Philip's beatific smile indicated her sweet little boy had returned.

"Yes, sir." Maggie reached over to ruffle her son's hair. "The recipe is going to be published in the new *Silver Leaf Cookbook*."

"Such good news, ma'am. Congratulations." Mr. Starks's

uncharacteristic grin showed his pleasure at her good news as he climbed into the driver's seat.

"Thank you, and remember, it's just plain Maggie Galloway to you, sir." A chuckle tunneled her throat.

If she weren't a thirty-two-year-old widow and mother, she would most improperly throw off her hat and enjoy the spring breeze in her hair. She closed her eyes and breathed in the sweet scent of budding leaves while the vehicle bumped along the road toward Apple Blossom House and the estate's nearby cottage.

"Maggie." Her sister-in-law's voice, calling to her from the roadside, broke her reverie.

She opened her eyes. Sophie McCormick waved at her. "Sophie." Maggie waved back. Leaning forward, she said, "Would you please stop the conveyance for a few moments, Mr. Starks?"

"Certainly, ma'am." The butler stopped the horse and alighted from the buggy to help Maggie down.

"You mustn't go to such trouble for me, Mr. Starks." Maggie shook her head.

"I'm under the strictest orders from Mrs. Myles, you see, so I must." His eyes brightened a bit.

Maggie had grown up somewhat well off, but it chafed her to feel she was taking advantage of another family's servant or to think she was above anyone else's "station" in life. Gloria Myles had assured her it was their pleasure while Maggie and Philip leased Apple Blossom Cottage, and the arrangement had suited them all when her brother, Ian, had married the previous autumn. But she'd had time to think about other plans since.

Sophie's three-year-old daughter, Caira, jumped up and down. "Fiwip!"

"You look lovelier every time I see you." Maggie hurried

toward Sophie and kissed her on the cheek. "You're positively radiant." Then she bent to pick up Caira.

The younger woman blushed, touching a hand to her slightly rounded belly. "Well, I've never been more content."

"I don't suppose Ian has anything to do with that." Maggie teased, making her sister-in-law blush a deeper crimson. "Do not feel embarrassed. Being in the family way suits you, and I've never seen Ian happier, dear."

"Thank you." Sophie added a smile to her appreciation.

Maggie took one of Sophie's hands in her own. "Would you, Ian, and Caira come for the evening meal tonight?"

"We would be delighted to. May I bring something?"

"Just yourselves. I have excellent news to share."

~

*M*aggie had been impressed the first time she'd seen the guesthouse, tucked behind the garden in the shadow of blossoming fruit trees. Now, as she walked up the flagstone path, Maggie counted her blessings in having such a lovely little home. The clapboards almost shimmered with a coat of bright white paint. The hunter-green shutters and trim blended with the foliage. A small covered front porch had room for a chair and a porch swing. She and Gloria Myles had spent many pleasant evenings there chatting.

"Hi, Elise!" Philip waved at a little blond girl who stood on the back porch of the large Queen Anne-style Apple Blossom House. "Can I go play with her, Mama?"

"It's *may* I, and you certainly may not after your behavior at school today. Now, get inside, finish your chores, and do your homework." Maggie gave her son a warning look.

Since the orphaned Elise had come to live with her grandparents, she had been quite withdrawn. Piano lessons had brought her out of her shell a bit, but Gloria and Asa didn't think the child ready for the schoolhouse. Instead, they'd hired a private tutor. Philip was often the only companion Elise had close to her age.

Philip held the door for Maggie, a contrite look on his face.

"Now, you see, your ill behavior doesn't only hurt yourself, but others too. Elise will miss playing with you today." Maggie pulled one kid glove off at a time while pondering her dilemma. He'd made up with Zeke. Should she have him help Mr. Starks with extra chores in addition to helping Miss Oliver at the school?

He nodded. "I'll be good now."

She threw her arms around him, and he hugged her back with fierceness.

~

The cool evening demanded the warmth of a fire in the small sitting room's hearth, but Maggie grew quite warm enough as she stood by the coal stove to prepare supper. She passed the back of her hand over her brow and stirred the gravy for hot roast beef sandwiches with the other.

At a knock at the front door, Maggie left the kitchen, squeezing between the sideboard and the oak dining room table. The evening sun streamed through the large window and glinted off her Blue Willow plates. She missed the convenience of the gaslights she'd enjoyed in the parsonage, but a little candlelight would serve them well. Apple Blossom Cottage was a lovely little home, and the rent was more than reasonable. There was but one problem. The home wasn't hers. Maggie McCormick Galloway hadn't been taught to accept charity. If only she had a place truly her own, like the cozy bungalow she'd once shared with Robert.

Another more persistent knock sounded. "Philip! Go let Uncle Ian and Aunt Sophie in."

"Yes, Mama." The boy ran to open the door.

Maggie's brother and his family entered the cozy abode and surrounded Philip with hugs.

Maggie moved toward the dark-haired man who was more than a head taller than she and four years her junior with open arms and gave Ian a generous hug. "Little brother, how good it is to see you." She scooped Caira from Sophie's arms, holding her tight. "Come here, sweetheart."

"Supper smells delicious." Ian looked around as though wondering what was in store.

"I'm thinking Ian misses your cooking." Sophie shrugged out of her wrap with Ian's help.

"How can you say that? I love your cooking." Ian pretended a pout.

Sophie put a hand on one of her disappearing hips. "You and I both know I have a lot to learn in the kitchen."

"But I hear you're doing very well. I had a few good years of practice before I came to keep house for Ian. You're learning faster than I did, I'm sure." Maggie hurried them toward the dining room.

Over the meal, Ian related the challenges of refurbishing the old White farm so that it could become Hope's Place, a refuge for unmarried mothers and fallen women who needed a fresh start. Maggie told them of her eventful afternoon, but when she ended with the account of the slithering garter snake, the humor of it suddenly struck her. She chuckled. "It didn't seem funny at the time." Mostly annoying.

Then the face of the pharmacist came to mind, along with his twinkling hazel eyes.

Sophie paled. "Certainly not."

"I done." Caira wiggled, dropped her fork on the table, and then pushed herself away from it.

"Where do you think you're going? Hmm?" Ian took her tiny hand. "Eat up if you want some of Aunt Maggie's cookies."

Caira subdued as she took a bite with her mother's help.

"But I heard you had news for us," Ian said. "It couldn't have been only your snake story."

"How about some tea and snickerdoodles first?" Their crestfallen expressions made Maggie more anxious to share. "*Prize-winning* pecan snickerdoodles." She lifted her chin a bit.

Sophie's and Ian's faces both creased with smiles.

Maggie went to the sideboard where she had stashed her reticule. She fished for the letter, carefully pulling it from the envelope. "This afternoon's mishaps have all been made right by this." She held the letter in front of her.

Ian snatched the paper from her hand and cleared his throat. "'Dear Mrs. Galloway...'"

Maggie couldn't help a grin of pleasure while he read aloud. Hopefully, she wasn't being too prideful. After all, she did thank God for her baking ideas and skill. After plucking golden cookies covered with cinnamon and sugar from a cream-colored earthenware jar, Maggie placed them on a pressed-glass plate that had once belonged to her mother and took them to the table.

"Wonderful," Ian exclaimed. "I always thought your baking would bring you notice."

"Oh, Maggie." Sophie passed Caira over to Ian so she could round the table to give Maggie a hug. "I'm so happy for you." She took her by the hands. "When the Silver Leaf representative comes, we must have a luncheon to celebrate. We'll invite everyone. It's so exciting."

"Absolutely." Ian waved the letter. "It will be big doings for our little town. Who did the letter say was bringing your award?"

Maggie's face warmed. "Mr. Giles Prescott." Her hand went up to pat the back of her upswept hair.

"The name sounds familiar, though I suppose it could be a coincidence." Ian stroked his chin.

Maggie averted her eyes from his probing gaze.

"It couldn't be." He drummed his fingers on the table.

"Whatever are you talking about, dearest?" Sophie still held one of Maggie's hands.

"There was a young man sweet on my sister back in our hometown by the same name."

Maggie cleared her throat. "You mean we grew up with a boy with the same name, but this is a big country. There could be dozens of Giles Prescotts." She waved her hand.

"We both know he had his cap set for you until Robert came along, and you broke Giles's heart." Ian took on a teasing tone and smug smile.

Sophie placed an arm around Maggie's back in a quick hug. "Don't pay attention to him."

Philip tilted his face toward Maggie. "You had a beau before Pa?"

"Not exactly. Now look what you started, little brother." Maggie scurried around the kitchen, looking for a tin of green tea. "And where's my silver tea ball?" she muttered under her breath.

"May I help you bring out the tea or some cups?" Just when Maggie was prying the lid off the tin, Sophie's soft touch on her shoulder caused her to jump.

Maggie knocked over the container, causing tea leaves to spray all over the kitchen floor. Then all she could think of was when Giles had strewn red rose petals on her front porch the first time he asked to court her.

$\sim$

"*A*way with you now. Off to bed." Thomas Harper closed the leather-bound book with finality in the flicker of the gaslight. "We'll have to find out what happens next to Jim Hawkins on the *Hispaniola* tomorrow night."

"Papa, can't you read a little more?" Abby placed her hand on his forearm and stared up at him with pleading eyes. She sat close to him on one side, while Zeke snuggled with his head against Thomas's other arm. His youngest son yawned and struggled to keep his eyes open.

Josiah sat in a horsehair chair in the opposite corner from the couch while Lyle stacked blocks on the floor.

"Do we have to go to bed?" Lyle continued building.

"Yes. It's been a long day for all of us." Thomas failed to suppress his yawn. "Look at Zeke. Not even he is as chipper as usual."

"Come on, Pa. Couldn't you read a couple of more pages?" Josiah's pleading tempted Thomas, but he needed to put his foot down. Without a nanny, the task of disciplining this bunch fell on him.

Thomas stood. "What did I say?"

A chorus of disappointed chatter met him, but one by one, they shuffled toward the door.

Earlier, in his shop, that Galloway woman's piercing eyes had accused him of his lack of parenting skills. Like a little sergeant, she must have marched her son up to bed and had him tucked in already. But why did he even care what Maggie Galloway thought?

CHAPTER 3

*T*homas fought through the fog to catch up to his Bess. Thick mud sucked at his feet like magnets. Never enough air... He gasped. Bess gave him a teasing grin over her shoulder. Then disappeared around a corner. A floating brick wall blocked his view. Sent panic into his chest. Her musical laughter drifted in the heavy mist. Then he was alone. Again.

"Papa, Papa." A young voice broke through his dream, dragging him back to reality.

Thomas's heart pounded. He pried his eyes open one at a time. Even the dream was preferable to life without his wife.

"I don't feel too good."

"Zeke?" Thomas batted the sleep from his eyes and struggled to focus. "Must you shine that light right in my face, son?"

"Sorry." Zeke placed the lantern on the floor.

"What's wrong?" Thomas focused on his son. What a sorry-looking lad he was with a black eye and a bruised cheek.

Zeke coughed. "Abby said I was burning up." The boy inhaled through his stuffy nose.

Thomas felt his forehead. "You are quite warm. Come on,

let's get you some medicine." He could concoct remedies to make almost everyone feel better—except himself. There was no medicine for a broken heart.

Thomas stood and pulled his rumpled robe from the end of the bed. He wrapped himself in it and tied the sash against the chilling nighttime air.

Zeke coughed again.

"Cover your mouth, son."

"Do I have to take willow extract?" The boy's face scrunched with obvious distaste.

"I have some good news for you. The same medicine is in a tablet now. You can swallow it with some horehound tea." He chuckled at his son's face, the child's tongue hanging out in disgust. "Or a glass of water."

Despite the reprimand of the Galloway woman, Thomas felt quite confident the tablets he'd made would be just the ticket—though the thought of her indignation over the aspirin made him smile. Ah, well, she wasn't likely to darken his doorstep any time soon.

But the reminder of Mrs. Galloway...and his dream. Bess's hair had been auburn instead of blond. How odd.

"What about the sweet stuff with horehound and molasses in it?" The boy's eyes lit up beyond the glassy cast the fever lent to them while he licked his lips.

Bess had saved the more expensive bottled horehound medicine for customers and insisted the children drink hot tea. She figured it was better for them than the sickly sweetened potion. And if they had protested much, a sprinkle of sugar would have to do.

There he was, doing it again. Comparing his parenting skills to Bess's.

"Well, why not? It might do you some good, and you can get back to bed much quicker."

They padded down the creaky stairs.

"Pa, it's scary down here when it's dark." Zeke stopped short in front of him.

Thomas nearly knocked the boy over. The lantern's glow dispelled the darkness, but not the shadows. Piled crates with a jar atop cast the shape of a hulking monster. Even the blue liquid of the show globe reflected a sickly glow against the front window.

"Stay right by me. I'll have what we need in a moment." Thomas procured a small bottle of tablets and a dark-amber bottle filled with liquid. "Let's go back up to the kitchen to find a spoon and a cup." He handed his son the lantern.

Zeke nodded and followed close at his heels, taking two steps at a time. When he reached the top of the stairs, he turned, placed a hand on his chest, and exclaimed, "Whew! Nothing got me." *Hack! Hack!*

"Son, you must be more careful when you're carrying the lantern. And don't be silly. I wouldn't let anything get you. Besides, there's nothing, and no one, to hurt you in the shop. You know that. Go sit on my bed and wait for me." He took the lantern. "I'll turn the gaslight on for you." After setting the bottles on the dresser, Thomas adjusted the switch under the glass cup inside the doorway to his room until a low flame claimed the surrounding darkness.

He made his way to the kitchen. It was less than twenty-four hours since Mrs. Peaberry had left his employ, yet dirty dishes were stacked in the sink and books left out on the table. A loaf of bread sat outside the breadbox, its paper wrapping askew. Tomorrow would find things even less tidy, no doubt.

Thomas opened the cupboard to look for a cup. Two tiny beads of onyx stared back at him before their owner scurried away with a squeak. Thomas jumped back, inhaling a quick breath. Things were worse than he thought. He passed a hand over his hair. He simply had to make some order out of all this chaos.

With shaky hands, he grabbed what he hoped was a clean glass from the sideboard and pumped water into it. He rattled around the drawer for a teaspoon. At least he found the utensil without running into any more unwelcome creatures. Maybe the missing garter snake would find the mouse and enjoy a hearty breakfast, although he had to admit, the mouse was more pleasant to look at.

Once he had given Zeke a dose of each medicine, he covered the boy with a blanket. "You'll stay with me tonight. I don't want your brothers getting sick." Leaden weariness pulled at Thomas's frame as he climbed into bed.

"Pa, can I stay home from school in the morning?"

"Assuming you're truly ill, of course." Thomas turned over and closed his eyes while pondering how he would care for a sick child and any customers who came along during the day.

"Micah Bradley's sister said he came down with measles. Do you think that's what I have?" Zeke yawned.

Thomas's eyes popped back open. "Only time will tell." A measles epidemic? Had the other three children ever been sick with the disease?

A sick feeling crept around his middle. He recognized the long, dark fingers of fear. When influenza struck Bess down, hadn't he promised her he wouldn't let anything happen to them?

The morning after Ian, Sophie, and Caira came for supper, Maggie looked forward to a productive day.

"Dear Lord," she prayed as she closed the door behind her son. He often walked with the children from a neighboring farm. It was a good hike, but he was used to it. "Please watch over my boy today. Keep him out of trouble. Give him wisdom and strength to do what is right...and please comfort the Harper children."

Her eyes moistened at the thought of her son growing up so quickly. She had once hoped to have more children, but she should be thankful for her healthy boy. Besides, Maggie had grown used to the relative quiet.

She poured herself a cup of coffee from the pot on the stove and sat down at the table with a cookbook. Maggie flipped through the pages, some dog-eared, some worn by frequent use. Nothing pleased her more than creating delicacies to comfort and cheer friends and neighbors. Perhaps she should work on improving the scone recipe or the chocolate cake. Or increasing the vanilla in her favorite snickerdoodle recipe which had won second place in the contest, while adding toasted, chopped pecans to the dough.

She leaned forward, placing her elbow on the tiny kitchen table, and rested her chin in her hand. She yawned and scanned the neat little room. Beef barley vegetable soup simmered on the stove, using up the rest of Sunday's leftovers. A colorful braided rug covered the swept wood floor.

While Maggie kept house for her brother, she hadn't worried about keeping a roof over their heads. She'd gained a small inheritance from her parents and received some insurance money when Robert had passed. They might do all right if she was careful with her money. But she couldn't stay in Apple Blossom Cottage forever, living off Gloria and Asa's charity.

I may have to turn my favorite activity into a business. There are worse things in life.

The night before, as sleep evaded her, her conscience had stirred. Did she have to speak to Mr. Harper as sharply as she had? His kind eyes had held a depth of sadness she'd only seen matched in her own reflection, after the loss of her Robert to pneumonia. Dark circles and worry lines aged a face some would call handsome.

Images of the disorganized shop, the boy with a bruised eye, courtesy of her son, and the other motherless children in the background haunted her. Didn't Mr. Harper have any help with the household or the shop? Four children to bring up and a business to run... Would she have been able to handle such circumstances?

His superior attitude still annoyed her, along with his unwillingness to discuss things more rationally. But had he deserved her censure?

Now she drew in a sip of the bitter brown liquid in her cup, then nestled it back in its saucer and pushed it away. Her first and foremost concern was Philip, but she could pray for the Harper family.

Maggie rolled up her sleeves and stood to pull her apron from its peg. Baking always made her feel better, and she'd promised Philip a chocolate cake for dessert. When a knock sounded at the back door, she pushed the green muslin curtain aside.

"Gloria!" Maggie pulled open the door and ushered the woman, who was both her friend and landlady, inside with a hug. "What are you doing here?"

The elegant lady with graying blond hair and an apron uncharacteristically slung over her arm squeezed Maggie's hand with her finely gloved one. "Elise stopped Philip on the pathway to say 'hello' when he was on his way to school. He mentioned you would probably be baking a chocolate cake this morning. Is this true?"

Maggie nodded. "You caught me just in time."

"I would like to learn how again. It's been so long since I baked anything." Gloria's eyes lit up like a child at her birthday party, ready to open presents.

"Your cook, Flo, does a fine job." Maggie took her friend's light topcoat as she shrugged out of the garment.

"Very true. But I sometimes want for an occupation." Gloria

slipped the apron over her head and tied the strings in the back. "You keep the cottage so peaceful and quiet. It's a contrast to our large household. Even with only a couple of servants and a stable boy, I feel the busyness of it. We really don't need as big a home for only Asa, Elise, and me."

"Sit down for a minute. Let me pour you some coffee." Maggie procured another cup and saucer from the corner cabinet, along with a bowl of sugar cubes.

Gloria pulled a chair out to sit down. She folded her hands, waiting politely. "You know, this was the first house on the property. Asa's parents settled here before their business grew and they gained their fortune. I've tried to imagine what it was like for them, but I couldn't before you moved in. Now, I can imagine a family living and loving within these walls each day. You've made it a home."

Maggie felt a smile crease her face to match Gloria's. "I suppose it's much different from where you grew up?"

"Oh yes, simplicity is definitely lost when you live amidst great affluence." Gloria sat up straight and took the silver spoon Maggie handed her, stirring in the cream and sugar supplied. "Thank you." She drew in a dainty sip.

"But there is great blessing in not living with great need." Maggie topped off her cup with coffee.

"Truly I have been blessed. This gives me all the more reason to look forward to the work at the orphanage when it opens." Gloria set the spoon on the rim of the saucer.

"Then you will not lack for an occupation." Maggie smoothed her skirt and joined her friend at the table.

"No, I will not. It's a dream coming true to help orphans like our granddaughter, and have it be in the memory of my dear only daughter and son-in-law."

"You're welcome to help me with the cake." Maggie tapped her hand on the table before she stood. "And have you heard my news?"

"Philip mentioned something about a contest. I must say, he looked as though he would bust his buttons with pride."

Maggie filled in the details to Gloria's delight. Before long, they were sifting flour, beating eggs, and mixing cocoa, sugar, and butter to make a silky brown batter.

Once it was in the oven, they sat side by side at the dining room table and browsed the cookbook for a frosting recipe. "This is your lesson," Maggie said. "Would you like to make up a batch of plain buttercream? Or do you prefer a rich chocolate?"

Gloria took a whiff of the cake baking in the oven. "How about buttercream? Maggie, you have such talent. Have you thought of doing something more with your God-given ability?" She followed her into the kitchen.

A flash of warmth touched her cheeks, and she took a deep breath. Maggie found the confectioner's sugar in the cabinet and began to sift it into another stoneware bowl. She put down the sifter and wiped her hands on her white apron before she took one of Gloria's hands in hers. "You know I love it here."

The novice baker nodded.

"And you know how much I appreciate your letting the cottage to me so reasonably, don't you?"

"Why, of course." Gloria frowned. "What's wrong?"

"Nothing...and everything." Maggie could barely face the sincerity in her dear friend's cornflower-blue eyes. "I love Stone Creek and being near Ian and his family...and all of you, but simply put, I long for a place of my own. After Robert died, I was so bereft that when Ian needed me to keep house for him, I didn't think about it. I just came."

Gloria nodded.

"But Philip doesn't know Robert's family. I rather miss home and the memories it holds. There's a bakery for sale there. I think I'd like to try a hand at...at owning a business...if I could find the financing." The words finally tumbled out, and there was no taking them back. Maggie's heart pounded in her ears.

Gloria blinked her dewy eyes. "What a marvelous idea." She threw her arms around Maggie as though she would never let her go. "Of course, we'll miss you something fierce. You are truly a brave woman." She pulled back and shook her head.

Maggie swallowed hard. "I have a little set aside from what Robert left us, but I thought this award might recommend me to a lender, since it isn't so easy for a woman to get a loan. Perhaps I would be a good investment for them."

"But there's no reason Asa and I can't help."

Maggie held her palm out. "You've done plenty already. I could hardly expect more."

"We'll see about that." Gloria's eyes sparkled. "And I'm not sure we couldn't do something right here in Stone Creek."

Once her friend had a plan, it might be easier to stop an oncoming locomotive. Could she consider an alternate plan?

CHAPTER 4

A week later, Maggie snuggled in her feather bed, under the blankets. Still plenty cool in the evenings, it was another wonderful night for comfortable sleeping. She drifted off dreaming of what a perfect bakery showcase would hold.

As though from the other end of a long tunnel, a chesty cough woke Maggie.

She sat up. *Philip.* Scrambling out of bed, she pulled her wrap from the peg on the wall and pushed her arms through the sleeves. Her heart pounded like the drum corps of a marching band. In the moonlight, she fumbled to light a lantern.

Maggie hurried into the next room, finding Philip in a fitful sleep. She placed a hand on his forehead. "Oh dear." He was consumed by fever!

Philip pushed her hand away.

He had been acting rather lethargic and appeared a bit pale earlier in the evening. She'd figured he was overtired from extra chores. Truly, she'd been too busy writing letters to a solicitor in Buffalo and to the owner of the bakery she wanted to buy. She'd made one appointment with a local banker without much success. Thoughts of winning her prize, possibly taking over a business, and moving cross-country had preoccupied her. Since Robert's death, nothing had made her feel so alive.

And here was her fevered son with a cough, sounding like his father had before he died. How could she not have seen it coming on? Maggie clasped her hands and fell to her knees, trembling. *Please, Lord, let Philip get better. Don't let me lose him, too. I can't bear the thought.*

Maggie forced herself to take deep breaths and think of what to do next. She stood and almost tripped on her robe in her hurry to get to the kitchen. Inside the pantry sat a shelf where Maggie stored her remedies. She'd sold most of what had been left of Robert's collection to another pharmacist before she left home, but there were a few things she'd thought would come in handy. She searched for the bottle of white willow extract. Twisting off the top and peering inside, she found a few drops left. Perhaps the liquid would be enough for one child-size dose, but it wouldn't get her boy through an entire bout of illness.

Maggie set to preparing a cup of tea for Philip and one to fortify her. Mr. Harper never had given her the extract she'd asked him for, even after his pretense of businesslike behavior. *Tablets, indeed.*

Well, she wouldn't bother Mr. Harper with all his troubles and disorganization. She would go to Dr. Moore. Surely, he would be able to help her out.

～

Tendrils of pearly daylight made their way through the window and the airy muslin curtains. Maggie awoke, her legs stiff and prickly. She'd fallen asleep kneeling by the side of the bed, holding Philip's hand under her cheek as she rested her head on his blanket. She blinked, looking out the sliver of bare window between the creamy curtain panels. The sky, grayed by clouds, hovered between rain and sun. They would probably burst any moment...a typical spring morning in Michigan.

She felt Philip's forehead. Somewhat cooler. What a relief!

After buttoning up her simple cotton dress and putting on her shoes, she went to Apple Blossom House and knocked on the back door. The maid, Betty, opened it in her starched navy-blue uniform and crisp white apron. "Good morning, Mrs. Galloway. How may I help you?"

"I need to call Dr. Moore, please. Philip came down with something awful during the night." Maggie slipped through the doorway, rubbing the chill from her bare hands.

"Of course, ma'am. This way, please."

Maggie followed her to the hallway, where a telephone hung on the wall and a small table stood below it. She grasped the receiver and put it to her ear while speaking into the wooden transmitter box. "Hello? Yes, I need to make a call," she told the operator in a businesslike tone. "Put me through to Dr. Moore, please."

As the phone rang, time passed as slowly as molasses dripping from a spoon, but the doctor's housekeeper made a revelation worse than the wait. Dr. Moore had left recently for what promised to be the difficult delivery of a baby.

Once she hung up, Maggie wrung her hands.

Gloria burst into the hallway. "What's wrong, dear? Betty said you were here to use the phone."

Maggie shook her head. "It's Philip. He has a fever and a cough. I need something for the fever."

"Oh dear, I think we used up anything Dr. Moore gave us the last time Elise was sick." Gloria stood quietly for a moment, then touched Maggie's arm. "Why don't you go to the new pharmacy? I'll stay with Philip. Starks will take you."

Maggie's hands went down to her sides, forming fists. The

thought of going to Harper Apothecary and asking advice of its owner sounded about as much fun as having a tooth pulled. She shook her head again. "Gloria, I..."

"Whatever is keeping you from seeking out the help you need?"

Maggie bit her lower lip. *He just isn't Robert.* Her stiffened arms relaxed. "Very well. I'll go."

~

*T*homas sipped tepid water from a tin cup he kept in the shop—one of the few items his father had given him, a Union Army cup from the War of Rebellion. Despite the dented sides, the handle held fast, and the vessel was still sturdy. How young Army doctor Elias Harper had been when he'd served. What might he have seen? Sometimes in his father's dark brown eyes, a hint of sad memories had glinted. Perhaps the war had caused his father to grow a crustier exterior. And then Thomas disappointed him by not wanting to take over the practice. He sighed. Father's gruffness caused Thomas to purpose in his heart to be kinder to his children.

A metallic taste in the water stuck to his tongue. He should've remembered to add coffee to his list before he'd run out. The worlds of past and present clashed as Abby bounded down the stairs and into his thoughts.

She pecked his cheek with a kiss. "Good morning, Papa. I took breakfast to our invalids."

"Thank you, my dear." Thomas smiled through his weariness. "Where's Josiah?"

"With the quarantine, he thought he might as well sleep longer, but I want to get some schoolwork done, so I can read the books I want when I'm done." She pressed her lips together and braided her hair, frowning with concentration. "I can make him get up and do some homework too."

Thomas lifted a hand. "Don't bother for now. I'll deal with him later." He hated to see her saddled with mothering a boy only a year younger who should be helping her more.

Hack! Hack! The wracking cough sent painful shivers down his spine. A couple of days after the night Zeke awakened him with the cough, the rash appeared. Lyle had taken ill about the same time, answering Thomas's question about which of his children had already suffered from the measles.

He had no housekeeper and a store to run. But that wasn't the half of it. The children missed the gentle, loving touch of their mother.

There was a bright side to business being rather slow with the quarantine. He could accomplish more organization and take better care of the boys. Thomas downed the last sip of the cold water in his cup while picking up an inventory list. The dusty shelves wouldn't restock themselves.

He used a screwdriver to pry off the top of a crate from Parke, Davis & Co. and yawned. What was wrong with him? He'd actually gotten some sleep the night before, despite all of Zeke's and Lyle's coughing. He shouldn't feel so sluggish. The screwdriver slipped, and Thomas's third finger caught on the edge. "Ouch!"

His nail was torn half off. When had his nails become so brittle and paper-thin? He squeezed it tight so as not to drip too much blood.

After disinfecting the injury with iodine and wrapping his fingertip with a bandage, Thomas went back to work. Prying at the lid with more caution, he opened the crate.

As he placed a clear bottle filled with amber liquid on the clean shelf, someone pounded on the front door. Through the glass, he spied a woman dressed in green, holding her shawl to her throat while a matching reticule hung from the crook of her arm. A straw hat shaded her eyes.

Thomas stood with his mouth open. Mrs. Galloway was the

last person on earth he expected to darken his doorway. What should he say?

He opened the door a crack. "I really must insist, ma'am, you leave. Did you not notice the quarantine sign? Two of my sons are recovering from the measles."

When Mrs. Galloway's gaze connected with his, the green of her outfit brought out the splash of green in those aqua blue eyes, a shade darker than Lake Huron in July. Her furtive glances past him signaled her distress.

Her eyes snapped shut and then reopened as though she came out of a trance. "The fact is, my son is quite ill with a fever, and I am completely out of willow extract." Mrs. Galloway stood up straighter and shot an accusatory look at Thomas. "And quite frankly, I wouldn't be here except that Dr. Moore is attending a woman...in her final stages of...confinement. The fact is, I do need your help."

Was that a slight blush across her pale cheeks? Was it over admitting she needed his help? Or embarrassment about mentioning a woman in confinement? Thomas averted his gaze for a minute. "Mrs. Galloway, I apologize. You would not be without your key remedy if I had filled your order as you asked. I still have a few bottles left. Wait here." He stepped outside, guiding her lightly by the elbow to a bench on the boardwalk. Then he motioned for her to sit down.

"Very well." Mrs. Galloway sniffed, looked away, and remained standing.

He went back inside, closing the door behind him, and fussed among the shelves until he found what he was looking for.

Mrs. Galloway knocked again and rattled the doorknob. When he opened the door, she stumbled forward. He caught her in his arms, barely saving the glass bottle in his hand. A clean, lavender scent and the softness of her rounded form roused his senses, but he steadied her despite his panic. He couldn't let her get to him like this.

The feisty redhead righted herself, held onto the doorframe, and straightened her hat. "You didn't need to lock the door behind you. I'm well aware of the seriousness of your quarantine. Besides, I'm sure we've probably been exposed to the same disease."

"Mrs. Galloway, I only want to protect you. Now, these are the tablets I told you about yesterday." He held the bottle out for her to see. Let me wrap this up and send them home free of charge, please. However, I'm more than happy to give you the willow bark too."

The flicker of suspicion in her eyes softened.

Thomas smiled. "I only mentioned the aspirin because the tablets are easier for my children to take. This really is the same compound, but a different form."

The widow examined the bottle.

He shrugged, hoping to disarm her. "I understand your husband also came from the apothecary's trade. I can understand why you, of course, would want to use what he thought best." His lips hurt from the continued attempt at grinning when he really wanted to flee their encounter.

Mrs. Galloway nodded. "The tablets are truly easier to take?"

"Less bitterness to taste when you swallow the whole thing with a glass of water."

"I suppose. I guess I'm being resistant to yet another change. I trusted Robert with my life." She bit her lower lip and looked downward.

"I'd be happy to send a sample of the tablets home with you."

"All right, then." She nodded again. "But I think I would like to bring home some white willow extract as well."

"Wait, here, then." She was just inside the door, but Thomas wouldn't chance having her fall into his arms again. He found a small envelope.

"Please hurry, Mr. Harper."

One, two, three, four, five, six. Thomas shook half a dozen white tablets into the folded paper container. No, for this woman, he better make it a dozen.

Hack! "Pa! We're thirsty!" Zeke called.

Mrs. Galloway spoke with dread. "They still sound awful."

"Two of my boys, Zeke and Lyle, are almost over the measles."

Mrs. Galloway looked back toward the door "Are you sure?"

"I had the building quarantined, but yes, I'm sure they're no longer contagious at this point. Measles is a childhood illness. And I keep the boys far away from the customers"

"I see. I hated having to leave Philip this morning. I'm quite anxious to get back, but I'll also need some expectorant." She fished around in her reticule.

"Let me get you a sample of an excellent elixir containing horehound." He wiped his hand on his suit coat before he procured the bottle. After placing the bottle and envelope of tablets on a sheet of brown paper, he added a small amount of the white willow bark she wanted. Thomas's fingers tangled as he worked to tie up the parcel before the nervous woman got away and forgot her package.

Two aqua-blue saucer-sized eyes peered at him from under the brim of her hat. "That's kind of you. Thanks."

Thomas carried the package around the counter and placed it in her gloved hands, but she must not have grasped it well enough, as it slipped from her hold. He bent to catch it while she did, and they bumped heads. When they both stood, he steadied the parcel in her hands and still held them between his.

"How c-clumsy of m-me." Maggie withdrew her hands from his and stepped back. A slight blush colored her cheeks and

43

made her more becoming. She averted her gaze and clasped the package to her chest.

His face warmed. "Not at all. I apologize for not handing it to you more securely. I will put the extract and elixir on your account." He walked her to the door. "If Philip has started coughing, you may want to look for a rash in a few days...if he hasn't had the measles yet, that is." As her brows pulled down, Thomas placed his hands in his pockets.

"I've had measles, so I think I would know if my son has them." Her defensive tone irked him. Mrs. Galloway grasped the doorknob, but then she stopped. "I'm sorry for snapping at you. I'm sure you meant well. Thank you for your help. I won't be bothering you any longer."

"Mrs. Galloway..."

She looked over her shoulder as she opened the door. "Yes?"

"If there's anything else you need, let me know."

She sighed. "Thank you, Mr. Harper, but I'm quite capable of taking care of Philip. My husband taught me a lot, as I'm sure you taught your wife—"

"You misunderstand me. I truly hope your son is better soon, and I know how tough being on one's own with children can be."

Her eyes widened. Had his concern surprised her?

"And here I am being shrewish again. Only by God's grace will I overcome this tendency." She shook her head. "You've been nothing but kind."

Just then she straightened, masked her emotions, and looked away once again. "Please know I'm good for the credit on my account. Send me a bill when you can." Once again, the auburn-haired spitfire marched out of his store.

Had he disarmed the prickly woman even a little? He smiled at the possibility.

~

*M*aggie lifted the curtain of the sitting room window to find sunshine and a blue sky—a welcome spring day. Also, a stranger jaunted up the path to her front door. No...not a stranger...but Mr. Harper. What was he doing here just over a week since she'd visited his store?

After she'd been so snippy, Maggie was tempted to hide in the kitchen and pretend she wasn't home. Though Philip was feeling better, he sat in bed reading a book. Mr. Harper would be none the wiser. But his forlorn face wouldn't allow her the deception. She opened the door while he was yet on the path and stepped onto the porch.

"Good afternoon, Mr. Harper. What brings you out to Apple Blossom Cottage?"

He tipped his hat. "Fine day, isn't it?"

She nodded, waiting...

"I came to see how Philip fared. Was it—"

"Yes, it was measles." He probably had just come to confirm that very thing. How annoying. "You were correct in your assumptions." And she sounded snippy yet again.

Mr. Harper wouldn't meet her gaze. Was he embarrassed? But why?

"Please Mrs. Galloway, I only meant to check on the boy. You seemed very concerned, and a number of other children in the community had come down with it too."

Maggie's shoulders slumped. "I'm sorry. I don't mean to be so cross. We were fortunate that it was a rather mild case."

A dimple appeared with his shy smile as he looked up at her. "I'm relieved to hear it."

If Maggie's mother had been there, she would have chastised her for not being a more gracious hostess. "Please have a seat." Maggie motioned toward the swing. "Would you like some coffee or tea?"

"Why, thank you, but I'm afraid I must get back to my shop."

"At least rest your feet for a few minutes before you turn around and walk back."

"Very well." He stepped up onto the portico and seated himself.

Maggie sat in a chair across from him and folded her hands on her lap. "And your children are healthy?"

"They're quite fine, thank you. But it gives a parent a start, doesn't it...especially after losing one's...companion in life?"

"Yes." He'd hit a tender spot. Their gazes met, warmth and understanding in his eyes. Perhaps their situations weren't so unique from one another. "The one you'd hoped to grow old with."

A frown, a flicker of sadness, crossed his eyes. Maybe the wound was still too fresh to talk about much. Best to change the subject before they both wound up wallowing in melancholy. "How do you like our little town?"

"It's quite different from living in Detroit. My pharmacy had nary a quiet day there, and the millpond is a mite smaller than the Detroit River. The children miss the library. It's a grand place."

"Oh?" Maggie smoothed her skirt.

"Don't get me wrong, it's quite peaceful here, and the people have been kind so far." Mr. Harper took out his pocket watch and flipped the cover open. "Dear me, I really should be going. We'll have to continue this conversation another time." He stood, then patted his chest as though feeling for something. "Ah, I almost forgot. I brought you some more aspirin tablets." He pulled a small package from inside his suitcoat.

Maggie stood as well. "Thank you, but I still have the willow extract."

"Since your visit to the pharmacy during quarantine was so

hurried, I didn't want you to run out of whatever you needed." He thrust the package toward her. "Please, take it."

She pushed it away. "Mr. Harper, you're too kind, but I believe I have everything I need here." Her pride just wouldn't give way. While he meant well, she wasn't about to concede that he might know better what her son needed for medication. Or that she might need anything from him.

CHAPTER 5

homas surveyed his little shop before closing. The package he'd taken to Mrs. Galloway the day before sat near the register in case she changed her mind. He'd place it beneath the counter for now. The shelves were stocked minimally, but neatly. Tomorrow, perhaps he'd have Josiah help him hook up the soda fountain.

The things a modern druggist was expected to have in a growing town amazed him. The old chemist in Detroit, Mr. Eldon, had told tales of dried herbs which hung on a wall where he had been apprenticed. The apothecary's space had been barely bigger than a shack. But turn-of-the-century customers expected so much more.

Eventually, the walls would need a new coat of paint. Abby, with her artistic flare, had helped him place an attractive arrangement of goods in the window. Things were beginning to shape up. He stood straighter and stretched. His limbs ached from the busy days of caring for sick boys and setting up his business.

The store lit up with lightning, and a crash of thunder followed, shaking the building. When had the storm begun? He

walked over and turned the sign hanging on the door to the
closed side. He liked watching the rain. Streaks of lightning
brightened the sky. Electricity crackled in the air. Heavy raindrops bounced off the street until they thickened to a torrent.
Ah, well, they needed it, to purge away the last of the dirty piles
of snow and to water the fields.

Thomas pushed the door all the way shut and turned the
key in the lock. He shivered as an unusual chill overcame him.
He turned to walk wearily toward the counter. The tightness in
his chest gave way to a cough. What was this all about? He'd
been sniffling all week and fighting a bit of laryngitis.

"Papa!" Abby's sweet voice carried down the stairs. "I've
made split pea soup. I used Mama's recipe!"

Thomas smiled. His dear girl tried so hard to fill in the gaps.
He sniffed at the scorched smell in the air and chuckled. He
wasn't very hungry, but he would eat a cup of it for her sake.
"I'll be right there, my little dove!"

This time, a cough overtook him. Thomas grasped the railing. How heavy his footsteps grew. Halfway up the stairs, he
tripped and remembered no more.

❧

*M*aggie yawned as she bent her head over her
mending. Her son had been tucked into bed.
His cough had quieted, and he'd had no further complications,
but that hadn't stopped her from fretting each night. Tonight,
she paid the price with exhaustion.

"I know you're always with us, Lord," she whispered, lifting
her head and blinking in the bright glow of the kerosene lamp.

Had more of the Harper children become ill? Had Mr.
Harper been able to reopen the shop? When Philip returned to
school, they would surely hear something.

As it turned out, Philip had preferred taking the aspirin

pills to swallowing her concoction. Mr. Harper had been more than generous, despite her anxiety about being exposed to measles and her insistence Philip didn't have them...when it turned out he did.

No, Thomas Harper wasn't Robert Galloway, but did every pharmacist need to be exactly like her deceased husband? Her brother, Ian, hadn't turned out to be like the grim Reverend Garrison of their childhood church, something she feared when Ian answered God's call. Being different could even mean better. Her prejudice, her memories of Robert got in the way of acceptance.

Truth was, she didn't care for change. "Hmm." But how would a new pharmacist in town really affect her? Thomas Harper wasn't going to be a part of her everyday life as Robert had, any more than any other merchant, so what about his presence unsettled her so much?

The man's face wouldn't leave her mind. His pleading smile as he handed her the package and offered another suggestion —as though he cared. And the strength of his hand upon her arm as he guided her to sit down that morning, combined with the look in those hazel eyes. They'd shone with tenderness... and concern. Hadn't Thomas...no...Mr. Harper...just been going through illness with his own children? He would know what she needed.

Robert's gentleness and sense of humor had smoothed over her rough edges. He'd listened to her—maybe too often. *Lord, I know I've asked you to work on my pride and my sharp tongue.*

Perhaps someone who challenged her yet did so with such kindness was more what she needed. Had God brought the handsome Mr. Harper into her life for such a purpose?

Maggie's breath caught. What was she thinking? She needed a cup of chamomile tea and a good night's sleep.

~

*P*ounding awoke Maggie Saturday morning. Lazy raindrops hit the bedroom window in slow rhythm. The gray pallor of the sky peeking through signaled the early dawn. Perhaps it was only thunder. She closed her eyes again. The knocking persisted.

Maggie sat up, trying to get her bearings. She'd better answer the door before her would-be guest awakened Philip. The boy still needed his rest. She pushed straggling hairs from her face and her auburn braid over her shoulder. Once her feet were firm upon the floor, she found her robe and wrapped it tightly about her as she marched through the kitchen toward the back door.

She pulled it open. "In all the world, Ian, what is it?"

Before her stood her brother in a dark coat, water dripping from the brim of his hat. His mouth agape, he held his hand in midair as if poised for yet another series of loud knocks. He dropped it down to his side. "I'm sorry to bother you so early, but we need to talk."

"What is it? Is little Caira sick? Is Sophie all right?"

"They're both well."

Maggie clucked her tongue. "Come in out of the rain and dry off. I'll start some coffee. Or tea?" Her mind began to clear, and her heart pounded.

"Either would be welcome." He removed his hat and let it drain onto the porch.

Ian stepped through the doorway, and Maggie handed him a towel. As he dried off, she filled the cast-iron hopper with coffee beans and cranked the handle on top, then pulled the drawer from the grinder and took the contents to prepare a pot of coffee.

Her brother pulled out a chair at the kitchen table and plunked into it. He leaned forward, resting his elbows on his knees and clasping his hands under his chin. Concern emanated from his eyes. Whatever her brother had to say, she wasn't going to like it.

After placing the coffeepot on the coal stove and lighting it, she sat in the chair across from him.

"Maggie, this isn't going to be easy to tell you...or should I say...ask you." Ian averted his gaze.

"Out with it now. You didn't get me out of bed for nothing." Her little brother could be so irritating.

The pace of the rain's pitter-patter picked up as they sat there in silence for a minute or two. Ian was going to make this more painful than it needed to be.

"Well?"

"Thomas Harper collapsed last night," Ian finally blurted out and took a deep breath.

"What?" Maggie found herself tying the sash of her robe tighter as though to protect herself from the mere mention of the man.

"Poor Abby found her father unconscious and went for Dr. Moore. Amazing how the girl kept her wits about her." He shook his head. "Dr. Moore says Thomas has a concussion and pneumonia, no less. He's going to be laid up for quite some time."

A prickle went up Maggie's spine. "But what does that have to do with me?"

Ian cleared his throat. "I...that is...we all thought you were the logical person to come to for help."

"What can I do, Ian? And who is this 'we'?" The moment the words left her mouth, Maggie realized they'd sounded accusatory, not filled with any desire to show compassion.

"Well, both Dr. Moore and Sophie recalled how well you took care of her when she had a bad case of the quinsy last year. The doctor was very impressed with your knowledge of medicinal preparation, and well, you know, with Robert having…" Ian paused.

She shut her eyes. "Yes, with Robert having pneumonia—yet he passed away under my care."

"But Robert taught you quite a bit, and Dr. Moore believes your knowledge is a real asset."

The walls of the tiny kitchen seemed to close in. The coffee would boil soon. Maggie stood and paced, pulling her braid over her shoulder and smoothing the ends. She would hear Ian out before she sent him away looking for help elsewhere.

Ian wiped a stray drip from his temple. "The fact is, Maggie, Thomas Harper is a very sick man. He needs round-the-clock care if he's going to recover."

"I'm not a nurse." She yanked open the cupboard and banged two ironstone cups and saucers onto the table.

"And your knowledge of his business would be helpful. He really needs help getting organized."

"I have plenty to keep organized here. Besides, I'm thinking of moving back to Buffalo and buying a business of my own." There, she'd said it!

Ian looked as stricken as if she'd slapped him. "I…I…had no idea." A muscle moved in his jaw before he spoke again. "Maggie, the man needs help. Someone he can rely on, who can take his rambunctious lot of children into hand. There's no finer mother in all of Stone Creek. You've done a capital job with Philip—"

"Oh, right." Maggie waved a hand at him before she poured the steaming, pungent brew into their cups. "My son goes to fisticuffs with the new boy in town and likes to play with slithery creatures. He's quite the little gentleman, and I'm just a paragon of virtue." She plunked the enameled pot back onto the cast-iron stove and crossed her arms.

"All the Harper children have left is their father, and

everyone knows he's struggling." Ian rubbed the side of his face. "Look, I can't ask Sophie to help out in her condition, except with meals." He stood and held his arms out to her. "It's only temporary, for maybe a couple of weeks. Besides, no one else has your qualifications."

Maggie shook her head. "It just can't be. Harper and I are like...like...oil and water. We just don't mix." She bit her lower lip again. "Besides, Philip needs me. And what about the contest? And the rest of my plans?"

"It's not as though I'm asking you to give Thomas your whole life, Maggie, only a few weeks of it."

"*No*. Absolutely not."

"I don't know what's wrong with you, but this isn't like the older, compassionate sister I know." Ian swung around and walked away.

She bristled. "What about your coffee?"

"Keep it."

"But where are you going?" Maggie followed her brother as he moved to the back door.

"I'm going somewhere to pray." His gaze seared into her.

Maggie's face warmed.

"And I'm going to ask the Lord to knock some sense into you or to bring the kind of miracle worker Thomas needs into town."

As Ian slammed the door behind him, Maggie should surely still feel angry—indignant, even—but instead, a leaden pressure lay upon her heart.

"Mama! Mama!" The tone of Philip's cry pierced right through her.

"What is it?" Maggie practically flew to her son's room.

He sat up in bed, sniffling and rubbing his eyes. "Mama, I dreamt I couldn't find you! We went for a ride in Uncle Ian's buggy. We were going for a picnic, but when we got there, you weren't with us! And I looked for you everywhere."

She sat down on the side of the bed and gathered Philip into her arms. "I'm right here, darling." His soft hair pressed against her cheek. She hugged her little boy even tighter.

"You're all I have, Mama." Philip sniffled again. "I can't *ever* lose you."

"And you're all I have. I'll be here for you as long as I live." Maggie had barely gotten the words out before her throat thickened and her eyes flooded. She savored Philip's warmth as she held him close.

Though the storm had quieted since the night before, the distant thunder rumbled low.

All they have left is their father.... Ian's words haunted her.

Philip had been frightened by only a dream, still grieved for the loss of his father. How did the Harper children feel with their father so ill? Pneumonia was serious. Some never recovered...like Robert.

Maggie swallowed hard. "Would you like some breakfast now?"

Philip looked up at her. "You promise never to leave me?"

"I don't know what God's plans are." She drew in a ragged breath. "But, as far as it's in my power, I promise."

"Yes, then." Her son smiled. "I'll have some toast, please."

Maggie roughed up his hair and returned the grin, but her heart grew heavier. *Lord, You're not going to let this go, are You?* No, He wasn't. Despite any argument she might have, she'd been appointed to assist a helpless, endearing man and his incorrigible children. *Then please give me guidance and strength, Lord, and Your love for these people. Without it, I don't know what I will do.*

"Come along, then, Philip. I'll have toast and jam with you, and then we have something to discuss, young man."

"Am I in trouble?" His eyes widened.

"Not at all, but I think you're well enough for a bit of an...adventure."

"Really?"

She nodded. "And after breakfast, I must go to the parsonage and call on your Uncle Ian. I believe I owe him an apology."

CHAPTER 6

*H*ad someone hit him with a rock? Thomas turned his head from side to side in a vain attempt to escape the throbbing pain above his temple. Muffled voices grew closer, but he was in a fog as thick as Abby's pea soup. A wracking cough caused an ache deep in his chest and worsened the smarting in his head.

A woman spoke in hushed tones with the doctor, his baritone subdued. What woman would be there to care for him other than Bess? Had he died? No, heaven couldn't feel this miserable. Could it be...the other place? *Perish the thought.* He pushed his eyes open for a minute. A flash of burnished copper hair. The brief sight oddly comforted him before his eyes closed against his will.

Auburn hair? *What on earth would bring Maggie Galloway to my side?* Somehow, the notion soothed the panic churning inside. And he was in good hands with Thad Moore. Maybe he would survive this earthly torture, after all. He tried to open his eyes again, to will himself back to full consciousness, but instead found himself pulled away, drifting off as though in a sailboat just a little too far offshore.

~

"*I*-I'm not sure how much help my nursing will be, Dr. Moore, but I'll do what I can." Maggie clasped her hands together, wringing them. She glanced at the patient. One moment a deep cough overtook him, the next minute he grew deathly silent and still. The sight of Thomas Harper transported her back to the side of Robert's deathbed. She could picture his thick dark hair. The sweat upon his brow. His shallow breathing.

"Maggie." Dr. Moore had hold of her upper arm.

"Hmm? I'm sorry, Doctor."

His eyes, as large as saucers behind his glasses, and filled with kindness, anchored her in the present.

"He had a bad fall yesterday evening, causing a concussion. I stayed with him for the night, and I've seen signs of stirring. Worried me that he was unconscious for a quite a time. But now it's the pneumonia troubling me. He has such a high fever."

"Yes, my brother did give me some indication of what was going on." Her glance flitted to Thomas and back to the doctor. As though the air had been sucked out of the room, Maggie closed her eyes and inhaled a deep breath while she held onto the back of a chair near the bed.

"Are you strong enough for this?" The doctor again took hold of her arm. "You're a woman of faith, young lady. I know you have it in you."

Please, Father, if I'm meant to be here, give me Your strength. Help me to forget about the past and stay in the present. The words of a Bible verse came to her mind. *I can do all things through Christ which strengtheneth me.*

Maggie steeled herself and opened her eyes. She nodded at the doctor. "I'm ready."

"Good." The older man went about showing her his remedies. He retrieved a fountain pen and wrote down the most important instructions, going over each one with care.

"May I speak to you outside this room?" The doctor peered through her eyes and into her soul.

The steps of her high-topped, buttoned shoes padded softly into the hallway as she followed Dr. Moore. She squared her shoulders. "I hope I won't disappoint you."

"My dear." The doctor took her hand in both of his. "Your brother informed me of your husband's sad demise. It was through no fault of your own, I'm sure. We do our best, but God is in charge of the results. I would have brought Harper to the clinic, but I didn't want to move him so far considering his concussion. I'm sure this is his best chance." A slight smile curved across his face.

"What of the children? I've never cared for so many. Gloria Myles is watching Philip for me today."

"My wife has the Harper brood for now. We'll bring them back later. A few choice commands from me should put the fear of God in them, at least for a while." He chuckled. "And Mrs. Moore will gladly advise you. We raised five high-spirited children—two girls and three boys. You'll do just fine." He patted her hand.

The doctor's encouragement, delivered in his soothing tone, calmed Maggie. No wonder all of Stone Creek loved their resident physician.

After he left, she rolled up her sleeves, scrubbed her hands with the strong lye soap, and returned to her new patient's bedside.

~

*M*aggie wrung out the cloth for at least the twelfth time and swathed it over Mr. Harper's fevered face, arms, and chest, which was sprinkled with tufts of dark-blond hair. Her face warmed, and she looked away, patted the patient with the cool cloth, and covered his chest again. While there was nothing unseemly about caring for such an ill man, who probably wasn't even aware of her presence, Maggie somehow felt as though she'd invaded secret territory belonging to another. She exhaled. How long had she been holding her breath?

Folding the rag, she placed the wet cloth on Mr. Harper's brow. Then Maggie rearranged another one around a melting chunk of ice she'd brought up from the icebox and held it against the darkening bruise alongside his forehead.

Not to examine his facial features at such close proximity would be difficult. Rich gold curls fell across his high forehead, giving him an attractive, though boyish look. The worry lines had relaxed, the depths of their troughs not so alarming. But all this was overshadowed by dark, well-formed eyebrows, a fine, straight nose, and a square jaw. Mr. Harper's eyelids fluttered open momentarily. His hazel eyes wandered, not focusing. His lips parted but didn't crease into the smile that usually revealed a dimple in his cheek.

Dear me—why am I thinking of his dimples and his unsettling smile?

A slight wheeze prompted Maggie to place her ear against his chest. Thank the Lord, it wasn't a death rattle. Heat poured from his skin. The fever still raged. She pulled her warmed cheek away. Shyness overtook her in the gas-lit room as she blinked.

"Well, Mr. Harper, it's the two of us, by ourselves. We might as well get to know each other," she whispered to him. "I'm originally from New York State, and my husband, Robert, as you know, was also a druggist."

A small portrait on a vanity table caught Maggie's attention. Edges of the gilt frame reflected the dim light. A beautiful young woman with very light hair sat on a settee, like a queen, surrounded by her babies. A younger Thomas stood behind with his hand on her shoulder. Maggie couldn't decide which one displayed the prouder look.

Picking the portrait up, a pang of loneliness reminded her of what she'd lost with Robert. A silent wish for more children also burned in her heart sometimes. And yet, as a widow, she'd been relieved in some ways. It must be God's wisdom that she only had one child. Maggie always liked things neat and in their proper place. The only dusted and well-cared-for item in Harper's room was this family photograph. Her heart ached with questions.

"This must be your wife. She's lovely." Could the semi-conscious man hear her?

Mrs. Harper's eyes glowed with contentment and spirit, as though she'd great difficulty keeping her expression serious. "I wonder how many years ago this was taken. Perhaps another day, you'll share all the facts with me."

Indeed, his wedded life must have been much different. His countenance showed calmness and joy. "She must have been quite a woman, Mr. Harper. You both look very happy."

He stirred, licking his lips. They moved as though he wanted to say something.

"Are you thirsty, sir?" Maggie sat near him again and placed an arm under his shoulders. She brought his head up far enough that she could spoon weak tea into the side of his mouth. Hopefully, enough would trickle to the right spot. The last thing she wanted to do was choke him.

Thomas's lips moved, and his mouth closed as though the liquid sufficed for the moment. Maggie placed his head gently back on the pillow. Bent over her suffering patient, her heart filled with...something. Surely, only compassion stirred in her breast, not romantic feelings. But as she swiped the rag across his brow again, the leaden blanket on her heart lifted. A closeness to this man she barely knew welled up in her as though their lives were entwined inexplicably.

"Ahem."

Maggie jumped. She straightened and turned. Abby stood with her back against the doorjamb.

"Mrs. Moore said I could come see if you needed any help. I was trying to be quiet like she told me to." The young lady's glance flitted from Maggie to her father and back again. Her brows furrowed as though stricken by something Maggie did.

"If it's all right with the doctor. I would feel terrible if you got sick."

The girl's chin went up. "Papa says I'm the healthiest one. *I* nurse everyone in the family."

So...Abby must feel she'd invaded her territory. But Maggie wouldn't have the child becoming ill. Mr. Harper wouldn't need to worry about such a thing during his recovery. What task could the girl to do instead? "First, let me properly introduce myself. I am Mrs. Galloway." She nodded toward the girl and extended her hand. "And you must be Abby."

Abby crossed her arms. "Mrs. Moore told me you would be here."

"I was asked by the doctor and Reverend McCormick to attend to your father. There's plenty of work to go around, and I appreciate your offer to help." Maggie took a step toward Abby.

Despite her confident posture, the girl refused to meet Maggie's gaze.

She was used to playful banter with Philip when getting him to do something he wasn't happy about. But how should she deal with a young lady? Maggie tried to think back to her own fragile emotional state at that age and add to it possible tragedy...when life should be filled with hope and dreams. How ironic she hadn't wanted to be there any more than Thomas's daughter wanted her to be. However, now Maggie was invested, compelled by a sweep of emotion she'd never intended.

"Abby, would you please get the table ready for dinner? I imagine the meal Mrs. Myles is sending will be here any minute." The image of the pile of unwashed dishes in the sink flashed through Maggie's mind. "Or perhaps you could wash some of the dishes as we will need them." She paused. "And though I'll be checking on your father periodically during the night, perhaps you could get me a blanket and a pillow so I can rest on the sofa tonight. All of these things would be a help to me and, consequently, your father."

The girl peeled off her coat and continued to avert her gaze. "I wish to stay with my papa, Mrs. Galloway."

Maggie sighed. This wouldn't do. She needed to buy time to ascertain Dr. Moore's opinion. She crossed her arms as well, hating she had to stand ground when she'd rather befriend the stubborn girl.

"Abby, you must try to understand. I simply must talk to Dr. Moore about whether you should be allowed in the sickroom." Maggie reached out, so wanting to comfort the girl, but clasped her hands together instead since the gesture might not be welcomed.

Abby's bottom lip quivered, though she jutted her chin forward. Perhaps no one had stood their ground with any of the Harper children for a long time. They were in for it now.

"I promise to take good care of your father. My husband came from the same trade and taught me much."

Abby flashed Maggie a glance. Then her eyes wavered to the corner where the family portrait stood. She was already being sized up against the cheerful Mrs. Harper, though Maggie promised to be a short-lived guest.

"Fine," Abby snapped and turned toward the hallway. Then, as if she'd remembered her manners, she looked over her shoulder. "Yes, ma'am, I will go set the table for dinner."

Maggie relaxed her rigid posture, dropping her hands to

her sides. That was one Harper child down. She had a feeling the boys wouldn't be so easy.

~

*A*t the top of the hour, Maggie attempted to rouse the semi-conscious man, whose eyelids fluttered open as he looked about blankly. "Away with you, now...off to bed. You need rest...you'll get sick...Bess? Child...ren..." Thomas's delirious ranting tormented her. The fever showed no sign of decreasing.

A knock at the door below interrupted her prayerful meditations. "Abby! Please get the door."

"Yes, ma'am." The girl sounded deflated as she tromped down the stairs.

Maggie walked about the room, folding what looked like clean laundry and tucking it into drawers. Dust flew as she swiped her hand across the more clouded surfaces. Her nose itched. She lined up pairs of shoes under the bed for the time being and stopped by the side of it, watching her patient.

She wrung her hands, unwilling to leave Mr. Harper's side for long until his fever came down. This was personal. The Harper children needed their father—the same as Philip and she needed Robert. Perhaps if she'd been more diligent, instead of worrying about household chores constantly, her outcome would've been different. Her work would have been there when he was better.

She smoothed her skirt. *I'm sorry, Lord. I must trust You that things are as they should be. But perhaps You had a lesson for me to learn, and I can do a better job with this man.* She blinked back tears.

Maggie bent and adjusted the thick quilt around him. It looked as though scraps had been pieced together frugally, and most likely, with love. Her mouth curved into a smile as she remembered having done the same thing for her and Robert. If only she could have known Mrs. Harper. The lovely blond woman must have had her hands full with all those children and a disorganized husband. What an interesting lady she would have been to know.

Beads of sweat appeared on Thomas's brow. Perhaps he was too warm. Maggie replaced the quilt with a lighter coverlet she'd found in a pile at the foot of the bed. She folded back the linen sheet, white next to Thomas's flushed countenance, and smoothed it beneath his chin. The covers hugged his sturdy shoulders—the kind of shoulders a woman could lean on.

"I hope you're comfortable now, Mr. Harper." She sighed.

Light footsteps ceased in the hallway outside the door. Gloria Myles stood there, her cornflower-blue eyes wide with worry. "My dear friend, is it as bad as they say?"

Maggie washed her hands quickly and dried them on the cotton towel hanging at the waist of her apron. She rushed into the hall, closing the door partway behind her. "Gloria, what are you doing here? You should have sent dinner with Mr. Starks and Betty." While she was concerned that her delicate friend might contract an illness, Maggie was relieved to see a friend, just the same.

"I wanted to talk to you for a moment. Since Philip is barely over his measles, you could let him continue to stay with us. Elise will enjoy the company. And she's already had that dreadful sickness a few years back." It was as though the words tumbled out before Gloria remembered to stop them. Although they'd found much comfort in the years since it happened, the memory pained her friend. And Maggie, herself, couldn't imagine the loss of a child. How precious a balm Gloria's grand-daughter was to her!

"If you're sure. I had promised him an adventure, thinking he would come stay with me and spend time with the Harper children. I'm going to miss him dreadfully, but I think he will be better off with you." Maggie continued to wipe her hands on the towel, then twisted it between her hands. Tension creased her forehead. How she hated to be away from her son.

Gloria nodded.

"I think I'm going to have my hands full for a while." She let go of the towel and smoothed it.

The warmth of Gloria's smile reached her eyes. "Yes, you will, and very soon. I saw Mrs. Moore sending the boys out the door with her husband only a few minutes ago."

"Pray for me, for all of us." Maggie paused. "Especially for Mr. Harper's recovery. These children need their father."

"I have been, but let me pray for you right now." Gloria took Maggie by the hands, and they bowed their heads in the dark, drafty hallway.

After Gloria prayed for wisdom, strength, and patience, along with healing for Thomas, she left. None of those character qualities had miraculously descended upon Maggie, but peace wrapped her heart with a comforting blanket. She needed this peace of mind. She'd been given a second chance... to save a sick man's life. Failure wasn't an option.

CHAPTER 7

"Pa!" More than one voice called in unison as the back door banged shut below the room where Maggie sat with Mr. Harper.

"What did I tell you, boys?" Dr. Moore's husky whisper followed. "Your father needs peace and quiet. Now take your shoes off. Right now."

"Aww, we thought he was getting better." The hard clunk of shoes sounded upon the wooden floor.

"Can we see him?" A hiccup after the question made Maggie chuckle. Was that the voice of Zeke, the troublemaker? She would learn soon enough.

"Do you young men want your father to get better?" This time, the doctor's voice boomed with authority.

The Harper boys sung out in a chorus of *uh-huhs*.

"What?" Dr. Moore asked more intently.

"I mean, yes, sir." Sounded like the oldest son. Younger voices repeated.

"Then I suggest you get to your chores and homework as soon as possible and obey Mrs. Galloway, or I will make sure I hear about it." The unusual bark of Dr. Moore's gentle voice carried up the stairway.

Maggie peeked around the corner toward the head of the stairs to find the doctor giving them a rather fearsome look over the top of his glasses.

"Yes, sir." All the boys looked down and shuffled their feet. Just how long would the brokered peace last?

She might as well make an appearance. Holding onto the stair railing with one hand and holding up her skirt with the other, she made her way down the stairs. The clack of her button-top shoes echoed the thump of her heart. *Dear Lord, please help me.*

"Ah, there you are, Maggie." Dr. Moore took her by the hand as she reached the bottom.

Had Daniel felt this way going into the lions' den? She was probably overreacting, but she steeled herself, nevertheless. She could not let them see her fear...lest they devour her.

"Josiah, Lyle, Hezekiah, do you remember Mrs. Galloway?"

"Hiya. You can call me Zeke." The boy grinned, and his brothers snickered.

Dr. Moore sighed.

Maggie gulped. She might as well act as though she was up to the task. "Pardon me, Zeke, what was that?" She trained her sights on the child, sounding more severe than she intended.

Josiah and Lyle put a hand on each of his shoulders, pushing Zeke forward. "Tell her what you meant to say, *Hezeki-ah,*" the oldest brother prompted.

"I-I meant to say, pleased to meet you?"

The other boys followed suit.

"That's more like it." Maggie lifted her chin.

"Let me know if you need any help." Dr. Moore took Maggie's hand in both of his and squeezed it. "Mrs. Moore or I can be here very quickly. And I will be back to check on our patient tonight." His brown eyes melted with sympathy toward her.

"Thank you, Doctor. I would appreciate that." Before Maggie could make a full protest, he'd disappeared out the door. She gulped against the fear tightening her throat.

She turned toward the boys.

Lyle bowed from the waist. "Pleased to meet you, Mrs. Gollywump."

"Yeah, so good to see you, Mrs. Galliwagg," Zeke doubled over with laughter.

Josiah rolled his eyes but stood up straight and shoved his hands in his pockets. "You can go home now, Mrs. Gaggy-what-ever. We Harpers can take care of ourselves. We don't need you here, so you can just leave instead of thinking you're going to do us some good deed." He glared at her.

Her heart shriveled like a little girl's who'd been picked on in the schoolyard. Maggie didn't consider herself particularly clever. Oh, she needed to keep the upper hand with the Harper brood. They couldn't be allowed to run willy-nilly, but the three boys in rumpled clothing, and their sister upstairs, all displayed nothing but false bravado. These children needed her compassion as much as they needed discipline.

Josiah, clearly the ringleader, was already taller than she. Gangly and blonde, like Zeke, his hazel eyes held a mutinous glint. Lyle, shorter, with his father's golden-brown hair and darker eyes, had a serious set to his mouth. He was perhaps the quietest of the three. Zeke, with his light-blond hair, resembled the woman in the picture. He shifted his weight to one foot. Something about the sprinkle of freckles across each of their noses reminded her they were more boys than young men, even Josiah. But Maggie still needed to tell them exactly what was on her mind.

Taking a deep breath and crossing her arms, she began in as calm a tone as she could muster. "My name is Mrs. Maggie

Galloway. You know this." She paused, taking the time to look each one of her foes in the eye. "Call me whatever you like, but I was asked by Reverend McCormick and Dr. Moore to nurse your very ill father back to health." She lifted her chin. "Now, everything you do to keep me from doing my job will hurt not only me but your father as well. Are you willing to take such a risk?"

Zeke's mouth fell open. Lyle scratched his head, and Josiah looked down, shifting his feet. A sob cut into Maggie's very heart. Abby had been listening, sitting halfway up the stairs. The girl turned her tearful face away, letting out another sob, then scurried back up.

"Now you went and made our sister cry. We don't need you here." So Josiah chose to take another stand of defiance.

"And your poor behavior hasn't?" Maggie desired to leave for the quiet comfort of her rented cottage as much as these children wanted her to go, but something in her heart kept her feet to the floor. *A soft answer turneth away wrath: but grievous words stir up anger.* The words from Proverbs came to her mind, and compassion flooded through her.

"Josiah, perhaps your father hasn't found the right house-keeper for your family yet, but I'm not planning on taking up the position. I'm only here until he gets better. You need to become a better example for your brothers. I'm sure you'd want to do your father proud by being responsible. But only you can make the choice. Come now. Are you willing to help me? We're on the same team, you know."

Josiah shrugged, looking down again. "I suppose."

"Why, thank you. May I count on the rest of you?"

Lyle and Zeke nodded. Did their widened eyes display fear-fulness or surprise in her handling of them? "All right, then. I'm sure you're all hungry. Mrs. Myles has brought us dinner. You're in for a real treat—"

Before she could finish, the boys stampeded up the stair-case to their living quarters.

Once Maggie made her way up to the kitchen, she found them shoving one another.

"Slow down," Abby commanded. Despite the way she turned her head away, Maggie caught sight of the swollen, reddened eyes behind the girl's spectacles.

At one end of the table, Abby had set four places. The head of the table was left empty. The rest of the table was piled with boxes and dirty dishes. This wouldn't do at all.

"Abby, pass me a clean bowl and plate, please, and some silverware." Maggie moved toward the head.

"You can't sit there. That's Papa's place!" Abby blocked the way to the chair as though it were some hallowed shrine.

"Very well, perhaps Josiah would like to sit there instead."

Josiah stepped to the other end and swept the piles off. The clink of plates and glasses breaking as they crashed to the floor filled the kitchen. "Now there's plenty of room for you, Mrs. Galloway." The eldest Harper boy crossed his arms, head held high.

The other children sat with widened eyes, waiting. Had a mere moment or a half hour passed? Maggie's stomach quivered like jelly. Her legs wobbled like rubber. She swallowed. "Josiah, you're going to clean up this mess you've made, but first, you're going to serve us dinner. Abby, sit down. Josiah may eat standing up since there are no more clean places to set a chair." She moved her chair to the corner of the table, by Zeke. "It's been a long day. We're all hungry. Did everyone wash their hands?"

"*I* take good care of my brothers. Time to wash up, boys."

Josiah, Lyle, and Zeke all looked from one female to the other and back again.

Maggie needed to establish authority. "Well, Abby. I guess

we'll get awfully full eating without the boys, won't we? Go on. Wash up if you want some dinner."

The three of them shuffled toward the sink, where they pumped water onto their hands and passed a bar of soap around.

After cleaning up, Josiah stood like a soldier by the counter. Tiredness weighed Maggie down, and her first day as Mr. Harper's nurse hadn't even finished yet. "We can sit here until that delicious dinner grows cold, or we could begin eating while it's still warm, Josiah. It will be even colder by the time you eat." She sat up straight with her hands folded in her lap.

He looked from her to his brothers and sister, and then to the food on the counter. After wavering a bit, Josiah plunked a basket of yeasty-smelling rolls onto the table. The other two boys plunged in with their hands poised to fight over the freshly baked morsels.

Maggie lifted the basket above their reach. "It looks to me as though there is plenty to go around. Will you continue to fight like little savages? Or wait your turn like proper gentlemen?" She kept her tone gentle and calm, refusing to yell at them, though she would like to grab each one by the collar and march them off to bed.

Their hands hung in midair. The boys brought them to the table, waiting for the return of the basket until she put it down.

"Please hand me the tureen now." As soon as Josiah brought it to her, with the entrée spilling over the sides, Maggie ladled hearty Irish stew into their bowls. Each of the boys began shoveling the stew into their mouths.

"Ahem." Maggie cleared her throat. Each one, including Abby, stopped with their spoons halfway to their mouths. Maggie bowed her head and folded her hands. "We need to say grace." She followed with a simple prayer of thanks with one eye open. "Amen."

Zeke's tummy rumbled. "Can we eat now, Mrs. Galloway?"

"That's *may* we eat." She tried not to smile. "Yes, dig in."

Spoons scraped against the side of each bowl, except for Josiah's, who stood by Maggie, holding a dish out. "*May* I have some, too, please? I sure am hungry...uh...ma'am."

The boy's stomach rumbled, but she couldn't back down. She stared at him, hoping to convey her displeasure. "I believe I told you to clean up this mess. And about the time we're done eating, it will be your turn, won't it, now?"

Abby turned sympathetic eyes on her brother. "I'll help him, Mrs. Galloway—"

"No." Maggie placed a firm hand on the girl's arm.

Please help me win this one, Lord. I'm sure there will be enough battles to lose in the days to come.

Abby turned a pouty face toward Maggie but stayed put. "Whatever you say, *ma'am*."

Josiah rummaged around until he brought an empty box back near the table. Then he knelt and began picking up pieces of plates and glasses and putting them in one by one.

Her mother's heart made her cringe. "Be careful, Josiah. I don't want you to cut yourself. Shouldn't you put on some gloves?"

Josiah turned away as though he hadn't heard her.

Abby sighed. The glum little group chewed their dinner. Butter melted into the warm rolls, almost creamy in texture. Lyle and Zeke scooped bite after bite of the savory stew into their mouths, but Maggie struggled to swallow, and Abby picked at hers. Perhaps tea and a roll would be enough. Of course, she could imagine if Dr. Moore were there, he'd be scolding her to eat more because she'd need to keep up her strength.

Maggie let out a breath she hadn't even realized she'd been holding. The scraping of spoons against bowls grated at her nerves like a wet cloth squeaking across a glass pane. How she longed for a quiet evening by the hearth with knitting needles and yarn in her hands while Philip read aloud one of his favorite stories. How had she let Ian and Dr. Moore talk her into this?

"Ow!" A piece of glass rattled into the crate. Josiah muttered a few words Maggie wouldn't care to hear repeated. In fact, if they had come from Philip, he would be disciplined in short order.

Abby blushed at her brother's utterances.

Blood oozed from the young man's finger, though he tried to hold the cut closed.

Maggie stood up. "Abby, go look in on your father and come back directly to let me know how he's doing. Boys, if you have any homework or chores to catch up on, now would be a good time." For the joys of her evening seemed to only be beginning.

CHAPTER 8

*M*aggie guided Josiah toward the sink. "Lyle, do you know where your father keeps the iodine?"

Lyle nodded. "I think so."

"Then go find it. Josiah, let's wash your cut." Maggie's head dizzied. It had been a long time since she had helped Robert sew up a cut like this one.

"I feel sick." Zeke paled and held his stomach.

"We don't have time for that. Go find something constructive to do." Maggie stepped over to the sink.

Josiah clenched his teeth while drops of blood plinked into the sink. "I can take care of it."

"Let me look." Maggie grasped his wrist and cupped the injured hand in her other one, giving him no choice. As blood poured from the cut, she examined the incision for shards of glass. "It's a deep one."

Josiah looked away. Clearly, he tried to hide the fear in those ice-blue eyes beneath a frown. "What are you going to do? Call for Dr. Moore?"

Maggie pumped a gentle stream of cool water onto the cut. The boy sucked in his breath as she rubbed lathered soap over open edges. "I'm thinking the good doctor has plenty to do right now. I've helped my husband a great many times to close up larger cuts than this."

The boy slid a glance sideways toward her.

"Robert Galloway was a pharmacist, too, and a quite capable one at that."

Josiah shrugged. "Doesn't make you a doctor."

"Any more than your big mouth makes you a man."

"Mrs. Galloway, here's the iodine," Lyle interrupted and then began to back away.

"Thank you. Hand me that towel, will you?" Maggie reached out for the cleanest-looking white dishtowel she could find. After pouring the reddish-brown liquid over the offended area, she tore a strip from the towel, wrapping it around Josiah's finger as tightly as she could. She pulled out a kitchen chair. "Sit down before you fall over, Josiah. Keep putting pressure on it."

Maggie ignored the threatening look the young man gave her. "Come along, Lyle. I might need your help elsewhere."

The younger boy swallowed hard enough for Maggie to hear. His countenance had paled almost as much as Zeke's.

Abby sobbed in the hallway. "Papa's dying. I'm sure of it."

Maggie grabbed her by the shoulders. "Whatever do you mean?" Her thin-as-a-filament patience would snap with one more touch.

The girl sniffled. "He's awfully still, and I haven't heard him coughing. You should have let me stay with Papa. You've killed him!"

"Get a hold of yourself, Abby. Lyle, stay here with your sister." Maggie looked around for the other Harper child. "Where on earth is Zeke?"

"He's retching in the water closet. If you hadn't made Josiah pick up the broken glass, he wouldn't have gotten so upset. It's all your fault." Abby began her sobbing afresh.

"Let's hope he made it all the way to the water closet, or you will be cleaning it up." Maggie's head ached from the neck up. She definitely hadn't eaten enough, and now she'd completely lost her appetite.

First things first. Maggie hurried to Thomas's side. Though still quite warm, his forehead was cooler to the touch. Just to be sure, Maggie peeled the covers back and knelt by the side of the bed to listen to his heart. *Thud, thump, thud, thump.* Its beating sounded normal, still strong and clear.

"Mm, mm." Thomas's arm moved. His hand touched her shoulder, resting there. A comfortable, warm sensation melted her.

Maggie pulled away, readjusting the covers.

A look of peace took over his face. His cheeks went from ashen to pale pink.

"There now, Mr. Harper. You're looking better." Rinsing a fresh cloth from the pile on the dresser, Maggie wiped his forehead with gentle pressure. "We'll beat this fever before you know it. You keep resting and heal up." She kept her voice to a whisper.

Abby sniffled in the doorway. Lyle clung to his sister's arm.

Maggie stood and put a finger to her lips. "He's sleeping, and I think his fever is coming down. He's not dying." *Yet.*

Maggie washed her hands in the basin, scrubbing them as though she could cleanse away thoughts of failure along with the germs. Thomas Harper had to get better under her care. He *had* to. His four children depended on it.

"Abby, I need you to calm down. You and Lyle must help me find some suture and needles in all those boxes downstairs." She waved a hand. "I have no idea where your father keeps his supplies in all that mess." Maggie pushed the brother and sister gently ahead of her as though coercing a couple of stubborn donkeys.

Marching close behind them, Maggie headed toward the

first floor. When they reached the bottom of the stairs, she examined the room from floor to ceiling, the piles of unpacked and empty boxes, the unorganized cabinets. The dear man had his hands full, but really, did Thomas Harper believe little gnomes would come along and put the store in order while he slept? "Now think, where would he keep the things I asked for?"

Abby lifted her eyes to Maggie's. "I-I think Pa's needles and suture are in one of the drawers."

"Well, let's check there first." Maggie nodded in the girl's direction. "Lyle, I'll help your sister, but I would like you to check in the cubbies underneath the counter."

The boy darted out of her way, and Maggie surveyed the tall cabinets. She grabbed the drawer pulls, two at a time. Several were empty. Others contained materials inconsequential to her quest.

"Mrs. Galloway, this looks like Papa's suture!" Abby left a drawer open for her to see.

"The needle should not be far. Let me see!" Maggie pawed through the different widths of the thread-like substance. "There!" The glint of a thin piece of metal poked out from under the suture. "Good work, my dear."

Had the look in Abby's eyes softened? Or was it the reflection on her glasses from the westward moving sun streaming through the windows?

Maggie slid the drawer from its place and carried the whole thing up the stairs. In the kitchen, after passing a fine needle through a candle flame, she moved a chair so she sat almost knee-to-knee with Josiah. She grasped his hand and began to unwrap the bloody makeshift dressing. "You may not want to see this."

The young man grew paler, fastening his gaze toward the kitchen window.

"I can't promise you this won't hurt, but it simply must be done." Maggie bathed the bloody finger with iodine once again.

Josiah bit his lip and clenched his free hand into a fist.

"Can I help?" Abby asked from the doorway. Her lower lip quivered, but she stood straight.

"Check on Zeke, please."

"Yes, ma'am."

"And close the door behind you." Maggie had to concentrate on the job as she threaded the needle. *Robert, how would you do this*— She caught herself. No, she needed God's help to still her shaking hands and pounding heart.

She *would* mend this boy's hand and leave nary a scar. She worked the needle in and out in small and even stitches. Josiah closed his eyes. But he squeezed them tighter with each prick of the needle, blinking against the tears trying to escape.

"You're doing well, Josiah. I'm almost done." Would that she could mend his heart as well. This youth was no *viper* as that Peaberry woman had said.

Her own Philip had tried to take his father's place as man of the house. How would a boy feel with his ill father lying abed and his mother buried six feet beneath the cold earth? For that, Maggie had no medicine to offer but prayer and patience, kindness, and care.

CHAPTER 9

The next two days passed drearily as the rain pelted against the windows like tears down dirt-streaked cheeks. So much work needed to be done in the Harper home and apothecary. Maggie lifted a dusty curtain away from the window. It might as well have been a shroud for the heaviness of her heart as she listened to the fitful cries of Mr. Harper for his dead wife, Bess. The fever had waxed and waned. Every time Maggie thought he was turning the corner, he lapsed back into the depths of his illness.

Thankfully, Josiah's cut was in the process of healing with no signs of infection. Truly, the Lord, in His mercy, had seen fit to answer at least one of her prayers.

Thomas moaned.

Her heart jumped. Fear sent a current of shock from the crown of her head to her toes. She rushed to Harper's side in time to see him reach out. His glassy eyes searched. "Bess?"

Then he closed them, his head lolled to the side, and he fell limp.

Maggie grabbed him by the shoulders. "Mr. Harper, can you hear me?" She might have been talking to a dead man, but for his laboring breaths and the cough continuing to rattle his chest. She swathed his forehead again with a wet cloth.

Clicking open the cover of the watch pinned to her shirt-waist, Maggie wished away the hour before Dr. Moore made his usual visit. She could call him, but he had other patients. As nerve-wracking as Thomas's actions had been, there hadn't been change enough to worry the good doctor any more than he already did over this patient. When she wasn't pacing, Maggie was sure she wore grooves into the floor as she tilted the oak rocker back and forward.

"How's our patient doing, my dear?"

When Maggie finally heard the familiar heavy footsteps and baritone, she released a breath of relief. Dr. Moore's crinkled forehead told of his worry, despite the comforting smile he often wore.

After she explained the most recent happening, Dr. Moore examined Thomas's eyes, pulling one lid open at a time. "I believe this is a critical time. What if I stay here tonight, and you get some rest, young lady?"

Rest. Just the sound of the word brought visions of hearth and Philip nearby, warm blankets and chamomile tea. But Maggie would never forgive herself if she didn't see this through. She had to win the battle. "No."

"You'll wind up getting sick. What about Philip?" Dr. Moore opened his ominous black bag and lifted out his stethoscope, then placed it around his neck.

"I'll be all right. You'll see." If they could get through this next night, all would be fine. In some small way, helping to save Thomas would help her to redeem herself for failing to cure Robert. "I promise you, if he's not better by tomorrow, I will go home for a short rest."

"If you're sure." Dr. Moore arranged the stethoscope, placing the chest piece over Thomas's heart.

"If you could take the boys off my hands, that would be

good." She spoke in hushed tones. "Leave Abby in case I need help. We'll call if there's a turn for the worse."

"We'd be happy to—after you take a break and get something to eat." He motioned for her to assist in rolling the patient to his side so he could listen to his lungs.

"Of course." Maggie aided Dr. Moore in situating Thomas and then moving him back to a comfortable position.

While the physician finished up, she went to the water closet and ran cool water into the sink. After scrubbing her hands, she cupped them, splashing the liquid onto her face and patting dry with a cotton towel.

When she went to the kitchen, Lyle and Zeke were actually seated at the table examining a bug in a jar, while Josiah actually had his head in a book. Thank goodness, she'd found them working together and not being mischievous.

However... "That insect belongs on the back stoop." Maggie pointed to the door.

"Aww! Do we have to?" Lyle piped up.

Maggie suppressed a smile. She put her hands on her hips. "Yes, and let's get you ready for a night with Dr. and Mrs. Moore."

Josiah's book plunked onto the table as he stood. "Is Pa gonna die tonight?"

"It's 'going to' and no—not on my watch. But I think it would be good to have the house extra quiet. Your sister will stay and help." Maggie swallowed away any shakiness in her voice.

"She gets to do everything." Zeke crossed his arms.

"Come on, Zeke." Josiah cuffed his little brother on the arm. "Abby's not staying for fun and games. Let's get ready to go."

While Maggie would have liked to hear the words "yes, ma'am" as they obeyed, she would take this. Josiah's blue eyes softened as he searched hers, though the boy frowned with worry. She could only hope that respect grew, where once contempt reigned.

Maggie loosened a wedge of cheese from its wrapping and cut off a small piece to nibble. As she lifted the lid from the stockpot, the rich smell of simmering chicken soup reached her nose but did nothing to whet her appetite. Days of spooning broth into Thomas's mouth had taken away its appeal. She sighed as she ladled clear broth and a few noodles into a bowl. She'd be lucky to get half of this down him.

An unwanted crust of bread sat on the cutting board. With a little butter, it would more than do for her. She washed it down with cold coffee left in the speckled enamel pot from that morning.

Maggie spied a sheet of paper on the table. What she guessed to be Zeke's splotchy writing caught her eye.

Mother
Mother brought us sunshine,
Her cooking was terribly fine.
But Pa doesn't smile any more,
He's laying at death's door.
If only Mother could live again,
Pa's smiles wouldn't end.
We'll be good and not make a fuss,
If only Pa can stay with us!

Maggie turned away. The crumbs of bread became like sand in her throat. She choked back her tears and sobs. The children couldn't see her this way, or they would surely think their father wasn't going to make it. *Heavenly Father, preserve what's left of this family, I beseech You.*

Her reflection in the kitchen window showed her crown of auburn hair astray. She straightened it, rearranging the pins. There. She was ready to do battle this night and win.

~

*M*aggie read the Psalms, but her eyelids drooped even as she tried to cling to each word about how she must look to the hills where her help would come from or something to that effect.

"I'm done washing the dishes."

Maggie's beloved Bible slid from her lap as she jumped at Abby's words. She scooped the sacred book from the floor before she turned to see the Harper girl in the doorway.

"Is there anything else I can do for you? I could sit with Papa while you rest."

"Thank you, Abby, but you need your rest as well. You have school to attend. Your father wouldn't want you to get behind on his account." She bit her lip. How could she tell her the deep sense of responsibility she possessed for seeing this through alone? Would the girl understand how someone who was virtually a stranger a week ago would have so much concern for her father? "I'll call you if he gets worse."

"Yes, ma'am," Abby acquiesced. Her eyes, so much like her father's, shone with moisture.

The house became quiet, save the wind and the rain against the clapboard and the windows, along with the settling sounds of the building. Maggie paced to keep herself awake. Then she again checked Thomas's vitals. He indeed had a pulse, and his breathing was less labored, yet raspy. And his fever still raged. She bathed him once more, held his head up, and spooned the medicine in. Did his eyelids flutter open for a moment? Yet his eyes didn't register recognition.

Perhaps if she knelt and prayed, she would stay awake. Before she did, Maggie picked up the Harper family portrait once more, staring into the lovely face of Mrs. Harper. She sighed, set it down, and turned it around rather than feel as though she was being watched by his dead wife. *What has gotten into me, anyway?*

Kneeling by the side of the bed, she began to beseech God for Thomas's healing, both physically and in his heart. Something compelled Maggie to grasp his still-warm hand. "Mr. Harper, I know you loved your wife very dearly, probably still do. And I understand. I'll never stop loving my Robert. No one can replace him, but you see, I had to let him go."

She straightened her back, leaning forward. "You still have a treasure in your children. It's not the same, I know. You probably don't feel like going on, but they need you." The heart-wrenching poem written by one of the boys caused a catch in her throat as she tried to swallow a sob. It didn't work. Wetness flowed down her cheeks. "Please, Mr. Harper, they love you, and they want you to live. They deserve to have one parent left. Don't let go, Thomas. God will help you see it through."

The love Thomas had for his children and their loyalty to him warmed her heart. Perhaps this home just needed a woman's gentle touch. Indeed, during this time caring for Thomas, she'd grown in affection toward him. She rather liked being needed by a man—much to her distress.

Maggie poured prayers quietly from her heart until her eyes closed once again, this time for the night.

CHAPTER 10

*T*homas blinked. Light streamed in, and he closed his eyes against the brightness. How long had he slept? He shouldn't be lying here when he had a family to care for. He opened his eyes again, squinted, and allowed them to adjust to the yellow glow of morning sunlight pouring in through the window.

While it took a moment to register, a cool hand grasped his. He looked down to see a head wrapped in a halo of reddish hair. "Mrs. Galloway?"

"Hmm?" She lifted her head. Her eyelids fluttered open. As she focused, her eyes registered shock. She dropped his hand. "You're awake?"

Turning pink, Mrs. Galloway scrambled to her feet, straightened her apron, and placed a hand on his forehead. "This is wonderful! Thank you, Lord! Oh, I must tell Abby and call Dr. Moore."

"How long have I been asleep?" Thomas swallowed against the dry gravelly feeling in his throat. "What happened? And w-what are you doing here?" He pushed himself to a sitting position and then slid the covers half off. If he could only swing his legs over the edge of the bed and get up, but he found himself too weak as stars danced before him.

"No, no, Mr. Harper. You must stay in bed." Mrs. Galloway quickly covered him again, tucking the quilt around him while averting her gaze. Her blush grew deeper.

Was this a nightmare? Had he imagined the whole thing? Something had to be wrong if this woman who so disliked him was happy to see him alive and here to care for him.

"You've been very ill with pneumonia and a high fever, but you were also unconscious from a concussion. It was touch and go for a while, but I believe you're going to be fine. You even know who I am."

Thomas relaxed back into his pillow and pulled the covers up to his chin. "I think I shall stay put for a while."

"Oh dear, I must look like a mess." Mrs. Galloway patted her hair and gave a quick look over her shoulder. "Let me get Abby. She'll be ecstatic to find you better. And the boys are at Dr. Moore's. I'll call over there." She twisted up loose strands of hair into her bun as she rushed out the door.

"Abby, come see. Your father is much better." Her words echoed from the hallway, along with her quick footfalls.

His daughter's light footsteps came closer. She appeared in the doorway, pushing her arm through one sleeve of her robe and her glasses up her nose with the other hand.

"Papa!" Abby nearly flew to her father's bedside. "You're awake!"

Thomas patted her, surprised at the heaviness of his arm. He pushed his stiff, dry lips into a grin.

"You were so sick for so *long*. We were sure you were going to die. Oh, *Papa*."

"Nonsense." His tongue rasped like grains of sand against the roof of his mouth. He searched for a glass of something to drink.

The bell over the front door jingled as the door clattered

open and several feet pounded their way up the stairs. *That was fast.*

"Pa!" Josiah halted in the doorway with Lyle standing next to him. Zeke eyed him and blinked as though shocked to see him alive and breathing.

"I'm all right." He lifted his hand, heavy as lead, and beckoned them.

The three boys about knocked down their sister and piled on the bed.

Maggie Galloway rushed back into the room and clapped her hands twice. "Off the bed, boys! Your father is still getting better."

"Yes, ma'am. Do what she says." Josiah elbowed them, and Zeke pushed Lyle out of the way. What kind of magic was this?

His daughter's brows furrowed together. "Papa, did I hurt you? I wasn't thinking."

Thomas shook his head. "I'm happy to have you all here."

"I'm so sorry, Mr. Harper...I thought the children needed to see you were on the road to recovery. I should have had Dr. Moore look at you first. How are you feeling? You must be thirsty...and probably hungry."

The children moved away to make room for Mrs. Galloway. Nearly as miraculous as the parting of the Red Sea. "I'm very thirsty."

"Would you like some tea? A little sugar in it might help strengthen you." She felt his forehead again and then pulled her hand away as though she'd acted too familiar with him. Was that a blush on the usually cool and composed widow? He hadn't minded her touch, but she backed away rather quickly. "I'll be right back with what you need." She turned and went into the hallway.

How strange. Perhaps he was still unconscious, or worse, addicted to laudanum and imagined all of this.

But Abby perched on the edge of his bed, holding his hand. "Do you remember what happened, Papa?"

"You fell on the stairs!" Zeke waved his arms.

"Sh. I want to hear what he has to say." Abby shot a look of displeasure at her little brother.

"I remember not feeling well and walking up the stairs..." His throat was still dry. "Abby, some water...please." He wanted to talk to them, but he had so little voice and even less strength.

"Yes, Papa." Abby poured water from a pitcher on the nightstand and held a glass to his lips.

Thomas took sips of water. The tepid liquid refreshed his parched throat better than iced lemonade in the summer. When he'd had enough, he touched her arm. "Thank you."

Abby lowered the cup and smiled.

"When you fell, you bumped your head. I was so worried because you wouldn't talk to me, so I called Dr. Moore." Her look turned serious.

The front door clattered open, the bell ringing above it a welcome sound. He must get back to work—somehow—and soon.

"Hello!" A deep voice boomed up the stairway, and heavy footsteps approached.

"Dr. Moore, you're here. Our patient is *much* better." Mrs. Galloway's response from the kitchen sounded happier than he would have expected at the prospect of his recovery. His heart warmed.

"That's excellent news." Dr. Moore entered, carrying his black bag.

Mrs. Galloway made her way in behind the good doctor with a pot of tea and a cup. After she put them onto the nightstand, Abby helped her fluff Thomas's pillows.

"Are you able to sit up, Thomas? I mean, Mr. Harper." Mrs. Galloway blushed yet again as she placed her hand behind his shoulders.

He eased into a sitting position, suddenly shy with her so near.

~

*M*aggie stepped back so Dr. Moore could have a closer look, while Abby, who sat on the bed again, scooted toward the end. Thomas's hazel eyes met Maggie's, full of questions. She could barely tear her gaze away. She had tried to keep him cleaned up, but even the unshaven stubble and disheveled hair couldn't keep her from thinking him rather handsome, only adding to her discomfort. To find a man besides Robert attractive—well, this new feeling unsettled her.

The old doctor pulled a stethoscope from his bag and listened to Thomas's chest. "Much better. Now breathe deep for me." He moved the bell-shaped metal piece to his back to listen to his patient's lungs.

Thomas coughed.

"Good. It's loosened up some. You're improving. And I hope you know the reason." Dr. Moore raised an eyebrow at Thomas.

Thomas scratched his head. His hazel eyes, much less guarded than when she'd met him, implored them both for answers.

"Why, this young lady stepped right in when you needed the most care." Dr. Moore smiled and held a hand out toward her with a flourish.

Warmth surged up Maggie's neck and over her face. "Thank you, Dr. Moore, but I'm only doing my Christian duty." She turned to pour tea with a shaky hand. "Would you like anything in your tea...Mr. Harper?" It would have been so easy to call him Thomas after being in such intimate quarters with him.

She'd bathed him with Dr. Moore present, shaved him, and

fed him like a little child. The memories of cradling his head while spooning hot broth into his mouth flooded her mind. The closeness, knowing his children better, and seeing pictures of his wife—all of these things made her feel as though they should be close friends, not mere acquaintances. The Harpers' lives had enveloped her in a way which made her feel as though she'd invaded his privacy.

"I'll take it plain, thank you." Thomas reached out to take the cup and saucer.

"No, let me put it on a tray for you. You're weak." Maggie's gaze locked with his bewildered one as he searched hers.

"I beg your pardon." He sat straighter. "I'll be right as rain in no time."

"Of course you will be. I just meant you need to regain your strength after being so ill." Placing her hand on his shoulder, she coaxed him to relax against the pillow again.

Thomas grimaced.

She turned quickly to find the metal tray she'd left on his dresser. Her glance caught the turned-around picture of the young Harper family. She set it aright. *Well, Mrs. Harper, he's under your watch again.* Why did the thought sadden Maggie when she didn't belong here in the first place? Placing the earthenware cup and saucer on the tray, she gripped the handles and placed it on her patient's lap.

"Thank you, Mrs. Galloway." Thomas paused. "Not for the tea alone, of course, but for all of your care." He took a sip of tea. "Tell me more, Doctor."

"Maggie here barely left your side, except to care for your children, of course, for over a week. She fed you and made sure you got all of your medication. If I were you, I'd behave myself and keep her coming back as long as possible. There's not a better nurse in all of Stone Creek." Dr. Moore folded his stethoscope and tucked it into his bag.

"Really, Dr. Moore, I only did what anyone else would do to

help their neighbor." Maggie wiped her hands on her apron even though they weren't wet or dirty, then pretended to pick a piece of lint from it.

"Not everyone would, Maggie. That's why the reverend asked you." The physician's smile couldn't be wider if she'd been his own daughter.

"Well. If you'll be here a while, I'll take care of some other chores."

Perhaps she should boil an egg for Thomas. He'd need to gain strength. Had she really been here over a week?

The Harper children chatted quietly with their father and Dr. Moore as she left the room. She missed Philip so much. None of the Harper children could fill the spot in her heart he did. At least they had sent little notes back and forth with Mr. Starks, who often made deliveries to her. If Mrs. Moore could stay with the Harpers, perhaps she could go home and see her son.

She had plenty of eggs in the icebox. She could make pancakes for the children to celebrate. Every morning, she had struggled to cook a pot of oatmeal or get a little tea and toast on the table. Thankfully, Gloria's efforts to round up dinners from the ladies at church had proven fruitful. Her friend also made sure they had eggs and dairy products.

She pumped water into the heavy pan she'd placed in the sink. Her back ached, and weariness overtook her. How she would love to go home and sleep in her own bed. Sighing, Maggie carried the pan to the stove, where the fire had dwindled. She stirred the remaining embers and shoveled more coal from the bucket into the belly of the stove.

Come to think of it, would it be proper for her to spend time at night in Thomas's room now he was awake? Maggie flushed. Perhaps she could come and check on him during the day, do a few chores and cook a meal or two, but she couldn't stay here any longer.

She smacked the egg against the edge of the bowl, spilled out its contents, then cracked another egg. Finding a whisk, Maggie beat them together. Nothing unseemly had happened, so why blush at the thought of being in close quarters with the man since he was getting well? What made her heart flutter as she recalled her time with him?

Dr. Moore's lumbering gait brought him toward the kitchen. "Well, my dear, you've done an amazing job with not only Mr. Harper but also his children." He cleared his throat. "You know, though I'm sure he's through the worst of it, he will need help around here."

"Doctor, I do feel a need to spend some time at home. If the children help Thomas—I mean, Mr. Harper—with his medicine in the evening, I can bring dinner and clean for them during the day. You know, make sure the children get home all right and have something to eat." Maggie paused to take a breath. "Quite frankly, Philip needs me. I've been away long enough."

"Slow down, my dear." The old gentleman chuckled. "You are quite right. We wouldn't want people to talk." Chair legs scraped along the floor, and the doctor lowered himself into the seat. "Philip is doing quite well, you know. He and Elise are having a grand time. The measles have cleared up. Your son is stronger than ever."

"So Gloria tells me."

Hopefully, the canister contained enough flour to make a nice stack of golden pancakes, but she would need to replenish it soon. Even as she scooped it into the measuring cup, the ladle slipped from her fingers, spreading a dusty mess.

"Maggie, you're tired. Please consider going home and resting today. That's what I came in here to tell you. The children will be at school. Mrs. Moore will stay and see to his needs. Once he's up and about, I promise to look in on Thomas and make sure he is resting too."

"Let me feed them first, and put on some dinner for them to come home to. By the time I'm finished up here, Philip will already have walked home from school."

He nodded. "It sounds as though you have everything in hand."

Indeed. And now that she did, her presence would be superfluous at best—a notion that unexpectedly squeezed her heart.

~

*T*homas's eyelids grew heavy listening to his children's chatter. As delightful as their company was, his illness had left him weak.

"Come and get your pancakes." Maggie appeared in the doorway. Her musical call grabbed the boys' and Abby's attention.

Zeke rubbed his tummy. "I'm starving."

The others followed him to the kitchen, but Maggie brought a tray to Thomas. "I'm afraid you only get a poached egg and some toast, sir." She set the tray on the table next to the bed.

Her lavender fragrance and closeness as she tucked a napkin into the front of his nightshirt perked him up. "But the pancakes smelled so good."

"Let's see what your stomach can tolerate and get you stronger, then we can talk about feeding you something tastier." She cut his toast into four pieces. "This will make it easier to dip it into the yoke."

"Yes, ma'am."

Maggie placed the tray on his lap. "If you think you're up to eating on your own, I can leave and check on you in a few minutes."

"No..." Thomas placed his hand over hers. "I mean...please

94

stay. We never finished that conversation we started on your porch."

She pulled her hand away but sat on a chair near the bed. "Perhaps you're a little weak and I should stay. Or maybe not thinking right?" A half smile appeared on her face.

"What?" He popped a bite of toast dunked in yoke into his mouth, chewed, and swallowed.

"I could have been more appreciative of the package you brought me. I'm surprised you still want us to continue the conversation. I thought..."

"You figured you'd upset me? I'm not quite that easily rattled. In fact, I have the very package I brought you waiting for you under the counter downstairs." He winked.

Maggie shook her head. "That figures. You thought I would give in."

Thomas swallowed another bite. "Didn't the aspirin help at all?"

She fiddled with the hem of her apron and didn't look at him. "Yes, but I'm not convinced the old-fashioned way doesn't have its merits."

"Fair enough." What else could he say? He really wanted to know more of her—this woman who Thad claimed had saved his life.

When he reached for his tea, she held the cup out to him and steadied it. The liquid soothed his dry throat and tasted better than he'd remembered. "Have you lived in Stone Creek all your life?" He took a deep breath. How could he keep her engaged in conversation when he tired so easily?

A chuckle resonated from her throat. "Why, no. I'm originally from Buffalo. Still have family there—er, my in-laws, anyway."

"Do you miss it?"

"Sometimes. In fact, I'm considering buying a bakery there. Some way to provide for Philip's and my future." Her eyes brightened as she shared about her contest placement and how she loved to create confections her family and friends enjoyed.

Thomas nodded and murmured his encouragement as he sipped his tea. He'd had no idea the woman was such a talented baker. Was there anything she couldn't do?

Finally, Maggie opened the cover of the watch pinned to her blouse. "Oh my. I've been going on and on. And I see you still have half of your breakfast left. You can't eat anymore?"

His second wind had ebbed, and he yawned. "I'm afraid that's all I can get down for now." Wooziness threatened him.

"Pa!" Lyle stood just outside the doorway. "Can you read us a book?"

"Later."

Maggie wiped Thomas's mouth and removed the napkin. "Your pa needs his rest, but maybe you could read to *him* later."

"I'll do it." Josiah stood tall next to his brother.

Maggie nodded her approval. "Rest well, Mr. Harper. I'll be here for a while, but I'll be going home for the night." Her expression turned stony, unreadable. Was she hiding the same disappointment that had settled in him?

Thomas ventured a telling statement. "I know the house will feel your absence."

"I'll be back during the day, but your children will be instructed on how best to help you when I'm not here. You'll be fine, no doubt." She averted her gaze.

The warm, caring nurse turned into the aloof woman he so easily annoyed. If that was how she played it, so be it. But the hollowness in his heart returned.

CHAPTER 11

*A*pple Blossom Cottage beckoned her with pink, white, and yellow tulips along the pathway right up to the cozy front porch. Mr. Merton, the Myleses' gardener, had already begun his seasonal work making the small yard tidy and welcoming. Rays of sunshine poked between the budding branches of the trees surrounding the little house.

Gloria and Elise burst out the front door, waving, but Philip dashed past them both and ran to Maggie with open arms. "Mama! I thought you weren't ever coming home! I prayed you wouldn't get sick." Her dear boy collided with her, burying his face against her coat.

"Let your poor mother come in and sit down to rest. She's had a hard time at the Harpers'." Her friend laughed, shaking her head at Philip. "I've made some tea and brought sandwiches from the manor house."

"You're all a sight for sore eyes." Maggie could barely blink back the tears of happiness.

"We make your eyes hurt?" Philip scrunched his nose and stared up at her.

Elise giggled. "No, silly, your mother means she's glad to see us."

"Elise is quite right." Maggie tousled the red hair she loved.

Philip shrugged but smiled with two new front teeth almost too big for his freckled face.

Once Maggie removed her coat, dizziness overtook her. She leaned against the wall to steady herself. She rubbed her temple and forehead. "I guess I didn't realize how tired I am."

Gloria rushed to her side and took her by the arm. "You've worked so hard to get Mr. Harper better. And now he has a chance."

"By God's grace." Maggie nodded.

"You need to sit down, my friend." Gloria led Maggie toward her favorite rocking chair.

She took her place there, relaxing into the soft cushion. Philip brought in the mail she'd missed and set it on the table next to her.

Gloria smiled and pushed a diminutive footstool under her feet. "You just sit, now. I'll bring you something to eat and drink."

"Gloria, I don't expect you to wait on me." She shook her head.

"You're worn out, I'm sure. I'm happy to help you." She headed to the kitchen. "You've certainly earned a rest."

Maggie couldn't stifle a yawn. "I'm used to being busy, even with only the two of us."

Gloria bustled back in with a tray. "There, see now, you're exhausted. After you have a little lunch, I'm going to take Philip back to the manor, and you're going to take a nap. Then you and Philip will have a lovely dinner with us."

"First, I think I will take a warm bath. My back is aching after I fell asleep kneeling by the bed." She bit her lip even as Gloria's eyebrows went up. She'd said too much. "I was praying for poor Thomas." How wretched! Heat crept up her neck and face yet again. Why did mentioning the man do this to her? Nobody since Robert had brought a blush to her cheeks and a flutter in her stomach...until Mr. Harper. How could a man in such a helpless condition stir these long-buried feelings?

"It seems the Lord heard your prayers, didn't He, now? Such good news that Mr. Harper is still with us." Gloria's eyes sparkled as she placed the tray across Maggie's lap. "I'm going to send the maid to draw your bath, so you don't have to lift a finger."

"No, no, you're going to too much fuss." Maggie shook her head. "I'm not an invalid."

The sweet tea slid over her tongue and warmed her dry throat. Then she bit into a sandwich filled with roasted chicken. It took effort to chew. Once she swallowed, she was ready to continue the conversation. "I'm afraid I'll get spoiled and won't want to work so hard anymore."

Gloria took Maggie's coat from the back of the chaise and hung it up on the coat tree. "Maggie, I'll put your things in your room." She reached down for Maggie's carpetbag and scurried from the sitting room.

After taking her time eating what she could—she really was more tired than hungry—Maggie folded her linen napkin and placed it over the partially empty plate. "I'm positively stuffed." She reached for the envelopes Philip had placed on the side table for her. "Let's see. A letter from my cousin Lettie. Maybe there's something from the real estate people. Hmm."

Gloria returned to the room.

"Look—a letter from the Silver Leaf Flour Company. Maybe it's the information about the gentleman they're sending with my prize."

"Why don't you open it? I can't wait to hear more about it."

Maggie reached for her silver filigree letter opener and gently pushed the pointed end between the flap and the upper edge. She read aloud.

Dear Mrs. Galloway,

We sincerely apologize for our delay in reaching your fine town. I will arrive in Stone Creek at 2 p.m., a week from this coming Saturday. Please gather your friends and acquaintances to celebrate your impressive accomplishment of earning a second-place Silver Leaf pin. The Silver Leaf Flour Company aspires to encourage only the finest cooks and bakers to reach the utmost heights in their culinary abilities.

Until then, I await my time in Stone Creek with great anticipation.

Most sincerely,
Giles Prescott
Midwest Regional Manager

"*T*hat's good news, but you have a pained expression on your face. Whatever is wrong?" Maggie lowered the letter to her lap.

Her friend's eyebrows met in a frown. "You're not going to be happy with this, but while you've been busy with the Harpers, Gertrude Wringer and Mrs. Neuberger have been busy cooking up something. Pardon the pun."

"Yes?"

"They want to hold a Stone Creek cooking competition and have the estimable Mr. Prescott head the panel of judges." Gloria swept her long skirt under her as she gracefully sat on the sofa nearest Maggie.

"Gloria, how did they know about all this?"

"Ian has been quite proud of you. And, well, I announced it to the Ladies' Aid Society."

"You didn't."

Her friend's sheepish grin told all.

Maggie leaned back, and her lips curved into a grin. "I'm guessing the Silver Leaf Flour Company would be pleased with such publicity."

"I'm relieved you don't seem upset." She exhaled and returned Maggie's smile.

"Piffle." Maggie refolded the letter and waved her hand. "Why would I be? They should be following the rules of the original baking contest, though, if they want Mr. Northwest Regional Manager's help. They can't expect to make up their own rules."

"But Maggie, this was your moment to shine. I don't like to see them take it away from you. Of course, Gertrude is sore her recipe for cherry corn muffins which she entered didn't win."

"I'm not in the least bit ruffled. My special moment was receiving the letter which told me I won. After that, well, I'm happy to share my celebration. Isn't that what life is all about?"

"You're not telling me something." Gloria tilted her head to the side.

"It's a long story." Maggie swallowed, not prepared to discuss what the name *Giles Prescott* meant to her.

"Only because you're tired, I'm going to let you off the hook and let you get ready for your bath right now."

"After a bath and a nap, I'll pen a letter to the paper, inviting all the ladies to join the contest."

Wait a minute! When was this posted? Maggie reread the letter. A week from this past Saturday was less than a week away!

CHAPTER 12

*T*he next morning, Maggie awoke to a rapping on her front door. Who would bother her this early except for Ian?

"I'll see who it is, Mama." Philip popped his head through the doorway and rubbed the sleep from his eyes. What a sight he was with his ruffled hair. Then he scurried to look out a front-facing window. "It's old Mrs. Wringer. Should I let her in?"

"Oh bother. No, Philip, you get ready for school. I'll get up." Maggie sat and swung her legs over the side of the bed. She pulled her robe from the end of the bed, then stood and wrapped it around her.

The rapping continued, as incessant as a woodpecker looking for bugs in a tree trunk.

"Just a moment, please." She raised her voice.

Maggie smoothed her hair and wrapped it into a loose chignon before placing pins. She couldn't wait to hear tomorrow's gossip about how awful she looked in the morning.

She reached the front of the cottage and grabbed the knob to pull the door open. Gertrude stood with an umbrella handle —her implement of torture by repetitive door knocking—

poised in midair. Couldn't the woman knock on the door with her hand like a normal person?

"What is it, Gertrude? I just woke up." Maggie gestured toward the east, where the sun lit the pearly clouds with a glow.

"Meanwhile, that fellow from the Silver Leaf Flour Company is due to arrive any day now. We need to start planning while the day is young."

"Only yesterday, I got back from caring for Mr. Harper and his children, and there's much to catch up on here, but I'd be happy to meet with you later this afternoon." Maggie crossed her arms, blocking the entrance.

"Yes, yes, I heard about Harper's little bout of illness." Gertrude waved her hand as though she dismissed the subject like brushing a crumb from her skirt. She leaned in a little closer. "I've already called on my friends last night to tell them to meet here this morning. You better get ready."

"Aunt Gertie!" Nora Armstrong, the older woman's niece, yelled and waved as she hurried to the front steps of the cottage. Her light hair escaped from its braid, and her pale face grew pink from exertion. A hand flew to her thin chest as she took a deep breath. "I'm so sorry, Mrs. Galloway. I tried to get her to stay put this morning. Aunt Gert, you shouldn't be running out of the house without telling me. Uncle Edmond won't like this at all. Now let's go home and let Maggie get ready for the day." Nora touched Gertrude's arm, but she pulled away.

"We have work to do." Fierce determination burned in the older woman's eyes.

Maggie's heart squeezed with compassion for Nora, a gentle-hearted soul trapped with her unkind aunt. Only months before, Gertrude had received her comeuppance after trying to run Maggie's sister-in-law, Sophie, out of town and attempting to block the establishment of a home for unwed mothers. The hen-pecked Edmund had humiliated her in front of most of Stone Creek by telling her she needed to mind her own business. Unfortunately, he still struggled to break out of his subordinate habits. For the whole town's sake, he needed to put her in her place again.

Gertrude tried to slip past Maggie, but Maggie stood her ground. "You will not come in right now, Gertrude. I don't even have Philip off to school. You may come back at ten o'clock this morning if you must."

"Very well, but you're wasting valuable time." Gertrude sniffed.

"You can sit here on the porch or go to the comfort of your home to make a list of what you think is important."

"I have one already." She plucked a folded piece of paper from her reticule.

Maggie snatched it from her hand. "Thank you. This will give me a chance to go over it first."

"You're growing much too independent, Maggie Galloway." Gertrude arched an eyebrow and pointed a bony finger at her. "Maybe since you were taking care of another man's children, now you think you're in charge of this little event. I—"

"I am the second-place winner in the Silver Leaf baking contest. Not you." Maggie paused, letting the truth sink in. "And remember, I can send Mr. Prescott packing if I'd like and put an end to this whole celebration." She thrust the list back toward the antagonistic woman.

Pale, Nora ducked her head. She pulled on Gertrude's sleeve. "Aunt Gert, you and I can work on the planning and share what we have later today."

Maggie inhaled slowly and closed her eyes for a moment. "Please forgive me, Gertrude, Nora. I don't mean to be a brag-gart. I do want the town to be part of this. Please, let me get dressed and have some breakfast. For that matter, I need to get a bit more organized. Would you care to meet over at the church instead? I'm sure my brother wouldn't mind."

"Of course. You understand, don't you, Aunt?" Nora spoke

softly into the older woman's ear as though coaxing a stubborn donkey.

Gertrude pushed her list back into her reticule and stepped away. "Fine, suit yourself, but it won't be my fault if this whole thing is a disaster, hmm?"

∼

*T*homas Harper sat on the edge of his bed and breathed deeply, only to cough again, while Dr. Moore listened to his lungs.

Dr. Moore removed the stethoscope's earpieces from his ears and let the instrument hang from his collar like a necklace. "You're a lucky young man, Thomas, but I don't have to tell you such a thing, I suppose. I was afraid we were going to lose you."

"With a fine doctor like yourself, I didn't have to worry, did I?" Thomas meant his compliment.

"I think we both know you probably wouldn't be sitting here if it wasn't for a certain lady." Dr. Moore cleared his throat.

Thomas nodded and rubbed his hand over his scruffy chin. Dr. Moore expressed what he didn't want to admit to himself. She wasn't Bess, but she had a caring heart and way about her. Her firm hand had reigned in his mischievous children. He pushed away thoughts of her gentle touch lest palpitations overtake his heart.

"Were you even aware how much time Mrs. Galloway spent by your bedside?" Dr. Moore took his stethoscope from his neck and folded it into his black bag, snapping it shut with finality. "She could help heal your heart if you let her." The doctor had a twinkle in his eye.

"I didn't know who was here with me at first. I'm relieved Abby wasn't left to handle it all." Warmth crept up his neck. Did Dr. Moore expect him to ask Maggie to be his wife in payment for her healing arts?

"Come, come, man. You need a wife, and she needs a husband." He spoke as though having read Thomas's thoughts. "You've both been through enough sorrow."

"You're not adding a matchmaking fee to payment for services rendered, are you?" Thomas tried to draw the conversation away from uncomfortable territory.

"Thomas, both of us are involved in healing others, but sometimes we overlook what's most important." Dr. Moore thumped his chest. "As a young man, I lost my first wife in this treacherous territory many a year ago. She had a bad case of the ague. Frail thing, she was." He shook his head. "I didn't really heal until Sarah came into my life."

"I appreciate the sentiments, Doctor, but I need a nanny or a housekeeper. I don't plan on marrying again." He'd believed this with all his heart a few weeks ago, but something had changed, though he wouldn't admit it aloud. He never thought he'd meet a woman of character whom his children liked, but Maggie fit both criteria. And her loveliness didn't hurt.

"Well, you'll be in my prayers." The doctor's eyes looked bigger through his spectacles and made Thomas feel as though he were a bug being examined through a magnifying glass. "Maggie will come by later. But you better find yourself some full-time help soon. Maggie has her own life."

Thomas sighed. No use explaining how often his housekeepers had resigned.

~

*A*fter seeing Philip off to school, Maggie readied herself for meeting with the townswomen who wanted to be part of the Silver Leaf Award festivities. She caught her reflection in the small mirror by the front door and stopped to make sure her blue felt hat sat straight.

Who stared back at her? Dark indentations accentuated the

circles under her eyes. Looking like that, there were certainly no worries about her reigniting the spark Giles Prescott once had for her. *Not that I want him to notice me. Do I?*

Thomas and his difficult brood flashed through her mind. He was so different from the carefree Giles Prescott.

Maggie quickened her pace as she strode toward the road. The misty rain had lifted. Sunny spring filled the air. The grass grew lush and green again. Blooming lilacs filled her nose with their perfume.

She had been cooped up in the Harpers' dingy apartment above his shop for too long. Yet she couldn't help but wonder how they were doing. Affection bloomed at the thought of the widower and his brood.

Thomas...again. Well, she had spent a fair amount of time there.

When Maggie entered the church, a small group of townswomen sat in pews near the front of the sanctuary and chatted with good humor. Or was the cackling laughter of Gertrude and her friends at Maggie's expense? As the door clanked shut behind her, the women grew silent.

"It's about time you got here." Gertrude waved her finger at Maggie.

Maggie slipped into a pew a couple of rows behind them. She forced her lips to form a smile, albeit a fake one. "Well, then, what did I miss?"

"We were thinking of asking Mr. Prescott to be our judge for our baking contest." Gertrude smirked.

"I rather hate to see him put out when he has no warning." Maggie stiffened. She shouldn't have come.

"As long as he's here, we might as well have a little fun, don't you think?" Mrs. Neuberger's smile was as forced as Maggie's had been. "By the way, we learned you know Mr. Prescott from the past...and were wondering if that had anything to do with your placement in the contest." The awful woman pursed her lips and fussed with the gaudy filigree pin on her blouse.

Warmth crept up Maggie's face. She'd never outgrown that tendency to blush.

"Do tell." Gertrude lifted her chin with her usual smug grin again plastered across her face.

Whatever Maggie said they wouldn't believe. "What does it matter to you, Gertrude?"

"The rest of us would like a fair chance at being judged by the Silver Leaf Flour Company."

"I don't know if he was even on the panel of judges." Maggie shrugged. "He's the regional vice-president from the Chicago office."

"But you don't deny you know him personally?"

"I did know someone by the name of Giles Prescott before I met my husband. He was a family acquaintance." Maggie glared back at Gertrude and her cronies. What business was it of theirs? Yet if she didn't tell them some of the truth, the gossip would only grow worse.

"But how do you know he didn't have some influence over the judges?" Gertrude smiled like a cat that ate a mouse.

"Gertrude, I haven't seen the man since before I was married. How do I know if he even remembers me?" Maggie gripped the back of the pew in front of her. "Besides, hasn't your husband asked you to mind your own laundry?"

Half the women gasped, and the other half tittered with light laughter.

Gertie's face reddened. "Then perhaps you should stop stirring up the past. What my husband said is none of your concern."

Maggie blew out a breath. She wouldn't rise to that bait. "If you want to give the women of the town two days to get ready for a baking contest, then so be it. Let the best baker win." She sat back in the pew. "But I don't know whether Mr. Prescott will oblige you or not. Perhaps as a goodwill gesture of the flour company, he'll help. What about other judges?"

"I'm sure you can count on my husband." Etta Stout waved her hand.

"And Dr. Moore, no doubt," someone else added.

The women buzzed with ideas for decorations. Millie Wilson would make sure her son and his friends would be available to set up tables.

Maggie shook her head. She really didn't want all this fanfare. Sunshine momentarily lit the rear of the sanctuary through the door as Gloria walked in. Finally, a voice of reason.

Maggie waved her over. "Tell them we don't need such a production—a simple contest, tea, and cookies is enough."

"If anyone deserves celebration, it's you, my friend. The lilacs are blooming, and there are other flowers we can cut to decorate the tables. And we must have festoons at the railway station." Her animated smile and waving arms indicated she wouldn't help tone things down after all.

Maggie rubbed her throbbing temples. The air inside the sanctuary had become stifling. Somehow, this celebration didn't matter much anymore. She stood and made her way toward the door.

"Where's she going? We've just begun." Gertrude wouldn't give up.

"Plan whatever you like. I need some air!" Maggie pushed open the heavy oak door and fled outside.

CHAPTER 13

$\mathcal{M}$aggie hadn't meant to be so abrupt, but she would explain things to her friend later. Perhaps taking a walk would calm her nerves. Why she'd allowed the ladies' plans to upset her so much was anyone's guess.

Yet she'd pictured the whole event differently. The Silver Leaf representative would no doubt be on a whistle-stop tour, spreading goodwill for the company. He'd stop to award Maggie her prize and be gone by nightfall. The town would be there to cheer her on with cake and cookies.

Giles Prescott. She'd been the envy of the other young ladies in town when the handsome Mr. Prescott began paying attention to her. With his hair parted in the middle and slicked down, a wayward ebony curl had always escaped the pomade and made him appear rather rakish. His warm brown eyes had penetrated right through her. He'd had Maggie believing she was the only woman he cared for—except when his head turned as a prettier girl walked by.

She sighed.

Her mother had told her she'd never go without if she

married such a clever young man as Giles, someone with a future. After all, his father was a so-called self-made man and expected no less from his son. But then Robert came along. Not as tall or handsome, but he was a hardworking man of godly character.

She mindlessly wandered over by the millpond and stopped to stare into the murky waters. If she had married Giles, she wouldn't be a widow now, would she? Yet not having Robert meant no Philip or the wonderful, precious years she'd spent with her husband. Her heart squeezed with the familiar grief. Yes, the love had been worth the pain.

A muskrat poked its nose above the surface, rippling the water and breaking into her thoughts. The animal peered at her with shiny eyes as if to ask her what the problem was. What was her problem, anyway? They were well-fed and safe, and Philip had regained his strength after his illness, but still she was a widow, and her son had no father.

"Maggie!" Gloria strode toward her. The elegant feathers in her hat ruffled in the gentle breeze. "Are you quite all right?"

"Yes." She averted her gaze.

"I was concerned something was wrong. It's so unlike you to run off in such a hurry."

"Like a child. I know. I'm sorry for my outburst. I couldn't take any more of Gertrude and the others. I know you're all excited about this, but I really didn't expect such a large celebration. I don't want all this focus on me."

Gloria smiled like a beneficent angel, blond hair circling her face like a halo. "How often do we have an important visitor from the big city? I know you don't care about these pretensions—"

"No. But we shouldn't presume upon Mr. Prescott either."

"He'll be here to promote the Silver Leaf brand. He'll probably be honored, even flattered."

"Very well." Maggie clasped her hands together. "If he

minds, I suppose we can still have a party with all the sweets the women bake." She paused. "But you're in charge of the decorations. Hopefully, they won't get out of hand."

"You never know." Gloria's conspiratorial arch of an eyebrow made Maggie laugh.

~

*N*obody would run Thomas Harper's business for him. He had work to do and was still minus a housekeeper. He sat and swung his legs over the edge of the bed, seeking his slippers with his feet but finding the cool wood floor first. A shiver slithered up his legs.

Taking his time, Thomas stood, holding onto the nightstand. Inhaling a deep breath without wheezing reminded him to be grateful for surviving his bout with pneumonia. His heart pounded at the exertion.

He caught a hint of a sweet scent. Was it vanilla touched with lavender? Something Maggie Galloway had left behind. What had she seen when she cared for him? What had he said under the influence of fever? She'd nursed him back to health, been there for his most personal care.

Thomas trembled as thoughts of Maggie threatened to take over his mind. Not only because he feared letting someone into his heart, but also from an appreciative affection growing for her. Holding onto the dresser, he staggered to where his robe hung and wrapped himself in it.

He made his way from holding onto the doorframe a few paces to the stairway and clung to the banister as he placed one foot on the tread, making sure his legs held. They did. Thomas exhaled. When he reached the bottom of the steps, he surveyed the pharmacy. The gaslight sputtered until it blazed to life as he turned the knob below the wall sconce.

Thomas shook his head at the disarray. Crates still needed

unpacking. Specks of dust floated across beams of light and coated the shelves. If only Maggie weren't so opinionated, he could ask for her help around the shop.

Holding onto the counter, Thomas inched his way toward a lone wooden crate against the wall. Nearly out of breath, he lowered his weight onto the makeshift seat, then placed his elbows on his knees and his head in his hands. He'd made a mess of things by leaving his business in the city. At least Bess had left it well organized, and the children had friends and their grandparents nearby. Why had he thought running from his past life with Bess would result in anything good for himself or the children? How would they ever get back on their feet? Perhaps he should just give up, sell the store, and work for someone else in Detroit.

Knock! Knock! The sign on the door had been turned to the *closed* side. Instead of waiting for an answer, the person on the other side of the door rattled the knob, shaking the bell above. A key went into the lock and turned with a click.

Maggie Galloway barreled through the door. "Mr. Harper? What are you doing up already?"

CHAPTER 14

*T*homas Harper had no common sense. Maggie glared at him. He'd nearly died, but he was up puttering around, likely before Dr. Moore had given him permission.

"I couldn't stand to be bedridden one day longer, Mrs. Galloway." His eyebrows went up like a guilty child's. Wrapped in a long green robe, he hunched on the edge of a crate, thinner than before his illness. He needed a shave again, and an unruly mop of sandy brown hair flopped onto his forehead.

"I don't think Dr. Moore would be happy finding you down here." She crossed her arms.

"How am I going to get my strength back while sitting in bed? I have a business to run." He raked a hand through his hair, pushing it back into place. "What are you doing here, anyway? I was fairly sure I'd seen the last of you for a while."

Maggie could barely contain a smile. "Yes, well, I'm so glad to see you, too—among the living, that is."

Thomas's eyebrows went up before he let out a chuckle. "Have a seat on the bench or pull up another crate."

Looking around, she pulled out the pin holding her hat in

place and removed her waistcoat. She hung them on a peg near the door.

"What are you doing, Mrs. Galloway?"

"It's rather stuffy in here. I'll tell you what. I'll help you get a few things organized if you'll promise to go rest again."

"I couldn't impose on you any more than I have." Thomas stood and leaned against the counter. "Why, before you know it, I'll be fit as a fiddle and won't need any help at all." His grin was less than convincing.

"Mr. Harper, I don't know how you arrange your store, but perhaps you could give me some direction. After all, I used to help my husband run his shop."

Thomas averted his gaze, appearing to study the marble counter surface. "I hope you won't think any less of me than you must already, but you've seen our family firsthand. I've had three housekeepers leave my employ. Between the poor behavior of my children and our messy house, I can't say I blame them." He paused. "I'm certain the only reason you stood your tenure is the fact you knew it would only last until I got better." His greenish eyes searched her out.

"Mr. Harper, I...I don't know what to say." The man had bared much of his heart to her.

"I'm not sure why I told you all this, except my deceased wife was the one who organized my stock. I'm afraid we'll be learning together." He placed both elbows on the counter as though leaning his full weight on the marble slab.

When once she might have laughed at his disorganization, Maggie found any humor melted into a pool of empathetic warmth near her heart. They were more kindred spirits than she'd realized. "We're each missing our better half. You're at a greater disadvantage with four children. As difficult as it has been bringing up Philip without Robert, my brother has been a good male influence."

"I'm certain he has."

She swallowed, remembering the lovely blond woman in the photograph upstairs. "You've been rather alone here."

"Yes."

An awkward silence fell between them.

"Why don't I open the front window shade and some of the windows before we get started?" Maggie tugged on the string hanging from the shade and pulled it partway up.

Flecks of dust danced among the afternoon sunbeams streaming through the window. The rain had stopped. The corners of her mouth pulled upward in a smile, despite the poignancy which flooded her.

Crash!

She jumped as a crate tumbled to the floor. "What do you think you're doing? Are you trying to hurt yourself moving those crates?" Maggie cringed. She could only hope any break-ables in the crate were well protected.

Mr. Harper's childlike, sheepish grin disarmed her. "I didn't intend for that to happen. Maybe I should start with moving one crate at a time?" Then Mr. Harper stood straight and cleared his throat. "I propose we get to work."

"Of course, but I will help you with each crate." Maggie approached with a smile. Could helping him in the pharmacy be more difficult than taking care of him and his children?

~

Three hours later, Thomas leaned an elbow on the counter, surveying the miracles Mrs. Galloway had wrought. Bottles of tinctures, tablets, and powders were grouped behind the glass-paneled doors of the upper cabinet according to their curative properties and then in alphabetical order. Clear, amber, and brown bottles stood like beacons to the sick since she had also cleaned each container to a shine.

Tins of dry goods were arranged as artistically as in your

mother's kitchen. The tireless woman wiped a cloth across the gleaming marble as she hummed. Then she went about setting the carefully dusted jars of candy sticks atop the polished countertop.

"There. Your shelves are much neater now." She lifted the lid from one jar and sniffed the sweet scent which wafted from the opening. "Mmm. Don't you love the smell of sassafras candy? Mr. Harper, you need a soda fountain installed here. You know they're all the rage." Maggie replaced the lid with a little too much enthusiasm.

Thomas grimaced in response. "Of course, but I must get up and running first." Bess would have been pushing him to do the same.

Maggie's hand went up as if in defense. "I'm only trying to help here. You have wonderful stock and the latest remedies, such as the aspirin tablets." The way she arched her right eyebrow made her far more alluring.

"Mrs. Galloway, you have outdone yourself. I can never repay you for all your work." He coughed.

Maggie's gaze softened. "Sometimes it takes a partnership—"

The back door opened and closed with a slam, and a cacophony of voices let him know the children were back from school.

When they reached the front of the store, Abby gasped.

"What?" Zeke blinked a couple of times.

Josiah shook his head, and Lyle rammed into his side, eyes widening.

Stepping forward, Abby put her hands on her hips. "Pa, what are you doing up? Mrs. Galloway, why are you here? Don't you think my pa should be resting?" His daughter's eyes narrowed, shooting darts of accusation at Maggie.

"Abby, you apologize to Mrs. Galloway this instant. Your mother and I didn't raise you to be so disrespectful."

"That's just it. She isn't Mama, so why is she helping you set up the shop? I wanted to!" Abby's chin quivered, and her eyes flooded with tears.

Thomas ambled over to his daughter and brought her into an embrace though she stiffened and swallowed her sobs. "Mrs. Galloway was of the same opinion about my getting more rest. She was kind enough to stop by and check on me, but fool that I am, I didn't listen to her advice. I couldn't stay in bed any longer, and we must get the business up and running. I can't keep working out of crates and boxes. And you've helped in many other ways, Abby."

Maggie placed a hand on Abby's shoulder, but his daughter shrugged it away. She patted the girl in an awkward gesture before drawing back. "I'm so sorry. I didn't know, Abby. I thought you should have time to keep up your studies along with everything else going on."

"It's not your fault. Pa never lets me do much around the store, anyway. I'm sorry, Mrs. Galloway. I shouldn't have spoken to you with such a tone." Abby averted her gaze.

"I understand. I should go now." Maggie went to the door, lifted her hat and waistcoat from the peg, and pushed her arm through a sleeve. Was that a dejected expression on the strong woman's face?

"Abby, stop crying!" Zeke poked his sister in the ribs.

"I'm *not*." She pushed Zeke away.

Both Josiah and Lyle stood there, looking at the ground with their hands in their pants pockets. A lump grew in Thomas's throat. He'd allowed another woman to fill their mother's shoes, and it had hurt his children.

Maggie cleared her throat as she arranged her hat on her head. "I must get home to Philip, though he'll probably be happy to have a chance to play with Elise while he's waiting." A short-lived, perhaps forced smile crossed her face.

"Thank you for your help, Mrs. Galloway. Please let me know if there's anything I can do for you."

"Getting better would be a good start. Goodbye, children." She nodded toward Thomas.

As the door swept closed behind her, the spring breeze chilled Thomas. Exhaustion overtook him. Her company had meant more to him than he realized. Even when he was surrounded by the children, it was becoming obvious they could never fill the hole which his former soul mate left behind.

~

*M*aggie sauntered down Main Street with her head down. How tempted she was to take a detour to the church, or the parsonage on Bradford.

"Afternoon, Mrs. Galloway."

She'd nearly run into the owner of the mercantile. "Oh, I'm sorry, Mr. Neuberger. I didn't see you coming."

He took her elbow to steady her. "Not a problem. But be careful out here on the boardwalk. I wouldn't want to see you get hurt."

"Thank you." She smiled up at the large man with dark eyes and beefy arms. "I'll watch where I'm going."

Isaac tipped his hat and stepped around her.

Why was her heart so heavy? Had she been hurt by Abby's statement? The accusatory look of all the Harper children? After all, she could have been back at the cottage, happily baking rather than checking in on Thomas.

Thomas. What compelled her to feel responsible for the man? Philip needed her, so why did she also feel needed by this grieving family?

CHAPTER 15

*T*wo days later, the weather in Stone Creek couldn't have been finer to welcome the representative of the Silver Leaf Flour Company. Maggie carried a large platter of her winning cookies to the party. Ian and his wife flanked her as they walked from the cottage toward the modest carriage he'd procured for his growing family.

Philip and Elise dashed ahead, giggling, each holding one of Caira's hands as she ran to keep up with them. Maggie pictured Gloria's worried face as Elise had left her and Asa behind after asking special permission to go to the ceremony with Philip's family. Gloria trusted Maggie and Ian, but it cost her every time she let the child out of her sight.

"Slow down. I don't want you to get your Sunday clothes dirty." Her son needed to look his best. This was her special day. All eyes would be on them, and she didn't want to leave room for the town's criticism. Besides, if this Giles were her former beau, she wanted him to see her and Philip at their finest.

The contents of Maggie's stomach turned over, and her palms drenched her nicest ivory gloves. After Sophie had been situated on the leather seat, Ian helped Maggie into the carriage, and she offered her sister-in-law an anxious smile. Caira sat next to her mother, and the other children were on either side of Maggie while Ian drove.

"A penny for your thoughts." Sophie winked at her. "Are you a bit anxious about meeting your old beau? I would be."

Maggie shrugged, though her tummy fluttered with nerves. The possibility of seeing Giles wasn't the only thing getting under her skin lately.

If Sophie only knew it's Thomas who consumes my thoughts.

"We don't know if it's truly the same Mr. Prescott, so don't get any romantic ideas." She shifted her weight. "I'm just nervous about all this attention and formality. While I'd hoped to win the contest, I thought it highly unlikely. I'm sure there are many other fine bakers across our country."

"You deserve such a party. Besides, it's another chance for the town to celebrate." Sophie patted her knee. An interesting change of roles since Maggie had often comforted her in the past. At one time, Maggie had been the one with a settled life and some of the answers to life's challenges.

~

*M*aggie grabbed her wide-brimmed hat as the breeze lifted it, though the hatpins kept it securely in place. The train whistle pierced the chatter of the crowd, reaching them before the acrid odor of the exhaust from the coal-fired steam engine did.

The exhaust temporarily clouded the sun, and sparks flew as the train slowed to a stop. The town's band played "America, the Beautiful." Festive bunting hung from the train station. What would they find at the town hall, where the reception was being held?

Maggie's heart pounded in her ears like locomotive wheels rolling on the track. The chattering dimmed around her. Even the pinched face of Gertrude Wringer and her solemn welcoming committee didn't bother her.

A few people emerged from the passenger cars one by one. Wind gusted a puff of smoke in front of the stairs, but no one who looked like Giles Prescott stepped down.

The band finished their piece and stood silent, waiting. The only music came from a horn squeaking and the chug of a horseless carriage motor on Main Street, a block away. The strange vehicle rounded the corner, coming toward the railroad station on Third Street. The driver waved as dust rose in a cloud around him.

Maggie shaded her eyes with her hand as she looked in the direction of the sun as the automobile came toward them, almost too close for comfort before it came to a stop in the middle of the road. *Well, he's putting on quite a show for us all. Could he be...Giles?*

The tall man alighted from the padded carriage-type seat of fine leather. He stood wearing an odd cap and goggles which reminded Maggie of a frog. She moved her hand to her mouth to cover her smile.

He removed the hat and leather-bound goggles and strode with confidence toward her. He unbuttoned his long duster, and it billowed out behind him. Yes. Giles...Mr. Prescott, who took the hand she'd extended automatically and kissed it. "You look as lovely as ever." That black curl escaped onto his forehead as it had all those years ago.

"Why, Mr. Prescott, you haven't changed, have you?" Her hand flew to her throat, where her pulse sped beneath her fingertips. When had the air around her grown so thin? And what was this swimming feeling in her head? *Steady.* She inhaled. His eyes, dark as a cup of coffee without creamer, penetrated her soul.

"Shall we stand on formalities, Maggie Galloway, when we

were once good friends?" His eyebrow cocked with a look of reproach.

"But it's been so long." She swallowed. "Shouldn't we get reacquainted before we use our Christian names?"

The warmth in his chuckle startled her, and before she knew it, Mr. Prescott had tucked her hand into the crook of his elbow.

Ian cleared his throat from behind her. "Giles, nice to see you again."

"Ah, Master Ian." Giles's eyes sparkled with humor. "I believe I remember your younger brother, Mrs. Galloway."

"That's Pastor or Reverend Ian McCormick now." They shook hands and, ever Maggie's protector, Ian's expression turned grim. "I would like to introduce you to my wife, Sophie." Ian placed an arm around her.

"Pleased to make your acquaintance, Mr. Prescott." Sophie tipped her head toward him.

"Most enchanted." Prescott tipped his hat and bowed.

The music began again, and the townspeople started to gather around them. Gertrude Wringer pushed her way to the center of the commotion. "We, the people of Stone Creek, Michigan, would like to welcome you to our town." She gave Prescott the closest thing she was able to give to a smile. "Mayor Wharton would like you to join us in his barouche for a ride to the churchyard, where we'll begin our festivities." Gertrude extended an arm.

"Thank you for offering such an honor, madam." Giles bowed toward Gertrude. "However, I would prefer to drive myself. Maggie, er, Mrs. Galloway, would you care to join me?"

"Really, I'm not dressed appropriately for such a thing, without a duster, but thank you. Perhaps another time." Maggie's heart pounded. Thank goodness, the excuse had come to mind. "Besides, after driving all the way here, you must be tired. Wouldn't you rather ride with us?"

Giles guffawed. "Heavens, no. I had some business in Detroit, so I had my car shipped by train there. I thought it would be a positively lovely drive here. And it was. But our destination in town can't be far. And I have a blanket stored in the back. Please reconsider."

Giles always could be rather forceful when thwarted from getting his own way, but Maggie had to put her foot down. Gertrude would see it as some collusion and make sure the rest of the women of the town would as well.

"Mr. Prescott, I really must insist I meet you at the church, though your offer is most flattering." She kept her voice in an even tone, tilting her head in polite deference.

"I see how it is." Gertrude turned toward her husband. "Edmund!" she screeched and then stopped when it grew quiet and everyone stared. "They're going to meet us there." Her tone carried her displeasure.

Maggie bit her lip to keep from smiling. She was almost sure she heard Gertrude Wringer grind her teeth.

Like an informal parade, everyone walked or rode toward the church, which had also been decked out with red, white, and blue bunting above the doorway and the front windows, as though a president were visiting. Maggie couldn't help but roll her eyes.

"Do you have a dignitary arriving on the next train?" Giles asked once they had all arrived in front of the church.

Gertrude furrowed her brows as though offended. Then again, when wasn't Gertrude offended? "Why, Mr. Prescott, there is nothing more wholesome, and all-American, than the Silver Leaf Flour Company, and you're their representative."

"I thank you, but you shouldn't have gone to all this trouble for me." He tugged on his ascot.

Maggie smoothed imaginary wrinkles from her skirt, averting her gaze from Gertrude's perusal as she leaned toward Giles's shoulder. "If it were up to me, they wouldn't have made

124

all this fuss. You would have gotten lemonade and snickerdoodles." At her whispered words, he smiled.

"Ahem!" Gertrude cleared her throat. She crossed her arms as she scowled at Maggie before turning to their guest with her imitation of a smile. "We trust you will judge an impromptu baking contest this afternoon. Wouldn't it be nice to have more than one prize awarded today?"

Giles's eyes widened. "Such an honor." He glanced sideways at Maggie, who hid her smile behind a gloved hand.

Gertrude stood there gawking. "Now, Mr. Prescott, let me show you what has been prepared in your honor."

"And in Mrs. Galloway's honor, as well, I would hope." He arched an eyebrow and smiled at Maggie as their gazes met.

Almost before she realized it, her hand was tucked into the crook of his elbow again as they strolled closer to the church. It was as though they'd repeated the action through the years. Amazing.

"Of course, and we're using any proceeds from sales of baked goods and lemonade to support the Ladies' Aid Society." Gertrude sniffed, her nose high in the air, as usual.

A verdant lawn and colorful flowers flourished on either side of the walkway leading to the front of the church. The coneflowers and pansies set out a riot of welcoming color in front of the humble white building. From the right of the walkway, where they stood by their table of baked creations near the hedges with heads high, Etta Stout, Millie Wilson, and Hyacinth Blanding all glared at Maggie, which could have cut her like a cake knife if she let it bother her.

Sugary scents of vanilla, cinnamon, ginger, and nutmeg wafted on the gentle breeze. The smell of bittersweet cocoa made Maggie's mouth water. All manner of sweets piled the table, from cookies to cakes and pies, golden with perfection or bursting with the color of berries.

"Mrs. Galloway!"

Maggie turned to find Abby Harper rushing toward her, holding up a plate with something on it. Several paces behind her walked Thomas, carrying a walking stick and flanked by Josiah and Lyle.

"Am I too late to enter the baking contest?" The girl waved at her, her hold on the dish precarious at best.

"What's this?" Gertrude scurried over. "There's not much room on the tables as it is. You should have been here more than an hour ago."

"What Mrs. Wringer meant to say was..." Maggie looked the spiteful woman in the eye. "We can move some things around and find room for your cake."

"Humph!"

"Please, Mrs. Wringer! It was my mother's special buttery pound cake. There's nothing like it. I know it's not very pretty." Poor Abby blushed. "But I brought raspberries we picked from the bush in the little garden behind the shop."

Maggie tilted her head. "Mrs. Wringer, don't we want to see the young people participate?"

Gertrude arched an eyebrow. "Fine," she said as she stomped off.

Maggie smiled with triumph back at Abby, only to find the girl's father hovering nearby. Thomas covered his mouth as he coughed. She'd never seen him all cleaned up, wearing such a fine suit. With his contrasting waistcoat, he cut quite a dashing figure, in fact.

She pulled her hand from the crook of Giles's arm under the guise of taking Abby's cake plate. Discomfort prickled Maggie's heart. What would Thomas think of her on another man's arm? *And why do I care?* "Let me help you with this."

Abby relinquished her creation. "Thank you, Mrs. Galloway."

"Mr. Harper, let me introduce you to an old friend from my hometown. This is Mr. Giles Prescott." Maggie nodded to her old beau, who raised his eyebrows in a curious expression as she moved away from his side.

"How do you do?" Thomas shook Giles's hand when he offered it.

"Very well. Pleased to meet you." Giles poured on the charm as usual.

Did he even notice the narrowing of Thomas's eyes? And should she even care?

~

Thomas's gaze trained on Maggie's back after she excused herself with his daughter in tow, admiring the swirl of her lilac-colored skirt. She possessed a fine form. He blinked. *What am I thinking? And what would Bess think?*

"What? I'm sorry, Mr. Prescott, I didn't quite hear you." The man's incessant chatter pulled him from his daydreams.

"Are you well-acquainted with Mag—um, Mrs. Galloway?" Prescott grinned as though he were a child hiding a stolen cookie.

"Not for very long. She's assisted me...in my shop...at her brother's urging." The whole truth was none of the stranger's business. He cleared his throat. "If you've known her a long time, then you are aware of what a generous heart she has." As warmth crept up his neck and over his face, Thomas tried to loosen his collar.

"Yes, yes, she was quite a little mother to Ian—that is, Pastor McCormick—and she was always ready to help a tired mother with their little ones or take cookies to the elderly widows. Quite the role model for my sister, Penelope." Was Prescott wearing a smile or a smirk on his face? The man was much taller than Thomas, lean and muscular. Without a doubt, the better specimen. "I've known her since our youth...before she met Robert."

"Who?" The name seemed familiar, but Thomas couldn't place it.

"Her dearly departed husband." Prescott's eyes seemed void of sympathy but held satisfaction instead. "What do you do for a living, Mr. Harper?"

"I am Stone Creek's new pharmacist. Still settling in."

"Ah, I see. Did you know Mr. Galloway was also a chemist or pharmacist? Or whatever they call purveyors of these medical tonics and potions these days?" Giles rubbed his chin.

"She may have mentioned it." Thomas leaned on the walking stick his sons had made for him. He knew all about these city fellows. These executives looked down their noses at anyone who they might consider a snake oil salesman.

"Maybe we'll have more time to chew the fat later. I really should be sampling the women's baked goods since they would like me to judge them, don't you think?"

Thomas nodded his dismissal. "Later, then."

The man's presence caused a prickled of unease. Just how well had Maggie known this flamboyant character? To think of her in his arms made Thomas sick...and perhaps a little jealous. Thankfully, the man would be leaving town soon.

~

*M*aggie did her best to make room for Abby's creation, even removing her plate of prize-winning cookies to another table and less prominent place. She looked down at the sad little cake, lumpy and lopsided, which probably hadn't been mixed well enough. Maggie did her best to distribute the raspberries Zeke brought to her in the most attractive way possible.

"It wasn't quite that uneven when I left home with it. I guess running here made it worse." Abby's hazel eyes carried such a forlorn expression. Sandy-brown hair popped out from her braids. A lace collar stood out around the neck of her slightly wrinkled brown frock, contrasting with the simplicity of her outfit. She took a raspberry and tried to help with the arranging.

"Here." Maggie handed Abby a handkerchief from her reticule so she could dab the beads of sweat on her forehead. As the girl's face fell, Maggie placed an arm around her. "Presentation is only part of it. Taste is the most important. Don't give up heart."

"I wanted to think Mama would have been proud of me. And if I won, maybe it would cheer up Papa." She shrugged, giving a slight smile as she swiped at her cheek with the white cloth.

"Of course, but you know your father is so happy to have a lovely daughter like you around, don't you? You're all going through a hard time right now." Somehow feeling a presence behind her, Maggie turned and startled to find Thomas so close, his brows furrowed. "Oh, were you looking for me?"

"I didn't mean to sneak up on you." His gaze searched her face with a more penetrating look than before. "You look very... elegant today, Mrs. Galloway."

"Do I?" Her thoughts were jangled. *Fuss and bother! Why do I feel as flustered as a schoolgirl today?*

"Yes, your outfit reminds me of...those flowering bushes."

"Thank you." Maggie averted her gaze. "By the way, shouldn't you be home resting?"

"I didn't think a bit of fresh air and sunshine would hurt me. In fact, it should make me feel better. Don't you think?"

"In small doses, Mr. Harper."

"Oh, there you are, Thomas." Dr. Moore tipped his bowler hat. "I'm so glad you took my advice and are getting out for a bit."

"There, you see, I'm physician approved." Thomas gave her

a most annoying smirk. If she hadn't noticed the teasing glint in his eye, she'd be so irritated.

"I was only concerned you're moving too fast, but I'm sure Dr. Moore knows best." Maggie plastered a smile on her face.

Dr. Moore guffawed. "I've interrupted something here, haven't I? Maggie, he's doing better than he looks. I mean, you still look a bit tired is all, Thomas."

Abby bounced on her feet, then clasped her hands behind her back, craning her neck to look around her father at the other tables. "Please excuse me, Papa. I'd like to check out the competition."

"Certainly, dear."

"Well, I must go cheer my Sarah's efforts on. Her chocolate cake is the lightest and tastiest in the county, I'd wager—that is, if I were a betting man." The older man grinned, the corners of his eyes crinkling as he turned to saunter away from them.

"Mrs. Galloway, I don't appreciate your scolding me in front of my daughter." Thomas gave her arm a coaxing touch and pointed her away from the crowd. "You know I have enough trouble keeping my children respectful."

"And whose fault is that?" Maggie could not but help mumble under her breath as she crossed her arms, pulling away from his light grasp.

"Pardon me?"

"Mr. Harper, I can truly understand the temptation to give in, but they need a firmer hand. All of you are grieving a terrible loss. I've been there—waiting for my Robert to return at the end of the day, expecting to see him at every turn. And do you think it's easy to be a widow with a son who needs a father? Little boys tend to want to take on the responsibility of being the protector much too soon. I point him to the Heavenly Father every day." She aimed her first finger upward.

Thomas stood with mouth agape, leaning onto his walking stick with both hands. "Why that's doubtful. If He exists, He doesn't care a whit for me. Or else, He wouldn't have taken Bess when He did."

Did she imagine it, or did the brim of her blue hat droop under the noonday sun? Sweat beaded her forehead, and she pulled a small fan from her reticule. Her stomach churned. Between the scrutiny of Gertrude, the flirtations of Giles, and the absolute difficulty of Thomas Harper, she might as well be twisting in a vise. How could she feel any kind of affection for this infuriating man? Maybe it was only pity, after all.

For even now, dark circles rimmed Thomas's hazel eyes, though they sparked with anger. He'd looked exhausted even before he was sick, and in fact, his skin looked dry. Fanning herself, Maggie peered at him. "Are you cold all the time, Mr. Harper? Have trouble swallowing?"

"Whatever are talking about?" He narrowed his eyes.

"Have you taken your temperature? You may have symptoms of a goiter. You should know this. After all, we live in the goiter belt. Perhaps you should speak with Dr. Moore if your training hasn't apprised you of such a fact." Her tone was quiet, nearly a whisper. No sense in embarrassing the man further.

Ian and Giles chuckled companionably, strolling toward them like schoolboys with hands in their pockets. Regaling the old days, no doubt, but she saw concern in Ian's eyes, and a question in Giles's when they both glanced toward her. Her brother always seemed to sense her distress a mile away, sometimes to her frustration. He'd show up before she could sort out the situation at hand. However, she wouldn't mind a break in the tension.

Thomas made a scoffing sound. "Here we go again. You're bent on discrediting me, aren't you?"

Maggie sniffed. "Don't be silly. It's easy for us to overlook ourselves when we try to care for the children. I was merely suggesting—"

"How are you feeling these days, Thomas? I hope my sister's

care has set you back to rights." Ian clapped the man on the back.

Maggie placed her hands on her hips. "I'm afraid he's tired of a prickly old nurse like me."

Thomas's lips tightened into a straight line, and his eyes never left her face. "Oh, I can't get along without her help, can I, Mrs. Galloway?" A slight smile went with his gentle tone, so the sarcasm was lost on her brother and Giles.

The breeze relieved the stifling heat but not the tension between them.

"Maggie, I have more entries to test. Would you like to accompany me?" Giles offered his arm.

"With pleasure." She turned on her heel and looked over her shoulder. Was it her imagination? Or did Thomas look even more miffed as she strolled away on the arm of her former admirer? Somehow, she enjoyed the thought of making him jealous.

CHAPTER 16

Thomas glared after Maggie and the arrogant upstart who'd rolled into town not two hours before. He hoped they were happy. They deserved one another.

Ian cleared his throat. "Maggie can be rather...opinionated. I don't know what you were discussing, but she has a way of exasperating a man, especially her brother." The pastor rubbed the side of his face.

Thomas inhaled and attempted to regain his composure. "Mr. Prescott hasn't seemed to notice." Why did he care, anyway?

"Yes, well, he's never had to live with her." Ian chuckled and patted Thomas on the back. "How are your children adjusting to our little one-room schoolhouse after living in the Paris of the West?" Ian shifted his weight.

"As well as I could expect. Perhaps I shouldn't have taken them from the environment they were accustomed to, but everything reminded me of...of my wife." Thomas could hardly believe he was opening up to someone who was nearly a stranger, but there was something about this boyish pastor. Perhaps it was the sincerity in his gaze as he furrowed his eyebrows. Thomas didn't have much use for religious hypocrites. The only people he knew who lived out their faith were his younger brother, Daniel, and his sister-in-law, Isabel.

"I'm sorry. I'm sure that was difficult."

"Yes, well, I thought a business in a small town with lakes nearby would be a good place to heal. I wanted some peace and quiet, a place to think." Thomas leaned a little harder on his walking stick.

"We all have times we need a new beginning. I've been there myself." Ian rubbed his chin. "I did hear your Zeke is getting on famously with my nephew, Philip, since they made up after their spat."

"Yes, your nephew is a good sort." A smile came unbidden. Philip had befriended the most difficult of the lot.

"You know, we'd love to have you visit our church. Perhaps your children would become more a part of the community if they had more fellowship. And the moral guidance couldn't hurt."

Thomas shuffled his feet a bit as he adjusted the position of his cane. "No offense, Reverend, but I haven't had much use for organized religion...or hypocrites. Bess, their dear mother, used to round them up for Sunday school, good soul that she was. But since she's been gone, I don't know what to believe. Give me a good reason I should send them to learn about a God who's supposed to hear their prayers and yet still took their mother away."

Ian barely blinked. "Are you sure it's not you who is so disappointed with a deity who won't always give us what we want?"

Thomas stiffened and clenched his jaw. "Look here, Reverend—"

"Please don't misunderstand me. I couldn't imagine life without my Sophie, nor would I want to. But as a minister, I've watched many good people lose loved ones for no apparent reason. You're not alone in your sorrow and frustration. I'm extremely sorry for your loss. Don't forget the Father gave His own Son for us. Do you think it made sense for Jesus, who'd done nothing wrong, to die for our sins? And I'm talking about my sins as well."

"So what is your point?" Thomas's wool suit coat made him itchy under the early-June sunshine. The discomfort stretched him nearly beyond politeness.

"Thomas, I'm only suggesting the very one who understands and can get you through this valley of sorrow is the one you're avoiding." Ian reached out to clasp Thomas's shoulder. "You're always welcome at my church."

"Pa! Come and watch us play baseball. We're rounding up some other fellows." Lyle nearly barreled into both men. "We're starting up a team!"

"Lyle, watch your manners. You nearly knocked us over. You must apologize." Thomas held him in place by the shoulder. He would have liked to prove the point that he could bring up a family well enough without organized religion, but Lyle wasn't helping.

"Sorry, Pastor McCormick." The boy tipped his head in deference for a moment, then peeked at his dad and put one foot forward.

"All is forgiven. Go have some fun." Ian cocked a thumb toward the empty green area where the young men had begun assembling.

Lyle wiggled out from under Thomas's grasp. Any kind of stability stayed elusive, except...except when he'd been ill in bed. Somehow Maggie Galloway, that insufferable, yet beautiful woman, had managed to hold his family together.

The mirth of her musical laughter from the other end of the churchyard hit Thomas where he least expected it. In his gut.

"Maggie certainly appears to enjoy becoming reacquainted with Mr. Prescott." Ian rolled his eyes, which didn't exactly signal approval. "At one time, we thought those two might make a match. But once Robert came into my sister's life, no other man could turn her head."

Indeed, the couple gazed happily into one another's faces as Mr. Prescott handed Maggie a forkful of Abby's cake. *Bess's recipe.* So Maggie and Giles did have a history—one they appeared to be reviving.

"Papa!" Caira tackled her father's leg with a hug. Sophie panted as she caught up.

"Come wif me?" The child hugged her daddy's legs and stared up at him with devotion.

Thomas flashed to a miniature Abby with light-brown hair tied back in a bow. Bess, pregnant with Josiah, was never far from their sides. His throat thickened with emotion. Perhaps he would have been better off allowing the children to attend this event by themselves.

The crack of a bat brought him back to the present.

"Excuse me, Reverend, Mrs. McCormick." Thomas tipped his hat and wanted to pat Caira's head, but emotion threatened to overtake him. He plastered a grin on his face. "I've been invited to watch a baseball game."

Thankfully, the poignant memories weren't as frequent, nor did they cut as deeply as they once had.

~

Giles plunked a coin on the table so he and Maggie could partake in the cold lemonade the Ladies' Aid Society sold to raise funds.

Maggie took the ice-cold glass that Giles offered her and took a sip. Her heart quickened from his proximity. She tried not to stare into his coffee-colored eyes or to become enchanted by the way that dark curl escaped from under the brim of his hat. While he hadn't lost his boyish good looks after all these years, there was something even more alluring about the stronger, more manly jaw and the breadth of his shoulders. A scent reminiscent of a pine forest emanated from him. How intriguing...a city boy still carrying the smell of the deep woods.

His closeness made her keenly aware of how long it had been since Robert had held her. Hadn't those feelings been tucked away, though they had rippled during her caretaking of Thomas Harper?

Giles brushed a crumb from her chin. "So what do you think about the entries?"

She stepped backward. "Why, Mr. Prescott, I don't believe I should be influencing your vote toward any of these delightful confections." Maggie quickly found a napkin and went about rubbing not only her chin but patting all around her mouth.

"Maggie—"

She raised an eyebrow and placed her hand on her hip.

"*Mrs.* Galloway, if you prefer." He spoke in a low tone. "You know your cookies are undoubtedly the most delightful offering. You're an expert baker. I remember your cakes and pies from when we were not much older than children. It's your great talent."

"Pshaw, Mr. Prescott, I'm afraid your memory doesn't serve you very well. Don't you remember my disaster, which was the lumpy, sunken cake I made for Rebecca Purl's birthday? Or the watery blueberry pie I brought to the church potluck?" Maggie paused. Had she been acting too coquettish? She cleared her throat. "Then again, I've always loved baking."

A grin spread across his charming face. "You never let a little failure set you back, did you? You always came back with something even better."

"Excuse me while I check on how Sophie is doing. She probably should have stayed home." Maggie spied her sister-in-law sitting at one of the tables fanning herself. Good thing Ian had charge of Caira and Philip and was enjoying his time with the Harpers. In fact, was that Thomas out on the field helping Philip handle a bat? How interesting.

Maggie took one of the lemonades to Sophie, handing her the dripping glass. She didn't dare look back at Giles for concern of losing composure. "You should have something cool to drink." Maggie also took a clean handkerchief from her reticule and handed it to Sophie after giving her the glass.

Sophie smiled her thanks. "I've been trying to sit in the shade, but the sun keeps moving faster than I am." She wiped beads of sweat from her forehead and smiled.

"Hopefully, Mr. Prescott will make his decisions soon, and we can get on with the dreadful ceremony." Maggie sighed as she sat down next to her sister-in-law.

Sophie's eyes sparkled with amusement. "You don't seem to mind his company."

"Oh, not you, now. You're almost as bad as Ian." Maggie smoothed her sateen skirt and tried her best to catch the beads of moisture from her glass which dripped onto the lilac fabric. "I must admit, as a girl, I was quite infatuated with young Giles, but that was a half a lifetime ago. Even if we could pick up where we left off, so much has happened since then." Her ice had quickly melted, but she swirled the cloudy liquid and stared into it as though it had answers.

"Though I never met Robert, from what Ian's told me, he'd want you to be happy." Sophie used the handkerchief to wipe some of the condensation off her cup.

"I am happy," Maggie snapped. Then she turned to Sophie and touched her arm. "I'm sorry, Sophie. I'm used to being alone. Keeping things to the two of us is probably what's best for Philip. Don't you think?"

"Maggie, I have some idea how you feel. When I was alone with Caira, I wished she could have a father, but I never thought it possible. Then Ian came along."

"And you were right for one another. A successful relationship has to work for both parties." Maggie traced the rim of the glass with her finger. She shifted in her chair, turning away from the table. "I wish this whole miserable day were over."

"Is it really all that bad?"

"I just wanted to have Mr. Prescott stop, give me my pin, and be on with his trip. I would have been happy to stand in front of his horseless carriage while everyone looked on. Then I could have shared some of my cookies and my recipe...and everyone would be on their way."

"And you could go back to Apple Blossom Cottage, back to your old life?" Sophie giggled. "You're a minor celebrity in these parts now. Stone Creek wouldn't let you get away with that."

"Please, Sophie. You know a few spiteful women wanted to prove I wasn't really deserving of the prize." Maggie leaned forward, taking Sophie by the hand. "I had hoped it would recommend me to investors. I'd like to buy an old bakery in Buffalo, back where Ian and I are from, and rebuild the business."

"Oh. We would miss you so, but it's good to dream." Sophie squeezed her hand.

"No, not dream, Sophie. I have a plan for a home which truly belongs to Philip and me." Maggie returned the squeeze with affection. "And I would miss you as well...but you would have to visit and see where Ian grew up."

"Of course." Sophie let go of her hand, sat up straight, and touched her belly. Her amber eyes took on a wistful gaze. Then she grinned at Maggie. "I never tire of feeling new life kicking within me."

A desire to partake in the mysteries of motherhood surged again in Maggie's heart. How long had it been since she gave up on even the thought of having more children?

"It will be so nice to have a new niece or nephew." Maggie hugged Sophie, eager to hold a baby again someday.

After another half hour of the judges tasting baked goods

under the unrelenting sun, wilted contestants and their families took seats in front of the steps to the church to await the results. There Giles Prescott was officially introduced by the mayor of Stone Creek, and the townspeople applauded.

Abby Harper squealed with delight as Giles handed her the white third-place ribbon. Gertrude Wringer grinned smugly, reminding Maggie of a wrinkle on a dried apricot as she received the red second-place ribbon. Gertie's pleasure only lasted until Leona Packer was awarded a blue ribbon for her apple pie with its delectable streusel topping. The shy woman beamed. Her round face and warm brown eyes lit up with the announcement.

As Miss Packer took her seat, Giles turned back to the crowd. "And we mustn't forget the main reason I came to visit the lovely village of Stone Creek. I've truly been made to feel at home, though I've been here less than a day."

Everyone grew quiet.

Maggie hadn't thought she could sweat more than she had already. Nerves shook her.

"Mrs. Maggie Galloway, please come forward. Your recipe for pecan snickerdoodles, with their subtle spice and crunchy sweetness, are surely an accomplishment to be celebrated in kitchens around our nation. Women everywhere will covet such a recipe."

Maggie took her place by Giles's side, hands folded, gaze cast downward.

"Let me congratulate you on winning second place in the third annual Silver Leaf Flour Company's Don't Rest on Your Laurels baking contest. Because of your esteemed placement in this prestigious contest, I am awarding you the sterling silver laurel leaf pin." Giles leaned a little too close as he shook her hand and held an opened navy blue velvet box out for her to admire its contents.

She snatched the box from his hands and studied the pin

rather than let him offer to pin it on her lapel. The Silver Leaf logo rested in the center of two laurel leaf crescents and shone with a small bright gemstone in the middle. Probably just a rhinestone.

"Thank you, Mr. Prescott, for this generous show of appreciation for my small contribution."

"But I am not finished, Mrs. Galloway." He put up a forefinger as though asking her to wait for a moment. Giles had a book tucked under his arm. In a fluid motion, he retrieved it and an envelope from an inside pocket of his suit coat. "Here is Silver Leaf's nationally known and distributed cookbook, which includes your delicious and original recipe for pecan snickerdoodles. We are honored and delighted to present this edition to you. And of course, a check, which will insure you may replenish your supply of Silver Leaf's finest all-purpose or cake flours for months to come."

Her beloved fellow townspeople cheered her on, applauding and whooping. You'd think she'd won the first prize laurel leaf crown. Maggie ignored the crossed arms and frowns of Gertrude and her cohorts, yet she was aware of Thomas Harper's puzzled stare. Was he still miffed at her over their earlier conversation?

She cleared her throat once the applause died down. "Thank you, everyone, for showing up today for the celebration. I've always enjoyed baking for you—my family, friends, and neighbors. Without your encouragement, I wouldn't be here today." More applause began afresh. She curtsied, feeling like an opera star or a political candidate. This would certainly be a day to remember.

As the people collected their belongings and dispersed, the usually shy Abby Harper beamed at Maggie. The child stepped close as though to hug her but then held back. "Thank you, Mrs. Galloway, for getting me into the contest. This ribbon means a lot to me. She clasped the white badge with its fluttering tails close to her heart.

"I only gave a little push, dear. Mrs. Wringer was in charge of this affair."

"Abby! We really need to go home now. Come along." Thomas tapped his cane, annoying Maggie with the gesture.

"Yes, Papa." Abby sighed and waved a quick goodbye.

Maggie nodded toward her and restrained herself from telling Thomas to go take a nap. She couldn't decipher the coldness in his hazel eyes. Thomas had gone from nemesis to patient to friend. Were they back to near-enemies again?

"Mother!" Philip bounded into her presence, breathless. "Can I go home with Zeke today? We're gonna look for snakes."

"It's 'may I' and 'going to' and no, you may not."

"Aww..."

Her furtive glance noted Thomas's stare, which convinced her further. "You need to come home with me and clean up. We're having dinner at the Myleses' house." Maggie patted her son on the back. "No more pouting."

"Yes, Mama." He hung his head and pushed his hands into his pockets.

But she'd been shrewish once again, earlier. Maggie took a quick glance around. Good. Gertrude and her cronies surrounded Giles for the moment. "May I speak with you for a moment, Thomas?"

"What is it? As I'm sure you'd agree, I've been out and about long enough for today." He frowned.

Maggie withdrew a handkerchief from her reticule and dotted her forehead and neck. "Please accept my apology. I could have chosen a better time to speak to you of your health or your children...and I could have said those things more nicely." There. That wasn't so hard, after all.

His brow relaxed. "Very well...I suppose I could apologize

for questioning your beliefs as well. I only wish I had that kind of faith."

She nodded and smiled. "Accepted."

His grin didn't reach the hurt still lodged in his eyes, but he tipped his hat. Ever the true gentleman. "Good day, Maggie. Perhaps Philip can visit the boys another day."

"Of course." If only she'd learned to keep her opinions to herself once in a while.

He turned, and his children trailed behind him off toward the pharmacy.

"May I escort you home?"

She jumped, as she hadn't heard Giles come up alongside her. How quickly he'd escaped Gertrude's grasp. Impressive. He again crooked his arm toward her, his eyes twinkling with amusement.

"Aren't you staying at the Pink Hotel tonight? I imagine you must rest up for the next leg of your journey."

"Quite the contrary. I've delayed the rest of my trip so we may get reacquainted, my old friend. And Mrs. Myles has kindly invited me to dinner."

"Oh. I'm glad you met her." Maggie found herself slipping her hand into the crook of Giles's arm as though it were the natural order of things, despite the uneasy thump of her heart. He certainly knew how to flatter a lady, but was his prolonged stay a good idea? What if things had gone differently with Thomas? Would she have been on his arm instead? The fleeting thought stirred disappointment. Or maybe the heat caused her to feel muddleheaded.

CHAPTER 17

"*P*apa!" Abby's smile and eyes bright with happy tears warmed Thomas's heart, and she handed him the silky white ribbon as they strolled across the field toward Main Street. "Do you think Mother would be proud of me? Even if the cake didn't look as good as hers?"

"Abby, your mother would be proud of you whether or not you baked her cake or won a ribbon." He chucked her chin. "I hope you know that."

She stepped back. "Papa, I am not a little girl anymore!"

Indeed, she wasn't. Her face under the straw bonnet was quickly losing its baby fat, and she'd grown taller, her willowy form a reminder of Bess. Her smile said she forgave him, though she placed a hand on her hip with indignation.

Laughter distracted Thomas as Maggie walked off on the arm of Mr. Prescott. With such ease. A screw tightened in his gut. A moment before he was thinking of Bess. *How have I let Maggie Galloway push her way under my skin, anyhow?*

"Ha! Got your dumb old ribbon!" Zeke snatched Abby's pristine treasure from Thomas's hand and spun it above his head while sticking his tongue out at her.

"Give me that right now!" Abby stomped in her brother's direction. Though she was taller and had the longer legs, Zeke was too fast for her. He turned and ran. "Give it to me! Papa, tell him to give it back!"

"Zeke Harper! Give your sister her ribbon immediately!" Thomas rubbed his forehead, doing his best to avoid the gawking faces around him.

"She has to catch me first!" Zeke turned to reveal his mischievous grin and then shoved the prized ribbon under his cap.

"Stop it right now!" Abby managed to grasp her brother's waistcoat and ran into him.

Zeke bent over, holding his hat down over the ribbon.

"Give it to me!" Abby tackled her little brother, and soon they were sprawled on the grass.

Thomas sighed and made his way toward his errant children.

Abby pried Zeke's hat from his head and grabbed her ribbon. She clasped her prize in her fist while Zeke lay in the grass chortling.

"Oh, look at my ribbon. You've ruined it." Streaks of dirt marred the shiny surface of the material. "How could you? I hate you!"

Thomas grabbed her arm before she could pound her fist into her little brother's nose. "Abby, you must get up and stop acting like a hoodlum. I'll take care of Zeke. Brush yourself off." He pulled her to her feet.

Unmistakable fury clouded her eyes. An angry little girl, with hat and hair askew, replaced the young lady he'd observed just moments before. So much for his worrying Abby was growing up too fast. More likely, he was going to have to find someone like Mrs. Moore or Mrs. Myles to teach Abby how to behave like a young lady.

"Tsk! No wonder Mrs. Peaberry left your employ and you

can't keep a housekeeper. Such ill-behaved children." Gertrude Wringer stood with arms crossed and one raised eyebrow.

Millie Wilson towered next to her, barely covering her smirk. "Anything we can do to help?"

"Thank you, ladies. I believe I can handle this."

But his chest burned. Another parenting failure. And this one quite public.

~

*M*aggie turned toward the commotion, but Giles grasped her hand. The pang in her heart nearly held her back. *Abby, what are you thinking?* Though there were wonderful people in Stone Creek, there were others who would ridicule a newcomer for a mere lack of etiquette, let alone the hint of rumor. She'd seen dear Sophie go through such poor treatment before.

"Maggie?"

She blinked. "Yes?"

"Let me drive you to the Myleses' house."

"Very well." Though reluctant, she smiled up into the warmth of his eyes. Thomas Harper's problems were not hers, and he needed to learn to manage his own family affairs. She took Giles's hand and didn't look back.

~

A few hours later, Maggie sat with Philip and Giles in the large dining room of Apple Blossom House. The wallpaper with its pattern of floral crisscrosses had a background of English red, with a warm pink hue. The old Federalist-style dining room chairs, square and mahogany with hunter-green upholstered seats, were Gloria's nod to tradition.

She had told Maggie how much she loved the dining room set Asa's parents had left to them.

"Your cook has outdone herself, Mrs. Myles." Giles dabbed his mouth with the finest of white damask napkins, which matched the luxurious tablecloth.

"We are very blessed to have her and the gift of her skills, Mr. Prescott." Gloria nodded toward her guest. "The day went very well, indeed. I'd venture to say even the children enjoyed themselves." Her silverplate fork clinked against the edge of the bone-china plate adorned with a delicate pattern of green flowers.

Philip, who'd been pushing the last of the sweet potatoes around his plate, muttered under his breath.

Maggie cleared her throat. "Philip, dear, if you have something to say, then be polite about it." She sent a stern look his way.

He continued to poke at the remains of his dinner with his fork. "That baseball game was so fun. Wish I didn't have to leave so soon."

"Well, what did you like most about the fine game of baseball, young man?" Giles nodded toward her son.

"Playing with my friends. And Mr. Harper gave me some pointers on throwing the ball the right way and batting too."

"I see." Giles nodded and loosened his tie a bit. "Didn't your father teach you how to throw a ball?"

Philip's eyebrows scrunched together. "I don't remember everything he taught me." No longer frowning, he looked wistful. "I'm not so good at baseball, but Mr. Harper was really nice. He knew just what I needed to learn. Did you ever pitch at a baseball game?"

"Afraid I'm not much of a baseball man."

"Mr. Harper says it's an all-American game. You're American, aren't you?"

Gloria covered her mouth, barely concealing a giggle. Asa pinched his lips together, no doubt suppressing a grin.

"Philip, don't be rude to Mr. Prescott." Maggie grasped her son's arm.

"Of course, born and bred." A look of amusement spread over Giles's face. "Baseball is a most enjoyable pastime for some folks. However, I won awards in rowing and golf at Cornell. I'd be glad to teach you how to golf."

"No, thank you, sir. What's so hard about using a stick to push a ball that's standing still on the ground?" Philip shrugged, and the frown returned.

Maggie stifled a groan. Things weren't going well at all.

"If Grandma and Grandpa will excuse us, I'll show you my new puzzle. Would that be all right with you, Mrs. Galloway?" When Elise spoke with her tiny voice, everyone stopped to listen.

"Both of you may be excused." Gloria gave them an authoritative nod.

"It's fine with me, but first, you will apologize to Mr. Prescott." Maggie grabbed the neck of his vest.

"I apologize, Mr. Prescott." He scowled as he averted his gaze.

What had gotten into him? Other than the impertinence of the Harper children?

"A bit of a misunderstanding, is all." Giles stabbed his meat with his fork. "I'm sure Philip is usually much better behaved."

"I should hope so." Maggie gave Philip's collar another tug. "You better mind your manners the rest of the day, young man."

"Yes, Mama." He left the dining room behind Elise.

Maggie sighed as she folded her napkin.

White tapers flickered, perched in crystal candelabrum at either end of the table like elegant sentries in the ensuing quiet.

"Perhaps we should take coffee and dessert in the other room. We are so glad to have you as guests. Here you are practically in our backyard, and we've hardly ever entertained you, Maggie." Gloria's statement broke the tension in the room.

"I wouldn't expect such a thing. You are kind enough letting us stay in the cottage."

Gloria smiled, her eyes filled with mischief. "Well, we're rather selfish as Philip's friendship is one of the balms which have been helping to heal Elise."

"I'm afraid if he continues acting so rudely, you won't think him suitable company for your granddaughter." Maggie looked into the glass of water in her hands.

"A firm hand and some guidance from a gentleman should be the right cure. You would know much about that." Giles smirked.

Maggie bristled. "Perhaps, but we were getting on fine until recently. No one can replace Robert in his life." She caught Giles's gaze. Would he catch her meaning? While she sometimes still missed male companionship, and Philip could use a closer male example, she hadn't planned on remarrying just to fill a gap in their family.

"Of course not." Giles's smirk turned into a grin. "However, I only meant to suggest that even your brother could be a good influence over the boy."

"Oh...I see." Heat crept into Maggie's cheeks. How could she immediately assume her old beau was hinting at being that special gentleman? "In fact, Ian has been an excellent influence in my son's life."

After an awkward silence, Asa cleared his throat. "Perhaps this would be a good time for us to adjourn into the parlor for dessert as you suggested, Gloria?"

"Why, yes." Their hostess stood. She glanced at Maggie and nodded.

Maggie crushed her linen napkin in her hand before she pushed back her chair and came to her feet. After placing the serviette atop her empty plate, she smoothed her long skirt.

Giles rose, hurried to her side, and offered his arm. "Shall we?" He motioned toward Gloria's parlor. "After dessert, I would like to escort you back to the cottage as I have an idea I would like to run by you." He spoke close enough for only her to hear.

~

homas sat in the kitchen eating a cold supper with four silent children. When one opened their mouth to speak, he sent them what he hoped was a withering look. Each one seemed to know they'd met their father's limit of patience. He forked the last bit of cold ham on his plate into his mouth.

"Abby, I will speak to you downstairs when you're finished eating."

"Yes, Papa." She pushed her plate away, stood, and trudged toward the stairs.

"Lyle and Josiah, you will clear the table and dry the dishes. Zeke, you will do the washing."

"Pa, do I have to?" Zeke's whining grated on him.

"After how you behaved today, you shouldn't even be asking. Unless you prefer for me to punish you...another way." Thomas crossed his arms and stared his son down. The boy's furrowed brows told him his son understood.

"Now get to it," Thomas ordered with more conviction than he felt. Would being a single parent ever get easier?

Chairs scraped against the pine flooring, and the boys scurried to do his bidding. He turned to leave the small kitchen, weariness filling his chest as he sighed and held fast to the stairway railing. The tread of his feet on the bare wooden steps echoed with the emptiness of his heart.

How had Maggie kept his children in order? Though she often provoked him, she also emanated compassion. In the darkest moments of his illness, her care had brought calm. But it was more than that....

The sight of his sweet daughter, Abby, sitting on a stool at the soda fountain and sobbing jarred him. She took off her glasses and folded them neatly before placing them on the counter.

"I'm sorry!" Her apology burst forth before he could even begin his lecture. "I know I've embarrassed you. I've acted as no proper young lady would." She sniffled.

Half of Thomas's job was done for him already.

"Abby, I will always be proud of you, though today's behavior did leave something to be desired. Yes, you're responsible for a lack of self-control, but Zeke set out to get a reaction from you—"

"Yes, he did." Abby scowled. "How could he be so hateful when I just won a ribbon for making Mama's pound cake?"

"And I will deal with him." He reached out to pat her arm. "But you will need to remember your mother's code of behavior. She is the best example of a lady I can give you."

"But, Papa, that's what bothers me. I'm having a hard time remembering what she said...or even what she looked like." Abby bit her lip and stared down as though the floor held something fascinating. Her sobbing resumed. "Sometimes I have to go look at her picture and try so hard to hear her voice in my head, the things she would always say. What's wrong with me?"

"Nothing." Thomas shook his head, gathered his beautiful child into his arms, and let her tears soak into his shirtsleeve.

If he admitted the truth to himself, Thomas had been struck by the same thoughts. It was as though he could only remember Bess as a whole when she visited his dreams. Such dreams were so raw and real—her smile, her touch, the loving way she spoke to the children, visions of their home in Detroit. And when he awoke, the aching emptiness returned.

"Maybe it's just the way of grief. If we remembered everything so sharply all the time, then it might hurt all the more." He could think of no other reasons for the cruel tricks their memories played on them. Thomas stroked Abby's hair, not sure what else to do.

"I don't like it, Papa. I don't want to ever forget her."

"You won't. There are some memories so dear they never completely leave us. And she'll continue to live in you." He held her a moment longer, then drew back, taking her hand and patting it.

He couldn't think of one woman, other than Maggie Galloway, who'd taken time to care enough about the children, but how could he expect her to teach Abby? After all, Maggie was quite busy with that upstart from the big city.

Perhaps Reverend McCormick had a point, and he should at least send the children to church. After all, they had to learn how to be better behaved somewhere.

CHAPTER 18

*a*n early evening breeze and the lazy golden orb in the sky moving west stirred Maggie's heart. Glancing up into the coffee-colored eyes of Giles Prescott didn't help her ache of longing. She really missed their family days of the past. Sensing how much Philip missed his father was only part of it. Having the warmth and strength of a man by her side comforted her, even as it pointed to her loss.

They approached the cottage. She never tired of inhaling the fragrance of lilacs. "What a pity their blooms only last a couple of weeks." She fingered the delicate blossoms on one of the bushes near the modest porch. "I wish they lasted longer."

"But you, Maggie, are still in your blossom."

"What?" She swung toward him.

"You've hardly changed at all since I saw you all those years ago. Motherhood, and the maturity which comes with it, becomes you." Giles's grin—did it reach his eyes? Was there sincerity in what he said?

She averted her gaze and clasped her reticule tightly. "If you're only going to puff me up with flattery, I will have to ask you to leave, Mr. Prescott." Maggie pressed her lips together and turned away from him.

"I promise to behave if I may stay and visit, but I do speak nothing but the truth." His eyes twinkled when she glanced up at him again.

"Well, you're not coming in, if that's what you think. Though I'm no longer an innocent maiden, I am a widow of good reputation."

"I wouldn't dream of calling your reputation into question, Mrs. Galloway." Giles placed a foot on the lowest step.

"Have a seat on the porch swing, then, and I'll bring you something cold to drink." Maggie still had a pitcher of tea waiting in the icebox.

"Thank you." He put his hand out to help her up the steps ahead of him and then parked on the porch swing.

The door swished closed behind her, the breeze whispering past Maggie's ear. Getting reacquainted, the almost flirty repartee between them, stirred new sensations. Not to mention, the pound of her heart as she wondered what idea he had only for her ears.

When Maggie returned a few minutes later with a crystal glass from her punchbowl set for each of them, she swallowed. She'd never realized how narrow the swing was when she'd only shared it with Philip or Gloria. Giles, who had removed his suit coat, had flung an arm across the back of the contraption and comfortably sprawled his legs in front of him.

He scooted over, making room for both of them. That was better. She sat next to him but as close to the arm on her side as possible.

"Glad you made yourself at home." She handed him the iced tea she'd poured for him. His large hands nearly swallowed the delicate vessel, his fingers too long for the diminutive handle.

"Maggie, you are ever the elegant hostess. I remember

having dinner with your family and how you made such a fuss about the dishes on the table." He winked at her.

"Ancient history." She studied the amber liquid in her cup rather than return his gaze. If she looked too long into his eyes, the warmth of memories would flood her. The last thing she needed was to entangle her heart in infatuation. When was he going to reveal the secret he had for her?

Birdsong punctuated the silence along with the sound of Elise's and Philip's laughter as they burst outside through the back door of Apple Blossom House and ran around the yard in the distance. The quiet struck her as companionable, sitting here with an old friend, albeit a handsome one. Although, why did he stay in their sleepy little town when he clearly had more important things to handle for the Silver Leaf Flour Company? In concert, they pushed the swing back and forth.

"Maggie, as soon as I saw you'd placed in our national contest, an idea came to me." His eyes went from mischievous to thoughtful, a line creasing between them as he furrowed his brows.

"What?" She took a sip and swallowed, waiting for him to finish his thought.

"Since you're not keeping house for Ian anymore, there can't be anything tying you here, can there?" He didn't give her a chance to answer but leaned a little closer. "There's a wonderful opportunity at our test kitchen at our regional offices in Chicago. We need someone to help manage these tests, choose recipes, create new ones. What do you think? I mean, I imagine you're in need of some kind of a paying occupation."

Maggie gulped. She would have been less surprised had he gotten down on one knee and asked for her hand. After setting her cup on the arm of the swing, she played with the cuff of her sleeve.

"Dear me...I don't know what to say." She sat up straighter.

"Make no mistake, Robert left me with a means to support Philip and myself for a time. I've been trying to gather the funds to buy a bakery in our hometown. I figured if it went well, I could sell it someday and live off the profits, or it would be something to leave for Philip. And baking is something I love to do."

Maggie squeezed against the arm of the porch swing, making sure their legs didn't touch. His fresh pine scent and tanned countenance made her more aware of his masculinity. "In fact, it was because of the contest I had the idea, thinking it may give me some clout. It's so hard for a woman to start a business on her own—getting approved for a loan and all that."

"Chicago has many more opportunities, even for women. This would supply you with a decent income and..."

"And?"

"It would give us a chance to see one another occasionally and get reacquainted." He lifted a questioning eyebrow.

There it was. Giles's interest went beyond business. A warm tingle went up her neck and her face again. She was no longer a swooning seventeen-year-old. What was her problem, anyway? His good looks and sense of humor had captivated her all those years ago, and there was no doubt when he arrived in his horseless carriage, she still found him attractive. Robert wouldn't have expected her to stay alone for the rest of her life, but could she forgive herself for such thoughts?

"You're awfully quiet."

"Naturally, I'm flattered, Giles, but I'll have to think about it. For that matter, I'll have to pray about it."

The glint in his dark eyes turned dull. He still lacked understanding of her desire to take everything to the Lord. She shifted on her side of the swing the best she could and gripped the arm. She had prayed for him even after she'd decided against him in favor of Robert.

"If you're going to be in Stone Creek a little longer, you

should come to church with me tomorrow. I'm sure Ian would take it as a compliment if you took the time to hear one of his sermons." Maggie smoothed her skirt, looking up through her eyelashes. Too coquettish?

Giles cleared his throat. He reached for her hand. "If you would consider my proposition of offering you a decent job where you could showcase your talents, I would gladly come with you." The mischievous light reached his eyes again.

"Sounds more like a challenge than a deal to me." She lifted an eyebrow in return. "But, yes, I will consider your plan."

"Very well. Then you have yourself a deal." He squeezed her hand, then raised it to his lips and placed a tender kiss on the back of it.

Maggie pulled her hand away. This was the second time today in which her charming former suitor had taken such liberties. Her heart gave a little thump as though reminding her it still beat within her chest. Why did Giles's presence always come at the price of a conflicted heart?

~

Thomas herded his children toward the door of their house. He yawned. With the shenanigans Zeke had pulled on his sister the day before, he couldn't trust them to go to church on their own. He'd wanted to send them to Dr. and Mrs. Moore, but they were both under the weather.

Glancing sideways, he caught Abby sticking out her tongue at her youngest brother, and the favor returned. Bess wouldn't have allowed such behavior, especially on a Sunday morning.

We are a family, and we must bear one another's burdens. If your brother or sister won't look out for you, who will? Now, let's put aside our anger, especially on the Lord's Day. Her sweet but firmly delivered words had often brought the children from cross looks and crossed arms to near tears of repentance. They inevitably drew a truce for a while, but Thomas didn't seem to have the method down. He was forever pulling Zeke up short by his collar and making Abby cry, even when he tried his best not to be gruff.

Were the children even presentable for such an excursion? Abby had her hair neatly in pigtails. His dear daughter had done her best to iron her Sunday frock and her brothers' shirts and pants.

Abby reached to slick down Lyle's cowlick in front with a saliva-moistened finger.

"You're disgusting!" His middle son pushed his sister's hand away.

"That's what Mother used to do!" She snapped right back.

"You're not Ma!" Lyle's scowl rivaled an insulted cat's.

"Come on, now." Thomas placed a firm hand on his son's shoulder. "Abby is trying to help. Have you thanked her lately?"

"Thunderation, Pa! Why do we have to start going to church again, anyway? It's boring." Zeke, the troublemaker, wasn't going to make this easy.

"Young man, I've had quite enough. And I don't like your language either." He wagged a finger toward his youngest son.

The other three suppressed giggles, even Abby.

"All of you young men need to straighten up." Thomas walked the length of the floor in front of them, with hands clasped behind his back, much like his father had years ago. "You need to fix your ties and comb your hair. Your mother would have liked you—us—to go to church. And not looking like ruffians." He hated to play the guilt card, but what else could he do? "Come on. We're going to be late."

The boys shuffled off, murmuring.

Abby's crestfallen expression tugged at his heart. He put an arm around her. "Those words weren't for you, little dove," Thomas whispered in her ear. "You have done well."

"Thank you, Papa." Her eyes glistened, and her pout turned into a smile as she soaked in the little bit of praise.

A short walk later and the Harpers trudged through the entry of Stone Creek Community Church. Thomas sighed. Each of them had a reason not to want to be there. They hadn't been to church since they had left the Presbyterian Church on Fourth Street in Detroit, shortly after his wife's death. That Abby missed Bess terribly was evident as she wiped a tear from the corner of her eye. The boys didn't want to sit still and behave for an hour or more. As for himself, Thomas knew exactly how God felt about him.

If only he could have the simple, happy faith of his brother, Daniel. The young doctor and his wife, Isabel, could still believe God loved them through their trials, and they'd had their share.

The congregation was already singing. Miss Nora Armstrong played the piano. Strains of "It is Well With My Soul" met his ears. He wanted to turn and dart out of the sanctuary. This had been one of Bess's favorite hymns. They'd even sung it at her funeral. Reverend Ian McCormick looked up at him and the children with such delight in his eyes and a welcoming grin on his face that Thomas feared he must find a seat.

The pews in the back of the sanctuary overflowed. Shuffling forward, Thomas gave Josiah a nudge. To his horror, the only pew with enough space was right behind Maggie and Philip Galloway. And there stood Mr. Giles Prescott in his well-tailored suit, a bit too close to her. Oh, yes, he had noticed that ridiculous horseless carriage outside. *Huh, what do I care?*

"Please be seated," Ian directed the congregation. "We are so pleased today to welcome some guests to our humble little church. Would you care to introduce your family to us, Mr. Harper? I'm not sure everyone knows all of you."

Thomas cleared his throat, glancing around the congregation and not meeting anyone's eyes, taking in the smiles, the looks of expectancy, or of surprise. Of course, he had to be polite. "I'm Mr. Thomas Harper, and these are my four children, Abby, Josiah, Lyle, and Hezekiah." Perhaps using his full biblical name would cause his son to behave better.

A little girl snickered behind them.

"Zeke," his youngest growled.

Laughter erupted, and his son did his best to push past Thomas, who pressed his hands on either of the boy's shoulders. "Sit," he whispered.

Zeke plopped into the pew next to Thomas, wedged between Abby and him.

"Welcome, we're happy to have you here." Ian's voice boomed, and the people quieted.

Thomas wanted to slouch down in his seat as Zeke had. Should he bother to tell his boy to sit up and behave like a gentleman? *Behave.* How many times had he said the same word every day?

The service took place around him as though he were in a dream. Ian preached something about the newness of spring unfolding into summer and putting on a new person in Christ. How did one become a new person, anyway?

Maggie's auburn hair, showing beneath her green velvet hat, glinted under the daylight streaming through the stained-glass windows. The scent of lavender drew his thoughts to gardens and their last conversation. She truly meant to help. He knew that.

Thomas shifted in his seat and crossed his arms. He shouldn't let the woman unnerve him. Yet her presence reminded him of Abby's need for guidance and how much help she'd been in the store. Perhaps she'd been sent by God to help them. Bess had probably been beseeching God to send aid to his family. He smiled to himself at the thought.

And what of this fellow from the flour company? Was he

worthy of her? At least the annoying man would shortly be leaving Stone Creek, but not soon enough.

~

*M*aggie sensed a need to turn around and greet Thomas after the benediction, though she wasn't entirely comfortable with the prospect. How could she offer to lend a hand to guide Abby and help with the other children, and not insult the proud man?

"It's nice to see you and the children here." Maggie extended a hand of reconciliation to Thomas. They hadn't parted on the best of terms the day before, but there was no sense in prolonging ill feelings. Perhaps if she continued to show kindness, he could forgive her impertinence of the day before. It was an excellent thing he'd brought his family to church.

"Thank you. This has been a bit difficult for the children. I'm sure church brings memories of the funeral." Speaking quietly, Thomas took her hand for a moment before he shook it.

"And for you as well, I'm sure." Maggie allowed her hand to rest in his grip a moment longer than necessary.

He dipped his chin in agreement. Their gazes met, and she turned to watch the boys.

Philip and Zeke had greeted one another, and all four boys headed toward the door. Caroline Mallory, a sweet young girl Abby's age, had come to welcome her. Giles was distracted by curious townsfolk greeting him. Maggie and Thomas stood alone in the crowd. Their gazes locked. She understood his sadness, remembered the first time she and Philip had entered a sanctuary after Robert's casket had sat at the front. Life went on, yet Thomas seemed to be stuck in his past. Was there some way to reach him and bring him forward?

"Of course, I understand." Maggie nodded. "I hope it helps the children that they are in a different church today."

"Well, I'm not sure how much." He shuffled his feet like an overgrown boy.

"I see Abby is acquainted with Caroline Mallory. You know, her parents have a Sunday school lesson for the children and youth before the church service. Perhaps if you brought them earlier, they could get to know some of the others better."

"Perhaps." Thomas shrugged. His noncommittal attitude grated on her.

He shifted his weight and held his hat in front of him like some kind of shield. "Mrs. Galloway, this may not be the time or place to speak with you on this subject, but I feel a need to approach you sooner rather than later."

"Yes?"

"I need more help organizing the store..." He lowered his voice again. "And quite frankly, Abby needs a bit of training...in deportment. Only a year without a mother, and I fear the boys have influenced her more than the other way around. She's tried to mother them some, but..." Thomas's eyes glazed over. Was he in a faraway place called the past?

"She's not meant to be their mother, really, but it's good she tries to take on some responsibility." Maggie bit her lower lip. "Perhaps I could come by around the time the children get home from school a few days a week. I'll bring Philip with me. I'll work around the shop first and then spend some time with Abby."

"Would you? I'd be willing to pay, of course."

"Don't be ridiculous. Philip and I will enjoy helping you out."

The tittering giggles of three young women took her attention away from Thomas. Mr. Prescott was surrounded by admirers, and leading them was Irena Blanding, who had recently returned after a very long visit with cousins. Prettier than her younger sister, Helena, she fluttered her eyelashes and smiled, fanning her face with a lace fan as if she was trying to hide from Giles.

"Excuse me, please. I must get the children home." Thomas narrowed his eyes as he cast a wary look toward Giles. Did he want to say something more? Maggie stopped him as he opened his mouth.

"Of course." She nodded toward him before she went to rescue Giles from those silly girls.

"Why, Mr. Prescott, certainly you could find it in the generosity of your heart to take my little sister, our friend, Cecilia Neuberger, and myself for a little excursion in your horseless carriage," Irena crooned, leaning a bit too close to Giles.

Maggie waved away the waft of her strong jasmine scent. Where had the girl gotten hold of such noxious perfume?

Maggie leaned toward her and gave her upper arm an affectionate squeeze. "Hello, Irena. How are you? I didn't realize you were home. How was your trip?"

"Why, Mrs. Galloway, how kind of you to inquire as to my health." Irena snapped her gaze away from Giles to narrow her eyes at Maggie and closed her fan. She grinned, not unlike a cat that had just lapped up a saucer full of rich cream. "I'm quite well. Perhaps you could persuade your friend to take us on a little adventure. I mean, I've ridden in a horseless carriage before, but they haven't." She nodded toward her sister and friend.

"That's entirely out of my realm. Mr. Prescott must make such a decision." Maggie adjusted her hat and averted her gaze. She had chosen to ignore the gossip about Irena's extended visit with relatives, the insinuations she had been with child by her former beau. But now she found herself wondering. Tendrils of jealousy spread through her. Maggie didn't care for the ire which arose inside.

Amusement sparkled in Giles's eyes as he examined the young woman in front of him. Maggie moved closer to his elbow, but he didn't automatically offer his arm, though they almost touched. Was he mesmerized by Irena's fresh looks? Her caramel-colored hair curled softly around her oval face. Her complexion was peachy pink. Her neck was long and graceful, reminiscent of the rest of her figure. The blue flowery print on her pale gray walking suit warmed the coolness of her gray-blue eyes.

Maggie glanced down at her own skirt. How long had it been since she'd taken the time to buy something new? Her hips had grown somewhat wider from her love of baking, and her waistline strained against her newest corset. She always swept her hair into the practical up-do of a matron, a simple pompadour. When was the last time she'd actually tried doing something stylish with her tresses?

Though disappointed Giles might find the younger woman attractive, she had no claim of her own on him. But Irena Blanding? The thought of the snobbish young woman throwing herself at him was more than annoying. Maturity counted for something.

"I appreciate your request, but I'm certain we must have a particular chaperone for such an outing, and of course, your parents must consent." A hearty chuckle rumbled in his throat.

"Why, I'm sure *Mrs.* Galloway is old enough to properly chaperone us, Mr. Prescott."

"What's this?" Georgina Blanding, the girls' mother, pushed her way into the little group.

"We were hoping Mr. Prescott would take us out in his automobile." Helena patted the back of her hair. "Please allow us to, Mother."

"You may certainly *not.* Your uncle and aunt will be coming for Sunday dinner, and I'm going to need your assistance around the house."

"But, Mother—"

"And you, sir, are no gentleman, putting ideas in my daughters' heads that they should be gallivanting about town in that *contraption* of yours." Georgina pointed her index finger toward Giles's face while turning red as if for emphasis.

"Madam, you mistake my intentions. Your charming daughters were merely interested in the adventure of riding in a motor car. I did not suggest such a thing to them." He chuckled.

Maggie stepped back. Though he lived in the big city, did mothers there care any less for the reputations of their young daughters? He wouldn't make friends with such an attitude.

"Very well, see that you don't." Georgina's head snapped down in a nod. "Come, girls." She sent Maggie a withering look as though to suggest guilt by association.

The Blanding girls wore sullen expressions and followed behind their mother, and Irena looked over her shoulder, casting a longing glance at Giles.

"And you, too, Cecilia," Georgina called to her. "Your mother is looking for you."

Whether the girl emitted a sigh of admiration for Giles or exasperation with her friend's mother, Maggie could not tell. She found herself gripping his lean, muscular arm, giving it a tug even as her hand settled in the crook of it. She would not comment on the number of admirers he'd seemed to gain. He would think her petty and jealous.

"If you will escort me home, I will gladly feed you, and the Myles family, dinner."

The hungry look in his eyes as his gaze lingered on the retreating young women was concerning.

"Giles?"

"Yes, what did you say? Dinner at your house? I'd like nothing better. I'm positively starving."

CHAPTER 19

*M*aggie opened the door, surprised to find Gloria with her hand poised to knock. Her dear friend wore a guilty grin and held up a telegram. "They dropped it off at the house for you."

"You could have sent one of the kids—or Mr. Starks." Maggie closed the door behind her. "You just caught me. I'm on the way to see the Harpers. Have a seat on the swing, but I'm afraid I don't have time to be much of a hostess right now."

Maggie took the offered envelope as Gloria handed it to her. Gloria leaned forward with hands clasped in front of her like a child waiting for Christmas.

Maggie rolled her eyes. "You couldn't be more obvious. You should have steamed the envelope open and saved me the trouble." She chuckled, and Gloria followed suit.

"I know, I know. But I am hopelessly curious as to whether you have news on the bakery."

The summer scent of fresh-cut grass wafted on a lazy breeze as the two settled into the porch swing. The chain creaked on its hinges.

"I'm afraid it's rather on hold. I sent a letter to the lawyers and the bank to let them know if an investor or a loan doesn't come through soon, they will lose my offer." Clinging to the missive, she reached up and adjusted the hatpin pulling at her hair.

Gloria returned her news with a crestfallen expression. "I had such high hopes for you. And you know Asa and I want to help."

"I know." Maggie looked away. "And I appreciate it. But Giles's offer has changed things."

"You can't catch me!" Philip's voice traveled as he came trotting round the corner of the house on long legs as agile as a colt's.

"Oh yes, I can!" Elise followed close, her blond hair flying behind her.

"Do you ever wish life was still as simple as it is for them?"

"Sometimes I wonder why I was in a hurry to grow up." Gloria sighed.

Maggie smoothed the envelope. "I suppose I should open this. It's from Mr. Prescott, as I suspected." She read quietly.

Maggie, hope you are considering my offer. You are in my thoughts every day. Work keeps me from returning as soon as I like. Anxiously awaiting your decision. Hoping to convince you soon. Yours, Giles

"He wants an answer, but I can't give it yet. I've barely had two good nights' sleep in a row since he left." Maggie folded the telegram and shoved it into her reticule. She closed her eyes for a moment, allowing the balm of the children's laughter to soothe her.

"Take your time, my friend, take your time." Gloria patted her hand and smiled.

Maggie had the feeling Gloria preferred her leaving for Buffalo to leaving for Chicago—and Giles.

~

*O*pening the door to Harper's Apothecary and hearing the friendly bell was a comfort, something to take her mind off decision-making. And the buggy ride on a beautiful summer afternoon had helped calm her.

The strong scents of valerian root to calm nerves, horehound to soothe the throat, and peppermint candy swirled together and met her nose as the smell of familiarity. Perhaps being in the apothecary shop was a comfort because of her past work with Robert.

Light shone through the large window, illuminating the polished oak paneling and the glass knobs on the soda fountain. The marble counter gleamed as well. Maggie had been stopping by a couple of days each week for only a few weeks. With her help, the store had gained a more settled feel. The shop had been organized and cleaned until spotless.

"Hello, Mrs. Galloway!" Zeke surprised her by running to hold the door open for her, bowing with a flourish.

"You're becoming quite the gentleman. Thank you."

Zeke chortled as though it were some great joke.

"Ignore him." Abby rearranged jars on the shelf, wiping up any spilled powders with a dust cloth.

"Where's Philip?" Zeke hopped from one foot to the other.

"Playing with Elise today, but I will bring him next time." She patted Zeke on the head.

"I hope so. Guess I'll have to do my chores." His posture changed as he trudged toward the back door.

"Where's your father?" Maggie craned her neck as though she might find him hiding behind the counter.

"Papa's in the back, going through a new order that came in today. What do you think, Mrs. Galloway?" She gestured toward the counter with both hands, palms open, and dishrag dangling from her right one.

"I was just going to remark on how pleased I am to see what a beautiful job you're doing keeping things cleaned up."

"Thank you." Abby's eyes sparkled at her approval as she leaned on the counter and folded the cloth. The girl continued to blossom under Maggie's tutelage.

And Maggie couldn't help but smile at how things in the store had been shaping up. The pile of crates and boxes were put away, the shelves were well stocked, each bottled physic or jar of herbs in its place according to what it was needed for and, further, in alphabetical order. She'd also made sure the newer stock was in the back, and the older moved to the front. She'd been shocked to see how many older jars had lingered in the back. They needed to keep things moving.

Maggie lifted her chin. "Well, now. I suppose I should see if your pa needs any help."

~

*H*ow fetching Maggie appeared, wearing a pale-green blouse, as she walked toward Thomas as he stood outside of the office in the storeroom. Her auburn hair was curled in such a becoming fashion around her face. Her deep aqua eyes shone like two prettily cut sapphires. What an odd thing his heart did as the sunlight framed her from the back when she strolled toward him. She reached toward the hook on the wall for a white apron. As she pulled the already-tied straps over her head, they caught on a hairpin.

"Ouch! What a nuisance!" She fumbled with the strings, trying to untie them.

"Let me help you with that."

Their fingertips met, her small hands brushing his. She tried to pull her hair out of the way. The scent of lavender and something else jolted his senses. He wound up pulling the hairpin away, releasing Maggie's auburn locks on one side as they fell to the shoulder of her blouse.

"I'm so sorry. I'm afraid I'm making things worse." Thomas stepped back. His hand shook a little, mimicking the thump of his heart. How long had it been since he'd touched a woman, felt the silky softness of her hair?

Maggie pulled the ties down around her neck and then tied the others around her waist in a crisp, fluid motion. She swung around to face him as he stood after picking up the offending hairpin which had fallen to the floor. She reached for it.

"Thank you. I'm a mess now. Excuse me while I fix my hair again. Perhaps Abby has a mirror I can borrow." She gazed up at him, pink grazing her cheeks, making her look even lovelier.

He tore his gaze away and cleared his throat, sensing an unusual vulnerability in Maggie. Had she ever needed him, except to pick up this hairpin?

"You could never be a mess, Maggie Galloway." The words slipped unasked from his lips, and just as naturally, Thomas put his hand on her shoulder while her left hand touched his right in the hairpin exchange.

Her eyes widened. Unmistakable warmth emanated from her gaze.

Thomas cleared his throat. "Allow me to help, if I may."

What is this boldness overtaking me?

He coaxed her to turn around and took the lock of fallen hair. He twisted it around the mass of hair fixed into a bun as he'd seen Bess do. *So soft.* He pointed her toward a very small mirror on the wall near the corner. "There, you look just as lovely as before."

Their eyes met in the reflection, and Maggie took his hand from her shoulder and turned around to face him. Her lips parted.

Thomas's throat grew dry, and his heart ticked faster than

the wall clock. He cupped her face in his hands. "Maggie...I...
must thank you."

"For what?" Her voice had become light and breathy.

"I don't think I'd be alive or have the shop running properly
without you."

"It's...nothing...I..."

She gazed up at him. "Please, don't feel obligated. I was only
doing what was right."

But his arms went around her back, and he drew her closer.
Her arms went around his waist.

If only he could kiss her. *What am I thinking?*

Catching himself, he laid his cheek atop her head instead.
Her warmth melted into his being, and he let it.

Steps came their way, and Thomas straightened.

"Thomas, are you back here?" Dr. Moore—Thad, as
Thomas had come to think of him—appeared in the doorway,
moving the stem of an unlit pipe between his lips. What timing.
"Abby said I'd find you working on an order."

Maggie pulled away. "Excuse me." Her glance flitted to the
doctor. "I'm getting ready to help Mr. Harper in the shop, and
he kindly retrieved the hairpin I lost." She patted the back of
her hair and stepped back gracefully. "I need to find Abby
again."

"Good to see you, Thad." Thomas shook his hand, feeling
much like a boy with his hand in the cookie jar. "What can I do
for you?" He bent to lever up the corners of a crate one by one
with the end of a screwdriver he'd retrieved. He palmed a bottle
from inside, inspecting the blue label.

"Ah, Mrs. Winslow's Soothing Syrup." Thad nodded from
the doorway. "I've begun to give a warning before dispensing
that. I've heard stories from my colleagues of children dying
after too large a dose."

"If disease hasn't gotten them first." Thomas paused. "Actually, I've heard this myself. And I'm wondering if they're not

being forthright in listing all the ingredients." He shook his head.

"We have to balance how much to give to relieve these little ones without hurting them. That's certainly been my mission." Thad rocked back on his feet. "I actually came to see how you're faring. Your color is much better. In fact, you're downright rosy." Dr. Moore's eyes twinkled.

Thomas rolled up his sleeves and gathered the crate into his arms. "I'm feeling stronger every day."

"Things are looking much more organized this last week." Thad raised an eyebrow and barely stepped aside to let him pass to the storefront. "She's been good medicine for you."

"Thad, it's not what you think." He lowered his voice. "I was merely thanking her for taking such good care of me. My children depend on me. I can't go about courting these days."

Despite his words, he'd allowed his emotions to get the better of him. Then he'd enjoyed her embrace, and that made him all the guiltier.

"Listen, young man...her son could use a father as much as your children could benefit from a mother." The doctor waved his pipe in the air as though calling up evidence.

Thomas set the crate on the front counter before retreating once again into the storeroom.

"Let's discuss this with some privacy." He shut the door behind him and motioned for the doctor to sit at his desk in the makeshift corner office.

Thad lowered himself into the squeaky wooden chair, removed the pipe from his mouth, and sported an amused half smile.

"You've been married much longer than I was." Thomas crossed his arms. "Could you imagine life without your wife beside you?" He smoothed his hair back.

"Of course not."

"Well, then, you must understand I still—no—we *all* still

miss Bess. She was the heart and soul of this family." His hands fisted involuntarily, and he brought the right one to his heart. "She was truly my better half. I can't begin to compare any woman to her. Besides, I don't think the children would take kindly to such a thing." Though without Maggie, where would they be?

He paused. "Maggie Galloway's a fine woman, but you've seen what my brood has done to each successive housekeeper. They've tucked tail and run—every one of them." Thomas sat on the corner of the desk and crossed his arms again. He couldn't find it in himself to look into Dr. Moore's eyes because he couldn't face the pity he knew he'd find there.

The doctor shook his head. "Maggie Galloway is made of sterner stuff than some flighty housekeeper."

Silence encompassed the little room like stale air. Heaviness weighed on Thomas as he did his best to push the image of Maggie from his mind. Try as he might, he couldn't forget the softness of her hair or the creaminess of her skin, or the comfort of having her nearby. Even now, her laughter as she worked with Abby in the other room was like a salve to his weary heart. But what would be the point in further entertaining his attraction to her when his children needed him?

"And what do you think Bess would say about this? Do you think she would condemn you to a prison of fidelity though she's no longer here? Or would she want you to do what's best for the children, and frankly, for you?" Thad tucked the unlit pipe into his suit coat pocket.

"That's completely unfair, especially when I'm still missing Bess."

"You're past the time of wearing a mourning band on your sleeve."

"Barely. But I wear one in my heart." Even as the words came out, he knew they weren't completely true. This cut him more. He would always love Bess and would never forget her, yet he coped. He'd almost died—and wanted to, except for the kids—but he had survived. Maggie's deep-blue eyes arose in his mind, how he'd awakened to find her tending to him and she'd roused in him emotions he thought long buried.

"There's not much I can do for you, my boy, except to point out that God has put a woman who uniquely fits your needs right in front of you. It doesn't get much simpler." Thad stood, his movements slow as though the stiffness of old age was beginning to set in. He supported himself with one hand on the desk.

Thomas hadn't meant to sigh. Was he fighting Thad's suggestions? Or his own reasoning against Maggie?

"I felt it was my duty to let you know she may not be around forever. I wouldn't take too long to consider your options."

"And what do you mean by that?" Thomas slid from the corner of the desk, his shoes making a gentle thudding sound on the wood floor.

"Mrs. Moore told me she heard from Maggie herself that Mr. Prescott didn't visit only to hand out awards."

"What are you talking about?"

"They are old friends, and he offered her a job at his test kitchen...in Chicago."

Thomas licked his dry lips and combed his hand through his hair. "Ridiculous!"

"Is it, Thomas? She's a sharp woman, that Maggie Galloway is. Without Ian needing her to keep house for him anymore, what's going to hold her here?" Thad shrugged. "She's not from Stone Creek originally. Other than the family here, she is free to go anywhere she likes, don't you think?"

Thomas blinked at him.

The doctor met his consternation with a level gaze. "Unless, that is, someone gives her an inarguable reason to stay?" He finished with the shadow of a smile.

"She's..." What could Thomas say? Every compliment Thad

gave Maggie was true. "She is a singular woman. Any man would be lucky to have her, but that man...can't be me."

"Don't you think the timing of her presence in your life is quite providential? Come on, man, she saved your life." Thad's mouth became a grim line as his stare penetrated Thomas's soul.

"Why is everyone so concerned about my well-being? If God truly cared—if He even exists—how could He take Bess from us?" Thomas crossed his arms again as though he could protect his heart from further damage.

Thad touched his shoulder with a fatherly gesture. With the penetrating look gone, the man's eyes softened with a kind of sorrow in them. Or was it more pity? "Thomas, the Lord gives and takes away. I know you're hurt, but I hate to see you miss a blessing because you're angry with your heavenly Father."

Was God his heavenly Father? How long ago had he been a devout child, innocent in his faith? *Let the little children come to me,* Christ had said. As a boy in Sunday school, Thomas wanted to know a God who loved him, the Jesus who took children into His arms and embraced them.

His father had always been busy. His sister, Alice, and he had been adopted as young children by the Harpers, who didn't have children born to them—until their younger brother, Daniel, came along. When Alice died, he would have felt utterly alone, but for the grieving Daniel shared with him.

Then only Bess was able to make him believe God's accepting love was possible. When she left this earth, so had his concept of God.

The old bitterness rose in his throat, a sour taste like bile spread over his tongue, and he clenched his fist again. Thomas averted his gaze. "I don't know what I believe anymore, Thad."

"That's a dangerous spot to be in when you're responsible

KATHLEEN ROUSER

for the moral upbringing of four children." The timber of Dr. Moore's voice conveyed a keen disappointment.

Thomas took a deep breath. "But I can't lie about it either. I'll do my best."

"And what if it isn't enough?"

CHAPTER 20

Maggie stood in front of a mirror upstairs in Abby's room. She held an extra hairpin she'd borrowed from Abby between her teeth as she twisted her hair into a knot well above the nape of her neck. Thomas hadn't done the best job helping to fix her hair, but his attempt made her smile, along with the thought of his gentle touch.

"Do you need anything else?" Abby stood to her left shoulder chewing on a fingernail. Did she notice a hint of a blush still played on Maggie's cheeks?

The cadence of her heart had picked up at Thomas's nearness. His touch on her neck had been fleeting, but did she imagine the heat lingering there? Surprised by the tingling warmth it set off down her spine, Maggie had done her best to compose herself—until he'd cupped her face in his hands. *I was sure he was going to kiss me.*

"Mrs. Galloway?" Of course, Abby waited for her answer.

She pulled the pin from her mouth. "No, I think this will do it." She pushed the last one through the coil of her tresses and smiled back at the girl's reflection.

"Would you consider teaching me how to put my hair up like you wear it?" Abby clasped her hands together.

Maggie turned around. The girl was on the cusp of womanhood, more child than adult, but with an adult's responsibility often foisted upon her. She gathered the girl's hands into hers. How she would have loved to have a sweet daughter like Abby, a sister for Philip.

"What brings this on? You are still young and look pretty with your hair in braids."

"I'll be fourteen this autumn. I was hoping perhaps next April I would get invited to the Welcome Spring Social I hear Helena Blanding always puts on. I would love to wear such pretty clothes and ribbons like her and Miss Neuberger wear." Abby sighed, the longing for time's passage evident in her glowing eyes.

How could Maggie explain, without being too unkind, what snobby, spoiled creatures the other two girls were? She cleared her throat. "Perhaps I could show you how to put in a few pin curls. You could pull some back, but wear most of your hair down. It would be very attractive. And I like Miss Abby Harper much better than those other two girls. You're growing into a lovely young woman, but don't wish the time away. You have so many other things to look forward to before you're old enough for the social." Hopefully, by then, Abby would lose interest in such a pretentious crowd.

Had Maggie been spending enough time with the girl? "Why don't you come to the cottage later, and we'll cook dinner together? Your brothers and father can join us."

"That would be so helpful, Mrs. Galloway. I'm afraid the boys are tired of my cooking, and I can only try to placate them so many times with Mama's special pound cake." Abby giggled.

"Indeed. And it's probably not best to feed them cake all the time." Maggie chuckled. Besides, the thought of having Thomas on her territory for a change could prove interesting.

*T*homas fussed over the contents of the newly arrived shipment. After Thad left, he couldn't concentrate. Maggie leaving Stone Creek? And she hadn't even mentioned it to him. The cold, hollow area in his heart had begun to warm, but the thought of Maggie leaving cut him like a frigid knife.

What did it matter, anyway? He'd get used to it if he had to. Thomas rolled up his sleeves and set his jaw. He stood and paced, determined not to let another woman get the better of him or his heart. So what if he'd just declared she'd saved his life? Had she really? All those religious people like Dr. Moore would say God already numbered his days. He could very well have survived with Abby, or Zeke, for that matter, taking care of him.

Thomas searched for his hammer. Where had he put it? Finding it on the floor on the other side of a crate, he grabbed the handle and jammed its claw under the edge of the crate's lid, using it as a fulcrum. The top stuck, and Thomas forced it harder until some of the wood splintered apart. Useless, like his life. Dropping the hammer to the floor, he knelt and put his head in his hands.

Abby sang a happy tune Bess used to and knocked on the storeroom door, which was opened just a crack. "Papa?"

"Yes?" He stood and shoved the unopened crate out of the way for the time being.

"Mrs. Galloway asked me to come and learn about cooking with her this afternoon. Then you and the boys can come for dinner." His daughter's eyes glowed at such a prospect.

"I'm sure Mrs. Galloway has better things to do than entertain us." He grunted. "How could she have enough room for all of us in that little cottage?"

Abby's face fell. "But Papa—"

"It's no trouble at all, really, Thomas." Maggie appeared in the doorway behind Abby, peering over her shoulder, their faces both expectant. "And it's warm enough to spread a blanket and have a picnic in the orchard. It would be grand fun. You could use some fresh air."

He looked away for something to do, a tool to grasp, and clenched his fist. "If Abby wants to visit you this once to pick up some cooking tips, that's fine, but we don't want to be a bother." He did his best to present her with a smile, albeit a fake one.

"But you're no bother at all. It would be such fun for Philip and—"

"Not this evening." He held up his hand. "Perhaps some other time."

"But Papa..." Abby put on a long face like a puppy having been kicked out of the way.

"Abby." Maggie put her hands on his daughter's shoulders. "Why don't you mind the storefront in case anyone should come in? I'll see you in a few minutes."

Abby nodded, flashing a look of anger and disappointment at Thomas before she left the room. Once her footsteps disappeared toward the storefront, Maggie moved toward him with arms akimbo, stopping a few feet away.

❧

"I thought you wanted me to take the girl under my wing and teach her what it means to become a young lady." Maggie took another step forward, staring up into Thomas's face.

His eyes turned flinty. "She can't depend on you forever, can she?" He turned away and lifted one crate on top of another. With his back to her, the taut muscles in his arms tensed. Looked as though he was regaining some strength.

The warmth she'd experienced from his touch turned to ice in her gut. In fact, Thomas might as well have shoved her into an icebox and closed the door on her. Was that all he had to say?

"If you don't mind, I'd like to have Abby stay for a bite, and then we'll pack up some dinner to bring back for you and the boys."

"No need for that. We're fine...but Abby can stay awhile if you like." He shrugged. "But don't plan on doing this every day."

Insufferable man. Why is he being so stubborn and gruff? Moments ago, he'd embraced her.

"I have a little time to work around here today. What would you like me to start on?" Did he think she could be brushed off so easily?

"I'm not sure there's anything left for you to do here... today." He fairly growled at her.

"Really?" She crossed her arms. "You've made progress, but you don't even have the soda fountain up and running."

"What does that have to do with you?" Anger lingered under Thomas's even tone and pricked her heart.

Not willing to look him fully in the face, Maggie turned halfway around and placed her hand on the doorknob. "Abby has told me your wife thought it was important to business these days and would have had it in service by now." She slid a glance his way.

Thomas shifted his weight from one foot to another and passed a hand over his face. A jaw set in stone replaced the fleeting sorrow. His eyes went from misty to the glint of steel.

"Please leave. Now." He turned away from her completely.

Maggie's heart bottomed out. She'd gone too far. Again.

*a*bby's cheerful chatter on the way home helped lighten Maggie's heart, but still, the knowledge of what she'd done pressed on her chest as though the wind had been knocked out of her. Yes, at first triumph had risen in her. She'd gone for his Achilles' heel by mentioning Mrs. Harper.

"Mrs. Galloway? Are you feeling well enough?" Abby touched her arm, and Maggie jerked the buggy reins.

"Yes, I'm sorry. I'm somewhat lost in thought." She held the reins steady again. The groom, Mr. Phelps, would have a fit if anything happened to Lily, his prize mare, or the buggy, let alone her or Abby. Gloria often insisted Maggie have Starks take her into town, but she had missed having her independence.

"Now, what were you telling me?" Maggie forced her mouth to curve into a smile, though disappointment with herself gripped her conscience like a vise. Besides, Abby deserved better. It wasn't her fault her father had turned ugly on Maggie. No, Maggie had driven him to it.

"I was saying how Ma used to let me help sometimes, but the only thing I was good at was boiling an egg." The girl shifted in her seat and smoothed her skirt. "Eventually, I even stopped burning the toast." She snickered.

"We're not doing anything too difficult. I roasted a chicken, and I have the leftovers in the icebox. We can make up some nice sandwiches, and I insist you take some back for your brothers. We'll make a relish tray to go alongside and whip up a batch of cookies. Would you like to help me make some ginger snaps?"

"We don't get sweets every day. That would be quite nice. Although, I'm sure my brothers sneak a fair amount from the candy jar." Abby rolled her eyes. "Haven't you already had your baking day for the week?"

"Doesn't matter. I'd like to make our time together special."

Maggie pulled back on the reins a bit, glad for her kid gloves as Lily gave a little neigh and strained ahead on the smooth, dirt-packed road leading out of downtown Stone Creek.

"Mrs. Galloway..." Abby's voice trailed off, hesitant.

"Yes?" The jaunty rhythm of hoof beats picked up the lull in conversation.

"Thank you for being so kind to me, to all of us. My brothers and I didn't help much when you came to take care of Papa." The girl turned toward her on the seat.

Maggie blinked back the moisture building in her eyes.

"You saved his life, but at the time, I was jealous someone besides Mama or I was taking care of him." Abby twisted her hands together in her lap. She kept her head down.

Here Maggie was, not feeling worthy of any appreciation. The last thing she had wanted to do was nurse the annoying man back to health. If anything, she'd done it for the children and to redeem herself for her failure to keep Robert alive. Besides, she might have helped the family, but now she'd knifed the man in his heart. How would she have liked Thomas reminding her of Robert's plans in the face of her failure?

"Abby, that's understandable. I was pretty much a stranger to all of you." Children were expected to accept the decisions of their elders. Still, it couldn't have been an easy situation for any of them.

"Dr. Moore knew what he was doing. We couldn't have taken care of Pa on our own. If it weren't for you, we'd be orphans." Abby's voice trailed as she turned her head away as though studying the passing scenery. "Besides, we didn't think we could trust anybody. Mrs. Peaberry left us high and dry, like the others."

"That was plainly the grace of God." Maggie chuckled, having heard the woman was less than kind to the Harpers. "I didn't know what I was going to do, taking care of your father and all of you. Remember, before this, I only had Philip."

She tugged slightly on the reins, slowing Lily's gait further as they approached the orchard near Apple Blossom House. She guided the horse left into the drive and stopped in front of the barn. "Whoa."

The stable boy ran to greet them. Maggie handed him the reins.

Mr. Phelps came forward to help Maggie down. "I see you've returned in one piece, thank the Lord."

"As I predicted." She lifted her skirt so as not to catch it on her shoe, and he was kind enough to take her hand. Abby scrambled down, close behind her.

"Whoa, young lady, be careful there."

The stable boy quickly moved to help her as well while averting his curious glance.

"I'm all right, sir." Abby pushed her spectacles up her nose, also looking away while turning a little pink. So shy.

With a grandfatherly smile, the groomsman's gray whiskers twitched. He reminded Maggie of a thin version of Santa Claus.

Abby followed Maggie along the stone pathway around the barn toward Apple Blossom Cottage. The summer grasses grew up on each side, crowned with ripe seeds and interspersed with colorful wildflowers. A butterfly flitted from one blooming lavender-colored milkweed to the next. Subdued crickets announced evening's approach. As the pathway widened, Abby scooted up next to Maggie.

"Mrs. Galloway, what I'm trying to say is, I'm sorry for making things difficult." The cobblestones turned to gravel under their shoes as they strolled along.

Maggie stopped. She took Abby by the hands. "You had just been through a difficult time with the passing of your mother, and you'd left friends and family behind. You have nothing to be sorry about, but the apology is accepted, nonetheless." She let go of the girl's left hand and locked arms with her on the other side. They walked together like school chums.

"Thanks for understanding." Their heels crunched on the gravel as Abby continued. "Will I ever stop missing Mama?" She studied her shoes as though she could count her toes through them before looking into Maggie's eyes with a pointed gaze.

Had Maggie ever stopped missing her mother? Many years had passed since she knelt on a chair by the kitchen table while Hannah McCormick showed her how to roll out pie dough to the perfect thickness. Maggie's little fingers had fumbled as she pressed the dough into a fluted edge and Mother smiled, gently guiding her hands.

She'd only been gone a few years, but how Maggie often wished she was there to talk to, especially since losing Robert. Each little triumph, such as winning second place in the baking contest, made her think of writing a note to her mother. How many times had she picked up a pen and paper only to remember the truth?

"I don't think the missing, or the memory, ever goes away. It just changes." She let go of Abby and stooped to pick up a small rock with flecks of quartz and sharp edges. "See this?" Taking the girl's hand, Maggie rubbed the stone across her palm. "Feel how rough this is. But if this were on the lakeshore for a long time, the water and sand would smooth the rough edges. It would be bleached and faded, worn smooth by time. That's kind of how our memories are."

Abby nodded as Maggie closed her fingers around the rock. "That's a good example."

"It won't always hurt so much, but it will always be...in here." She placed a hand on her chest.

The soft look in the girl's dewy eyes gave away the closeness of the relationship with her mother as well as the sweet memories which must haunt—no, linger—like the sweet scent of hyacinth on a spring evening.

"You must be getting hungry. Let's get back to the cottage and start supper preparations."

"Sure, Mrs. Galloway."

Once inside the kitchen, Maggie lifted the hefty cutting board from its resting place against the wall and placed it on the small kitchen table. She took a loaf of bread from the sideboard, folded back the wax paper, and handed the bread knife to Abby. "Be careful with this."

"Mrs. Galloway." She shook her head and chuckled. "I'm the only one who can be trusted with a knife in our house."

"Ah, I suppose that's true." But she couldn't help mothering the young lady before her. Since she'd taken Abby under her wing, her braids were straighter and neater. A hint of curls escaped around her face. Her plain white shirtwaist had been well pressed by Maggie as she showed Abby how to iron.

Maggie took butter from the icebox and a stoneware bowl down from the shelf. She'd better start on the cookie dough. First, she would see how well Abby knew how to cream the butter.

"Mrs. Galloway..." Abby worried her lip, and the only sound heard was the soft thud of the knife on wood as it came through the bread.

"Yes?" Perhaps Abby needed a little coaxing. "Do you have a question for me?" She only hoped it wasn't about where babies came from or the monthly problems of women, as Maggie wasn't sure how she would approach the subject with another person's daughter.

CHAPTER 21

"When did you fall in love with Mr. Galloway? Did you know him when you were a schoolgirl?"

At Abby's questions, Maggie's heart slowed. She could speak on this subject with confidence. "I had finished school and then attended normal school. I was home after exam time and met Robert on a warm summer day, much like today."

"The stable boy here is handsome, but I don't believe I've ever seen him at school." Abby's face flushed like the tint on a pale-pink rose. She bent her head over the table while she brushed crumbs over the table's edge into her cupped hand.

Aha. "Nate is an orphan. Mr. Phelps was kind enough to take him in. He's a distant relative. He left school early to come here, but Mr. Phelps sees to it he works on reading and ciphering." The boy did love horses, so despite the older man's intentions for Nate to improve himself, he would be hard pressed to get him away from stable work.

Abby sighed with drama. "I don't suppose Papa would ever allow me to marry someone without an education, let alone a profession."

Maggie bit her lower lip to keep from smiling at such a

serious comment. "Character is important in a young man too. As long as he works hard and wants to care for you."

"Well, my Grandmother Harper wouldn't approve. She's a rich lady in Detroit. She was all against Papa taking us away."

Maggie put down the mixing spoon she'd lifted from a hook on the wall and squeezed Abby's shoulder. "I'm positive your father and grandmother only want the best for you. But you have much to learn before you can settle down as a housewife."

"I would like to teach...like Miss Oliver."

"Maggie!" Gloria knocked on the front door which was partially opened.

"Come on in!"

"Ma!" Philip's thumping footsteps followed his cheerful voice, along with Elise's quiet musical laughter.

"You need to take your shoes off, sir!" Maggie held up her hand in the kitchen doorway, not letting him come any farther. "Now, look what you've done. You must get a broom and dustpan and sweep up the dirt."

"I can help him." Elise's eyes sparkled with good humor as she unbuttoned her shoes by the front door. "Philip and I found tadpoles by the river, and I named them." She looked as pleased as a new parent.

"I told her not to bother." Philip rolled his eyes. "They all look alike."

Abby sighed. "I'll make sure they do the job right."

"Mr. Starks stopped at the post office while in town." Gloria waved an envelope in Maggie's face. "But I'm not sure if I should give this to you."

"Whatever do you mean?"

Though Gloria's blue eyes glinted with good humor, her slight frown gave her away.

Maggie wiped her hands on her damp apron. "Let me see that." She grabbed the letter from her friend, scanning it for the return address. "Mm-hm." She hiked up one eyebrow. "Only a letter from Mr. Prescott."

"That's what I'm worried about." Gloria sidled closer. She craned her neck as though making sure the children were out of earshot and tugged Maggie's arm to pull her away from the doorway.

"He's an old family friend." Maggie shook her head.

"And I'm sure he'd like to be more."

Maggie's stomach knotted at the thought. It was true. She examined the envelope in her hands. It could hold promises from an old *friend*—or rejection. He'd probably been expecting an answer sooner than she could give it. "He must have written this long before he sent the telegram I received this morning."

She couldn't lie. Viewing his name on the envelope conjured images of his dark, brooding eyes which could draw a woman to drown in their depths, as well as his strong chin, straight nose, and rather full lips. And he was tall. How many times had her heart fluttered as a young woman looking up at him, waiting for a kiss?

Then Irena's face invaded her thoughts, the way Giles looked after the younger women. The knot grew in her stomach.

∼

*T*homas fussed with the knobs underneath the counter. Hopefully, this would finally adjust the flow of carbonated water properly. He came up and pulled down the lever on the left side. Bubbling water squirted in every direction and then some. He pushed the lever back up and grabbed a towel to sop up the mess.

"Unbelievable!" His temple throbbed. The Lucky Soda Fountain Company had thoroughly falsified information by promising an *effortless installation with a most gratifying outcome* after congratulating him on the purchase and predicting he would make a fortune at his new endeavor.

A baby's wailing drowned out the chiming of the bell over the door. Cora Frost traipsed in with one-year-old Wyatt on her hip. His face was flushed, and he chewed on his fingers as though he hadn't been fed in days. A classic case of teething, no doubt. Wyatt wiped his runny nose with the back of his hand and gave a sad little cough.

Cora had Emmaline by her other hand.

"Wan' candy." Little Emmy pulled her thumb from her mouth and pointed to the jar of candy sticks.

Wyatt stiffened and threw himself backwards. His mother barely caught him.

A thud overhead hardly registered.

"Do you have anything for Wyatt's teething? He's worse than usual." The thin woman's dark circles attested to her lack of sleep.

Where was Abby when he needed her? He'd been training her to entertain the little children while he educated the mothers on the best choices.

He rolled up the towel he'd been holding and tossed it beneath the counter. He cast a glance over his stock. Where had Maggie put the paregoric? Yes, there it was, third shelf up to the right. Impressive how she'd organized expectorants separate from pain-relieving elixirs, remedies for biliousness, vomiting, and diarrhea. He had always kept them in alphabetical order. He rubbed the stubble on his chin. Maggie Galloway prickled like his whiskers—thinking she could take over things and then leave town.

"Mr. Harper, we need something now." Cora bounced the baby on her hip.

"Wan' candy." Emmy pouted and hid her face in the other side of her mother's long skirt.

Thud. Again. Thomas had to get what Cora needed and push her out the door so he could deal with his boys.

Thomas grimaced, no longer used to the shrill crying of infants. He procured a stout brown bottle from the shelf. "Rub a little of this paregoric syrup on Wyatt's gums, and he will feel much better."

"But will he ever sleep?" She pressed her lips together.

"Why, he'll sleep like a bear cub in a den in the middle of January." He pushed his mouth into what should appear a reassuring smile.

"I thought this was just for coughs." Cora grasped the bottle. "What about taking Mrs. Winslow's Soothing Syrup? Do you have any? I've taken some before myself."

"The paregoric helps alleviate diarrhea and numbs the gums nicely. I'm questioning the safety of Mrs. Winslow's Soothing Syrup for now."

"Oh...well, then I guess I'll take the—"

"Give it back!"

The unpleasant sound of bodies tumbling down the stairs silenced everyone. Even Wyatt quieted to a whimper.

"I don't have anything!" This time, Lyle rallied all his strength into holding the older Josiah down. For a change, Zeke wasn't involved—which wasn't always a good thing when Thomas didn't know where his youngest was.

He swung his leg over the half gate which kept his customers out from behind the counter and nearly leapt upon his sons.

"Boys, stop this right now." Thomas spoke through his teeth, grabbing each boy by the collar and doing his best to pull them apart.

"He stole my pocketknife, the little liar." Josiah frowned.

"Nah-uh." Lyle shook his head and stuck out his tongue. "Why would I want to steal that old thing?"

"Because you don't have a pocketknife of your own." Josiah

scrambled to his feet. His chin went up as he shrugged from his father's grasp.

Lyle's fist shot out toward his brother, but Thomas grasped his middle son's arms and pulled the child to his chest.

"Gentlemen, I've had quite enough."

He looked over his shoulder when Cora Frost gasped. She stood with mouth agape, her children wide-eyed and frightened by the ruckus. Wyatt rubbed his eyes and buried his face in his mother's shoulder.

"Josiah, go sit in my office and wait for me." Thomas pointed down the hallway toward the back. "And take the time while you're waiting to think about your behavior. Lyle, you will march up those stairs and wait in my room."

"But Pa." Lyle wiped his shirtsleeve over his bloodied lip.

"No *but*s, and while you're at it, find a wash rag and clean up your face in the water closet. And don't let that stain set in your shirt either." Wonderful. He sounded like their mother now. He turned around. "Mrs. Frost, I'm sorry for the boys' shenanigans." Glancing down, his remorse grew. His shirt was untucked, and a button hung from his waistcoat.

"If I wanted a show, Mr. Harper, I could've waited for the next medicine man coming to town. It probably would have been more entertaining." Cora set Wyatt on the counter while she dug through her reticule for the right coins.

Thomas straightened his shoulders. Hopefully, he looked a little more dignified as he opened the half gate to get back behind the counter. He smoothed his bowtie as well and tucked his shirt back in. "I really don't recommend one of those patent medicine hawkers. While some of what they peddle is harmless, some of it's quite dangerous and unnecessary." Thomas willed himself not to roll his eyes as he waited. Everyone was in a hurry to believe inflated promises rather than heed professional advice.

"Hmm...I thought I had enough money on me. May I put it on my account?"

Mr. Frost had likely imbibed away the needed earnings, or paid off the tab at the tavern, rather than worry about his children's needs. Thomas nodded. His own family was hardly perfect. Who was he to judge her situation? "I'll have a statement ready for you at the end of the month."

"Thank you." It was the first time he'd seen Cora smile, probably ever, though the expression didn't touch the shame shadowed in her eyes.

Oh, Bess would have said he couldn't give the whole store away, and a man needed to look out for his own family, but sometimes he made exceptions to the rule, and this was one of those times. It was such a small purchase and would bring them some measure of comfort. Besides, perhaps his kindness would curb the woman's tongue from wagging about the problems she'd witnessed.

After the Frosts left, Abby whistled her way through the back hallway. "Papa, I brought supper with me." Her cheery sing-song voice sounded so much like her mother's it conjured pictures of Bess. When she walked into the pharmacy area, Thomas found she was alone. He took up the towel again and swiped it over the counter and the floor where some of the soda water had dripped.

"Where's Mrs. Galloway?"

"Where are my brothers?"

It was fair that she countered. "Josiah and Lyle are here, though I've separated them after they caused a fair amount of trouble. Do you have any idea where Zeke is?" Thomas raked a hand through his hair.

Abby placed the basket on the countertop. The fragrance of ginger and spices wafted throughout the room. His stomach rumbled at the thought of eating the meal she and Maggie prepared. Maybe there were ginger cookies packed in there too.

"He's probably down by the millpond looking for more snakes. Do you want me to get him?"

"No, Abby. You set the kitchen table while I fetch Zeke." He patted her shoulder on the way out, not willing to meet his daughter's eyes.

What was it he didn't want her to notice? Perhaps the disappointment in not seeing Maggie with her? Or was it the inherent failure? He rolled up his sleeves another cuff length. Humidity pressed against him as the westward-heading sun left behind a burning trail on the earth. Perhaps it would be cooler by the pond.

Abby's new calm and maturity were evident in how she carried herself and helped around the shop since Maggie came to befriend her. Even the boys showed respect. Running to get the door for her. Fussing over the cookies she often brought. Minding her commands.

Worst of all, having her leave this afternoon, even in the wake of the sting of her biting remark, filled him with understanding. As much as his failure as a father was like a sinking ship, Maggie's presence, or lack thereof, moved in his gut like a storm on the Great Lakes, tossing his heart like a toy sailboat.

Thomas cracked his knuckles. She had stormed in with winds of change, stirring things up, bringing refreshment like the rain they desperately needed that summer. But if she truly left, they would be parched again. He needed the presence of a mother figure for his children. And what of a companion for himself?

Slipping his hands into his pockets as dusk neared, Thomas trod the ground carefully, walking closer to the pond's greenish waters. No, truthfully, if Maggie left Stone Creek, emptiness would probably consume him more than it did the children. They were pliable and resilient, but he was set in his ways.

How dare that woman enter our lives, stir things up, and then leave us? His heart squeezed as though a potter squished clay in his hands, letting the water drip out and leaving dry dirt. As much as the realization angered and hurt him, it stabbed him with guilt.

Thomas had once told Bess there was nobody else for him —that he would never marry again. Truthfully, she hadn't expected such a thing, but somehow, it seemed a betrayal—as though he put the final nail in her coffin. Her face faded from his memory more as time passed. How could he do that to her? How could God have ever put him in this situation?

He stopped, lifting his hand to protect his eyes from the evening sun, and scanned the bank for Zeke. He needed one vision of his light-blond hair to calm his anxious heart.

"Zeke."

"Over here, Pa." But as soon as he spotted his son on the dock, he lost sight of him.

Splash! The blond head disappeared into the depths below.

CHAPTER 22

*W*ith Abby returned home, Maggie sat in her chair while sipping a cup of chamomile tea. The shadows grew longer as the rays of sunshine retreated for the evening. A cooling breeze made its way through the open window and tickled her neck. The mantel clock ticked, announcing the passing of another day.

She set the cup on the small round table next to her and smoothed the envelope in her hand. She studied the fancy return address mark printed on the back which gave evidence of Giles's growing prominence in the flour company. The Silver Leaf emblem accented the uncommon labeling. Scrolling laurel leaves surrounded the address with Giles's name and the street number for the Chicago regional office. Flipping it over, she deftly slid the letter opener under the flap.

Her heart pitter-pattered a little as she unfolded the crisp sheets of paper to reveal Giles's writing.

Dearest Maggie,

I trust this missive finds you well. When you haven't been central in my thoughts, you have lingered on the edges, never far from heart or mind. Seeing you in Stone Creek is just what I needed. No other woman has been able to fill your place in my heart. My sincerest hope is you have felt it as well. I will return to Stone Creek soon with hopes of persuading you to work with me at the Silver Leaf Flour Company, a fine outfit if there ever was one. You couldn't do better. You would not be saddled with the troubles of sole proprietorship, and we could renew our acquaintance further. Perhaps with the intent of looking to our future? I will be confounded by desire until such a time as I gaze upon your fair countenance again.

Ever and only with fondness,
   Giles Prescott

Maggie caught herself exhaling with a little sigh, like a schoolgirl. She sat up straighter and fanned herself with the parchment. *Such foolishness.*

Yet she had to smile as she thought of chaperoned picnics with Giles and her other friends in the summer and skating with his hand on her waist in the winter. He guided her around and around the frozen pond. She chuckled when he almost fell and spun around, barely righting himself. And then she lost her balance and fell on her derriere. Giles sped to her rescue and helped her up with merely a teasing grin in retort. He'd swooped her to her feet just in time to avoid the thin crack spreading in the ice. When they made it to the side of the pond, they couldn't stop laughing. Despite the looming reality they'd escaped drowning or pneumonia, they'd found humor in their predicament and joy in avoiding it.

Still, how true were his words in his letter? Giles excelled at flattery. Then again, neither of them was getting any younger. Perhaps this time around, he meant the compliments. But would he ever be content to be a family man?

Then Thomas's handsome face flashed across her mind.

His love for his children was evident in the brightness in his eyes when they were present. His patience with them amazed her. Besides, he never minded having Philip around. If nothing else, the man was sincere, especially in comparison with Giles.

Did she want to trust Giles with her heart when he couldn't be trusted before?

~

"*P*a! Help!" Zeke bobbed on the water.

Thomas plunged from the dock into the murky pond. *God, if you're there, don't let Zeke drown.*

Thomas swam through the water, spewing and sputtering. "Come...on...keep...treading. Hold your breath. I'm...almost...there." The chill shocked Thomas as the cold water seeped through his clothes, weighing him down as he stretched each arm forth in an arc and kicked his feet until he could reach Zeke and grab him under the arm. He pulled his son close with strength he hadn't realized he possessed. His one free arm and legs propelled him back toward the dock. Grasping the slimy edge of the wood, Thomas maneuvered Zeke toward safety.

"Grab ahold." He nearly slammed his son into the boards, pushing him forward and upward. "Can you do it?"

Zeke coughed and sputtered. "Ye-ah," he said with a sob in his voice. "Think so."

And then the burden lightened as his boy climbed onto the dock. Thomas pulled himself up too. They sat, gasping for breath. Water ran off them as though eager to flow back where it came from and suck them down with it.

"D-dad, I'm s-scared." His arms clutched tightly around Thomas's waist.

"Son, you're out of the water now. You're not going to drown. You simply must be more careful."

Zeke coughed again. "I was praying we'd be okay."

Thomas looked away. Zeke had prayed too? Had God really answered? "What were you doing out here playing so close to the water by yourself? Hmm?" He pulled off one shoe at a time and drained each of them.

"I found an old fishhook and a string. I got a stick and thought I'd try fishing. Josiah and Lyle didn't want to help even though I found some worms for them." Zeke snuggled a little closer and stopped shivering for a minute.

His own goosebumps prickled, and not only from the chilling water. The thought of nearly losing his youngest—well, he couldn't abide such a thought. Maybe he needed to give God more credit for His mercies in this circumstance.

Thomas sighed. "Come on, away with you now. Let's get you home and warm you up."

"Sure, Pa." When was the last time Zeke had been this agreeable? They were both shaken.

"And next time, don't go fishing by yourself. You're still a little young to be here on your own."

Thomas took off his soaking-wet socks, picked up his shoes, and walked barefoot toward home with an arm around Zeke. At the sight of a colorful wagon on the opposite side of the millpond, fury raged through him, burning off his anxiety.

~

*M*aggie dabbed the tip of her fountain pen on her desk blotter, her hand shaking. Best she reply before she lost her nerve. As it was, her insides were as soft and gooey as custard. Was Giles's sudden reappearance in her life a second chance at love? Or just the remains of a schoolgirl crush?

Dear Mr. Prescott... She was beyond the point of being coy at her age and wanted her correspondence to reflect this. How should she address him? She crumpled the sheet of stationery and pulled a new one from the top drawer of her secretary.

Oh, bother. She chewed on her bottom lip.

Dear Giles,

I was most gratified to receive your letter and look forward to your next visit with much anticipation. I will inquire with Gloria Myles as to whether they would be inclined to provide accommodations for you. That way you will be nearby and able to become further acquainted with my son.

Was she being too bold at such a suggestion? As Maggie tapped the tip of the fountain pen on the blotter, the ink spotted the coarse paper. Perhaps she should suggest something lighter for the visit.

Verdi's Falstaff will be playing at a little opera house, not far from us, in the town of Kensington. Perhaps you would care to take this performance in one evening as you are, I'm sure, accustomed to much more sophisticated entertainment than our little town offers.

While I am most flattered by your offer, I find myself requiring more time to consider this possibility. I am taking this opportunity to pray every day, seeking the good Lord's guidance as to what plans would be in Philip's and my best interest. If you would indulge me with patience a bit longer, I would be most grateful.

Please allow me time to set a date at which time you would be most welcome to visit the Apple Blossom Estate. With thankfulness, I only expect your thoughtfulness in this matter.

And how was she supposed to sign this missive? Maggie didn't want to give Giles false hope, but she didn't want the sign-off to sound as cold as a glacier either.

Your friend? No. *Yours truly?* It was merely a saying. Or perhaps *fondly?* Maggie finally settled on:

With warmest regards,
  Maggie Galloway

Her bottom lip hurt from the indentation of her teeth. She folded the thin but tough and elegant paper into thirds before sliding it into an envelope and writing the return address Giles had supplied.

Absentmindedly, Maggie held onto the note as she climbed the stairs to her bedroom. Soft pink tendrils of evening light illuminated the room through the gabled window. She placed the letter on her dressing table before she reached for her robe and nightgown on the peg on the back of the door.

After readying for bed, Maggie sat in the bright kerosene light and uncoiled her auburn locks, placing the hairpins in a heart-shaped, flowered porcelain dish. She tugged her boar-bristled brush through the thick strands, staring at the woman in the mirror's reflection. Worry lines had begun to etch her forehead. Her eyes, the one thing which resembled Ian's, emanated sadness.

What was it? That she still grieved over Robert? Worried over Philip? Perhaps she was lonely, despite having dear friends and Ian's family nearby. Tugging the bristles through the tangles in her tresses, Maggie closed her eyes and pictured herself working shoulder to shoulder with this friend of her youth.

She could see him smile down at her, their hands brushing. Her heart quickened. In her mind's eye, she looked down and then up to meet his gaze. Instead of the moody and mysterious dark-walnut eyes which had once held her fascination, hazel eyes stared into hers. Disheveled sandy-brown curls begged her to push them off of, yes...Thomas's face. When she opened her eyes, Maggie put her cool palms to her heated countenance. Turning down the lantern light, she stood.

She placed the brush on the table, snugged the white cotton robe around herself, and stared at the envelope. Would sending this reply set off a chain of events she couldn't easily undo?

CHAPTER 23

a few weeks after Independence Day, Maggie relaxed on the porch swing outside the cottage. The wink of fireflies replaced fireworks. The chirp of crickets and birds substituted for the music of the town's band, and the march of the heroes in the parade was nearly forgotten. The chug of a car motor coming up the drive broke her peaceful reverie.

Maggie patted her hair. No time to run upstairs and look in the mirror. She pinched her cheeks. Her heart fluttered. Apprehension and hope fought to reign there.

Giles Prescott slowed his crazy contraption on the narrow dirt road leading back near the cottage. He swung his feet over the side of the car and brushed the dust from his traveling coat. He took off those strange-looking glasses which no doubt had protected him from the wind and dust covering the rest of his face.

"What are you doing here? You should have pulled up onto the drive at the front of the estate house." Maggie pushed her hands into her apron pockets. "Dear me, I forgot to take this off. I look like some kind of maid." She spread the white fabric out as though in apology.

"You look perfect to me." Giles took quick strides toward her and removed his traveling cap. His arms went out as though to gather her into them, but Maggie grabbed his free hand, trying to push away.

His dark eyes mesmerized her. His full mouth, curved into a slight grin, called to her longing for a man's touch, to let his arms engulf her and his mouth claim hers. But danger lurked in such actions.

Giles grasped her hand, not allowing her escape. He twirled her around and surveyed her, his eyes melting into warm desire. Maggie found herself dancing right into his arms, their old rhythm unforgotten.

"Did you think I would let you get away so easily?"

He was so close. She trembled at Giles's touch. Could he hear the beat of her heart? Did his beat as wildly as hers? So long ago, he'd held her close like this, their hearts almost in sync, but not quite. His musky, woodsy scent filled her senses, but she kept her eyes open even as his lids fell and his face moved towards hers. So inviting, but she couldn't.

Maggie inhaled, placing a hand on his chest to push away. She turned, looking back at the cottage. "We can't. Philip may still be awake." This was as good as an excuse as any, rather than leave them open to temptation.

He released her. The tension seeped away as the moment was broken.

He exhaled sharply, stepping back. "My darling Maggie, still as proper as a maiden." The soft lantern light emanating from the front window reflected the disappointment in his eyes. He chuckled. "Very well. I will go to my lodgings at the house, but I'm hoping your son will get used to such displays of affection between us."

She averted her gaze.

"I will steal that kiss soon enough. I have done it before. Or have you forgotten?" He chucked her chin.

Hardly. Thomas's embrace flashed into her mind. He'd avoided her since, but was she ready to commit her affections to Giles?

What would it have been like if Thomas had kissed her? The desire had been evident in his look.

A hint of that enticing bay-rum scent of him always lingered in the air of the pharmacy, including the last time she had been there to deliver a new recipe to Abby. The girl visited sometimes at the cottage, and they had pleasant conversations while Philip and Elise played. Abby was becoming a good cook. With Abby's help, the pharmacy was up and running smoothly. Clearly, Thomas didn't need Maggie's assistance anymore.

He had remained aloof when he saw her, hardly exchanging pleasantries. However the mystery behind his hazel eyes drew her, it was Giles who was an open book. She'd do well to remember that she had one man willing to bask in her presence while the other held back.

~

The following evening, Maggie perched on the passenger side of the automobile. She'd secured her emerald-green hat with a long white chiffon scarf. Though Giles had attached a top over the motorcar, he implored her to wear the odd goggles he supplied. Likely, she resembled some ridiculous dragonfly.

Her hands tightened on the edge of the seat as Giles applied the brake.

"So...what do you think of my little Packard Runabout? She's a beauty, isn't she?"

Beauty wasn't the first thought to enter Maggie's mind. "It's certainly sturdy." Her nerves grew taut from all the bumps as they bounced along the road. She couldn't believe they had made it to the opera house in one piece.

"You'll get used to it." He leaned close. His eyes shone with merriment. "You have to admit, it was fun."

"An adventure, to say the least." In lieu of a duster, Maggie had wrapped a shawl around her shoulders and covered her lap with an old blanket. Good thing she had too.

Giles guffawed as he came around to help her down, but she wasn't prepared for the people ogling them as though they'd just alighted from a ship from faraway lands.

Gloria waved, probably standing on tiptoe to get noticed in the small crowd outside the Kensington Opera House. She and Asa pushed through toward Maggie and Giles. "I'm so relieved you've made it. I would have felt so much better had you gone with us in the carriage." The older woman's brows furrowed.

Her concern touched Maggie.

"These new-fangled things make me so nervous." Gloria's glance shot daggers toward Giles.

"Your friend is in good hands. I've been driving such a 'new-fangled thing' for a while now." Giles took Maggie's shawl, folded it, and placed it on the seat.

She unfastened her scarf. Sweat trickled down her temples, the nape of her neck, and her back. While the windy ride had cooled her, she was relieved to be free of the extra layers.

"Are you overheated?" Gloria fanned her with one of her delicate ivory fans. "Perhaps this will help. I have an extra if you want this one."

"Thank you, but I believe I have one here in my reticule." After finding it, she looked up to the billboard attached to the three-storied brick building. What a treat to enjoy something as elegant as the opera, though she wouldn't understand the Italian lyrics.

After they were seated, Maggie surveyed the green walls and plaster sculptures of fleurs-de-lis...or were they shells? They lined the walls near the ceiling right under the moldings. The thick velvet curtains would soon open. A shiver of delight went up her spine. How long had it been since she'd done anything like this?

As the capers of the characters played out before their eyes, performers singing richly, Giles whispered the details into her ear, his warm breath hovering near her neck. Heat and electricity hung in the air. Giles scooted closer, slipped his arm around her, and rested his hand on her shoulder. Being in the company of a sophisticated gentleman who'd attended many such events made Maggie wonder how her life might have been different had Robert not captured her heart. Could she have been as happy all those years with the man sitting next to her?

"A penny for your thoughts."

"This is such a rare treat."

"There are so many more things to see in Chicago. A different theater show every week, if you want."

She averted her gaze, though Gloria caught it. A question formed in her friend's eyes, apparent even in the semi-darkness.

Maggie concentrated on the rest of the performance. Before she knew it, they were on their feet clapping for an encore. When she smiled to share the moment with Gloria, her friend didn't return the gesture.

~

"This is much better." Thomas paced the short length of his sons' room while the boys stood at attention. He was implementing his determination to impose order in their home. "Excellent job." He pointed to the blanket corners which had been neatly folded and tucked under.

"I'll bet Abby doesn't have to do this," Lyle mumbled and crossed his arms.

"What?"

"Nothing."

"Again?"

"Nothing, sir!"

"That's much better, or you would be scrubbing floors." Thomas paced again, holding a clipboard. "Now get down to breakfast. I'm sure Abby has the oatmeal ready. And then I will give you the chore assignments of the day."

Each son passed, their faces as long as a Bassett hound's. They dragged their feet.

"Step up, now, we don't have all day."

Josiah looked up for a moment and then away. Fear fell over his son's visage just as fast. The others' hooded glares remained fixed on the stairway. Thomas steeled himself against the sad and angry looks given him. While his heart threatened to melt like a plate of butter left in the sun, he needed to turn it into the ice that would give him the edge to control his unruly bunch. They were listening to him for a change. Once they got used to the new habits, they would be grateful for the parameters he set for them each day.

Nonetheless, his tender side threatened to take over. He wanted to chase after them. To tell them it was a joke. That he hadn't meant any of it. To allow these boys to express their *joie de vivre* and exuberant spirit. Yet allowing their unbridled spirit had led to chaos.

But was the quiet shuffle of their feet in obedience any better?

Maggie had brought about peace in his home when she'd been there, and without a cost. *Maggie.*

~

The fresh, dew-kissed morning air relieved Maggie from the humidity of the day before. Too bad it would likely be back in full force later in the afternoon. After breakfast with Gloria, Asa, and Elise, she waited by Giles's vehicle as he gathered his luggage from Apple Blossom Estate.

She rubbed her hand over the brass headlamp of the Packard Runabout. It had been polished to a shine, the dust from the weekend gone. The man took such pride in everything he did, but was it still all for show, as it had been back in Buffalo when they'd been an item?

Philip and Elise poured out onto the wraparound porch and down the steps. Their voices, as happy as the twitter of birds in spring, cheered Maggie. Did she want to leave this simple, charming town, and the little bit of family she had, for Chicago? Or Buffalo? Philip would stand to gain in getting to know his father's family, but she would miss the rich friendships she'd found in Stone Creek.

The door swung open as Giles appeared, handsome and polished, as usual, in a brown tweed suit with a patterned tie peeking out between his starched white collar and rich tan vest. His thick, dark hair was combed to perfection. The usual wayward lock fell across his forehead. His dark eyes shone with purpose as he strode toward her.

He dropped his luggage on the seat, his duster and hat next to the bags. Maggie stood silent, watching him. He'd stayed away from church, saying he had a headache on Sunday morning. That had been Maggie's greatest disappointment. But he had bowed his head respectfully each time Asa said grace. And he hadn't made fun of her *fanatical* ways as he had done as a youth. He offered to take Philip rowing on the millpond when they went for a picnic. The hint of future possibilities during their outings had been pleasant.

Today she'd dressed in her nicest day gown, her corset cinched tighter than usual. She'd taken pains to fix a braid over her shoulder while the rest of her hair was done up and curls arranged neatly around her face. She hadn't gone to this much trouble in years with her appearance. Indeed, Giles's presence rolled back time more than a decade.

Still, trepidation filled her as she patted her hair and smoothed the navy-blue chintz fabric of her skirt. Rather than meet Giles's gaze, she called to Philip. "Son, come here and say your farewells to Mr. Prescott."

Philip continued to chase Elise, her blond braid flying behind her. The once-shy little girl smiled with delight, and her son glanced over his shoulder. He'd heard her. Maggie was sure of it.

"Philip! Where are your manners? Come here, right now."

Giles's grin showed his amusement as he tried to take her hands, but she held them out to guide her son between this unsettling man and herself. She squeezed Philip's shoulders.

Giles didn't squat to her son's level, but he extended his hand to Philip. "It's been a pleasure getting to know you, young man."

"Thank you, Mr. Prescott." Another squeeze. "It's been nice getting to know you too." He took Giles's hand for a short shake. Then Philip looked up at Maggie. She could tell when her son stretched the truth as the misery seeped from his eyes and downturned mouth.

"Go on, now." She pushed him back toward his friend, who giggled and stood at a distance with hands behind her back. What girl wouldn't feel shy around this man's commanding presence? Soon their yelling and laughing rang out again.

Giles grasped both of her hands. "Let's walk for a bit. In the garden, perhaps?"

She nodded and let him place her hand in the crook of his arm.

"I was hoping you'd given more thought to my proposition." He tilted his head toward her.

The soft swish of parting blades of grass under their shoes turned to the scraping against the gravel path. They passed between hedges of Rose of Sharon in a riot of pink blooms and blue hydrangea fading away. The path opened to circle around a patch of flowers—yellow snapdragons and red roses, hearty daisies, and marigolds, to name a few.

"I have been thinking, but I still need time. It's a huge decision, and I certainly can't leave until Sophie's confinement is completed. She'll need help with an infant, besides her little one to care for."

"Understandable. But what else concerns you?"

She worried her upper lip, as her lower one was sore from chewing. "I don't know anything about Chicago. Where will we live? Besides, Philip is used to having me home here. If I were to open a bakery, it wouldn't be a problem as we would live above it. I know just the building in our hometown."

"Ah." Giles cleared his throat like a politician getting ready to deliver a persuasive speech. "There is a lovely town home not far from where I live. We can travel to work together. I'll see you're there safely each day. Your salary will be adequate to engage a housekeeper or, at the very least, a maid. Someone would be there to see the boy off to school and be there when he gets home."

"But it's not the same as having his mother there." She hoped her gaze held the sternness she wanted to convey. Her son often said how good her baking smelled when he arrived home from school. The conversation they had over cookies and milk or tea made her a greater part of his little world away from the house.

"We'll find a solution. I am looking forward to knowing you better as I once did, showing you the museums and other wonders the big city has to offer." His eyes glowed with a wolf-like hunger, and her heart skipped a beat. "You and Philip would want for nothing, Maggie. I would see to that."

"What are you saying?" She blinked as he stopped near the bench in the garden and folded her into an embrace.

"Do you think I would go to all this trouble if I weren't thinking long-term?"

"You mean—" Before she could utter the word *marriage,* he placed a finger over her lips.

"One thing at a time. We're not children. We've been in the world. No need to rush into anything." His hand slid to her cheek, then cupped her chin. His kiss was soft and gentle. He pulled back this time, gazing into her eyes.

"Could it be your eyes have grown more beautiful over the years?"

As he backed away, she left her lips parted, still tingling from the kiss. Then Maggie blinked again. She inhaled and came out of this trance being with Giles lured her into.

"I have to think of Philip. I'm all he has."

Giles gripped both of her hands. "Have you ever considered boarding school for the boy?"

Maggie's mouth fell open farther...for quite a different reason.

CHAPTER 24

'll be back soon. Giles's final words reverberated in Maggie's head with each revolution of the buggy wheels. His tone ominous and unforgiving, he'd misunderstood her tears. She gripped her reticule in one hand and a fan in the other as Mr. Starks steered the conveyance.

Giles Prescott meant for her to make a difficult choice.

Giles reminded her of home and the past, and the promises of youth all wrapped up together. His handsomeness didn't hurt. Plus, he still found her attractive. They could converse about Buffalo and all their old acquaintances and family for hours. He was comfortable in one way and dangerous in the other. And he lacked understanding about her conundrum over Philip.

Send him to boarding school? Unthinkable. I won't even entertain the thought.

Her gut churned, and her heart flip-flopped, but not in a good way. The increasing heat and her headache hadn't helped as the buggy pulled along. Each bump in the road a torture. What a time to be out of headache powder...and aspirin.

Thankfully, Mr. Starks drove the buggy into town as she sat back and fanned herself.

After the disagreement with Thomas over her dinner invitation a few weeks ago, an invisible wall had erected between them. Yet Maggie missed the Harper brood and welcomed the thought of seeing them. She hurt from keeping her distance. She was grateful Abby stopped by on occasion and they'd even made cookies together for her to take home, but she missed the rest of the family. What had caused the sudden coldness in Thomas?

"You can let me off at the pharmacy, Mr. Starks."

"Very well, ma'am." The stoic butler tipped his hat and slowed down in front of Harper Apothecary, where she alighted from the buggy.

Thud thunk, thud, thunk, thud, thunk. The loud noise came from around back.

Maggie hiked up the hem of her skirt as she stepped quickly across the boardwalk and onto the dirt path leading toward the rear of the building. Two skinny boys, Josiah and Lyle, to be exact, awkwardly wielded axes on a large log and made little progress.

"Oh, my." Maggie placed her hand to her mouth. She'd never seen the Harper children work so hard before.

Zeke plucked endless weeds from a long unkempt garden patch. His face lit with a smile when Maggie came into the backyard. "Mrs. Galloway." He waved the handful of greenery as he came toward her.

The other two boys dropped their tools and came running. "Hello, Mrs. Galloway," they called in unison. Josiah wiped sweat from his forehead. Lyle's and Zeke's faces were streaked with dirt.

One by one, their eyes grew dull with disappointment as they looked to her hands.

"You didn't bring us cookies?" Zeke piped up to say what

must be on all their minds.

"No, not today. Perhaps tomorrow. I came to see your father. What I mean is, I need some things from the apothecary. What is all this you are doing out here?" On such a fine summer day, these spirited boys needed some recreation.

"I'm glad you're here—even without cookies." Josiah bumped Zeke with his elbow as if to say his little brother should know his manners better. "You've got to talk to Pa."

"Yeah, he's acting like something's not right with his head." Lyle pushed his way to the front.

"You mean 'yes,' and you must be more respectful toward your father." She nodded toward Lyle. "What's wrong?"

"He's always punishing us." Josiah rubbed the back of his neck, and his gaze traveled to the ground. "He's been turning our house into an army camp, and he yells all the time."

How strange. Maggie didn't want to say the words aloud and fuel the fire of their disrespect. A breeze cooled her neck. The pounding in her head had calmed, now replaced by a fluttery sensation of worry in her chest. What was Thomas up to now? There was nothing wrong with hard work, but this was unusual for the Harpers.

"You best continue your chores while I go speak to him."

An almost comical collective sigh emanated from all three boys. They trudged back to their chores as though they were each a miniature Atlas carrying the weight of the world on their shoulders.

Maggie knocked on the back door, but nobody answered. Well, she'd let herself in many times before. Hopefully, it wouldn't be an affront to Thomas.

"Hello?" She cracked the door open and peeked into the darker interior, blinking as her eyes adjusted from the bright sunlight. The scrape of a brush on plaster drew her gaze to Abby in a stained apron, scrubbing the hallway wall. "Abby?"

"Mrs. Galloway, I'm so sorry I didn't hear you." She dropped the brush in the bucket, wiped her wet red hands on her apron, and nearly flew into Maggie's arms.

"Dear girl, what is wrong?" She hugged Abby tight, happy to be a comfort to her young friend, who sniffled.

Abby wiped tears from her face, pulling away a bit. "I don't know what's come over Papa. He's changed. I don't mind some chores, but he's given us so many. If we so much as give him an odd look... He used to be so patient. It's like he's not the same... Papa...I used to know. I hardly even have time to read anymore. If we don't do everything almost perfect, he won't even read to us at night like he used to. And he stopped smiling again." Such woebegone puppy eyes the girl gave her.

Maggie's headache pounded anew. Had this happened because she'd stayed away, hoping to give Thomas some breathing room to get over his ill-temperedness? He recovered well from his physical illness, but the children might be right about his head.

She marched toward the front of the store like a mother hen ready to defend her own chicks. "Thomas Harper."

There he was with a pencil behind his ear, rearranging stock on the shelves.

"Maggie?" The irritation in his tone almost equaled hers. "What is it?"

"Did you know Abby is crying? And the boys think you've lost your mind?" On the one hand, this wasn't any of her business. On the other, her great affection for the children—and she had to admit, for Thomas—prodded her into the middle of the situation.

"Because I've put them to work? Hmm? I'm finally keeping these children in order. I thought you would like that." He glared at her, his hazel eyes steely again.

"I-I only wanted to help you get organized. I wanted to give the children a united purpose in helping you, especially Abby." She crossed her arms, glaring back.

"All I've done is put a little order into our home, our lives. Look around you. Has the store ever looked better?" He swept his arm outward.

The marble-slab counter and glass knobs on the soda fountain gleamed as the sun's rays glinted off each one. Boxes were neatly stacked. Any trace of smoke had been scrubbed from the tin ceiling, the whitewashed walls, and any paneling. No mud encrusted the floor or the rugs.

"I'm quite pleased with the results of my experiment." Thomas snapped up a rag and polished the one slight streak from the counter. He pointed a finger at her. "For the first time, my sons are obeying me, and Abby isn't daydreaming constantly."

A suppressed sob escaped from the hallway.

"At what cost?" Maggie balled her hands into fists at her sides.

"At what cost?" He threw the rag under the counter after repeating her question. Then he laughed—in her face.

She stepped back and clasped her hands to her chest. "This isn't like you." She shook her head, blinking back unbidden tears.

"I'm tired of worrying about what they'll do next." He came out from around the counter to fuss with the merchandise on the shelves. "With snakes, banana peels, and...a near-drowning. They are busy and safe now. Idle hands are the devil's workshop."

"They are hurting. They want their true father back. Would it hurt for them to have a little fun? This is not you, Thomas." Maggie choked out the words with such emotion it surprised her. "They still miss their mother."

Thomas froze, and then turned slowly. "What business is it of yours, Maggie Galloway? Where have you been? You have practically deserted us while you sneak around with that dandy, Prescott."

He'd hit her with the truth like a brick thrown through a window. She clasped her waist. Her corset seemed to cinch all the more with the pain.

"And what do you know of my business?"

"My daughter, my children, can't afford to have their hearts broken again."

"I haven't exactly felt welcomed or needed around here lately." She fished a handkerchief from her reticule. "I might as well go to Chicago for the job Mr. Prescott offered me." Maggie turned on her heel before Thomas could see the flood which threatened to blur her vision and made her way toward the exit. "I don't understand you—having those boys chopping wood when you have a coal stove."

She slammed the door closed behind her. *Oh, bother, I've forgotten my headache powder.* Well, whatever home remedy she could cook up would have to do.

CHAPTER 25

As Maggie slammed the door behind her, the bell over the door clattered to the floor. Always something when the auburn-haired spitfire came around. Thomas left his work behind the counter to clean up the mess by the door.

Abby's stifled sobs sent a strange prickly feeling through his chest. Frustration overtook him and sadness flooded him at the same time. He turned to see his daughter wiping her eyes with the back of her hand. Her eyes widened, and she backed away as though retreating in terror.

"I'll g-g-get back to scrubbing the wall right away, Papa." She hastened back to her station. Her sniffling could be heard above the soft swish of the brush on the floor.

Thomas bent to collect the pieces of hardware. The bell had rolled across the floor, the clapper clanking its tinny sound against the sides. The discordant noise ceased when he picked it up, his hand closing around the offending item. He sighed. Gray light peeked through the front window while clouds partially obscured the sunlight, as they often did in Michigan.

He watched Abby over his shoulder for a moment. His sensitive daughter, who often smiled just at the chance to read another book. She showed her love for him, and her exasperating brothers, in a quiet way each day, as she made them breakfast or helped the boys with their homework. Now, she bent over the bucket like some beat-down washerwoman. Even the boys trudged around, too tired to fight him about bedtime at the end of the day, despite the lengthened daylight. Did he really like having such dispirited children?

Thomas picked up the hanger with its curved scrollwork and the nails which had held the bell in place. He'd depended on these pieces of metal working in unison each day, letting him know a customer had arrived. When the door was closed properly, there had been no problem. But once Maggie slammed it, everything had fallen to the ground, useless. Sure, it was old and probably should have been replaced or tightened properly before they'd opened shop.

Yet had he done the same thing to the children, coming down too hard on them? Nothing before had gained their cooperation. For once, they were all behaving. Plopping the items on the counter, he ran a hand over his face and then drummed his fingers on the counter.

Could he ever figure out the right way to be a father?

Thomas strode back toward his workroom and touched Abby's shoulder. "Take a break. That dirt will still be there later." He bent and patted her on the back. "Go tell your brothers to go fishing or find some game to play on such a nice summer day."

"Truly, Papa?" Abby's eyes brightened as she stood and wiped her hands on her apron.

"And I think you, most of all, need to find a good book to read. Get yourself some lemonade." Thomas couldn't help but smile at her obvious relief.

"Thank you, Papa. I'll dispose of this dirty water first, of course." She clasped her hands together and grinned.

"No, little dove, I will take care of the water. You go on now."

Thomas grasped the bucket handle. His heart crumpled a little. It wasn't that long ago, Abby would have thrown her arms around him in joy, but now she held back. What had he done to his little family?

~

*P*erhaps something in town caused Maggie's headache. After all, her eyes were watering something awful. She blinked away the blurry vision to no avail. *Oh, bother!* She fiddled around with the opening of her reticule, hoping to find a clean handkerchief.

She stared down at the skirt of her favorite day frock. The sheen of the cloth had grown lackluster. Washing and pressing helped little.

She walked several steps down the sidewalk before she caught a glimpse in the window of Millie's Fine Fashions of a gown in sage green with a delicate design in the weave, as pretty as damask, but perhaps lighter weight. The trim silhouette must be a newer fashion. While the mannequin boasted an *S*-shape, it wasn't as exaggerated as the Gibson girl. The wide, lace-covered lapels went from the neckline, one crossing over the other, down to the narrowest part of the waist. Not only smart but very feminine.

Such a lovely dress would be perfect whether visiting the test kitchens of the Silver Leaf Flour Company or meeting with the realtor in Buffalo. Would it hurt to go in and look at it? She only wanted a quick look. With the baby coming soon, Sophie didn't have the time or energy to make her a new outfit, and Maggie didn't possess that skill level in sewing.

Maggie pulled the door open quietly, so as not to take Millie Wilson's attention away from Georgina Blanding's conversation. She snuck around the corner toward the window as the two matrons cackled—over some unsavory piece of gossip, most likely.

"Shhh," Millie Wilson shushed her friend.

Maggie did her best to ignore them and touched the sumptuous sleeve with its matching lace trim around the opening. The slightly puffy sleeve ended around the elbow. This would be delightful for the coming days of August. As she was about to examine the price tag, Mrs. Blanding cleared her throat. Unfortunately, the sound moved in her direction.

Maggie looked up. "Yes, Georgina?"

"How are you today, Maggie?" The woman picked imaginary lint from her sleeve, or so it looked to Maggie.

"Quite fine, thank you. And you?" She dropped the sleeve on which the price tag was pinned, any pretense of buying the beautiful summery gown put aside after seeing the amount.

"Well enough." Mrs. Blanding squared her shoulders, and Mrs. Wilson stood behind her with a hand on her left hip and pursed her lips. With the two of them gearing up for battle, she was outnumbered but for the grace of God. Maggie remembered well why she preferred to pay Sophie for her services.

"Good to hear. I was admiring this gorgeous dress. I wish I had time to try it on, but I really must get going. If you ladies will excuse me, I'll be on my way." She flashed them a little smile and waved with a small flourish of the damp hanky she held. She wouldn't waste her time with Millie and Georgina's gossip or be interrogated by them.

"Not so fast." Georgina Blanding scooted sideways as though to block her exit.

"I have much to do." She could see the buggy parked a little way down the street as she slid her glance toward the window.

"Where is your gentleman friend? Mr. Prescott?" Millie took an ominous step toward her.

"Mr. Prescott is on his way back to Chicago."

"Well, next time you talk to him, please tell your profligate friend to stay away from the daughters of this fine town." Georgina narrowed her eyes.

"What? Giles Prescott has been nothing but a gentleman during his visits." Maggie wanted to say, *perhaps your daughters are too flirty,* but she pressed her lips together.

"He comes into town with his newfangled automobile, tempting our youth into thinking they can run off with no responsibility." Mrs. Wilson's chin jutted upward.

"Not that it's any of your business, but Mr. Prescott asked to court me as a young man and did nothing improper toward me...ever. You'll have to excuse me now." Maggie pushed past the other two women.

Her hand shook as she grasped the handle on the dress shop door. She would never enter there again.

The position in Chicago looked better by the minute.

CHAPTER 26

"So how are the plans coming with the orphanage?" Maggie asked Gloria over tea at Apple Blossom House the next morning. She stifled a yawn. She hadn't slept well since Giles left, and even less after her run-in with Thomas yesterday.

"Quite well. We didn't want it too far away from the unwed mothers' home or too far from town, so we found a piece of property in between." Gloria snapped a small napkin across her lap before she placed a slice of buttery-yellow cake on her plate. "And Asa has secured someone to do the brick work. The children will need a sense of permanence in their lives, and Lord willing, we shall provide it."

With the silver pie server, Maggie scooped a little cherry tart onto the plate offered her. Since she'd had her oatmeal early with Philip, her stomach rumbled. She'd not seen Gloria so animated—ever, as far as she could remember.

"We've had some generous donations to go along with the money we were able to set aside."

The sweet, tangy filling and delicate pastry nearly melted

over Maggie's tongue. Like life, the sour and sweet merged together.

Pounding on the back door resounded through the house.

"Dear me, it sounds as though someone is trying to break the door in." Gloria stood and folded her napkin, setting it on her plate.

"Like the big bad wolf, perhaps?"

The maid, Betty, came in. "A man has delivered a package from Mrs. Wilson's dress shop. I'm afraid he won't leave until he speaks to Mrs. Galloway."

"What?" Maggie stood, her napkin falling to the floor.

"I will settle this." Gloria waved her hand, but Maggie followed through the foyer and hallway to the generous kitchen in the back.

A large man, dusty from the road, smiled with a gap-toothed grin and tipped his hat, filling the doorway.

"I'm Maggie Galloway. How may I help you?"

"Greetings, madam. I've brought you this here delivery." He handed her a large box, then coughed and put out his tattered-gloved hand.

"B-but I didn't order anything."

"Don't know much about it, 'cept it's a gift." His acrid breath blew into her face, and she winced.

Gloria jangled a couple of coins into her own hand before dumping them in the stranger's. "Off with you now, back to the dress shop. And don't spend your tip on strong drink." Her quiet but stern command was enough to even unnerve Maggie.

Once the door closed behind him, Gloria clasped her hands together. "What is it?"

Maggie placed the box on the table and took the paring knife Betty offered. She sawed through the string, her heart pounding. Why would Millie send anything to her after what had occurred between them yesterday?

Finally, the fibers gave way with a pop. Maggie stared at the sage-green dress with its elegant lace-covered lapels.

"Ma'am?" Betty held the folded note card out. Gloria moved to look over her shoulder.

Maggie let the lid fall back into place before taking the message from the maid. She opened it with wonder. Who could have known she was looking at this gown just yesterday?

My dearest Maggie,

When I saw this elegant garment in the window of the dress shop before I left, I couldn't think of a better woman to wear it. With your auburn hair, green has always brought out your deepest beauty. You will bloom like a flower in it.

Highest regards,

Giles

Maggie gasped. Had Mrs. Wilson known all along that dress was meant for her? As much of a cad as the woman thought Giles, still, she happily took his money.

Maggie sank into a chair at the table with her hands grasping either side of the box.

"Betty, please clean up the tea." Gloria spoke more firmly than usual, but Maggie was relieved to be left alone with her friend.

"I can't keep it, can I?" She folded the note and held it to her chest.

"What is this all about?" Gloria's eyebrows met in a concerned frown. She sat in a chair next to Maggie and placed her hand on her arm.

"I saw this dress in the window yesterday. I went in to look at it and had to defend Giles against Georgina Blanding and Millie Wilson. They accused him of...well...of being a bad influence on the young women of Stone Creek."

Gloria averted her gaze and cleared her throat.

"What?"

Maggie's friend shook her head.

"Surely, you don't think the same thing of him, Gloria?"

"Maggie, I have my doubts about him."

"You barely know him."

"But do you know him like you used to?" Gloria quieted her voice. "He spent quite a bit of time under our roof, but he would leave from time to time. I would think he was with you, and then I would see you sitting alone on the front porch of the cottage mending or watching the children play."

A chill of dread lodged in her heart, like a shard of ice, but Maggie shook it off with memories of the warmth between them.

"Perhaps that was when he went on errands, such as to the shop to arrange to have the dress sent to me."

"There's not an easy way to say this, but the way he watched Irena at the opera during the intermission bothered me."

Maggie closed her eyes for a moment, steadying herself. The younger women had gathered and tittered like birds, swirling on the first floor with their different-colored gowns below. Irena had been swathed in a deep pink, layered with chiffon. They'd pointed toward Maggie and Giles, giggling like children. She'd done her best to ignore their silliness. Had Giles been flattered? Or shown any interest in them?

Opening her eyes, she creased his note. The crisp decisiveness of each letter seemed to take charge of the sheet of paper.

"Giles Prescott wooed me when I was a girl. My parents saw him as a young man with a future. For a time, I thought I might love him...but he was never serious about spiritual things...and then Robert came along." Maggie folded her hands on her lap, but not for long. She wriggled in the chair with discomfort. If she told Gloria that Giles had also been a flirt at times, the revelation would only give her friend more reason for concern.

The door bumped open with Betty carrying the tray with

the glasses of iced tea. Maggie gratefully took hers and nearly gulped it.

"Would you prefer a little water?" The sincerity in Gloria's eyes comforted Maggie.

She nodded in response, and Betty took her glass to refill it. "He asked me again to come work in the Silver Leaf test kitchen, offered me the proverbial sun and the moon..."

"And marriage?" Gloria tilted her head toward Maggie.

She swallowed, not caring for the answer she had to give. "Well, he hinted at it, as though it were too early to discuss." Maggie couldn't even bring herself to share how he'd suggested boarding school for her beloved Philip.

Gloria stood and paced a bit in the large country kitchen. "I don't like it, Maggie. I'm concerned he's taking advantage of you. You're lonely—"

"What?" Maggie rose and looked her friend in the eye as Betty set her glass of water on the table. "I have Philip. I'm not lonely."

"You know it's not the same. Besides, not so long ago, you wanted to open a bakery in Buffalo. But with your Mr. Prescott sweeping into town and having the gall to completely change your plans without any real promise of a future together...I don't like it." Unusual for Gloria to stand toe to toe with her and use such a tone of voice.

"Maybe the Lord sent him along to keep me from going completely off on my own. Besides, this could be a great stride for females in the business community. Who says I need him once I get settled in Chicago?"

Gloria shook her head. "I suppose this means you've made up your mind?"

Maggie shrugged, unsure of the right answer. What was most convenient didn't always line up with what was best, did it?

~

*T*homas Harper checked the bell to make sure it was secure over the door once more. He'd had the boys polish the brass pieces yesterday evening so they sparkled like never before. In fact, it looked almost brand new. But checking it made him think of Maggie.

She'd never purchased what she'd intended to. His fault? He kneaded the tense muscles in his neck. After what he'd said to her, she'd probably go to the next town before she darkened his doorstep again. All because he'd been stubborn, as usual.

But he couldn't afford to see the children hurt again. They needed more stability. Of course, he would let up on the chores a bit. And let them have a little fun during the summer. He'd figured out how to repair a bell over the door and was even getting the hang of dealing with the soda fountain and its many hoses, but he wouldn't let any of them suffer from a broken heart again any time soon.

Or am I more worried about my heart?

Thomas's heart beat in the quiet of the room. The children's voices floated down the stairs. For a change, they weren't fighting but working together on breakfast. Perhaps his little experiment had borne some fruit.

But he found himself alone, even surrounded by the children. How long had it been since he'd held Bess close? Felt their hearts beat in sync with one another? The children would grow up and leave. But so would Maggie, apparently. She was only too willing to take off. Hadn't they meant anything to her?

Maggie Galloway had marched into his store, nursed him back to health, and helped cheer and guide Abby. And now she had the gall to consider leaving them behind for Chicago.

Thomas opened a small drawer looking for a salve he wanted to put out on the shelf. It slid out smoothly. The interlocking pieces of the face and the sides fit together. If even one piece weren't quite right, the drawer wouldn't work properly. He retrieved the several small tins he'd been looking for. When Maggie left, things didn't work the same. He pushed the drawer too hard, and it stuck.

"Of course, you won't cooperate." Thomas spoke to the drawer, as ridiculous as that was. He grasped the handle and tugged it out, then took a deep breath and guided the drawer back into its grooves and slid it into place.

If only life were that predictable. Do things carefully, the right way, and everything turns out. But somewhere in the scheme of things, life wasn't like carpentry or chemistry. And the God Thomas once thought he believed in seemed farther away than ever. After all, He'd seemed to send Maggie, but then she'd probably leave, just like Bess.

"Mr. Harper?"

If the bell had rung, he hadn't noticed it, but he turned to find Mr. Frost in the doorway.

"Isn't the paregoric helping Wyatt?"

"It isn't my boy. It's my daughter, Emmy. She's got a fever. You have something for her?" The nervous man removed his hat and fussed with the brim.

"I can give you something to help her feel better right away."

Of all the medicines crowding his store shelves, none could fix his heart—or his life. Did God even consider his trials? As Thomas headed for his storeroom, he sent a prayer up. *Well, if you're there, God, I could sure use Your help.*

~

*A*fter a few hours of contemplating what Gloria had said and feeding her son dinner, Maggie decided it was time to do what she dreaded the most. Go to Ian for his advice.

The bloom was off her favorite rose along the picket fence in front of the parsonage. She fingered the wilting bright-pink petals, their edges rusty. Some fell to the ground, but she caught a few and brought them to her nose. Even the fragrance had faded, barely hanging on like a distant memory of something you thought was good, but maybe hadn't been, after all. Droplets of rain left from the afternoon's storm dampened the fingers of her gloves.

Laughter tickled her ears as she arrived at the front door and knocked. This had been her home for almost two years. Here she'd gotten to know her brother better, and she had gained a dear friend—eventually, a sister—in Sophie. She liked to think the Lord had used her to help them come together. So why was it so difficult to humble herself under her little brother's tutelage? Or, at the very least, his educated opinion?

Giving the door a little push, she announced herself through the crack. "Hello. I'm just stopping by for a quick visit."

"Aun' Maggie!" As Caira came running, Maggie swung the door open and caught the sweet little girl in her arms. "Cookie?" Caira grinned and held her hands up.

"No, my dear little one, but I promise to bring some next time I come."

Caira's lip went out, and she tilted her head, melting Maggie's heart even more.

"I apologize. She can be quite a tyrant about sweets." Approaching from the hall, Ian shook his head. "So good to see you." He bent to kiss her cheek.

"And you...dear brother."

"What? I've graduated, then? No more 'little brother'?"

She rolled her eyes at his mock-crestfallen expression. "You'll always be my *younger* brother, won't you?" She raised an eyebrow at him. "But for now, I need some grown up advice from my pastor."

The sweet tones of Sophie's beautiful voice wafted through

the air as she sang "Come, Thou Fount of Many Blessings." Water splashed about with the clanking of stoneware from the kitchen in the back of the house as she washed dishes.

"Sophie, I'll be in the study with Maggie," Ian called out to her.

"Hold on a moment." Sophie waddled into the parlor, becomingly pink cheeked, drying her hands on a towel. Dampness streaked the apron covering her blossoming abdomen. "Maggie, I didn't know you were stopping by. Would you like some lemonade? And I do have sugar cookies—your recipe, of course." She smiled, and as she drew closer, Sophie's dark circles showed more clearly.

"No, no. I stopped by unannounced. I only need a few minutes of Ian's time. You're welcome to listen too."

"Let me take Caira out of the way. It will be easier for you both then." Sophie reached for her daughter.

"No, Mama." Caira's bottom lip protruded.

"Maggie needs to talk to Papa. You and I will look at the kitten book and put together a puzzle."

"O-tay." But the little one looked with longing back at them as she held her mother's hand and went toward the parlor.

Maggie never thought she'd be one to sit across from her brother at his desk after he'd led her into his cozy study. "Really, we can sit in the parlor."

"I want to give you my undivided attention, Maggie. After all, it's not often you ask for my advice." He sat forward, placing an elbow on the desk and his chin in his hand. "You look upset." Ian stared right into her with brows furrowed.

She nodded as she took her seat. She removed her gloves and tucked them into her reticule.

"Would it have something to do with Mr. Prescott?" Ian turned away for a moment and picked up his pen, setting the nib in its stand. He moved the paperweight around while he waited for her answer.

She swallowed. He knew. Was she always so transparent? She couldn't meet her brother's gaze when it returned to her. Maggie stared at the dark paneling on the wall she'd once polished. Then she looked to the mahogany desk where the waning light of evening softened the light sheen of dust. Moving her fingers across the edge, Maggie drew a line and exhaled.

"What do I do?"

"What do you mean, exactly?" Her brother's eyes softened with concern as a wistful smile crossed his face.

Did she really expect he would know her thoughts? The line she cleared from the little bit of dust grew deeper. Where would she begin?

"I believe I've told you of Giles's offer of a job in the Silver Leaf test kitchen in Chicago."

Ian nodded as she explained the promises Giles had made as well as inferred and how she'd grown impatient for news about a loan for the bakery in Buffalo.

"Then this dress arrived at Gloria's door for me this morning. I don't even know when he asked for it to be sent. I saw the dress displayed in the window the first time yesterday, but I don't feel I should accept it. I mean, what does that say about me?" *What kind of woman would receive such a personal gift without a formal engagement?*

Maggie brushed the light coating of dust from her fingertips with her thumb.

"Was there anything else before I tell you what I think?" Ian moved the paperweight toward her almost like a chess piece on a board.

"Gloria thought she saw him flirting with some of the girls in town, but I can't imagine he would lower himself to such behavior, can you?"

Ian's eyes narrowed, almost imperceptibly, and his jaw muscles tightened. "Maggie, instead of answering your question, I'm going to ask you one. How does Giles feel about your faith? Has that ever changed?"

"Sounded more like two questions to me." Maggie curled her lips into a smirk.

Light rain struck the window. Ian stood and wandered toward the pattering on the glass pane. "You and I both know it was an issue all those years ago."

Maggie stood and turned around to face Ian. She leaned back against his desk. "He came to church with me...once."

"Yes, I remember." Ian wandered back toward Maggie and grasped the back of the chair she had sat in. "But I'm guessing there's more to it than that. What do you really believe about his spiritual condition?"

Maggie averted her gaze. "Must you be so formal about all of it? I need advice on the best thing to do. Should I go to Chicago?"

"Maggie." Ian tilted his head, his look imploring. "You're asking me to trust a man I have suspicions about with my only sister's future. I'd hoped you'd see it yourself."

"But what should I do about financial security?"

The room darkened as the rain beat harder on the window. The overcast sky echoed the shadow on her heart. Ian moved closer and took her hand.

"You cared for him then, and you care for him now. I understand, but I'm concerned about his lack of commitment to you, and to God." Ian paused. "You were unsure of his feelings toward you back then, though his intentions appeared to be honest enough."

At the sound of a throat being cleared, Maggie turned to find her sister-in-law coming through the doorway. "Caira's quite happy with her puzzle for the moment. I thought I'd see if I could help. Is this about Mr. Prescott?"

Maggie wanted to hug her for interrupting the tense

moment with Ian. Instead, she touched Sophie's arm. "You are always welcome."

Though quite a bit younger, Sophie had been through a great deal. She and Caira, her illegitimate daughter, the result of being raped by a cad, had run from town to town before they were able to settle in Stone Creek.

"There's something about him." Darkness clouded her amber eyes. "He reminds me—well, there's something about him that reminds me of Charles Warner." Her attacker. Her voice lowered to a whisper. She gripped the edge of the desk with whitened fingers. "Maggie, there's an arrogance about him...and I've seen how the other young women look at him."

And I suppose how he looks at some of them.

"He's handsome and successful. Wouldn't you expect them to?" Maggie countered.

Sophie shook her head. "I can't quite pinpoint it. But he seems almost too sure of himself, as though he expects to get what he wants and hasn't often been crossed." She paused, swallowing. "And there's always a possibility that if he doesn't get it right away, he'll find a way to take it at any cost." She let go of the frame and straightened, pulling a light shawl tighter around her shoulders.

"Don't be silly," Maggie sputtered. "I don't think he'd ever hurt someone, at least, not intentionally."

Sophie's eyes opened wider. Hurt etched her face. Maggie immediately regretted her comment when her sister-in-law had opened such a raw chapter in her life to her.

Ian pushed past Maggie to place an arm around his wife.

Maggie crossed her arms, loneliness enclosing her like a thick blanket. She stared at the floor, then made an effort to curl her mouth into a smile that probably came off more like a grimace. "I know you both mean well, but I'm not willing to give up on Giles yet. I've known him for a long time, Sophie."

"So have I." Ian's expression mirrored hers. "And I don't want him to take advantage of my favorite sister."

"Your only sister." She tried to chuckle, but an odd, guttural sound escaped her throat instead. "The rain is letting up. I'll head home now."

"Wouldn't you like to stay for tea? Perhaps some chamomile for your nerves?" Sophie's concern touched Maggie.

"I think I need a little air."

"I insist on walking part way with you." Ian's gaze brooked no argument.

Once Maggie had said her goodbyes to Sophie and Caira, she and her brother fell into step alongside each other, though she had to hurry to keep up with his longer stride.

Ian pushed his hands into his pockets, walking with his head down in the sprinkle of rain, reminding Maggie of him when he was a boy. Her heart softened despite her irritation.

"What's wrong now, besides not liking Giles?" Maggie scanned the street ahead.

"It's not only Giles's lack of commitment bothering me. We will miss you. I had hoped you would be around to help with the orphanage."

"It didn't bother you when I talked about going back to Buffalo to open a bakery."

"But the bakery was your dream, and Robert's family is still there."

"The most recent correspondence I've received isn't very hopeful about financing my dream. I have to think of financial security for Philip and me, you know."

Their feet squished along the moist dirt road as Ian shot a glance her direction. "And why can't you sell your baked goods here?"

She had no good answer for that—except that so many things would have to fall into place to make that happen, when it seemed Giles was already offering her the whole kit and caboodle. Besides, Ian would probably say something simplistic—that God would bring it all to pass here in Stone Creek if it was part of His plan. "I really must get back to the cottage. Thank you." Maggie gave Ian a quick hug, reaching up to peck him on the cheek.

"Pray about your decision, Maggie. Don't ever leave the Lord out of the equation," Ian called after her, and she bristled.

No one seemed to understand her need for security.

She'd sought Ian out for his advice. Had she really expected anything different from him? Or was she unsettled because of the niggling feeling in her heart that Giles's promises were too good to be true?

CHAPTER 27

Nibbling his apple pie, Thomas hid his glumness behind a copy of the *Stone Creek Herald*. Each time the door had opened since Maggie Galloway burst into his store four days ago, he'd looked up with the hope she'd come to apologize. Or, at the very least, tell him she'd changed her mind and decided to stay in Stone Creek. *Confounded woman.*

Beautiful woman. In heart as well as form. He couldn't deny that, even during her most irksome behavior. She'd even been right about his thyroid and, of course, his discipline of the children. Once he started taking medication for it, his energy had returned. How could she know him well enough to almost always be right about him?

He jumped at the pat on his arm. "Can we go?" Lyle wasn't usually as bothersome about things as Zeke or as likely to take charge of things as Josiah. No doubt, the other two had foisted the task of begging Thomas onto their middle brother.

"Lyle, how are you supposed to ask?"

"Can we please go, Pa?" Lyle waited with sad puppy eyes for the verdict. His imploring met silence. "Everyone's been telling us the show is so much fun."

"If your friends thought it would be fun to be bitten by a rattlesnake, would you sign up for that?"

"Huh?" Lyle scrunched his nose.

Thomas rubbed his chin. He'd like to finish his dessert in peace. "Where are your brothers and sister?"

"They're doing their evening chores." Lyle moved his weight from one foot to another and looked down.

"I see." Thomas folded the newspaper. The crisp sound of creasing paper punctuated the quiet between them. "And what about your chores?"

"I did them, Pa." The tone of his son's voice turned to a whine. "Can we?"

How many times had Bess taught them it was "may we" or "may I"? Thomas exhaled. "What is so *fun* about listening to a prevaricator of lies? He cheats people out of their money, giving them false hope over fake medicine." He sat straight in his chair at the head of the table and crossed his arms.

Lyle fell to his knees and clasped his hands as if in prayer. "I know Dr. Blaze isn't a real doctor or even a pharmacist, but he's supposed to be funny. And there's singing and dancing. It's a real humdinger!"

"The man is a swindler. He'll tell anybody anything to get their money." Thomas had a sense of being watched. He looked toward the kitchen entrance. Three more hopeful faces peered at him from the doorway.

His two older children snickered. "We told him probably none of it's true." Josiah waved away his little brother's comments.

Thomas stood, frowning. "Then why on earth did you send Lyle to do your bidding?"

Josiah shrugged with practiced nonchalance. "We all want to go."

Thomas stroked his chin. "I'll tell you what. We'll go to see the show tomorrow night."

"Yay!" His children sang out in chorus. The boys jumped up and down while Abby clapped.

"We're going to see *Mr.* Blaze for one reason and one reason only." Thomas raised his voice above the cheers and wagged his finger at them. The children stilled. "I'm going to show you that it's all really a con game to make money."

And maybe, just maybe, he'd run into someone much more important at this sideshow.

~

When evening descended the next day, Main Street hadn't seen so much excitement since the Fourth of July parade. Patent medicine shows usually arrived with a flourish and so-called *Doctor* Blaze's was no exception. Two horses that must have been combed until their coats shone, with manes braided, pranced down the center of the thoroughfare, heads held high. Their hooves kicked up dust from the road, which had dried in the summer heat after recent storms. They pulled a shiny barn-red wagon, with its blue trim and bright-yellow letters, harnesses jangling.

Thomas adjusted his straw boater to keep the sun from his eyes. A girl in buckskins and moccasins, with long black braids, sat atop the wagon and waved. She shook a tambourine. A man of rather diminutive stature played a banjo. He held the instrument at an awkward angle, as though it was rather large for him. His oversized suit hung on him. He wriggled his handlebar mustache. It nearly matched that of the wagon's driver who sat on the lower bench. They played a rousing chorus of "Oh Susanna."

"Whoa!" the driver called. "How-dee, citizens of Stone Creek!" Dust flew as he tipped his cowboy hat. "We're so happy to be here." He stood with the reins in one hand, though the wagon rocked a bit. When he raised his hand, the musicians above him stopped. "I'm Dr. Blaze. My crew and I are here to amaze and entertain you with miracle cures and jocularity. Don't go away. As soon as my horses are cared for, I will return."

One horse bucked a little and then the other.

Dr. Blaze had difficulty maintaining his balance. His backside slammed into the seat of the wagon. He winced, righted himself, and straightened his hat. "My mighty steeds are feeling their oats, or should I say, hungry for some. Let's give a hand to Maisy and Goldenrod." The large gentleman bowed to the chuckling crowd and dismounted before things got worse.

"Maybe you'll need some of your liniment!" a heckler called.

"Why, I've already covered my whole body in it. I am feeling almost no pain."

Thomas rolled his eyes. He couldn't help but say something to Abby, who held onto his arm. "I'll bet."

The little man and the girl in the buckskins scrambled down and took care of the horses while *Dr. Blaze* disappeared into the wagon. People of the town crowded the whole block.

The little man and the Indian maiden returned, bursting once again into song. At the back of the wagon, a plume of blue smoke exploded. As the vapor drifted away, Dr. Blaze appeared in a fresh suit, a bowler on his head.

"Hear ye, hear ye! Citizens of Stone Creek, I have traveled far and wide, from the mysterious mountains of west and east, and the plains where the buffaloes roam." He strutted around to the side of the wagon while the young woman shook her tambourine. "I come with the secrets of the great medicine men, the proven cures of the women of the mountains."

"Unbelievable," Thomas mumbled under his breath.

"Papa, behave." Abby smiled up at him, mischief in her eyes.

The boys paid rapt attention, along with everyone else.

"Allow me to introduce my illustrious companions. Princess Firefly, daughter of the chief of the Kickapoo tribe."

Yeah, right, more likely the daughter of the president of the Kickapoo Indian Medicine Company. Thomas couldn't help the cynicism that crept into him.

As the sun faded toward the west, it illuminated a familiar face across the street. Maggie Galloway had removed her straw hat. Flowers overflowed the brim, and ribbons trailed from the back. She held her hand up over her eyes. Auburn curls lifted in the breeze and landed again to gently frame her face.

Philip stood next to her, waving at Thomas's sons. She'd spent so much time with his family, caring first for him, and then the children. How well did he know her son? Not as well as he'd like, admittedly.

But how good of a father would Giles Prescott be? Would he relish the idea of having a new son, or relegate the boy to some far-off place like David Copperfield?

Why do I even care? I have enough to do with my four children.

The crowd clapped, pulling Thomas from his reverie.

"And I also want you to meet Pint-size Pete, the fastest jig in these here United States."

The wiry man twirled, his feet a blur as he danced to the lively jig Princess Firefly played on the pipe. Pete flipped twice and accomplished not only a handstand but walked on his hands as though they were a second pair of feet.

Almost everyone clapped as Pete righted himself and tipped his hat to the crowd, bowing profusely.

"Yes, sir-ree, we are setting the world on fire with my patented Fire Elixir. Old Pint-Size here was confined to a bed with severe dyspepsia, symptoms of dropsy, and even the ague. His family thought he wasn't long for this world when I visited the town of Lungworm Gulch, Montana." Dr. Blaze strutted back and forth, holding up a bottle in one hand and a large spoon in the other for all to see. "They took the few coins they had left over from paying the doctor with. Then they came to me to buy a bottle of Fire Elixir for Pete. Within minutes, my friend here was up and about, and you see him now today."

Pint-size Pete repeated a jig to more applause. Princess Firefly shook the tambourine above her head.

"Today, yes sir-ree, this could be your day to be cured. Who wants to take a chance?" Blaze's voice rose and fell in cadence. "Well, do I have a volunteer?"

A middle-aged man Thomas hadn't seen before limped toward the wagon. He coughed as he reached toward Blaze. "I will." He wavered like a man about out of strength.

"This gentleman is a shill," Thomas told Abby, loud enough for the boys and anyone else to hear.

"And what is your name, sir?" Dr. Blaze put his arm around the man.

"Gus."

"And have we ever met before, Gus?"

"No, Dr. Blaze. Never." He shook his head so hard Thomas thought it might fly off.

With laborious movements, the charlatan unscrewed the cap off the bottle and poured a spoonful of dark liquid onto the silver spoon. Pete and the princess lit torches and planted them in holders at the corners of the wagon behind Dr. Blaze.

With a shaking hand, Gus took the large spoon and gulped the contents. "It's delicious." He croaked out the words as he held up the spoon. Then with a sputter and a wheeze, he smacked his chest. Waiting a few minutes, he made more loud sounds with his effort to breathe. He cleared his throat. "I can breathe clearly! My cough is gone.'"

Dr. Blaze patted his back. "Why, that's wonderful, sir."

"I feel tingles." Gus shook one leg and then the other. He walked in a circle. "My knee doesn't hurt no more neither!" He jumped up and down.

Several women gasped. "It's a miracle!"

"You've seen it for yourself, folks! Yes sir-ree, my Fire Elixir has healing properties like no other." Dr. Blaze's grin reminded Thomas of a snake going in for a kill.

"And if that don't convince you, I have somethin' else to show you!"

An older woman stepped out of the crowd toward the "doctor," waving a cane in one hand and holding an empty bottle in the other. "I used Fire Liniment on my back and knees, and I don't need this here cane anymore." She nodded, then held the bottle close to her chest. "Thank you, Dr. Blaze. May the good Lord bless you."

Something wasn't quite right about the old lady. What was it? She tossed the cane in the air, and Blaze caught it. Pint-size Pete took hold of the woman's arm, and they began to dance a jig. Where had Princess Firefly disappeared to?

Ah. The old woman patted her hair—no—a gray wig. Her dark eyes matched those of the supposed Indian maiden.

"Who wants to experience some miracles of their own? Two bits per large bottle and a dime for a small. The large is a bargain. More miracles than you can imagine in one bottle."

People pushed forward, holding up their coins. Blaze unlatched the top half of a door and folded down a board. Pete appeared in the window, ready to hand out the product.

Thomas could hold himself back no longer.

"Stop!" He pulled out of Abby's grasp and stepped around his sons to weave his way through the crowd. "Please, friends and neighbors!" He pushed to the head of the throng clamoring for these so-called cure-alls.

"Papa, no!" Abby called after Thomas while the boys each groaned.

"Why do you want to spend your hard-earned money on this false medicine?"

The large group quieted.

"But you've seen with your own eyes three examples of

cures. Do you want more?" The snake smile returned. Blaze was unmoved.

"You, sir." Thomas pointed in his direction. "Are a charlatan. And so are the rest of your crew."

Blaze threw his head back and guffawed. "Visit any of my customers tomorrow, and you will find them feelin' much better."

"Perhaps for the day." Thomas stepped closer, almost face to face with his opponent. "Anyone can convince themselves a pill, a potion, or a poultice will make them feel better for a time."

"Is that the kind of stuff you sell at Harper Apothecary?" a man's voice called out. Someone snickered.

"You and Dr. Moore are the only ones to lose out here!" someone else yelled out.

"Yeah!" A chorus of voices surrounded him as the sun slipped farther to the west, the sky growing darker.

In the face of confrontation, Thomas wavered. Then the flame of fury surged through him. He balled his fists and set his jaw.

"Have it your way, then, all of you. Allow this charlatan to sell you his panaceas. Waste your money, and then you'll be knocking at my door, or Dr. Moore's. But let it be known, I've warned you."

An arm went around Thomas. "Son, I think you need to let this one go." He turned and blinked in the waning light. Thad Moore nodded at him and pulled him aside as gently as one would guide a blind person. "For now."

"But—"

"Come along. Save your passion for when you need it." Thad patted him on the shoulder, pointing him toward home.

His children had disappeared from where they once stood.

"Mr. Harper!" Maggie dodged her way through the crowd,

showing up at Thad's side. "You did a brave thing confronting that charlatan. Didn't he, Dr. Moore?"

"Well, yes, but I'm concerned—"

"I know, the townspeople don't understand right now." She touched Thad's arm as though to stop him. "They're here for the show. But they may thank him someday. Right, Doctor?" She smiled, cheeks tinged with pink.

"Eventually." Thad grinned and looked between the two of them with understanding.

As the doctor turned away, leaving Thomas and Maggie alone on the fringe of the crowd, Thomas forced himself to set aside his embarrassment. Once again, Maggie had come to his rescue. He sighed and swiped his hand over his jaw. "I appreciate your encouragement, Maggie."

She smiled. "Of course. I think you did the right thing by speaking up, Thomas. It's hard to do so in a crowd like this, but who else would have told them the truth?"

The air hummed with a connection between them Thomas couldn't deny. Much as he'd like to find an excuse to linger at her side, to offer his arm and invite her for an evening stroll, awareness of his responsibilities nudged him. "Well. I must find where the children are off to." Not that they'd be happy to see him, after he'd made such a scene. "Have a good evening."

"You, too, Thomas." Maggie smiled with what looked like... admiration? Was it possible?

~

Thomas had shown more fortitude in the five minutes he'd stood up to the medicine man than Maggie had seen in him all during their acquaintance. There he'd stood in his slightly rumpled suit, making a stand against the chicanery of the snake-oil salesman taking advantage of the people of Stone Creek. As lines furrowed across his handsome face and his square jaw tightened with anger, a new side of Thomas had appeared.

It must've been inside him all along.

Back at home later that evening, Maggie smiled at the memory and wiped her brow with a clean handkerchief. The evening air hung like a damp blanket being wrung out from heaven above one drop at a time. The cool of the shade trees protecting the cottage offered blessed relief. She settled in while Philip went to Apple Blossom House to check on Gloria and Elise, who'd been unable to accompany them to the show due to feeling a bit under the weather.

The front door banged, and she stepped from the kitchen to intercept her son's running form in the hallway. "Philip, slow down, you're in the house now."

He tugged on her sleeve, breathless. "Mama, Mrs. Myles wants you to come see her. She said as quickly as possible." He spat the words out between the spaces of missing baby teeth.

"All right, then. You go wash up for bed, and I'll be back to say prayers with you shortly." Maggie intended to give Philip a quick hug, but her arms curled around him in a fierce gesture. The sweaty sweetness of his hair met her nose. The realization of time slipping through her fingers like so many grains of sand in an hourglass squeezed her heart into panic. "Give me a good-night kiss in case you fall asleep before I come back."

"Okay, Mama." He smiled and gave her a peck on the cheek.

She took her boy's face between her hands. The chubby baby cheeks were becoming leaner. Maggie planted a kiss on his forehead and met his eyes, wishing to convey all of a mother's love she could. "Go on, now."

She made her way across the yard and up the back path. Her steps faltered as Apple Blossom House came into view, for Gloria stood on the stoop, waving her arms, her face twisted into a look of terror.

CHAPTER 28

"*D*on't come too near." Gloria, whose complexion was usually a lovely peach color, had blanched to resemble her high-necked, starched white blouse. She pressed her lips into a straight line and blinked, though her eyes glistened, and she held her chin high.

"Whatever is wrong?" Maggie cried.

"Elise is very ill. I've sent for the doctor." She choked back a sob. "I've never seen her with such a high fever."

Oh no. "Is she delirious?"

"No, but she is listless. She was playing marbles with Philip earlier today. Oh, dear me, I hope he won't get sick now." Gloria covered her mouth.

"Gloria. You are one of my dearest friends. You're like a sister to me. Let me help you through this." Maggie stepped closer to her friend before she could protest and hugged her. Gloria would do the same for her.

Please, Lord, please heal Elise. Don't take her away when Asa and Gloria need her so.

"'The Lord giveth and the Lord taketh away.'" Gloria's tears brushed Maggie's face. "I know I must be brave and trust Him."

248

Life was tenuous at best. They'd all suffered the loss of loved ones and had to take care of one another. She took Gloria by the hand. "Let me see Elise now. Maybe I can help make her comfortable until Dr. Moore arrives."

As though Maggie was the elder, she pulled her friend along, passing a servant as they padded up the carpeted stairs between the thick oak banisters. A sturdy oak table stood between rooms in the hallway. Gloria stopped and grasped the edge of it, taking a deep breath, as though it fortified her before they walked farther.

When they reached the room at the end of the hall, Maggie found Asa in an oak rocker pulled close to the side of his grand-daughter's bed, his head bowed. He looked up when they entered, his eyes red-rimmed. "We thought she had a cold the last few days, but now she's so sick."

"Asa, get some rest. I'll help Gloria." Maggie waved him toward the door.

Frilly down comforters and a fluffy white pillow engulfed the child. Belgian lace trimmed the pillow cover, but all the finery in the world couldn't hide her sickness. Elise's cheeks, usually rosy from play, were flushed, her underlying pallor sickly. Maggie touched the girl's head, sweat pasting strands of blond hair to her forehead.

"I'm so cold, Grandma," Elise whimpered and gave an odd little cough.

"First of all, these are too many blankets. We have to get her cooled down." Maggie unbuttoned her sleeves and rolled them up.

Betty brought in a fresh pitcher of water and poured some into the bowl on the stand. She placed clean linens over a wooden bar on the stand.

"Would you mind bringing me an apron and some wash-cloths, please, Betty?"

"Yes, ma'am, Mrs. Galloway. I'm happy to." Betty gave a

slight curtsy, relief written on her smooth forehead and in her eyes. No doubt she was afraid of the illness and probably with good cause. "Our cook, Flo, already made some broth. Shall I bring that as well?"

Maggie nodded. "Wonderful. We have to get fluid down her."

Gloria stood, one hand pressed over her mouth, the other grasping a lace-edged handkerchief. Something had changed in her. Was this the time of year at which she'd lost Anna and Jared?

Maggie gave Gloria's elbow a soft tap as though trying to pull her back to the present. "Elise needs you. You need to think about her."

"Of course." Still, Gloria continued staring at her grand-daughter, tears making trails down her cheeks as she blinked, a faraway look consuming her eyes. "This makes me think of when Anna got measles as a little girl."

Elise inhaled and coughed and made a strange whooping sound at the end of her coughing fit. Maggie took the clean washcloth Betty had brought and doused it with cool water. She bathed the child's head. Poor Elise lay as limp as a dishrag, whimpering like a puppy after her coughing fit.

"So cold. Stop." Elise batted at Maggie's arm, trying to escape her ministrations by twisting her head away, but her weakness left her captive to Maggie's care.

"I'll hold her head up, but you must bring the cup over and help her take sips, Gloria."

As though in a trance, Gloria nodded and moved like an automaton. Taking a beautiful crystal glass, she poured from the pitcher and sat on the other side of the bed. The brightness of the kerosene light on the dresser reflected the concern in her eyes. Lines in her forehead gave away the worry over her precious granddaughter.

They'd kept her home with a tutor because of her shyness,

but Maggie suspected it was more than that. This way, they could protect their granddaughter even more, despite Naomi Oliver being a fine schoolteacher.

Maggie would stay the night if that were what it took for Gloria to get her legs under her again. "Has she had any white willow yet?"

"We're all out."

"Have Mr. Starks go to the cottage and ask Philip for the aspirin. My son will know where they are. We must get this fever down. And would you mind sending one of the servants to stay with him tonight until we know what we're dealing with?"

"Of course." Gloria nodded.

Maggie rinsed and wrung the cloth again, swathing the child's forehead, though she whimpered at the cool touch. She peeled off the top quilt, leaving only a cotton sheet over the little girl's shoulders. She would need that aspirin Thomas had convinced her take—and fast.

$\sim$

The day after the medicine show debacle, Thomas took the locked box of money from his office to stock the cash drawer for the day. He prepared the soda fountain and straightened the shelves. He'd gotten the hang of taking care of the shop, and Maggie's touch was obvious on every group of medications.

A twinge of guilt hit him in his chest...like an invisible hand had reached in and squeezed it until he could barely breathe. He ran his hand over his face and looked up at the clock. It was already noon, and not one customer had come through the door. Because of the way he'd refuted "Doctor" Blaze?

In a sense, even his children had turned away from him. All morning, their feet had clunked above as they scuffled around doing their chores. When it was very quiet, he'd worried they were up to something, but had found them reading, frowning every time they looked his way. Could they be terribly upset over the scene he made the evening before? After all, Thomas had been standing up for what he believed in...what was right.

"Pa?" Abby peeked around the corner at him. Her eyes were magnified through her glasses and growing prettier every day.

He couldn't help but curve his mouth into a grin as she entered the shop.

"I'm sorry, Papa." She ran to him, and they both opened their arms to an embrace. She buried her face in his shoulder. "I was kind of scared yesterday that everybody would wind up in a fight, but I should have stayed by you."

When she pulled back a bit, Thomas held her chin. "I'm afraid I embarrassed you children." He paused. "I'm sorry. I'm concerned about Blaze selling his overpriced poison...and possibly hurting someone."

She nodded. "It's all right, Papa. I know you meant well. The boys will come around."

"Good, then." He let his daughter go. His hands went up. "Look at this. No business this morning. I'm afraid I've caused a problem when I need to make sure there's enough for you to eat." He shook his head. "Maybe we should think about moving back to the city. Business hasn't taken off the way I thought."

"Papa, Mama always used to say you needed to be more patient." Her mouth quirked into half a smile. "Dr. Blaze will leave town, and everybody will forget about what happened. They'll be back."

The octagonal wall clock ticked as another minute passed. Thomas rubbed his chin. "I don't suppose anything would bring them back right now except for free samples of soda."

Abby grinned and her eyes brightened. "What an *extraordinary* idea."

"Did you think I was serious, Abby?" He couldn't help but

roll his eyes at her enthusiasm. "You, my dove, would give the whole store away."

"I would." She chuckled. "If it meant that people got to come in to realize how wonderful you are."

"I'm afraid you are prejudiced." Thomas shifted his weight, looking up again at the insufferable clock, contentedly clicking the seconds of his life away, reminding him how long the days were. "Since I have nothing but time at the moment, perhaps I should clean the clock."

He pulled a folded step stool from the corner and secured it against the wall below the clock. As he stepped onto it, Abby cleared her throat.

"Since we're not busy right now, could I go visit Mrs. Galloway?"

"It's a long walk, Abby." Thomas removed the timepiece from the wall, anxious to cease the incessant ticking for a while. He went to place it on a table he kept at the back of his storefront. He blew off the thin coating of dust.

"Maybe Miss Oliver would like to go with me." Abby moved behind him and folded the stool for him. It warmed his heart the child did it without even being asked.

"If Miss Oliver would go with you, then I would be fine with it." Thomas reached below the counter for a small wooden box. He opened it and extracted a small screwdriver. He turned the clock over with care. Perhaps he'd manage not to upset the balance of at least one thing in his life.

"All right, Papa."

Once Abby left, the boys slipped out the back door to go fishing. Thomas silenced the annoying clock, taking the works apart, oiling them, and putting each piece back with careful order.

Three hours later, his daughter burst through the front door. "Papa! Something terrible has happened to Elise!"

CHAPTER 29

"$\mathscr{E}$lise has whooping cough...and Miss Oliver told me that's what Emmy Frost has, and she's not doing very well." Abby gasped for breath as though she'd run all the way home. Her hat had fallen to her back, held fast only by the ribbons around her neck. She closed the door behind her, and a warm breeze whooshed its way inside the store.

"Abby, calm down." His heart pounded. How was another disease creeping through their quiet town? No sense in upsetting his daughter any more than she already was.

"But remember when Josiah and I had it? It wasn't any fun." She wiped the beads of sweat from her forehead with the back of her hand.

Somehow Bess and he had managed to keep the other two children from getting sick. They'd stayed with Bess's mother until the all-clear came from the doctor. A cloak of fear settled over his heart.

As Thomas climbed the step stool to place the clock on the wall again, the door swung open, jangling the repaired bell above it.

"Hello, Mr. Starks. May I help you find anything?" Abby

hung her bonnet on a hook and found her shop apron on the hook next to it.

Thomas stepped down. "It's all right, Abby. You need something cool to drink after your long walk. I'll help Mr. Starks." He did his best to smile at the grim butler.

"Yes, sir. Mrs. Galloway...that is, Miss Maggie." He stopped before continuing. "She sent me for a bottle of aspirin. Something to bring Miss Elise's fever down." Mr. Starks stood as stiff as an undertaker, unflinching. He removed his hat as though an afterthought.

"Aspirin, you say?" Thomas couldn't help himself. Only the grim news of Elise's illness kept his satisfaction in check. So he'd convinced the indomitable Maggie of the advantages to the tablets. He retrieved a jar of aspirin powder from the glass-doored cupboard. "I have a few tablets made in an envelope, but I'll gladly make some more and have Josiah bring them over shortly."

The man took out a pocket watch. "I will gladly wait, sir. It is a ways for the boy to go." He closed his watch as quietly as though closing the front glass casing on a fine grandfather clock.

"Have a seat, then." Thomas gestured to the nearby chairs before pulling his tablet press from the cabinet below the hutch.

"I'm quite fine standing, thank you." Starks gave a perfunctory, wooden smile. He paced before stopping and checking his pocket watch.

When at last the package had been properly wrapped, Thomas handed it over the counter.

"How much?"

"Let's put it on the Myleses' tab, why don't we?" Knowing Maggie listened to him for once was enough payment for the time being.

As Starks left, hopeful rays of sunlight illuminated the

white powder remaining on the work surface. Thomas cleaned up. In the corner of the counter, one lonely strand of hair shone in the sunlight. He lifted it with his index finger and thumb as though it were a china teacup handle. *Auburn.* The lone hair danced in the gentle exhalation of his breath, reminding Thomas of Maggie's curls tumbling around her face. The softness of her hair that day as he'd helped fix back into place haunted him.

"Papa? What's wrong?" Abby's question caught Thomas off guard.

He closed his fingers around the delicate filament and pushed his hand into his suit coat pocket. "Nothing. I'm almost done cleaning up." He looked away, keeping his hands busy restacking little boxes.

Why did he feel so guilty about his attraction to Maggie?

Concern and care for those in her life emanated from her with each smile. He admired her willingness to roll up her sleeves and help others. Along with the inner beauty she possessed, her skin was peachy, translucent as porcelain, and soft. Her eyes, like water infused with hues of a sapphire, sparkled with a light of kindness, even in her prickly moments. Her strength of character and obvious love for her son and her friends touched him.

Would she truly leave Stone Creek? Had his jealousy pushed her away? The handsome face of Giles Prescott appeared in Thomas's mind, erasing Maggie's kind smile. He'd observed them rowing in the creek like a perfect little family, laughing and no doubt finding a spot for their picnic. He clenched his fists. He didn't trust something about the man. Hadn't he seen Prescott's eyes wander to some of the younger girls, even though he had the lovely Maggie on his arm?

What did Thomas have to offer, anyway? A tiny apartment above his business, four rambunctious children—well, if he didn't count Abby, three. The dubious security of a less-than-robust pharmacy. And himself—what a prize. Of course, she'd prefer to leave the swampy lands of Michigan for the bustling city of Chicago and all that Prescott offered.

∼

"*D*efinitely whooping cough, Maggie." Dr. Moore spoke with her in the wide upstairs hallway of Apple Blossom House.

"I suspected as much." Maggie blinked and yawned.

"You need some sleep, young lady." There was no humor in his somber tone.

"I finally got Gloria to take something to calm down and rest." She paused, worrying her lip. "She was with me most of the night."

"I'll be back to have a talk with her later. She's been through a lot, but this isn't like her. She's let her fears get a hold of her."

"I couldn't agree more."

"And she's going to need to steel herself if she wants to house orphans. There are some tough cases." Dr. Moore folded his stethoscope, placing it into his black bag on the oak table before closing it. "Even though Philip doesn't show signs of illness at this time, I think it would be wise to keep the house and the cottage under quarantine."

"Philip had whooping cough a couple of years ago, and I had it when I was a child."

"That may not be enough to protect you." He cleared his throat. He unrolled his sleeves since he'd already washed his hands in the basin in Elise's room.

"I've thought as much. I'm mostly concerned about Philip being a little weaker since he had measles last spring." Maggie pushed loose strands of hair behind her ear. Once the doctor left, she would recoil and pin it again. Her fingers shook as she thought of the threat of Philip becoming ill again. She smoothed her skirt.

Dr. Moore took hold of one of her sweaty hands. "Maggie, if you save the entire Myles family and the Harpers but become ill yourself, who will Philip turn to?"

Maggie nodded. "I know."

"Go back to the cottage and rest in your own bed. I'll instruct Betty on how to care for Elise until Gloria is up and capable. I think some rest and the tonic you gave her will help her nerves. But nobody can replace you as a help to her or a mother to Philip."

A lump formed in her throat as she studied the kind older man before her. His face had grown a bit thinner recently, making his jowls hang more than usual. Many looked to him like a father or a grandfather, but he relied on the women of the town to carry out his orders.

She squeezed his hand. "I know you don't need any more patients right now."

He chuckled and pushed his glasses up on his nose, letting go of her hand. "You are an excellent nurse, and I may need more of your help soon." He reached to pick up his bag and then looked at Maggie again. "Provided you stay in Stone Creek?"

"What makes you think I'm leaving for greener pastures, Doctor?" Maggie clasped her hands behind her back and tilted her head.

"That depends on whether you find they actually are greener pastures, my dear." He turned to the chair by the table to pick up his hat and suit coat. "There are some things which cannot replace family and friends."

Dr. Moore's common-sense statement jolted her. Was leaving for Chicago—or Buffalo, for that matter—really worth the loss it could incur? And would anyone miss her...Thomas, perhaps?

CHAPTER 30

wo weeks later, Thomas peeked between the blinds of his front window, looking down onto the street from his apartment. Headlines in the local paper about how President McKinley hung between life and death after being shot with a possible assassin's bullet added to the funereal atmosphere that shrouded Stone Creek. With all the whooping cough which had spread throughout the town and the number of children ill, he'd seen fewer parents than he expected.

A diminutive figure swathed in gray, wearing a large-brimmed, dark hat covered with blue flowers, rushed down the street toward Harper Apothecary. Thomas slid his arms into each sleeve as quickly as though his limbs were slathered with butter. Sarah Moore pounded at the door.

The children were off to school except for Lyle, who'd stayed behind with a stuffy nose. He sat in the kitchen practicing his ciphering so he wouldn't get too far behind in his schoolwork.

Thomas scrambled down the stairway. Each knock, punctuating the quiet, seemed to become more frantic.

"Coming!" Thomas straightened his tie and folded his over-starched collar down once again as he hurried toward the entrance.

He turned the sign to *open* before he grasped the doorknob. As he opened the door, the pleasant breeze of a September morning chilled him as he stared down at Mrs. Moore's dewy eyes and her mouth, set in a grim line.

She blinked. "Thomas, it's not good."

"What, not even a good morning?" As soon as the words came out of his mouth, he was sorry for his attempt at levity. "What's wrong?"

Her eyebrows came together with the crinkling of her forehead. "I'm afraid Thad has done himself in." The older woman wrung her hands. "He's not as young as he used to be, and he's overworked."

"Please, come in and sit down. Would you like something cool to drink?"

"No, no, thank you." She fairly collapsed onto his bench, though, gripping the arm on one side.

"What happened?" Thomas sat next to her.

"He's been working day and night. His face was so red this morning, and he was holding onto furniture to get around. He was that weak and dizzy. Oh, he wouldn't admit it, but I could see it." She fanned herself with the hanky she'd pulled from her reticule.

Thomas's heart sank. "That doesn't sound good."

"Little Isaac Blanding passed away late last night from the whooping cough, but Thad said there was no reason he shouldn't have recovered. And there's a baby on the outskirts of town, Berta Coping's little one, who got it too. She was teething on top of it all. Poor Berta." Sarah shook her head. "Thad is worried they are getting a different remedy than what he is recommending, though the parents haven't been forthcoming."

"What *was* he able to find out? Anything?" Thomas frowned. Whooping cough wasn't an uncommon childhood disease, and many children survived it, especially very healthy children like Isaac Blanding.

"They told Thad about some miracle syrup they thought was making their child better, but they didn't mention where they'd gotten it. He wants to know if you'll check in on some of the families for him. We know this is unusual, but he is so concerned and believes you could discover the cause better than anyone." She brought her hands up as though beseeching him.

"Tell Thad to get some rest and not worry about a thing." He patted her on the back as he would soothe his own mother.

After they went over details for each of the patients he might check on, Sarah Moore left. Her eyes had brightened with hope, and she stood straighter as she retreated down the boardwalk.

Ira Blanding owned the local bank. He and his family were educated, God-fearing people. What would have gotten into them to try some strange potion? He rubbed his chin. *Blaze.* The fraud must have sold them something. Yet he had no proof. It had been a couple of weeks since he'd seen that sorry excuse for a man.

Thomas scanned the list he'd written out at Mrs. Moore's instructions. When Abby returned in the afternoon to watch the store, he would start his rounds. He only hoped it wasn't too late.

~

*M*aggie carried a basket in one arm and a bag containing herbal poultices in the other along the boardwalk to the Blanding home. She choked back a sob.

No amount of roasted chicken or biscuits would ever soothe the broken hearts there, but Maggie would do her duty.

Yesterday, she'd taken dinner to the Copings. Such a forsaken place to visit, the little wooden house was not much more than an old ramshackle cabin. Three children, wearing mended but clean clothing, had greeted her. Berta Coping had rocked her dead infant until Maggie took her and helped prepare the tiny body.

After handing the basket to the grandmother at the back door of the Blanding home, Maggie turned back to the street. The sound of keening women made her look up. *Why, Lord?* She scanned the tall clapboard house, whitewashed, with hunter-green shutters, tall columns on either side of the front door proclaiming that Mr. Blanding provided well for his family. Yet that had not kept death away.

Maggie pulled her shawl tighter around her neck, warding off the slight breeze foreshadowing the coming of fall. Yellow and gold-tipped maple leaves rippled above her.

Leaving behind the fine home, the largest on Fourth Street, Maggie dragged her feet, not wanting to look anyone in the eye. Between what she'd learned from her grandmother's remedies and Robert's healing work, Maggie had lovingly picked herbs from the garden and sewn pouches for applying them. But would they do any good?

God, please let these herbs help the children. I'm probably better at baking than applying remedies, but I know they're safe to use on youngsters.

She picked up her feet and hurried toward the Lawdles'. As she rounded the corner, a large man in a garish coat looked both ways before he stepped off the front stoop at her destination. Maggie squinted. It couldn't be—but it was.

Why hadn't that Blaze fellow left town yet? Her stomach grew heavy at the thought of what he might be selling to the suffering families of Stone Creek.

~

*T*he small store practically suffocated Thomas later in the morning after Sarah's visit. He loosened his tie a bit.

Blocks tumbled and hit the apartment floor as Lyle built and rebuilt with the wooden shapes. Was he coughing now too? Thomas tightened his fists.

"Pa!" Lyle called down the stairs.

"I'm coming, son." The sound of his shoes on the steps echoed like the rhythm of a heavy heartbeat.

Lyle stood waiting for him at the top, sniffling and rubbing his eyes. "Everything hurts."

Thomas's chest constricted. "Let's get you in bed. I'm afraid it's your turn."

He ruffled Lyle's hair before prodding him into the room he shared with his brothers. Not quite as orderly as it had been during the discipline experiment, but the quilts were pulled up neatly enough, and their clothing was off the floor for the most part, other than the odd sock. The walls were bare except for the wooden cross Bess had put up in their room in their previous home. Books were stacked in a haphazard heap on the bureau. A current of warm air lifted the gauzy gray curtains.

Thomas pulled back the covers for Lyle. "Into bed with you now, son."

"Could I have a book to read, Pa?" The boy squinted. Perhaps he needed spectacles as well.

"You need your rest. After a nap, all right?"

Lyle yawned and coughed again. He grabbed for Thomas's sleeve as he turned to leave. "Would you stay until I go to sleep?" His eyebrows came together.

"Of course. Scoot over." Thomas lowered himself onto the edge of the bed.

Lyle closed his eyes and curled up on his side. Then his eyes popped open. "Am I going to die...like Isaac?"

Steady yourself. Nothing could have prepared Thomas for that question, especially coming from Lyle. He must not entertain the possibility.

CHAPTER 31

*T*homas exhaled as though to dispel his sudden fear. "You heard Mrs. Moore, then?"

His son nodded.

"Don't worry about such a thing. You are hardly ever sick." *Like Isaac.* He paused. "You may not have the same thing. Only a cold, perhaps?"

Lyle scrunched the edge of the white cotton sheet between his fingers. "Why did he die?" He stared up at Thomas, his eyes begging for an answer.

Lyle was asking for a spiritual reason, not a medical one.

"Son, there are some things I just don't know." His conscience pricked with guilt. But what could he say? He'd not unraveled the mystery of losing Bess. Or anyone else.

"Will you pray for me like Mama used to?" Lyle rolled over on his back and grasped Thomas's hand, his small one warm from fever.

Thomas sighed. *I'll try.* He looked at the ceiling. "Dear God." *Are you really there?* "Please give Lyle strength. And help him not to worry, but to know we're taking care of him. Amen." Thomas squeezed Lyle's hand and met his gaze.

Lyle smiled for the first time all day. "Thanks, Papa. Now I can sleep."

Thomas tiptoed out of the room once Lyle's breathing grew even and calm. Tears came unbidden to his eyes. He locked up the store before he went to his room, where he fell to his knees, shaking at the side of his empty bed. He clutched his hands together, and another, deeply genuine prayer welled up.

"God, if You're there, please let me know somehow. Bess knew You so well, I thought I knew You too. Maybe I didn't." He swallowed and wiped the moisture from his cheeks. "I've been angry You took Bess, but what good has it done me?" He blew out a puff of air like a humorless laugh. "I've made a mess of things. And I've probably driven Maggie away." His chest squeezed tighter than he thought possible, like bandages wound too tight around a sore.

And I don't want Lyle to hear me, but he doesn't seem as strong as his brothers. Please don't take him from us. Please give me a sign everything will be all right.

A gentle breeze from the window he'd left cracked blew Bess's Bible open on the bureau. The thin pages fluttered like butterfly wings.

Thomas had forgotten he'd even left it there next to their family picture, untouched except for an occasional respectful caress of its worn leather cover by Abby. As though it beckoned him, a piece of paper floated out from between the pages and fell to the floor. Or was it a small envelope?

Thomas rose and touched the Bible's cool dark-brown cover with his fingertips. The tears flowed unbidden again as he lifted the book and held it next to his heart. He bent to pick up the envelope, a bit yellowed. Turning it over, he found the words, *My Thomas,* written in Bess's elegant and exact script. He lifted the envelope to his nose, but her scent had dissipated. Only the businesslike smell of paper and ink remained.

He tucked it back in the Bible, not ready to face whatever

she'd written. The envelope contained the last bit of his deceased wife in a way. If he opened the envelope and read the letter, he was admitting she was truly gone. For the rest of his life.

Thomas choked back a sob. The sorrow he'd swept under the rug, keeping it out of sight for his children's sake, could no longer be forced down. Not wanting to awaken Lyle, he trod as softly as possible down the staircase and made his way to the back door. He opened it and inhaled the fresh air deeply.

Stepping outside, he closed the door behind him and sat on the stoop, still holding Bess's Bible, and wiped his eyes with his free hand.

The distant rush of the millpond, the call of restless geese as they flew overhead, anticipating the change in the weather, and the leaves, starting to dapple with color, calmed his soul. *I've failed you terribly, Bess. And the children. I don't know what to do.*

Thomas lowered the once much-loved Bible to his lap. Opening it, he fingered the pages with their worn edges. How had his wife ever found time to read, let alone contemplate, the Scriptures?

Corners of pages were bent over. Ribbons were tucked in to mark Bess's favorite passages. Gentle ink marks were few and far between because of her respect for the book and its words. But she'd drawn a diminutive cross by each of the verses and stories she loved most.

There were so many bent-cornered pages in the Gospel of John. The story of Lazarus being raised from the dead captured Thomas's attention. After losing her brother, Martha went out to meet Jesus.

"Lord, if thou hadst been here, my brother had not died. But I know, that even now, whatso-

ever thou wilt ask of God, God will give it
thee."

Jesus saith unto her, "Thy brother shall rise
again."

Martha saith unto him, "I know that he shall rise
again in the resurrection at the last day."

Jesus said unto her, "I am the resurrection, and
the life: he that believeth in me, though he
were dead, yet shall he live: And whosoever
liveth and believeth in me shall never die.
Believest thou this?"

She saith unto him, Yea, Lord: I believe that thou
art the Christ, the Son of God, which should
come into the world."

Thomas pressed a hand to his mouth. How many times had
he thought that if God had truly been there, Bess wouldn't have
died? And here was Martha, practically accusing Him of the
same thing. But did he have the faith to believe Jesus was the
resurrection and the life?

Thomas continued reading until he came to two words that
stopped him—*Jesus wept.*

Amazing. Jesus had grieved as deeply as Lazarus's sisters,
Martha and Mary.

Thumbing through more pages, Thomas read in chapter
two of Ephesians, "by grace alone through faith" men were
saved so that no one could boast. Everyone was equal in God's
eyes. They'd all failed, but faith was the remedy, and the grace
that came through faith from God.

"I can fight You no longer," Thomas whispered as he
rubbed his forehead. "If it's not too late, God, I'd like to accept
Your gift of grace and forgiveness for my sins."

A fledgling spark of faith spread in Thomas's chest like the
warmth of sitting near a fire on a cold day, while peace settled

over him as a blanket. Something real was taking place and renewing him. The feeling was better than his mother's hugs after he skinned a knee, and deeper still than Bess's embraces. A comfort beyond description.

~

"May I get you some tea, Maggie?" Pearl Lawdle asked from the doorway of her twins' room.

"No need, Pearl. I only wanted to see if you need anything more for the children." Maggie peered over the young mother's shoulder.

"Thank you, but I believe Ruby and Russell are on the mend." Pearl was missing the dark circles beneath her eyes and the pallor of a worried mother. Her thin pink mouth turned up into a smile as she patted her neat chignon.

Everything in the equally neat little home was in its place. The afternoon light cast a bluish hue on the white walls. The oak floors shone. A savory aroma wafted from the pot on the coal stove, tantalizing Maggie's nose and causing her stomach to rumble. Only a large amber bottle with a pink label, which sat on a pewter tray on a side table in the hall, a spoon next to it, appeared out of place.

"I'm so glad the children are doing much better. I did bring two poultices, as I'd heard they'd come down with the same malady as Elise."

"Why, thank you, Maggie." Pearl pulled the bedroom door shut.

"Pearl, what kind of medicine are you giving the children?" The words spilled forth before she had a chance to stop them.

"Why do you ask?" The younger mother turned away, performing a task hidden to Maggie, but when she faced her again, the bottle on the table lay flat, covered with a cloth. She carried the tray toward the kitchen sideboard.

"I think you know." Maggie set her hands on her hips.

"Whatever do you mean?" Pearl busied herself, but as she reached the kitchen and went to sneak the bottle into a cabinet, Maggie followed her.

"Please, Pearl. I'm concerned about what that Blaze fellow might be hawking to the good people of this town. He's no doctor, and he may not even know what he's selling."

Pearl swung around. "It's none of your concern. Besides, you wouldn't understand how tiresome it is being up with two sick children. You only have one child." Anger lit her eyes, and she set her jaw.

Maggie backed away so fast she almost tripped over the hem of her own skirt. "I'm not accusing you of anything. I'm only trying to help, but I can go elsewhere." She snatched up her bag of poultices.

Pearl softened her stance. "I apologize, but I love my children. I would never try to hurt them. I just wanted them to sleep and get better."

"Then tell me what you've given them."

"Oh, very well." She pulled the cabinet door open and held out the bottle she'd withdrawn. "Here."

Mrs. Whitcomb's Sweet-water Tonic. Maggie turned the bottle over in her palm. *Soothes the teething infant or the coughing child for a pleasant night's rest.* She unscrewed the cap.

"What are you doing? The remedy isn't cheap, you know."

"Just tasting it." Maggie put a fingertip to the opening of the bottle and then touched her index finger to her tongue. Despite the added sugar, a bitter taste lingered. Laudanum or morphine, or any number of opiates. She waved the opening below her nose. The alcohol vapors stung her sinuses. She replaced the cap. "Pearl, if the children have been sleeping all day, let up on the dose." She paused for emphasis. "For their sakes."

"What if they can't sleep? Or start coughing a lot again?"

"Wait until tomorrow and give them half if you must, but if you give them any more tonight, they may not wake up."

Pearl gasped. "What?"

After placing the bottle on the sideboard, Maggie took the other woman by her arms. "Use the poultices tonight. That should help relieve the congestion in their chests. And I'll check with Dr. Moore—or even Mr. Harper—to find you a better remedy. Something safer for your children."

"I wasn't trying to poison my children. That's not what you think, is it?" Pearl's voice hitched higher in panic.

"Of course not, but Blaze preys on tired mothers, and old people, to get their money for something which may seem to work but could be dangerous."

From the next room, Ruby and Russell coughed, ending with whooping sounds. They echoed one another's coughing fits.

Maggie sensed the other woman's fear as her demeanor turned to that of a frightened animal on alert. "Let me help you before I leave."

~

By the time Maggie stepped off the Lawdles' porch, the weariness hit her as though her poultices had become oversized sacks of flour. Perhaps she should stop at Dr. Moore's house and tell him her concerns.

She trudged along the side of the road where little puddles gathered. In her tiredness, she wound up stepping in one. Water seeped through her hem, mud splashing her. Cool, dirty water seeped its way up around the ankle of her stocking.

Well, that's just fine.

Maggie picked up her sodden hem and walked faster toward town.

Quiet enshrouded the Moores' usually cheery brick house. Maggie applied the knocker. "Hello? Anyone home?"

Sarah opened the door a crack, shushing her with a finger over pursed lips. "So good to see you, Maggie." The older woman's eyes brightened as she took Maggie by the sleeve, nearly pulling her inside.

"Hello, Sarah, thank you. Good to see you too. I was hoping to speak with Dr. Moore."

"Come sit down, dear. You look exhausted. I can't have you falling ill like my Thaddeus."

"Oh no. How can I help?"

"I think he'll be all right. But he gave me a scare this morning. I insisted he rest up. I gave him one of his own draughts to put him to sleep." Her eyes twinkled as she straightened cushions on the horsehair chaise and went about picking up any books sitting out, along with an abandoned cup of tea.

"You mustn't trouble yourself, Sarah. I should be helping you."

"The quiet has been getting to me. I gave my cook the day off and have had to turn away patients for everything but the simplest things. Ailments I could help with, which are few." Sarah shook her head. "Come sit down."

"Thank you."

"I'll brew a fresh pot of tea, and we'll have a little bread and cheese perhaps?" She bustled into the kitchen.

Maggie removed her shoes and went to sit down. The front room was as safe and cozy as her mother's. The pine floors had been scrubbed, and even the braided scatter rugs complemented the cheery Persian rug of faded burgundy, gold, and blue. She set her large cloth bag on the floor. Relief settled on her as she rubbed her shoulder. She lowered herself onto the overstuffed sofa.

Maggie closed her eyes, and before she knew it, was sitting bolt upright at the sound of Sarah's voice.

"Poor child, you must be so tired."

Maggie blinked the sleep from her eyes and adjusted her hat, which had slid forward a bit. "At first, I worried Philip would get whooping cough, but he's well enough. And I thank the Lord that Elise recovered."

"And now?" Sarah poured amber liquid into two china cups and held one out to her.

Maggie took comfort in the ritual of adding sugar to the brew and stirring it with a teaspoon. Then she took a sip and let the hot liquid slide over her tongue and down her parched throat. Her mouth watered at the yeasty scent of fresh bread and sight of cheese stacked in neat slices. Her stomach rumbled. When, and what, had she last eaten? A little oatmeal at breakfast?

"Sarah, you are too kind when you've been busy with your husband all day." Maggie slathered butter on a thick slice of bread before adding the cheese.

"Maggie, you can tell me what's bothering you."

"I'm afraid that Blaze fellow is peddling strange remedies. Well, not so much strange, but dangerous." She continued describing what was going on at the Lawdles. "I mean, what if that syrup caused the demise of Isaac or Daisy? The man should be arrested." She wiped the corner of her mouth with a napkin, placing it back on her lap. "I'd hoped to talk to Dr. Moore about this, but..."

"Honey, you should talk to Thomas. He's going the extra mile to help Thad out this week." Was Sarah wearing a self-satisfied grin, partially hidden by her teacup?

Maggie gulped. A dozen reasons leaped to her mind as to why she couldn't...or wouldn't darken the door of the Harper Apothecary again. Her feelings pulled her in so many directions, like a four-way tug of war. The warmth of sympathy she'd experienced when watching him confront Blaze. The confounded way in which he reacted to the possibility of her leaving town. The endearment his children brought out. Was it just the affection of a friend she felt for them? Or was there something more between Thomas and her?

The thought of seeing Thomas again made the bread and cheese in her stomach churn. How could she face him when he'd dismissed her so easily? Then again, was there really a choice when children's lives were at stake?

"Perhaps I'll do that." Maggie gathered her things and hugged the doctor's wife. "Thank you, Sarah. Goodbye."

When Maggie opened the front door on her way out, she stepped onto something, losing her balance. She slipped. Maggie's arms windmilled. Losing the battle, she looked up to find Thomas reaching out to catch her.

CHAPTER 32

Thomas launched up the Moores' porch steps in time to catch an astonished Maggie in his arms. Her softness and warmth pressed into him as she righted herself. He moved his hands to her bent elbows as he helped steady her.

"M-Mr. Harper, I'm s-sorry." Her stormy dark-aqua eyes flashed with something. Horror? Or embarrassment? She pulled away, one hand resting on the doorframe, and checked the bottom of her boot. She stomped her foot and used the heel of her other boot to push the clump of mud away.

"I'm glad I happened to be here to keep you from getting hurt." He removed his hat and swallowed. "I was stopping by to see if there was anything the Moores needed. After that, I'll be checking in on some of the children with whooping cough." He cleared his throat. "I don't usually make house calls." His chuckle died in his throat.

She opened her mouth for a couple of seconds, then closed it and blinked. As she stepped off the porch, he offered his hand. Maggie took it before averting her gaze toward the steps as he walked down with her. Once on solid ground, she pulled away, but not before tipping her head toward him in an appreciative gesture.

What else could he say? Was it worth it when she might leave town? But this beautiful specimen of womanhood before him set his heart pounding like a steam locomotive. The electricity between them was palpable, but was he ready for more than friendship? Was she?

"A good day to you, then." She seemed to drag her steps, and he stood as though glued to the spot, watching her retreat.

"Please, wait a minute." He combed his hand through his hair.

"Yes?" She whirled to face him and lifted her face. Was that hope which rose into her gaze?

"Is Philip well?"

She nodded. "He is. Thanks be to God."

"I'm glad to hear it." He paused. "And Elise?"

"Regaining her strength."

"I heard your fine care helped her heal all the faster."

Maggie's full pink mouth curved into a smile. The fire in her eyes subdued to the pleasant warmth he'd grown accustomed to. Gripping his hat in his hands curbed his growing desire to hold her again. The circles under her eyes and thinning of the rounded oval of her face signaled her weariness. Her hat tilted, a bit askew. So unusual for Maggie. How stressed she must be.

"And you, Maggie...are you well?"

She hesitated. "I'm fine. Just a bit tired from calling on people, bringing them my herbal compresses." She looked down. "Of course, I wouldn't attempt to take your place in providing remedies." When her gaze again met his, she wore a surprisingly shy smile. "But my poultices may provide some relief from chest congestion."

"You are the woman who nursed me back to health. I think I can trust your good medicine." He paused. "You know, Lyle's not feeling well. I'm concerned he's coming down with whooping cough too. If you have any poultices left over when you're done with your visits..."

"Oh, please, take one now." Maggie drew a paper-wrapped packet from her bag and handed it to him. Before he could thank her, she took a step closer. "But there's something you need to know." Her floral scent wafted toward him. Her auburn curls gleamed in the waning light of a gray late afternoon, framing the peach perfection of her face.

"What is it?" His heart leapt that she might still trust him. After how he'd treated her, she had every right to tell him to leave her alone.

She pressed her lips together for a moment. "That charlatan, Blaze, is at it again, but I'm afraid he's not so harmless anymore."

"What happened?" Thomas's heart pounded. A knife twisted in his gut at the thought of that fraud hurting anyone in Stone Creek. He found a handkerchief in his pocket to wipe perspiration from his forehead.

"I was at the Lawdles' a while ago. Russell and Ruby seemed awfully calm, so I asked Pearl about it, but she hesitated to tell me. But then she showed me the bottle of Mrs. Whitcomb's Sweet-water Tonic. I smelled it and tasted it. I don't think it's a far cry from Mrs. Winslow's Soothing Syrup, which I've heard has caused problems—"

"Yes, death in some instances." Thomas shook his fist. "I'd like to get my hands on him."

"That's precisely what I'm concerned about." Maggie adjusted the bag over her shoulder, shifting her weight to one side. "Without instructions for proper dosage from you or Dr. Moore, these children are in a dangerous place. Although I believe Pearl will do as I asked and reduce the dosage since I told her the danger of the tonic."

"I planned to see Russell and Ruby after stopping here.

Thank you for letting me know what to expect. I'll visit Sarah later." Thomas rubbed the back of his neck.

"It's very fine of you to help Dr. Moore out.." Admiration shone from Maggie's eyes.

So he hadn't completely pushed her away with his past nonchalance and rudeness? Thomas exhaled softly as his lips curved upward. Anyone else in the vicinity faded into the background. Main Street belonged to them alone—until a figure in a dark suit rushed around them.

"Excuse me." The man gasped for breath.

Thomas turned to him—not a stranger, but Mack Frost. How far had he run? "Looking for Dr. Moore?"

"Yes, we have an emergency." The young man bent to place his hands on his knees while catching his breath.

"He's quite ill right now. Is there something we can do to help?" Maggie used her calming tone of voice.

"No, no." Terror filled Mack's dark gaze. The laborer rubbed his hand over the shadow of whiskers. "This can't be happenin'." He gulped. "Emmy had whoopin' cough, and we thought it was finally gettin' better. But now Cora can't wake her up."

"Calm yourself. Take us to her." Thomas looked directly into the younger man's eyes.

"But what about the doctor?"

"Trust Mr. Harper. Dr. Moore does." Maggie's cheeks flushed as she glanced at Thomas.

He grasped her hand for a moment and squeezed it.

Her eyes widened.

As they hurried toward the Frost residence a few blocks east, gray clouds gathered. Large drops of rain hit Thomas's face. While once they would have reflected his tears over the sadness of his life, the losses which haunted Stone Creek, instead they were like cleansing waters. His past was washed away, and he could trust God again. Maybe he had never known or understood what Christ had done for him. Thomas had been given a new lease on life, and he intended to make the most of it. Starting now—with the people he could help. And with Maggie, if she would receive it.

When they grew close to the little yellow house, the cries of a small child emanated from inside. The interior was sparsely furnished. Mustiness mixed with the smell of tobacco smoke, and perhaps onions. Doilies underneath lanterns and polished candlesticks on the table showed Cora's care for the little home despite Mack's lack of concern.

Frost likely made decent wages with his carpentry. Thomas had heard his work was good. But too much of his earnings went into the bottle. Mack shoved an empty one under the sofa with his foot and wiped his mouth with the back of his hand. His bloodshot eyes and red nose alone would have been enough to tell the tale.

"I keep tellin' God I'll never drink again if He will save Emmy."

Wyatt's cries turned to whimpering when he laid eyes on his father, and he toddled into the bedroom.

Mack led them across a woven rug and the pine floor, smooth and swept.

In the small bedroom, Cora sat on a stool by a trundle bed, bent over the limp form of little Emmy, pushing back her curls, then holding her hand and patting it. "Wake up, little one, wake up. Come on." Cora sniffled, her eyes dewy with tears when she looked up at her husband. "Where's Dr. Moore?"

"Sick. The 'pothecary has to do for now."

"May we lift her to your bed so I can get a better look at her?" Thomas pointed to the taller piece of furniture.

Cora nodded.

"I'll do it." Mack lifted his daughter like a feather. Even the slight man overshadowed the child as he placed her on top of the quilt.

Maggie lingered in the doorway, letting Thomas take the lead for once.

He took off his suit coat, laying it on the foot of the bed. He rolled up his sleeves, stalling for time. *Father, please help me, especially if this is what I think it is.* He'd stitched up cuts and pulled slivers or shards of glass from a wound. He'd even looked at an occasional sore throat and advised a medicament, but this was new territory.

He pushed away the child's baby-fine locks of hair and placed his hand alongside her petite neck, feeling for a pulse. Emmy's breaths were shallow and her pulse a tad fainter than he would like to hear. He was no medical doctor, but he'd gained some skill working with his father. He opened her eyelids and found her pupils were the size of pinpricks.

"Has she been given the Sweet-water Tonic that Blaze fellow was peddling?" Thomas tried to curtail his confrontational tone.

Cora clung to her daughter's hand. Wyatt did his best to hide behind his mother but continued to peek around to study Thomas.

"You can tell me the truth. You won't get in trouble. I need to know."

She looked up, tentative. Tears rolled down her cheeks. "Yes." She nodded, barely looking up at him. "We—well, my husband—thought it best if she slept. We had given Wyatt a little for his teething and thought it couldn't hurt our little girl. We just wanted her to get better." Extracting a hanky from her pocket, the dark-haired woman wiped her eyes and blew her nose. "Tied bags of chopped onions to her feet last night to bring the fever down too."

So that's what he'd smelled. "When's the last time she took the tonic?"

"A couple of hours ago." The poor woman looked as guilty

as a man waiting to be hanged, but likely, it had been an accidental overdose due to her husband's prodding.

"How much are you giving her? Let me see the bottle—please." He reached out, and Cora handed him the good-sized bottle. She trembled and sobbed.

"A spoonful each time she needs it." She handed him the spoon next. "Since I got this a few days ago."

Thomas held up the bottle, and Maggie gasped behind him. More than half was gone. He closed his eyes a moment, then faced Cora. "Do you have any ipecac, Mrs. Frost?"

He prayed it would be enough to help.

～

As Cora sought the medicine Thomas requested, pushing past her husband without looking at him, Maggie followed her into the living room. She hung her hat on a peg, removed her shawl, and unbuttoned her sleeves. Rolling them up, she returned to the bedroom doorway and asked Thomas, "How may I assist?"

"Pray with me for God's grace and help." Thomas's gaze at Maggie as she washed her hands at the basin seemed so full of meaning. He'd never talked to her quite this way before. A new light in his eyes formed a connection with her soul.

"Here it is." Returning to the room, Cora held a bottle out to him.

"We'll need a small spoon. I think she can swallow still. Let's get a towel, a small bowl." As Cora hurried to oblige, Thomas glanced at Maggie. "Maggie, can you help me prop her up?"

She climbed over the trundle bed to sit next to Emmy, fluffing two pillows behind her. The little one mumbled and drooled. Her head lolled to the side. Maggie bent and placed an arm behind Emmy's head and neck.

The little girl sputtered as Thomas spooned some medicine toward the back of her throat, then pinched her lips shut so she had to swallow it. Maggie got a hold of her arms as the girl attempted to flail them but fell limp again.

"This isn't a pleasant task, but if we can get some of the accursed tonic out of her system by vomiting, that will help." Thomas rose and reached for his coat. "Can you handle this, Maggie?" He motioned her into the other room and followed.

"Of course." Though she cringed inside, she wouldn't let him see any of her weakness.

He slid his arms through his coat sleeves. "I have to go back to the shop for a few things. Between myself and Dr. Moore, we should be able to supply what Emmy needs."

"How long will it take? What if my little girl is dyin'?" Mack stood before him, shaking.

"Please, don't go." Cora sobbed, following him from the bedroom.

Thomas replied as he crossed the sitting room. "I must. She has had an overdose of a dangerous drug. I have to get a different medicine to combat it."

The front door closed behind Thomas, leaving a void. And yet, his confidence had strengthened Maggie. When she turned away from the door and toward Cora, Maggie offered her a reassuring smile. "If anyone can help Emmy get well, Thomas Harper can."

CHAPTER 33

*T*homas returned from his shop to the Frost residence out of breath. He wiped beads of sweat from his forehead with the back of his hand. He plunked down a leather case and removed his suit coat. The silence in the bedroom, but for the ticking of a distant clock, made his movements seem slower, more deliberate. He opened the case, removed a syringe, and passed the needle through a candle flame.

"You may want to leave the room for a moment." Thomas withdrew the solution of cocaine while Maggie tied a tourniquet around Emmy's tiny arm.

"After I saw what the ipecac syrup did to my baby, I can handle anything. I won't leave the room again." Cora stood at the foot of the bed with one fist to her mouth. Her other hand gripped the piece of furniture.

Thomas held the syringe up, studying it as he pushed the air bubbles out. Thankfully, little Wyatt slept under a blanket in the sitting room while Mack paced near him. As long as the nervous father was on the other side of the door, it was better for all of them.

A quick prick in Emmy's arm and Thomas administered

only enough cocaine with the plunge of the needle to neutralize the overdose of the opiate. His heart thumped in his ears as the silent hope in the room engulfed him. He exhaled after he withdrew the needle.

"This solution of cocaine should counteract how the narcotic has slowed her system down. I gave her a minute amount, but I hope it will be enough to bring her back. She won't feel very well for a few days, but you *must* not resort to giving her any more of that Sweet-water Tonic. Do you understand, Mrs. Frost?" While he didn't like using the stern tone of voice he reserved for scolding his children, Thomas wanted to make sure Cora absorbed the gravity of the situation.

"Yes, Mr. Harper, I understand." Cora nodded, a dark and earnest look passing across her face.

He rubbed Emmy's arm and removed the tourniquet.

The sound of boots treading the wooden floor stopped. Mack stood in the doorway. "Well?"

Within a couple of moments, color returned to Emmy's cheeks, and her breaths became deeper and more regular. Her eyelids fluttered open. "Mama?"

"My little darling. You've come back to us." Cora rushed around the side of the bed and pulled her daughter to herself. "You're going to be all right. You're going to be all right." She stroked Emmy's hair.

"Our little girl is goin' to make it?" Mack pushed past Thomas. "What do we owe you, Mr. Harper?"

"Nothing." Thomas took the syringe apart. He ran the needle through the flame on the candle for the time being. Echoes of Bess telling him he couldn't constantly give away his services and make a profit ran through his head. He pushed those thoughts aside. Today, God had used him to save a life, and it was enough.

"The Frosts are good for whatever we owe you. We don't take no charity." Mack crossed his arms and shifted his weight.

"I'll tell you what. Make good on your credit with the store and give me what's left of the bottle of Sweet-water's Tonic. That will be plenty of payment for me." Thomas couldn't imagine he had anything to pay with, anyway.

"Suit yerself." Mack shrugged.

"Shall I stay and make sure everything is all right?" Maggie sidled up alongside him.

"I'm quite sure she's going to be fine, but we'll stay a little longer. You can manage alone, right, Cora?"

"I've been doing it all along, haven't I?" She directed her question toward her husband. Plain disgust was written in her expression. "You might as well go to the tavern and celebrate."

"Maybe I should." Mack's shoulders slumped. The hurtful dart of sarcasm had met its mark. "I'll leave after I get the bottle for you, Mr. Harper."

After retrieving the bottle, he turned it over in his hand before he gave it to Thomas. Mack squared his shoulders. "You know what? I tol' God I'd stay away from that stuff if He saved our little girl. I'll stay here and help. You and Mrs. Galloway best be goin'."

Cora didn't move. She sat holding her daughter, her face emotionless, no doubt afraid to believe her husband.

"Very good, Mack." Thomas slipped the nearly empty tonic bottle into his pocket.

Someone was going to pay, and it wasn't going to be Mack and Cora Frost.

~

When they stopped in front of Harper Apothecary on the walk home, Thomas turned to Maggie. "Why don't you come in and visit Abby while I deal with some business? Someone has to get rid of that fraud."

Before Maggie stood a different man. His strong jaw set

with determination, while a dark-blond curl fell across his forehead. If only she could push it back. And...kiss him? She looked away.

He was like a new man this evening—one she'd like to spend time with.

"Wait a minute. Shouldn't you get the sheriff to help you with this?"

"All I have is circumstantial evidence." He pulled the tonic bottle from his pocket, the waning light reflecting off the brown glass.

"Then let me go with you." Maggie gripped his arm.

"I need to do this, Maggie. I don't want you to get hurt."

"Thomas Harper, I can hold my own with your three rambunctious boys and your precocious daughter. I am certainly capable of standing up to a fake princess, an acrobat, and a dishonest businessman." Her hands went to her hips. She pursed her lips to keep from grinning, but she couldn't help but return his smile.

"Very well, then." Thomas chuckled and ushered her forward. "I think I know where they're hiding."

Maggie followed him around the building, assuming he didn't want to disturb the children. They trod through the yard behind the pharmacy and the mercantile until he stopped short. She almost ran into his arm but stopped herself in time.

"There, see?" Thomas pointed in the direction of faint firelight on the other side of the millpond, partially hidden by bushes and trees. His hand went around to the small of her back as he urged her forward. Being so close to his side made concentrating on what he said nearly impossible. His clean citrus scent blended with the heat of the evening. His eyes, reflecting the soft moonlight, lit with a purpose she'd never seen before.

Laughter and intermittent banjo music traveled their way, faint but distinct.

"We're going to go out to the road around back, and they'll never expect us. With this moon, I'd rather not take a lantern."

"Well, we can only pray the clouds continue to flee, can't we?" She couldn't help but grin up at him.

Above them, the moon shone an ivory-yellow as it claimed its spot in the sky. When had it last looked so bright?

Thomas stopped, pulling her aside, and turned toward her. For a moment, Maggie only felt her own heartbeat. Thomas's breath grazed her ear. She closed her eyes and swallowed, steeling herself. This was no time to let her emotions take over.

But when she opened her eyes again and gazed at Thomas, her longing was mirrored in his eyes. Crickets played a soft symphony in the gathering dusk. She was perfectly dizzy with emotion, not knowing what to say. With her hands held against his coat, his solid chest beneath gave needed support.

"You must be careful," she whispered. "I don't want to see you get hurt."

His other arm slipped around her back. "You've been looking out for me all this time, but it's time I looked out for your well-being." He paused. "If I had any shred of decency, I would send you back."

She stood transfixed as his lips curved into a slight smile and a dimple appeared. Both were so inviting, but...

"Thomas, I'm not sure..."

"Not sure of what?" He stroked her cheek with his thumb before taking a lock of her curls and bringing it to his lips. "I should have done this a while ago." His voice grew husky, and he bent his head closer. She closed her eyes as his lips brushed hers.

CHAPTER 34

"Woof, woof, woof!" One of the largest dogs Maggie had ever seen barreled toward them, almost knocking them both to the ground.

She gasped and backed away as the dog jumped up, lunging at her face—but thankfully, with his tongue extended rather than his teeth. Then it was Thomas's turn.

"Buster, no!" A young man came out of the shadows. "Down, boy!"

Thomas pushed the dog down. The boy grabbed the mutt by the scruff.

"Sorry about that. He's too friendly. I didn't know he got away until a few minutes ago." The tall, gangly lad hung his head in apology. "Come on, boy."

The relentless dog and repentant boy retreated, but the moment of emotional rapture was broken. Maggie burst into laughter, and so did Thomas.

"Let's go. We have a job to do." He grabbed her hand, and they trotted out toward River Road.

Maggie held up the front hem of her skirt, abandoning herself to the moment. She didn't care about her high-topped shoes sloshing through puddles. She would clean them off tomorrow. Her breath came in spurts. A few minutes later, as they neared the campsite, Thomas slowed down. What a relief. She could barely keep up with his longer strides.

They went around the back of the garishly colored wagon, illumined not only by the moon but also the campfire several yards away. Wooden steps led to an open door at the back. Thomas nudged her toward the shadows. Thank goodness, the grass wasn't dry and crunchy.

Thomas climbed into the wagon. A stump of a candle burned almost down to the end in a dirty lantern.

"Here, take this." He hoisted a small crate down to Maggie. She took the box while he made his way off the platform with care. He landed softly and then took the crate from her arms and motioned her out behind the wagon. As Blaze's little band continued to practice ballads, Thomas and Maggie snuck back to a copse of trees.

"Nobody else in Stone Creek will die from this stuff on my watch." After setting down the crate, Thomas lifted the first bottle with a grand gesture as though he were going to toast, unscrewed the cap, and poured the liquid onto a grassy spot.

"Why, Thomas." Maggie covered her mouth. *I didn't know he had it in him, Lord.* The words had almost slipped out, but she caught them.

He unscrewed the next bottle and handed it to her with a perfunctory nod. "You may do the honors."

Maggie held her bottle in the air and nodded in return. "Happy to oblige." She emptied the bottle, then placed it back in the crate.

The dozen or so bottles were easily emptied, but for the one from the Frosts which Thomas removed from his pocket and placed with the others back in the crate. At Maggie's questioning look, he whispered, "Proof."

When he picked the loosely packed crate up, the bottles rattled.

"Did you hear, somethin'?" Blaze's baritone belted out.

"Let me check, Pa."

Maggie froze. Should they run? Instead, Thomas motioned with his head to follow him, and he went forward, exposing himself in the firelight. They met a young man of small stature just around the corner. Pint-size Pete without makeup? She stifled a chuckle.

"Who are you?" the boy demanded.

"Thomas Harper. We met a couple of weeks ago." He made his way into the glow of the fire.

"What in tarnation is goin' on here?" Blaze stood up from the log on which he sat.

"No need to get up." Taking hold of the Frosts' partially used bottle, he dumped the crate with the rest on the ground with a clatter. He tossed the empty containers into the fire. The glass crackled, and a flame shot up.

"Ah!" A young girl with long, dark hair loose, wearing a plain dress and shawl, screamed and jumped up. No Indian princess here.

Thomas raised an eyebrow. "I wouldn't breathe the fumes of this poison. Would you?"

A middle-aged man, the plant from the show, stood, and a tired-looking older woman, most likely "Mrs. Blaze," went to Blaze's side with widening eyes, looking at Thomas as though he were a crazy person. "Get in the wagon, children."

"You're nothin' but a thief." Blaze stepped around the fire, closing the distance between himself and Thomas, who stood unflinching. "Why, I ought to git the sheriff right now."

"Should you? Because I know Sheriff Baxter. And if you're not out of this town—no, this county—by tomorrow morning, I'll see to it that he runs you out of Stone Creek."

Blaze guffawed. "You're the dad gum criminal here."

Thomas held up the bottle from the Frosts. "I'll have you know, this nasty potion you've been hawking nearly killed a little girl today."

"What are you saying about my husband? He's a good man." Mrs. Blaze clasped onto her husband's arm.

"I'll tell you what. This upstanding citizen here has seen you peddling it elsewhere." He placed his arm around Maggie and squeezed her close for a moment. "Perhaps this is what killed Isaac Blanding or Daisy Coping? She was just a baby!"

Blaze blanched and pulled at his bolero tie. Even in the semi-darkness, his sickly pallor became evident. "I never meant to hurt anyone. I was only tryin' to help those mothers and children. They were sufferin'—"

"And now they're suffering more. Would you care to go to prison for manslaughter? I can have that arranged."

Blaze winced, then jutted out his chin. "What proof do you have?"

"This very bottle is from the family of the little girl who almost died today. Do I need any more proof than that? Once I start talking to the townspeople, whose side do you think they'll be on? I'll get enough proof for a hanging. That is, if you don't think prison is enough." Thomas placed one foot forward and clenched his opposite fist.

Blaze spit into the fire. "What about the bottles you just stole?"

Thomas tugged a handful of coins from his pocket and tossed them at Blaze's feet. "Now, get out of town."

Blaze trudged away, grabbing his wife by the arm. "Let's get packed up. Gus, put out the fire."

"I'm on it." Gus nodded, not even glancing at Thomas.

"Come on." Thomas grasped Maggie's hand, tucked the one bottle back into his pocket, and patted it. "I'm holding onto this for evidence."

"A good idea." Maggie pulled her shawl tighter as the evening air grew cooler.

Bang! She jumped and screamed. Her ears rang. Thomas pulled her to a stop. She turned to look over her shoulder. Pint-sized Pete held a firearm straight in the air.

Thomas pointed at him. "You don't fool me, young man. I bet all you have in there are blanks. You have a lot of nerve frightening a lady like that." Thomas let go of her and stalked toward Pete. "Give me that thing."

"Put it down, boy." Blaze stepped in front of Pete and put up his hands. "Fair enough, Mister, but you've destroyed a good portion of our merchandise, and I'm not about to lose a good prop."

"Then you ought to teach your staff to be more polite. Nothing is proved with violence."

Maggie trembled as Thomas returned to her. He shed his suit jacket and placed it around her shoulders. "I'm sorry about that."

"I-I'll be fine." His arm around her as he led her away stilled the pounding of her heart but led to a whole new sensation of warmth coursing through it.

On the way back, Thomas led her by the pond. Bullfrogs sang and plopped into the water as they neared. The rippling water reflected the moonlight like yellow topaz. She sighed, happy to get farther away from Dr. Blaze's Medicine Show camp.

"Do you think he'll stop selling that awful stuff?"

"If he gets far enough away, he might sell it again, but hopefully, with a warning attached. He might have hidden the bottles if I hadn't destroyed them and sold them somewhere else." Thomas hefted a sigh. "I'll still report him, but I don't think I have enough evidence to have him arrested."

"Why did you pay him?"

Thomas stopped and took both of her hands. "Maggie, I

may have made lots of mistakes in my life, but I won't have him accuse me of stealing any of his accursed inventory."

She could no longer suppress her chuckles.

"What is it?"

"When I saw you throwing those bottles into the fire, I could see where your boys got their streak of mischief."

"Perhaps." He shrugged, and a smile tugged up one corner of his mouth. "But I always thought Abby took more after me with her bookish ways."

"You were brilliant, the way you confronted him. I don't think he'll come back to Stone Creek any time soon."

"Let's hope not." He inhaled and exhaled as if in great need of air. He tucked her hand in the crook of his elbow, and they resumed walking.

She cocked her head his direction. "Are you all right?"

"I was thinking how *you* were magnificent helping out the Frosts. You always seem to be there when people need you. I— well, this whole town—will miss you when you move to Chicago."

Maggie's throat went dry. Feathery clouds moved across the face of the moon. An owl hooted. Mud squished beneath her feet, and whatever spirit of camaraderie which had bound them together that evening ebbed. Thoughts of Giles's moody, dark eyes flooded in.

Who did her heart belong to—Giles or...Thomas? Especially if there was no spoken agreement with either of them? She had more in common with Thomas, but why would he want her, when she'd been nothing but critical of him until recently?

∽

*T*he next morning, Maggie luxuriated in a bath, using lavender-scented soap cakes to scrub each inch of her body. Gloria had insisted Betty come to fill the tin tub with kettles of heated water, some from the rain barrel, perfect for washing her hair. With a partition set up in the kitchen, it helped take the place of an indoor bathroom.

After lathering her long tresses, she sunk all the way down so that all of her, from head to foot, was rinsed. She emerged into the cool air refreshed in heart and soul after soaking away the grime and sweat of yesterday's efforts. She stepped out and rubbed her skin dry with a fresh towel. How nice not to have to wait for Saturday evening when she usually took her weekly bath.

Maggie smiled to herself. Philip would resist taking a bath this early, realizing he wouldn't be allowed to get dirty the rest of the day. She'd have to find something quieter for him and Elise to do.

Dressing in a long skirt of blue chintz with a hint of green, Maggie matched a shirtwaist just a shade lighter than the skirt and wove the pin of her mother's jade brooch through the material to fasten it at her neck. How nicely the gold filigree pin would have decorated the front of the sage-green dress. When Giles returned, she would have to explain why she couldn't keep it.

After towel drying her hair, Maggie sat at the dressing table in her room. She'd leave her hair down to finish drying, but she combed through the tangles. That brought to mind the evening before.

How gently Thomas had lifted her locks to his lips, as though they were sacred to him. He'd almost truly kissed her. A gentle shiver went through her at the thought. His lips had brushed hers...warm and inviting...so close. If only he had a moment sooner—before that huge dog interrupted them. She sighed.

A little while later, Maggie ruffled her son's freshly washed hair as they approached Apple Blossom House for supper. "Philip! Look. Starks brought out another table for us so we could play checkers. And Elise is waving to you from the front porch."

"Just the ticket." Philip ran ahead and scrambled up the steps.

"Slow down, or you'll fall and get all dirty again."

"Come have some cider with me." Gloria patted the seat next to her on the porch. Two high-backed wicker chairs faced one another at an angle with a round marble-topped table sporting a crystal pitcher with two glasses between them. Gloria poured for them and handed one to Maggie.

Maggie smoothed her skirt behind her as she eased into the chair and took a sip of the cool liquid. "Mm, I can tell Flo added her favorite spices."

The children settled on the front corner of the porch, Elise on the swing while Philip plopped into an oak rocking chair on the other side of the table. Their giggles as they *taught* each other the *right* way to play checkers were like gems one might save in a pouch and take out to savor. Someday, memories of her son would be like that, but she wasn't in any hurry for it.

"Have you made a decision?"

"And there it is...the proverbial elephant in the room. Why don't you try being more direct?" Maggie rolled her eyes, and Gloria threw back her head in laughter—an unusual thing for her to do.

"Well?"

"I'm still not sure." Maggie worried her lip.

At one time, her plan had been so clear—buy a bakery and return to Buffalo, but then the job in Chicago came, along with

Giles...and there was the unpredictable Thomas and his family. She liked what she'd seen in him the night before. If she were truthful, she'd liked him all along, but perhaps didn't understand him. Maybe Gloria could advise her or even pray with her.

"Gloria, I'd really like to..."

Chug, chug chug. A motorcar barreled up the drive. Giles Prescott waved.

"Oh dear." Gloria groaned and plunked down her glass. "I suppose he's here to further persuade you."

Maggie rose and went to greet him, each step stiff with indecision. He lifted the goggles from his face and cut the engine. He hopped out of his horseless carriage wearing a wide grin.

"Maggie, dearest, it's so good to see you. Did you receive my gift?" Taking her in his arms like a rag doll, he swung her around, set her on her feet, and brushed the hair from her face. He must have noticed her scrunched-up, sour look. "I'm sorry, darling. You look perfectly lovely, and I've soiled your...outfit. How come you aren't wearing the dress I had sent?"

As though she lounged about in it every day, waiting for him. "For one thing, I didn't know you were coming, but we do need to talk." Dizzy from being spun around, Maggie tried to keep her balance but found herself leaning on Giles.

"I sent a message days ago." His full lips formed the pout of a boy who'd been indulged greatly over the years.

"There's been so much going on. We've been under quarantine here, and it's just recently been lifted."

He took one of her hands and looked down as though studying her fingers. "Hm. I see. Well, I'm glad to find you well. I've come for my answer about Chicago."

Oh. Well. Maggie looked around. "Where are your bags?"

Giles coughed. "You don't think me a cad who'd show up at the last minute and expect lodging, do you?" He barely met her gaze.

"Well, no, but I just assumed…"

"Don't worry yourself. I'm staying at the Pink Hotel. Why don't I take you into town? We have much to talk about."

She went for her hat, gloves, and a light coat and steeled herself for the bumpy ride.

After lunch at the hotel, they walked along the millpond arm in arm, as serene as old times—until he brought up the job.

"Well, what is your decision, Maggie? I've been quite patient."

"Giles, you're asking me to completely uproot my family to go to a strange city. I'm afraid I need more time." The idea of working in Chicago grew less appealing, but she had to think of the job, the opportunities.

He clenched his jaw. "What more is there to consider?"

Maggie sighed. "For one thing, I positively don't want Philip in boarding school."

Was he trying not to roll his eyes? "I'm sure we can work around that." And did she detect a less-than-sincere tone in his voice?

The rest of the afternoon and evening, the conversation continued to return to the position at the Silver Leaf test kitchen, no matter how she tried to change the subject. He would expect an answer by Monday.

As Maggie crawled into bed that night, weariness overtook her. She only hoped Thomas hadn't seen her on Giles's arm. She smiled into the dark as she realized how much she truly cared for the town's pharmacist.

CHAPTER 35

On Sunday morning, Giles sent a note to the church via the bellboy, pleading a headache. Despite Maggie's disappointment, his excuse wasn't surprising, though the fact that he'd also declined the invitation to dinner at Apple Blossom House was a bit more so.

Still, Monday morning, when she'd promised to deliver her decision, came far too soon.

Gloria hovered outside Apple Blossom House as Mr. Starks helped Maggie onto the wagon seat. His morning errands were taking him into town, making it convenient for her to surprise Giles early, after delivering a pie to the Blandings.

"I'm concerned for you, Maggie."

"I understand. And I appreciate it." The butterflies in her gut had not only grown but now flew in formation. Was it nerves or doubts over what she was about to do? She'd tossed and turned the night before and wound up deciding to make the pie for the grieving family since she couldn't sleep.

As she had sliced the paring knife through an apple's skin and peeled it off, she'd decided she must do what it took to work through the veneer on her own heart and down to the truth about her feelings. Her doubts grew about the wisdom of being courted by Giles.

He was offering her a once-in-a-lifetime opportunity and perhaps permanent independence. And more possibilities for Philip's future than this town or even Buffalo had to offer. Yet she had so many considerations before she could commit to anything.

She'd layered the apples, sweetened and mixed with cinnamon, in the bottom crust and dotted the filling with butter. In the nighttime silence by the light of a kerosene lamp, she prayed. *Father, please give me clarity.*

Giles must know her well enough to say whether he would consider proceeding toward an engagement. She would expect certain assurances before going forward. But what about faith and church?

That question still haunted her as she settled into the wagon.

"Gloria, don't worry. I'll be careful." *Of my heart.* Maggie shifted in her seat and reached down to her friend, who grasped her hand.

"I'm here for you." Gloria's eyebrows furrowed, and her eyes were dewy with affection. Maggie was blessed to have such a dear friend.

"Pray for me." Maggie waved as Mr. Starks pulled the wagon forward.

Another beautiful fall day for a drive. Each tree they passed was like an old friend. The pastoral scene of the Masons' farm with its bright red barn and speckled dairy cattle always brought a smile to her face.

As they drew nearer to town, the homes with their white picket fences and gardens grew a bit closer together. They reminded her of the home she'd shared with Robert. She would miss that certain ambience of home that Stone Creek held.

"Hello, Maggie." Leona Packer waved as she stood from tending to her garden.

"Good morning to you!"

Yes, all of these little things she would likely miss about Stone Creek, including the Harpers. If only she and Thomas were better suited to one another. If they could work together as they had at the Frosts. He'd confronted Blaze in a most amazing way, taking charge so decisively. No more wishy-washy Thomas. Even so, she had found him endearing from the start —though sometimes frustrating.

"Where to first, ma'am?" Mr. Starks still couldn't get into the hang of calling her Maggie.

"I'd like to deliver this pie to the Blandings. And it's a fine day, so I'll walk to the Pink Hotel from there. Please feel free to go about your business and back to Apple Blossom House whenever you're ready. I'm sure Mr. Prescott will drive me home in his...contraption."

They shared a chuckle as Maggie alighted, and he handed her the covered pie dish.

"This smells delicious, ma'am. I'm sure it would rival Flo's."

"Don't let her hear you say such a thing. But it's my mother's recipe. Nobody can beat that."

"Be careful, ma'am." Did she detect worry in the expression of the usually aloof servant?

She nodded. Everyone seemed so concerned about her. Was she missing something? Maggie was used to being the caretaker.

After she dropped the pie off, she would announce herself at the hotel and wait for Giles to come down to the lobby. They could walk around the Stone Creek millpond again and talk things through one more time. The stillness and quietness of the morning would provide them with some privacy.

As she neared the Blandings' stately white home, her feet grew leaden. The shades and blinds were still drawn. As she strolled up the front walkway, despite the sun and refreshing coolness, foreboding settled on her. Perhaps she should go around to the back where the servants would likely be available to receive her offering.

A bee grazed her hair, circling the pie plate, and then buzzed in her ear. "Shoo." Shooing the bee with one hand and balancing the dish in her other made progress slow as she inched her way around the side of the house. The bee finally received the message and wound his way around tall zinnias as he looked for nectar.

Familiar voices drew Maggie closer to the corner of the house, but when she rounded it, her eyes widened at the shocking sight before her.

~

Thomas leaned on the shining marble counter at Harper Apothecary. As long as it was early on a Monday morning, while many women did their wash, he could take a little time to read. He opened his Bible to the Psalms. Every day now, he looked forward to the refreshment and encouragement of God's Word. He longed to hear the voice of his heavenly Father as though he'd finally come home.

The Lord is my shepherd, I shall not want. Yea, though I walk through the valley of the shadow of death I will fear no evil. He never tired of reading Psalm 23, as it had a whole new meaning to him. He smoothed and refolded the bent corner of the page.

Thank you, Father, that Lyle only had a cold.

He smiled with satisfaction and peace. The Lord saw his joy and relief. The crisis was averted, the epidemic had passed, and the quarantine nearly lifted on all the homes.

Thomas lifted a mug of tea to his mouth, which he had poured from the pot of tea his daughter thoughtfully made earlier before leaving for school. He turned a few pages, finding Bess's letter still tucked there. Should he open it?

Did he imagine a chill as he touched the envelope? As though death once more sent out its evil tendrils and laughed at him? *It's time for me to overcome these thoughts.*

Thomas pulled his letter opener from the drawer. He slid it underneath the flap, making a neat tear. With shaking hands, he extracted the letter, unfolding the delicate sheaf of paper to read her gentle script.

My Dearest Thomas,

I fear I am waning, though it seems I've rallied. I dreamt of running to Jesus last night in a field of grass. He is my Shepherd, and I am willing to be home with Him, except for my sadness in leaving you and the children behind.

I know you think you cannot manage on your own, but you are a stronger man than you realize, and God will help you if you ask Him. When I no longer dwell in this earthly tent, I will still keep you and the children in my heart.

You may not want to hear this, but I want you to be happy. Please, make sure that if you marry again, the woman you choose to become a mother to our children will find it in her heart to love them nearly as much as we do.

I grow tired and must finish this now, but remember you have made me happy and I have always loved you.

Always, with a full heart,
Your Bess

Thomas's eyes clouded, and his throat constricted. To the very end, Bess had been selfless. Yet he'd done nothing but pity himself since her death. He folded the paper, tucking it back into the envelope and set it next to the Bible.

Make sure...that the woman you choose to be a mother to our children will find it in her heart to love them nearly as much as we do. Her voice echoed in his mind as clearly as though she were in the room with him. But the vision of Bess faded, and Maggie emerged in his thoughts. *Beautiful Maggie.* If anything, she liked —no, loved—the children more than she even cared for him.

Thomas's sorrow doubled. Not only did his throat constrict with emotion, so did his heart. Though there would always be a place in it for Bess, Maggie was alive, and warm, and caring. Had he ever shown her the proper appreciation for having nursed him back to health? Helping in the shop? Or spending time with Abby? Not really. He'd said a few words, but he hadn't shown her enough friendship, except for the other night.

He loved Maggie Galloway, but she was lost to him. Soon she would undoubtedly leave for Chicago. It was too late.

CHAPTER 36

aggie gasped, and the pie plate slid from her hands, landing with a crash at her feet. Giles Prescott held a weepy Irena Blanding in his arms.

Giles pushed the girl away as she stared up at him with adoring eyes. "Maggie, it's not what you think." He rushed down the back porch steps toward her.

She froze with her hand over her mouth. As he neared, she lifted leaden feet and backed away. "No! Don't you ever come near me again."

Irena lifted her chin with a smug look on her face. She fastened the two top buttons of her black high-collared mourning dress and smoothed her clothing.

"Listen to me." Giles grasped at Maggie's arm, but she turned on her heel and marched away.

"Not what I think? Pray tell—I can't imagine what your legitimate reason could be." She raised her arms in a dramatic gesture, only stopping for a moment.

"Just let me explain, Maggie." Giles tugged on her sleeve like an insolent child.

Maggie turned back to face him.

Irena disappeared into the house and slammed the door. How typical of the haughty young woman.

"All right, I confess, I did begin some correspondence with the girl as she was awfully interested in learning more about my horseless carriage."

"Ha! You expect me to believe such a ridiculous premise?"

Giles held his hat in his hand, his eyebrows furrowed into an almost contrite expression. "When I heard her little brother had passed, I wanted to comfort her."

Nausea rose in Maggie's belly.

"I hadn't planned on seeing her again, but she sent a note to me at the hotel." He rubbed his chin and shifted his weight from one foot to another.

"All while we talked of renewing our acquaintance in Chicago." Maggie clenched her fists.

"You and I had no formal agreement." He averted his gaze and shifted his weight again.

"Isn't this why you came back for my answer? So we could discuss our possible future? Well, there is no possible future for us *ever*."

He drew closer and lowered his voice. "Do you have to make a spectacle of yourself?"

She pointed a finger to her chest. "Me? I'm a widowed woman of decent reputation, but you have made my humiliation complete. What is there left to be embarrassed about?" She swept her hands outward.

"Fine. Set that aside for now. Are you interested in the job? The position is still open. There's no one better for it." He nodded and smiled, then straightened one cuff at a time as though nothing unsavory had transpired.

Maggie's guffaw brought the people around those four corners of the intersection on which the Blandings' house stood to their windows as curtains and shades lifted a little, allowing the curious onlookers to be discreet. "Giles Prescott, don't ever darken my doorstep again."

"But Maggie," he whined. Almost comically. Pathetic.

Maggie turned on her heel, meaning it that time. Overwhelming anger kept her tears at bay. Betrayal twisted within her, taking a slice from her heart like a hot knife. She was seared against any future trust of Giles Prescott.

She strode away. She wouldn't stop until she reached Ian and Sophie's house. This time, she never wanted to see Giles again.

Ian opened the door as she pushed the gate inward and trod up the path. "Maggie, what are you doing here so early on a Monday morning? Is Philip all right?"

She extended her arms, and her tall, strong brother and pastor enveloped her in a hug.

"You were right, Ian. Giles Prescott is an absolute cad. I found him embracing Irena Blanding."

"Oh, Maggie, I'm so sorry. And I want to hear all about this later."

They pulled apart, and she met Ian's sympathetic gaze, tinged by...what? Worry?

"I was on my way to find Dr. Moore. Sophie's baby is on the way. Will you stay with her?"

~

*A*rabella Faith McCormick was born that afternoon. The nickname "Bella" suited the unusually beautiful newborn. Maggie helped clean up after a better-than-expected labor and delivery. In the late afternoon, she brought a cup of tea to her sister-in-law.

Sophie was propped up on pillows and wore a pink-flowered nightgown and matching robe. "Thank you, Maggie, you can set it there. Tea sounds lovely. Would you like to hold Bella?"

The newborn seemed to stare up at Maggie as she took her into her arms and cradled the infant with as much gentleness as she could muster. She perched on the edge of Sophie's bed.

Maggie's parents' old cherry four-poster bed took up most of the room, looking stately in what had once been Ian's bachelor room. Sophie's soft chestnut curls spread across the white starched pillowcases.

"What will you do, Maggie? Are you still thinking about buying the bakery?"

"Sophie, don't worry about me. You just had a baby."

"But Ian told me what happened this morning, why you showed up before the doctor did." She patted Maggie's arm.

Inside, Maggie withered at the thought of facing the people of Stone Creek again. She itched to get back to Apple Blossom Cottage and pack up her belongings. "Robert's parents will gladly take us in for a time until I can find a place to live and wait to see if I'll *ever* get a loan. I'll figure out something." She sighed. "I have no other choice. I would have waited until you had the baby, either way. After you regain some strength, there's really no need for me to stay." *I can't.*

Bella's soft, mewling cries tugged at Maggie's heart. Leaving and not seeing her new niece grow up would be sad. Sophie reached for her tiny daughter, and Maggie handed her back.

"You know, Maggie, Stone Creek can be a forgiving place. I've seen it firsthand myself. Remember how, despite the gossip, most of the people accepted me and forgave my deceit? There are good people here."

Maggie could only stare down at her hands. While Sophie opened her robe and helped the babe latch on to nurse, Maggie looked for a burp cloth to give her. "But I feel so humiliated. Other than you and the Myles family, I have no reason to stay. A

fresh start might be good for me...and hopefully, for my son too."
Though truthfully, he would miss Elise and Zeke dreadfully. But
wouldn't it be good for him to make other friends as well?

"I understand how that feels, probably more than anyone
else in town." Sophie referred to the revelation Caira wasn't her
little sister, but her daughter. She'd had to make a decision to
come clean before the church or leave town. Ian had stuck by
her, and they both were stronger for it.

"That, I'm sure, is true." She met Sophie's empathetic smile
with one of her own.

"Ian and I, and of course, Caira, will miss you terribly.
Without your support and kindness, I don't think Ian and I
would have ended up married to one another."

Maggie's heart went as soft as butter melting into warm
bread. Liquid filled her eyes, and she didn't stop it from
pouring down her cheeks. "I will miss you more than you
know."

~

*N*early two weeks later, on a Saturday morning
before he opened the pharmacy, Thomas stacked
wooden boxes in the storeroom, and Abby swept the floor. The
boys were upstairs doing their homework. Usually, Abby talked
to him about her school lessons or perhaps a book she'd read,
but except for the thud of crate on crate or the swish of the
broom, an awkward quiet hung between them.

"Papa, a penny for your thoughts." Abby's light, cheery
voice was a balm for his oft-troubled heart as of late.

"I'm afraid my thoughts aren't worth even that." He rubbed
his chin.

"What is it, Papa?" Her earnest expression, the beautiful
eyes peering at him from behind her glasses pulled at him.
Should he tell her?

"I haven't said goodbye to Mrs. Galloway. Do you know when she's leaving?" He went back to the boxes and then searched for his accounting book under a stack of papers.

The swishing stopped. "Philip told Zeke they're leaving in two days. He wasn't happy at all."

"I'm sure he wasn't." The oatmeal from breakfast congealed in his stomach. Or had he swallowed a lead weight? Two days? He grew frantic in his search. Where was his confounded ledger, anyway?

Abby tapped him on the shoulder. "Looking for this, Papa?" She handed him the black leather-bound book. "It was up on the shelf where you usually keep it." She shrugged.

"So it was." Thomas sighed. "Thank you."

"You really should say goodbye to her. We all should. She was as nice to us as Mama used to be. Not like Mrs. Peaberry." Abby leaned on the broom and scrunched her face. "I wish you'd marry somebody like Mrs. Galloway."

Thomas placed the ledger on top of the pile of bills. "So now you're a matchmaker?" He had to smile, but he wouldn't let her see it. "Perhaps you should finish sweeping the floor before you take up a new occupation."

"Yes, Papa."

Thomas sat at his desk and opened the ledger. He procured a pencil from the drawer. The list of payments sent out and those received was indecipherable. Maybe he should leave the store and march right over to the parsonage where Maggie had been staying to help Sophie.

And when he got there, what would he say? *Thank you for all the kind things you've done? I wish you the best of luck with your new bakery?* At least his suspicions about that fop, Prescott, weren't unfounded. The way he'd treated Maggie infuriated Thomas.

He rolled the pencil between his fingers. Never mind that cad. Did he have the guts to tell her what he'd been fighting in his heart all along? That he was in love with her and wanted to join their families? He dropped the pencil and rubbed his eyes.

The door clanked shut as Abby came back in after emptying the dustpan. "Papa?"

"What is it, little dove? Can't you see I'm busy now?" Immediately, he regretted his snapping tone. He looked sideways at her.

"I just wanted to mention one more thing." Her shoulders slumped.

"I'm sorry. What is it?"

"Did you know Mr. Leonard is closing his shop next door and moving back to the city?"

He shook his head. He'd heard rumors, but nothing confirmed.

"We could use more room. Business will be booming come winter when everybody gets sick." She tapped her foot. "We could join the stores and maybe rent some of the space out to someone...who has something to sell." His daughter ran her finger along the side of his desk, not looking up at him.

"We'll see, Abby."

"Okay. I also have a surprise for you. You can say goodbye to Mrs. Galloway here. Leave it to me." She put her hands behind her back. At this moment, the mischievous glint in her eyes was pure little girl, but the confident demeanor of her head held high hinted at the young lady she was becoming. What was she up to?

~

That afternoon, as Maggie washed the dinner dishes, Sophie and the girls napped, and Ian was in his study, like old times. When she went to shake out the kitchen rug, Zeke and Lyle came up the walk with a card for her.

"What's this?" She opened the plain white card which said,

Dear Mrs. Galloway, please come to Harper Apothecary at 7 o'clock, p.m. I would like to speak with you. Please tell my brothers whether you can attend our meeting. How odd that Abby didn't come to the parsonage and ask for herself. "Please tell Abby I'll be there."

~

our hours later, Maggie stood at the door of Thomas Harper's store, where the *closed* sign faced out. She lifted her hand to knock, but Abby waved at her through the glass and motioned for her to come in.

"Hello, Mrs. Galloway." Abby came with arms open, and they hugged. "I'm so happy to see you. We've really missed you." Before she knew it, Abby had relieved Maggie of her shawl and reticule.

"Where's your father?"

"He'll be here shortly." The glimmer in Abby's eyes danced with mischief.

Josiah appeared in a clean shirt and properly affixed tie, his hair fixed neat and in place. "May I show you to your seat, madam?"

"W-what?"

The lanky boy revealed a toothy grin as he offered his arm. She held lightly to him as he escorted her to the storefront, pulling a kitchen chair away from a hexagonal, Jacobean-style table covered with a white cloth.

She sat, confused. "Thank you?"

Before her, the table had been set with two pressed-glass plates that almost matched. A lone white taper in a polished silver candlestick adorned the center of the table, along with a small vase overstuffed with little bright-yellow mums. Josiah pulled a napkin from the table and handed it to her.

Lyle tromped down the stairs carrying a tin of shortbread

cookies, which he deposited on the table and then bowed. Last, but not least, Zeke came around the corner from the hallway pulling his father by the hand.

"Come on, Pa."

Thomas ceased moving when their eyes met. They hadn't seen one another except from a distance since that night he'd confronted Dr. Blaze. His mouth hung open. "What are you doing here?"

"That's what I'm wondering...but I could always leave if you like." The children's crestfallen expressions kept her seated.

"N-no. I'm glad to see you, but I'm surprised. I heard a commotion while I was catching up on bookwork in the office, but I had no idea they'd dragged Bess's picture table down from the sitting room."

He stood awkwardly with a pencil behind his ear, in shirt-sleeves, a bit rumpled. The real, everyday Thomas before her endeared her more than Giles ever could've. How had she not realized sooner that he was the one who complemented her, who really cared about her? He unrolled his sleeves, refastening them, and came to sit at the table. Maggie pointed to his ear, and he swiped the pencil from behind it. A bit self-conscious herself, she patted her hair. If only she'd worn the pale blue-green shirtwaist instead of her old cream one.

"Have a seat." Josiah poured cups of tea for them.

"Would you care for sugar? One lump or two?" Zeke licked his lips.

"One, and yes, you may each have a cube." Thomas rolled his eyes.

Each of the boys took one cube to suck on.

"Come on, boys, leave them alone now." Abby motioned for them to follow and turned toward Maggie. "If you have found everything satisfactory, we'll come back to check on you later."

"Everything is beautiful. Thank you." Maggie couldn't

believe the trouble the Harper children had gone to on her behalf, but why on this particular evening?

Zeke took a bow before they scrambled away and likely out the back door, as it slammed behind them.

Maggie and Thomas each took a sip of lukewarm tea.

He smiled at her over the teapot. "I'm afraid Abby still has something to learn about serving things hot."

"I can't believe they'd go to all this trouble for us." Maggie found a spoon on the table and stirred the sugar around the bottom of the cup. He seemed as clueless about their plans as she, but thankfully, she had this time with him before she left. She'd wanted to say a proper goodbye to the children...to Thomas.

~

"*H*ave a cookie." Thomas pried the top off the tin and offered the buttery cookies to Maggie.

"Thank you." She reached in, took a golden treat, and nibbled on its edge before she put it on the plate in front of her.

The clock ticked away more seconds of his life, seconds of indecision. What should he say to her? How did he say good-bye, when he wanted to know her better and give her a reason not to leave?

Maggie cleared her throat. "You've made quite a lot of progress on Harper Apothecary."

"I had quite a bit of help." He had to touch her hand, even all the way across the table. "And I've never even properly shown my thanks. It appears my children have beaten me to it."

"No need to thank me. I was glad to help." She withdrew her hand and sat straighter.

Things weren't going so well, but he needed to say what he had to before it was too late.

"Maggie, I've been thinking." He swallowed and rubbed

sweaty palms on his trouser legs. He hadn't been this filled with trepidation since he'd asked to court Bess. "Are you sure you want to leave Stone Creek?"

"I don't see any other options." She lifted the cookie, this time snapping off a bigger bite.

He'd given more thought to Abby's suggestion. "The shop next to mine is going to be empty. If I expanded my store, I would have room for say...baked goods, especially when summer visitors are out here to stay at the lakes. Would you be interested?"

~

Maggie swallowed the wrong way, nearly choking on cookie crumbs. Grabbing her teacup, she knocked it over. She coughed and grasped at her throat. What a mess she'd made.

Thomas stood and soaked up as much tea as possible with their napkins. He patted her on the back and handed her his cup. "Are you all right?"

She took a couple of sips, coughed, and then nodded. Was he asking her what she thought? To be a business partner? Disappointment settled into her chest like the cookie crumbs, spreading discouragement throughout her being. Yet what had she expected? Had she really ever given him the idea she was interested in him romantically? Ideally, as a husband?

Maggie took another gulp of tea and stood. "I think I need to go. I only have a couple more evenings to spend with my brother and his family."

Thomas grabbed her hand. "Do you understand I'm trying to give you a reason to stay?"

"Are you?" Tears blurred her vision, and she looked away, but then he took her other hand. She wouldn't let him see her cry or let him know he'd hurt her. She tried to pull back but was caught between Thomas and the chair. "Really, I must go. Please tell the children goodbye for me, that I...love them... and Philip and I will miss them dreadfully. Thank them for me."

But it was no good. She choked on a sob. Before she knew it, Thomas had drawn her into an embrace.

"What is it, Maggie, dear?" His breath was warm above her ear.

"Thomas, is that the only reason I have to stay? To be your business partner?" She pushed against him, refusing to look in his eyes.

"Well, I suppose, if you'll have me, it might be easier if you married me first."

She swung her gaze up to him. "Do you mean it?"

"Maggie, from the moment I met you, I couldn't get you out of my head. I care for you deeply." He paused, and his heartbeat sped up beneath her hand. "I love you."

This time, when she parted her lips, tilting her face toward him, his mouth met hers fully, and with great tenderness. Lost in the moment, her form molded into his, fitting perfectly within his arms. When he stopped, he kissed her nose, then her forehead. One hand went up her back to her hair, where he entangled his fingers in her locks. The tender warmth of his hand on her neck brought comfort.

"Then, yes, I will be your wife," she said, almost breathless with a passion she had never expected to experience again, not just of physical attraction, but of spirit and soul. "You've changed," she whispered against his shoulder.

"The Lord has done a work in me. I no longer blame Him for my misfortunes but know they're meant somehow for my good."

Whispers traveled down the hallway. Maggie pulled back and looked around Thomas. There were Abby, Josiah, Lyle, and Zeke clapping as they came into the room.

"Yay! Mrs. Galloway is going to be my mother." Zeke jumped up and down.

Maggie and Thomas parted, but their hands remained intertwined.

"I suppose we would have had to tell you sooner or later." Thomas shook his head.

"All we have to do now is tell Philip. I wish he were here." Maggie leaned toward the man she loved.

"I am!" He popped around the corner and came running for them both with arms out wide for a hug. They embraced Philip, and all the children joined them in the largest hug Maggie ever experienced.

"I always wanted a big family." Philip's voice came up from somewhere in the midst of them.

"And it looks as though that's what you'll have." Thomas's grin spread ear to ear, endearing Maggie even more.

CHAPTER 37

*M*aggie and Thomas emerged from Stone Creek Community Church under light flakes of December snow on a sunny day. A shower of rice pelted them as they made their way toward the carriage. They climbed in, and she turned back to wave at her family and other well-wishers.

"Thank you, Ian, for a beautiful wedding ceremony."

He nodded at her with Caira in his arms, who blew kisses. Sophie stood next to him holding Bella wrapped tight in a blanket against her shoulder.

"You're most welcome." Ian winked.

Philip jumped up and down. "I wish I could go with you."

"You will, soon enough, son." Thomas's wide grin showed his pleasure at adding Philip to his family. "I'm taking your mother to a special place. We'll see you back at Apple Blossom House for the reception in a little while."

The small crowd with all of the Harper children, Gloria, Asa, Elise, Mrs. Fairgrave, and the group from the boarding-house, and even the Frost family had turned out for their ceremony. Mr. Frost waved as he stood clean-shaven with Wyatt in his arms.

"Where on earth are you taking me?" Joy bubbled up inside of Maggie.

"Did I tell you how fetching you looked in your dress?" Thomas gazed into her eyes like a lovesick schoolboy, holding her hand while Mr. Starks drove them.

"Why, thank you. Now, stop changing the subject." She rearranged the aqua satin of her skirt. She'd chosen the outfit with her husband in mind. "Where are you taking me?"

"I'll tell you when we get there." Thomas squeezed her hand, giving directions to Mr. Starks. They had only passed a few streets. "Turn right here, please."

"Yes, sir." Mr. Starks smirked.

"The last house on the block, on the right." Thomas pointed, leaning forward on the edge of his seat.

When Mr. Starks brought the barouche to a stop, Thomas popped up from the seat and pulled Maggie with him, lifting her down. Would she ever tire of the feel of his strong hands on her waist?

"There it is. I'd set aside money for a home, but the time didn't quite seem right until we were engaged."

"Thomas, it's beautiful."

A two-story red-brick house welcomed them. Lacey snowflakes created a powdery icing on the branches of a line of evergreens which stood like stately sentinals on either side of their new home. A wreath with a large red bow already hung on the front door. Maggie pointed at it.

"You put that up?"

"I had a little help from Abby and Josiah." He bounded up the front steps onto the generous porch. "Come along, my bride."

Maggie hiked the hem of her skirt, not wanting to get it wet.

Thomas opened the door and lifted her into his arms and over the threshold.

Maggie blinked, her eyes growing accustomed to the dimness inside the house. "It is simply beautiful." She took in the large marble hearth with an oak mantel. She looked forward to the times they would all gather together on cold winter nights. The house was emptied of furniture and would mean a fresh start for both families.

"I thought I couldn't feel any happier than I had at the ceremony, knowing you and I will be husband and wife for as long a life as the good Lord gives, but you have given me a new home...not only for my heart but also for our children." Maggie leaned against Thomas, listening to him breathe. "I couldn't love you more than at this moment."

"Nothing makes me happier than to know you are content." Thomas grinned down at her.

"Yes, more than ever. I do think we should get back to the festivities, though, don't you? The kids will wonder about us." Maggie tugged her new husband's arm.

"I have one more special Christmas decoration to show you." He led her to the archway between the parlor and the dining room and pointed upward.

Mistletoe dangled above their heads.

"I thought you'd never ask." Maggie stood on tiptoe, bringing her arms around Thomas's waist while he cupped her face in his hands and brought his mouth down to hers. Their lips fused together in a more urgent kiss.

The snowflakes flying outside the window became a blur.

THE END

Did you enjoy this book? We hope so!
Would you take a quick minute to leave a review where you purchased the book?
It doesn't have to be long. Just a sentence or two telling what you liked about the story!

Receive a FREE ebook and get updates when new Wild Heart books release: https://wildheartbooks.org/newsletter

SNEAK PEEK: SCANDALS AND MERCIES

Don't miss the next book in the Stone Creek Brides Series!

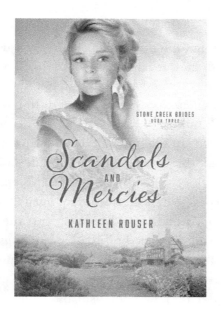

Scandals and Mercies
By Kathleen Rouser

CHAPTER I

OCTOBER 1902, STONE CREEK, MICHIGAN

A slight glow illuminated the sky through the window when Nora Armstrong awoke. She sat and rubbed her arms, shivering. She'd overslept and must hurry to accomplish her mission.

Nora reached for her corset, fastened it, and wished a lady had permission to curse such a contraption. She pulled on her petticoat and a simple long brown work frock. She then slipped on her most practical shoes, leaving the topmost buttons undone in her hurry. A hat would conceal her nighttime braid gone askew, and a shawl would cover her plain attire. A quick splash of clean water at the washstand would have to do for now.

Next, she lifted the dust ruffle from below the four-poster mahogany bed and reached underneath. She grabbed the smooth wooden chest and slid it toward her in the faint light. A creak made her jump as she opened the lid. Her heart pounded. Had Aunt Gertrude or Uncle Edmond heard the noise? She pulled out the small hidden burlap sack.

She slipped through the hallway and down the stairs, attempting to miss the creaky spot on each step, covered with well-worn carpet. When a squeak sounded under her light tread, she stopped and leaned back against the oak banister. Soft whiffling snores echoed off the high ceilings and came in concert from Aunt Gertrude's and Uncle Edmond's separate bedrooms. Ten more steps to the bottom of the grand staircase and she should make it without disturbing them.

"Miss?" Wrapped in a plain shawl, Eliza, the elderly maid, stood poised to defend herself on the edge of the shadows with a vase clasped tightly in her hand. Her white braid shone in the moonlight.

Nora put a finger to her lips. "I'm going for my morning walk early. Lots to do today." She carried the sack beside her as she reached the Persian rug at the bottom of the stairs.

"With that?" The maid pointed.

"Oh, this? I thought I'd drop off some old gloves at the box outside the church. Please, don't wake my aunt and uncle. I'll be back as soon as I can." Her dishonesty sent a twinge of pain through her conscience.

"I suppose, miss."

"Thank you." Nora gave the older lady a peck on the cheek and caught Eliza's smile in the dim light.

Nora made her way through the kitchen and out the side door. She only waited to close the wrought-iron gate behind her before she took off in a run, the sack swinging beside her.

～

James leaped off the back of the volunteer fire wagon before it barreled onto the path running alongside Hope's Place. Smoke poured from the rear of the building, above the unforgiving flames. He steadied himself, pulled his pad from his inner suit coat pocket, and scribbled down a description of the horrifying sight. Then he placed his pencil behind his ear. With a handkerchief, he covered his mouth and nose, seeking relief from the acrid odor of burning wood and plaster. Young women, wrapped in blankets, huddled together. They backed away when he tried to approach them.

A scream pierced the air as a girl tumbled out of the front door, coughing, her nightgown aflame. A nurse pushed her to the ground and pulled the blanket from her shoulder. She wrapped the girl, which put out the fire.

Firemen scrambled to unwind the hose, and another shoveled coal into the belly of the steam pump. A rather stout volunteer fireman pulled a ladder from the truck and hoisted it onto his shoulder.

"Come on, Cooper, we need more hands," Reverend Ian McCormick yelled. Soot streaked the minister's face and white shirt. His nostrils flared. His expression dared James to take part in the rescue efforts.

"Right." He ground his teeth. Helping put out the fire was, no doubt, the most important task. But did anyone in this sleepy town understand the importance of a reporter getting the news to its citizens as well? He removed his coat, throwing it onto the back of a wagon, and rolled up his sleeves.

"Let's go. We need relief in the bucket brigade." Ian turned to his wife. "Sophie, we have someone to take your place. The women need you."

The bright blaze silhouetted a line of men from town. They pumped water from the well into buckets, passing them along toward the fire and doing their best to help beat back the flames. He took the spot Sophie left empty, taking a sloshing bucket from the local carpenter, Mack Frost, who already appeared weary. How long had they been working?

Smoke rose in an ominous cloud. When they tamped it in one place, the bright orange flames ate up the wood in another. His stomach churned at the sickening sound of creaking wood and crashing glass. Though time flew, every purposeful movement seemed to take longer than needed until everything had calmed down. Still, billows of smoke rose as if to remind them the fire had won over a good portion of the house.

A group of young women huddled together; their faces etched with horror. "Where will we go?" A dark-haired girl on the front lawn spoke, half moaning. Some of them wept.

James wiped the sweat from his brow with his sleeve and left the line. Urgency called for him to obtain the details from Reverend McCormick.

"Reverend!" He waved to the taller man who was placing a coat around his wife's shoulders.

"What is it, Cooper?" The usually calm minister snapped at James.

As James strode nearer, McCormick held Sophie close. His eyes filled with sorrow as he studied the home's vulnerable occupants.

"What about these poor girls? They need someplace safe to stay." Sophie McCormick's voice caught on a sob.

"The Lord has got us this far, dear. I'm sure some local

farms and townspeople will take them in temporarily while we...rebuild." Ian scraped a hand down the side of his face. Seeing his dream that had only recently come to fruition go up in flames couldn't be easy.

Rose Sinclair, the head nurse of Hope's Place, coughed and caught her breath. "I salvaged a few blankets. Would you help me distribute them, Sophie?"

Sophie took half of her pile. "Of course, I'm just glad you got out all right."

James tapped his ever-present pencil on his pad. "Excuse me, Reverend, do you have a few minutes to answer some questions?"

Ian glowered at him. "Why are you still here?"

James clenched his fist around his pencil and drew in a breath. *Stay calm.* "I'm simply doing my job, Reverend. The people of Stone Creek deserve to know what happened tonight at Hope's Place."

"A tragedy happened tonight at Hope's Place. And right now, these young ladies are suffering. Now, you know as well as I this is a delicate situation. These women don't want to be named in your story. In fact, I'd like you to leave all of them out of it." Ian stepped closer, towering over him. He must appear as a knight-in-shining-armor to the handful of unmarried pregnant girls who'd taken shelter in the old farmhouse-turned-mission.

"Reverend, I can speak with him." Rose huffed. "Mr. Cooper, if you'd be so kind to wait for a couple of minutes while we hand out these blankets." She and Sophie hurried to the group of frightened pregnant girls.

"Our home is ruined." One of girls rocked back and forth on her knees. "Where will we go?"

"The fire is out. I need to survey the damage, Cooper. Walk with me if you like." Ian motioned toward the destroyed building.

James barely kept up with the other man's purposeful strides.

"Are you staying longer to help?"

"Sorry, Reverend. I've got a story to print. Maybe I can come and help with the rebuilding efforts later."

"I'm sure." The minister's sarcasm didn't go unnoticed.

Nurse Sinclair returned. "Reverend, I told him I had a few minutes."

James looked over his shoulder at the young woman, probably around his own age. Her brown hair framed a pleasant face. Dark circles revealed her exhaustion.

"I will leave you in Miss Sinclair's capable hands." Ian motioned toward her.

"Very well. Thank you." James nodded his agreement. He lifted his arm to escort the nurse to a quieter place where they could talk.

~

Nora jogged toward Hope's Place. The damp, cool morning air didn't bode well for her sister Lynnie's lung condition. She'd always been somewhat sickly.

Her senses awakened to electricity in the air. An ominous plume arose in the north. Fire? The heavy scent of burning wood, as though hundreds of hearths burned into the dawn, assaulted her nose. Hairs rose on her neck. Her heart lurched for a moment as she inhaled to catch her breath. Could it be Hope's Place? *No!*

Nora ran toward the old White farm. Lynnie had been there since it opened a couple of months before. Her sister should have been safe there. This was why she had advocated it, though they must hide the fact she was with child from Aunt Gertrude at all costs. Then again, Gertrude Wringer wouldn't go near a place that housed what she referred to as *fallen women.*

Poor Lynnie. Fallen woman wasn't a term Nora would say in the same breath with her sister's name. Deceived, yes. She'd loved the young man who'd deserted her, but she wouldn't tell anyone who the father was. Beautiful Evelyn, nicknamed Lynnie. She had been Mama and Papa's favorite. And now Nora had the responsibility of looking out for her sister, two years her junior at seventeen.

Shadows of Main Street's buildings fell across her path. More gaslights glowed than usual this early on a Saturday morning. The town already stirred. This didn't bode well. Nora slipped west another block, hoping to be less noticeable off the main road. The half hour it would take to get to their meeting place in Apple Blossom Orchard couldn't come soon enough. Nora slowed to catch her breath before taking off again in a sprint. She shouldn't have even bothered with her corset.

God, if You hear me, watch over my little sister. She needs You. A year ago, Nora wouldn't have questioned whether God heard her, but was she even worthy of His attention?

Her heart pounded to the beat of her own footsteps. She gripped her sack with a sweaty hand. A sack containing a much-needed medicine for her sister, bought with her stipend for playing the piano at the church. Hall's Catarrh Cure had to be better for her than some of the inhalers that contained mercury.

Light glowed through the windows of Apple Blossom House, showing her the way to the bench in the grove where she had permission to meet Lynnie. Her best friend, Sophie, had given her the idea. And Gloria Myles, owner of Apple Blossom Estate, along with her husband, Asa, gave them this privacy away from the eyes of gossip-mongering acquaintances in town.

Nora scurried to the path, straining her neck in an attempt

to catch sight of her sister's golden hair, darker than her own wheat-blond hair. Maybe Lynnie sat huddled on the bench in the cool morning air. Often, she stood, expecting their meeting, but she'd had to wait longer for Nora this morning.

The bench came into sight. Empty. Nora stumbled toward the seat and plunked down. She dropped the sack and bent forward, putting her head in her hands. "Oh, Lynnie! Where are you?"

She sucked in the smoke-tainted air, catching her breath. It would be a risk being seen at Hope's Place, but what else could she do? Fear for her sister's well-being spread its tentacles around her heart and squeezed.

She picked up the sack, stood, and set her face toward Stone Creek Road and Hope's Place. Her feet dragged her toward the inevitable. Less than another mile.

They had promised not to be seen together, but Nora had to know. The closer she trudged, the harder it was to take a full breath. She jogged until a pain struck her in the side and then walked the rest of the way.

The remains of Hope's Place stood twisted and malformed. Dissipating smoke blocked dawn's light as though a hazy cloud hung above. Fear seeped away as sadness gripped her. Nora's eyes blurred.

"Nora!" Sophie McCormick scurried toward her with arms outstretched. She engulfed her in a hug.

"Where is she?" A breathless whisper escaped her lips. "Is she all right?"

"She'll recover."

As they pulled apart, Sophie held her arms. Nora blinked away the tears. "What do you mean?"

"The smoke has been hard on her breathing, but she'll heal. Another of our girls received some rather nasty burns. They're being taken to see Dr. Moore."

Nora nodded. "I wish I could have been here to help. I was going to meet her in the orchard this morning."

"Come along, I'll have you talk with Rose. She can tell you more of Lynnie's condition." Sophie crooked her arm and held to Nora's, who drew strength from her friend's presence.

They strode around toward the barn, where Rose Sinclair stood close to a young man. James Cooper. The last man Nora wanted to see. Ever.

ACKNOWLEDGMENTS

Many thanks and appreciation go to Misty Beller and the Wild Heart Books team for your willingness to give *Secrets and Wishes* a new publishing home. And I'm so appreciative toward my editor, Denise Weimer, who has helped me hone this story into a much stronger romance.

I'm so grateful for the encouragement of my dear friend, Toni Price, who I think must be my biggest fan. Knowing you wanted to read the next book gave me another great reason to finish writing this story. Thank you to my dear friend, Shelia Sulkowski, who has cheered me on and reminded me for Whom I write. J'nell Ciesielski, you have been a wonderful critique partner. Your feedback has been invaluable. Elaine Stock, your help with my synopses is always a blessing. I appreciate your honesty.

Shortly after I wrote the first few chapters of *Secrets and Wishes,* my husband and I visited his cousin in Minnesota. Betsi Kolden and her husband, Tom, hosted us for a week and humored my desire to visit St. Peter, Minnesota, so I could visit the Soderlund Pharmacy Museum for research. There I could examine and photograph historical remedies, bottles, and antique pharmaceutical paraphernalia. We were even able to sample root beer from an old-fashioned soda fountain. Sadly, the physical museum no longer exists, but a virtual Soderlund Pharmacy Museum can be visited online. Thank you, Tom and Betsi, for a memorable visit and for taking us to St. Peter.

I'm especially appreciative for my husband, Jack, who has

often cooked dinner when I had a deadline, helped me work out plot points in a pinch, and helped also with historical information and dialogue. Thank you for your patience and support beyond the call of duty!

One of the reasons I chose to write a story about families with children is because of the joy I experienced as I brought up my own children. Family is so precious, time with our children when they're young is so fleeting, and they are such a blessing. Most of all, thank you, Lord Jesus, for my little family and for allowing me to write these stories and share them with others.

AUTHOR'S NOTE

Ever since I heard a story about how my father-in-law went to the local drugstore for emergency stitches in the 1950s, I have been intrigued by the historical role of the pharmacist, when the medical professions were perhaps a little less clearly demarcated. My curiosity was also piqued by colorful show globes in the window of the drugstore display in the Detroit Historical Museum.

So many medicines had their roots in herbal remedies (no pun intended), such as foxglove being made into digitalis for the heart. Guaifenesin, an expectorant used today, was originally derived from a plant but is now created chemically. Those are just two examples.

Unfortunately, other remedies at the turn of the nineteenth century into the twentieth were dangerous preparations made from derivatives of the opium poppy and were, unfortunately, unregulated. Customers gladly bought the over-the-counter products that seemed to give immediate results. Sadly, they came at a great cost. Mrs. Winslow's Soothing Syrup is one example. Containing morphine, it was used to relieve the symptoms of teething. Tired mothers accidentally overdosed their young children. Some documented cases resulted in death. Many other preparations caused addiction, as well as other problems. Mrs. Whitcomb's Sweet-water Tonic is modeled on such remedies, though a fictional product. Before the Pure Food and Drug Act of 1906, there were no federal regulations in the United States governing the pharmaceutical industry.

Sajou's Analytical Cyclopedia of Practical Medicine, Volume 5, from 1901, gave several instructions for the diagnosis and treatment of the overdose of opiates. Some of the advice given in the abovementioned book advised first administering an emetic to empty the stomach of any unabsorbed poison. Next, the physician might inject the patient with a solution of potassium permanganate or sodium permanganate to counteract the narcotic drug.

Sajou's includes the account of a father who saved his baby's life by giving milk and syrup of ipecac after the child accidentally ingested some morphine. The theory was that the emetic curdled the milk in the baby's stomach and "imprisoned" the drug. The reader will find similarities in Thomas Harper's treatment of Emmy Frost.

Depending on how badly the patient was overdosed, they may have needed more than one injection. Or the antidote might be administered through a tube to the stomach. It could have taken hours or days for the patient to recover completely. For the sake of moving the story forward, I made Emmy's return to consciousness a matter of several minutes.

While a pharmacist like Thomas Harper might still sell Cocaine Teething Drops or paregoric, these were common practices. The possible ramifications may not have been fully understood. Still, I would like to think that he would be concerned about any ingredients not fully disclosed and want to protect his customers, especially as a loving father himself. And that he would dedicate himself to educating them in the proper use of what he sold.

ABOUT THE AUTHOR

Kathleen Rouser is a multi-published, award-winning author of historical and contemporary Christian romance. She is a long-time member of American Christian Fiction Writers and a member of Faith, Hope and Love Christian Writers. She resides in southeast Michigan, a location which she often uses in her novels, with her hero and husband of forty-some years and two sweet cats who found a home in their empty nest.

GET ALL THE BOOKS IN THE STONE CREEK BRIDE SERIES

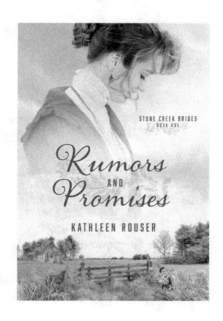

Book 1: Rumors and Promises

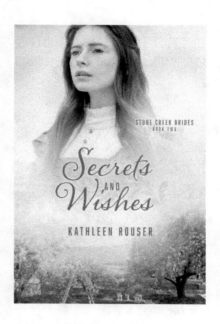

Book 2: Secrets and Wishes

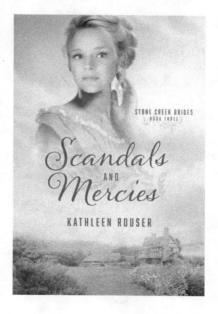

Book 3: Scandals and Mercies

If you love historical romance, check out the other Wild Heart books!

Lucinda's Defender by Blossom Turner

Can the depth of one man's love change a shattered woman's destiny?

Joseph Manning once watched his first—and only—love walk out of his life, right into the arms of a dangerous womanizer. Now he'll do anything to rescue her.

Lucinda Williams lives with the awful consequences of her impetuous youth. While she can't bring herself to open her heart to another, she can't stop her son from taking a shine to Joseph. But that only complicates what she must ultimately do. Even if Lucinda wants to admit that Joseph's ever-present kindness and respect are wearing away her resolve, she has a secret too shameful to reveal. She can't make Joseph pay for her tragic mistakes.

Only a miracle can bring true healing and a second chance at happiness.

~

A Season at the Grand by Sherri Wilson Johnson

Can the perfect picture reveal the truth before it's too late?

Photographer Amelia Harris has had enough of her aunts' meddling matchmaking. So when The Photographic Times commissions her to spend the summer on Mobile Bay taking portraits of the elite and capturing nature for penny postcards, Amelia happily accepts. But this job is not as simple as it appears, and Amelia must defend against naysayers if she's to ever gain respect in a man's world. And that doesn't leave any room for romance.

Point Clear Resort General Manager Titus Overton never wanted the position he inherited when his cousin passed away. If it were up to him, he would be traveling with the Audubon Society to far-off places, enjoying the solitude of nature instead of providing relaxation for his guests. And now he has to deal with the big-city photographer stomping her way through sand dunes that house the migratory birds nesting there. But when she reveals an admiration for his feathered friends, it reawakens a longing in his heart he'd buried after the death of his fiancé.

When threats arise against Amelia and the other resort guests, Titus knows he must step in to help. But she insists they trust God for deliverance. How can he turn to a God who took away his first beloved?

As the danger closes in, he must find the courage to overcome his past before someone gets hurt—especially the woman he's come to love.

~

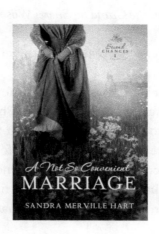

A Not So Convenient Marriage by Sandra Merville Hart

A spinster teacher...a grieving widower...a marriage of convenience and a second chance with the man she's always loved.

When Samuel Walker proposes a marriage of convenience to Rose Hatfieldso soon after the death of his wife, she knows he doesn't love her. *She's* loved *him* since their school days. Those long-suppressed feelings spring to life as she marries him. She must sell her childhood home, quit her teaching job, and move to a new city.

Marrying Rose is harder than Samuel expected, especially with the shadow of his deceased wife everywhere in his life. And he has two young children to consider. Peter and Emma need a mother's love, but they also need to hold close the memories of their real mother as they grieve her loss.

Life as Samuel's wife is nothing like Rose hoped, and even the townspeople, who loved his first wife, make Rose feel like an outsider. The work of the farm draws the two of them closer, giving hope that they might one day become a happy family. Until the dream shatters, and the life Rose craves tumbles down around them. Only God can put these pieces back together, but the outcome may not look anything like she planned.

Printed in the USA
CPSIA information can be obtained
at www.ICGtesting.com
LVHW082016050124
767981LV00025B/124

9 781942 265863